# BREAKING DEAD

# CORRIE JACKSON

twenty7

*For James*
*T. C. B.*

First published in Great Britain in 2016 by Twenty7 Books

Twenty7 Books
80–81 Wimpole St, London W1G 9RE
www.twenty7books.co.uk

Paperback ISBN: 978-1-7857-7045-6
E-book ISBN: 978-1-7857-7044-9

Produced by IDSUK (Data Connection) Ltd

1 3 5 7 9 10 8 6 4 2

Printed and bound by Clays Ltd, St Ives Plc

MIX
Paper from
responsible sources
FSC® C018072

Twenty7 Books is an imprint of Bonnier Zaffre,
a Bonnier Publishing company
www.bonnierpublishing.co.uk

*It seems she hangs upon the cheek of night*
*Like a rich jewel in an Ethiop's ear;*
*Beauty too rich for use, for earth too dear*

Romeo and Juliet, *William Shakespeare*

*Her skin is perfect.*

*Pink and plump. The way it puckers in the cold night air sends a surge of heat through my bones. It lights me up with longing, and desire, and fury. White fury, so intense it makes me itch.*

*She is spread-eagled on the mattress, eyes closed, her dark hair smeared across her forehead in wet ribbons. I suck on my cigarette. Watch her through the smoke. She turns her head away from me. No matter. I don't need to see her face. I know it like my own. Can picture the dusky curve of her eyelid, those apple-sweet lips.*

*A fox screams in the distance. I cock my head to one side, then roll the cigarette between my thumb and forefinger. The breeze coming through the shed window tugs at my hair like a sticky toddler. Reaching out, I drive the cigarette into the hollow of her throat.*

*A hot, red hiss of burning skin.*

*My body hums.*

*Someone shifts beside me, breaking the spell.*

*'Ready?'*

*His voice is gruff. Like velvet dragged across gravel.*

*'Take your time, she isn't going anywhere.' My eyes slide down to the restraints around her wrist; the slick of tape over her mouth.*

*Against the wall, more shadows watch, waiting their turn. The end is coming. I'm sure of it. These purple, pain-soaked nights aren't enough any more. She isn't enough. I see how fast their smiles drop, their eyes dull, once it's over.*

*He sweeps past me. I catch a waft of stale sweat and pear drops. Can hear him sucking. The click as the sweet skates over his teeth.*

*He kneels down beside her. Unbuckles his belt. I can't look away. She turns towards me. Begging silently in the dark. Her pupils are black and shiny, like liquorice.*

*Liquorice was my daddy's favourite. He always gave me a twist of liquorice when he finished touching me.*

*I stare at the wound blistering on her neck.*

*Now her skin is perfect.*

# 1

*February 2014*

A dazzle of frost had turned the grass white, and my feet crunched as I circled the police tape for a closer look. A sliver of the axe-head glinted in the wintery blue light. The rest was buried in the boy's skull. A brand of some sort was stamped on the buttery-wood handle, but I couldn't make out the word. I'd get it from the photos later. It's the kind of detail I like to include.

Inhaling deeply, I winced as the arctic air sliced through my lungs. It was eerily quiet. I'd been on the next street, doorstepping robbery witnesses with my photographer, when a shrill of sirens pierced the air. Sprinting towards the streak of blue lights, we skidded into Milton Way council estate moments after the police. The head-start meant the Scene of Crime Officers were only just starting their assessment of the body. Not that the cause of death was in dispute.

'Christ.' Ned Mason's voice sounded small and far away, even though he was close enough for me to smell his last cigarette. 'Is that an *axe*?'

He didn't wait for an answer. The frantic rat-tat-tat of his camera told me Ned had pulled himself together. It was crucial he nailed the details. The trouser leg that had ridden up, exposing a skinny black calf. The scuffed trainer lying on its side. The fuzz of hair amidst the mangled, red mess. My eyes snaked up towards the navy parka. A memory stirred, and I shook it away, focused on the kid's outstretched arms. His fingertips were still buried in the white-tipped grass where he'd tried to crawl away.

Ned shifted beside me, lowered his voice. 'Cavalry's approaching.'

A squat police officer I didn't recognise lurched towards us with a tarpaulin sheet under his arm.

'Can you tell me anything about the kid?'

His ferrety eyes swung in my direction. 'And you are?'

I held up my press card with a gloved hand. 'Sophie Kent, *The London Herald*.'

'Well, Sophie Kent, if you can find anything that resembles a face to ID, I'll let the Chief know.'

I pulled out my notebook, even though his expression told me it was a waste of time. 'Any word on who found him? Or how long he's been here?'

The police officer threw the sheet over the body and bent over to straighten it, pausing at the end with the axe. When he stood up, his pitted face was a shade whiter.

'Sorry, love, under strict instructions not to fraternise with your lot. Shame, though. I wouldn't mind fraternising with you.' His thin mouth spread into a leer that couldn't hide the tightness in his jaw. I ignored the comment. Tensions were running high, and for good reason. This was what my editor would call an IFM. An Important Fucking Murder. The twentieth teenager to be killed since the Commissioner of Police publicly declared a crackdown on London street crime nine months ago. This boy would become synonymous with their failure. No wonder they weren't talking.

He stomped back to the line of police vans, his boots leaving a trail of emerald footprints in the frost.

Ned wheezed beside me, squinting at his camera screen. 'I've got some of the body, some of the axe. What else do we need?'

I glanced at the kid's parka, at the gold circle branding his sleeve. I squeezed my eyes shut as an image of the same parka flashed through my mind – only this one wrapped around a skinny white boy with silvery-blonde hair.

I took a deep breath, forced my voice to sound calm. 'Get crowd shots. Mourners. They'll start laying flowers soon. Close-ups of personal messages. Anything that tells his story.' This kid may well end up symbolising the Met's weakening grip, but I was damned if he was going to be reduced to a statistic.

Ned pretended not to notice me struggling. He assessed the scene with shrewd grey eyes. 'Hardly your average street murder, is it?'

I cleared my throat, stamped my feet to keep warm, glanced at the green canvas rucksack flung open next to the body, its contents strewn across the ground. A plastic lunchbox lay next to a battered copy of *Romeo and Juliet*. The cover of a biology textbook flapped in the wind. 'He was young. On his way home from school, poor kid.'

My voice cracked. This time Ned threw me a glance.

'You OK?'

I glared at the darkening sky. 'I'm fine.'

Ned paused, then threw his camera strap around his neck. 'I'll come find you when I'm done.'

I watched him punch through the crowd, a boxer on a losing streak. At sixty-four, Ned was considerably older than your average crime photographer but what he lacked in finesse, he made up for in experience. Ned might be entering 'God's departure lounge', as he called it, but I didn't doubt his ability to get the money shot, not for a second.

A distant *whump-whump-whump* of a news helicopter rattled through the air. Heart thumping, I surveyed the unfolding chaos. Witnesses huddled in groups, clutching each other, their eyes dancing in the flashing lights. Reporters and news crews scampered round them like feverish squirrels. If I joined in, I'd end up with the same quotes. I needed a different tack.

I scanned the high-rise jungle. The murder had taken place behind a line of parked cars, on the grassy wasteland in front of the building. The clearest viewpoint would be on the third floor, over to the right. I sprinted towards the stairwell and took the steps two at a time, dodging a used condom and empty Burger King boxes. I paused at the top to catch my breath. The sour stench of urine filled my nostrils.

I knocked on the first door.

An elderly lady appeared. She was short, my height, and round as a barrel. A Saint Christopher chain hung around her neck.

'Hello, I'm a reporter with *The London Herald*. Can you tell me anything about the incident?'

'I didn't see nothing.' Her voice was high and bleating. She pushed her thick glasses up her nose and they left behind deep red welts. 'But it's obvious, ain't it? Drugs. I've lived here for over forty years; this neighbourhood used to be respectable. Do you know how many kids have been killed round here lately?'

I was sympathetic. I'd written about most of them.

Up ahead I spotted a tall brunette girl darting into her flat.

'Wait!'

She glanced back and her distress was so raw it wrong-footed me for a second. I glimpsed her face through a shroud of dark hair. Small elfin features and full lips, which she chewed between the gap in her front teeth. She stared down at the floor, as though to stop herself from crying. Her chin creased with the effort. 'Hey, are you OK?'

The girl wiped her puffy eyes with the palm of a trembling hand. A blue butterfly tattoo covered the lower part of her middle finger. She started to close the door but I put my hand out to stop it.

'Please, let me help you.'

The girl didn't speak. Instead, she left the door open for me.

I followed her into a tiny sitting room that was foggy with cigarette smoke. On the walls, yellow paint blistered like acne over patches of damp. Her flat was barely any warmer than outside. I pulled my coat tightly around me waiting for the girl to say something, but she collapsed on the grey sofa, wrapped one

long, skinny leg around the other and relit a half-smoked cigarette. The smoke twisted upwards and hit the ceiling.

'Did you know the victim?' She gave me a blank look. I spotted a Russian dictionary on the shelf. 'You're from Russia?' At
the mention of Russia, her violet-blue eyes flickered. 'What's
your name?'

She inhaled deeply, blew the smoke out in a long white
stream. 'Natalia.'

Her voice was deeper than I expected. Despite the chill, she
was dressed in a T-shirt and a short, flowery skirt that fluttered
as she twitched her bare foot.

'How old are you?'

She paused. 'Eighteen.'

'How long have you been in London?'

Natalia stubbed out her cigarette in the overflowing ashtray.
'Three months.'

She didn't elaborate and I didn't pressure her. I noticed a black
portfolio half-hidden under the sofa with gold lettering embossed
along the top: *Models International*. That would explain her bone
structure and willowy frame.

'Does anyone else live here with you?'

Natalia lit another cigarette with shaky hands. 'Eva. She at
casting.'

My deadline was looming and I moved to the window. The
net curtain felt damp between my fingers. SOCOs were erecting
a white tent over the boy's body. *The navy parka.*

I shook my head. 'Are you crying because of that? Did you see
something?'

Natalia uncoiled herself and joined me. Watery daylight filtered through the window, affording me a proper look at her face. Skin pale as a pearl, and an ugly purple bruise on her cheek. She peered through the window and her hand flew up to her mouth. A bracelet of bruises marked her wrist. She shook her head so violently, her dark hair loosened from its bun and fell around her shoulders. I led her gently back to the sofa.

'Natalia, what happened to your face?'

She shrank into the seat, pulling her skirt down over her milky thighs. Even then it didn't cover her birthmark, round and brown, like an old penny.

'It is accident. I slip.' She fixed me with a doleful gaze. 'Please, you go.'

'I'm not leaving until you let me help you.'

Natalia chewed her lip. 'I can't talk here. Somewhere else.'

'Where?'

She shrugged, her eyes cloudy with fear. I grabbed her phone and dialled my number. It rang in my bag. 'Listen, I have your number. I'll text you the address of a pub nearby. We can meet there tonight?' Natalia shook her head. 'Tomorrow?' A small nod.

I let myself out and leaned heavily against the cold concrete, willing my feet to move. Knowing what would happen if they didn't.

By the third door, I'd learned the victim was fourteen-year-old Jason Danby. A studious kid and an ardent Millwall supporter, raised by his aunt Mary, who lived in the tower block opposite this one. His older brother, Jermaine, belonged to a notorious gang called the Red-Skilled Boys, and often loitered around the council estate in his trademark coat: a navy parka. A man with sad eyes and peppery hair told me he heard a scream, looked out of the window and saw the boy's skull dribbling blood on to the ground. He thought it was Jermaine until he saw the rucksack. The man took my card and closed the door, shaking his head.

Sixty feet below me, a pathologist approached the tent. *Keep moving*. I closed my eyes, replayed the scene behind my eyelids. Bloodied face and sugar-white socks. Frozen fingertips, sticky axe. *Keep moving*. My hand moved to the small, silver T on a chain around my neck. I pressed the corners of its familiar shape into my fingers. Then all of a sudden, dread pooled in my stomach, heavy as wet mud. I squeezed my eyes shut, braced myself for the crash. Pounding heart. Ragged breath. Cold, iron fist around my heart. I dug my nails into my palms as I clung on, willing it to pass. Nausea gave way to pain. I howled into the wind and kicked the wall hard.

Stumbling forwards, I hammered on the next door. Cheap plywood reverberated against my hand. The door opened a crack and a wiry black man in a blue, zip-up hoodie peered out, eyes full of mistrust.

'Yeah?'

'I'm a reporter from *The London* –'

The door slammed sharply in my face. I knocked again.

A muffled voice, thick with anger. 'Get the fuck outta here.'

*Keep moving*.

I hurled myself against the door. 'Tell me what you saw. Stop hiding, you moron. I'm trying to help –'

'Sophie!' Ned's hand gripped my shoulder. 'What are you doing?'

I wrenched myself free, pulled back, staggered against the concrete. 'I got a name. Jason Danby.' My eyes were watering so much I could barely see. 'Fourteen, Ned. *Fourteen*. His aunt's in Tower Block C. I need to talk to her.'

'The aunt will be behind a wall of people. Besides,' Ned paused, raised his eyebrows, 'you shouldn't question family members. Not like this.'

'What the hell is that supposed to mean?'

Ned fiddled with his camera strap. 'Listen, it's your first day back, and this crime scene is –'

'Ned, there's a teenager over there with an axe through his brain. Can we not do this now?'

Ned shrugged and opened his mouth to speak, but I didn't wait to hear him. I turned on my heel and charged down the steps. Towards Tower Block C. Towards Mary Danby. Towards the story.

The icy air shredded my insides.

*Keep fucking moving.*

# 2

*One Week Later*

'For Christ's sake, Sophie, what were you thinking?' Philip Rowley's narrow face peeped over the mounds of paper on his desk like a mole coming up for air.

'She's not giving you the full picture. I rang the buzzer and she wouldn't speak to me –'

'So you yelled at her?'

I bristled. 'I didn't yell.' The sound of Mary Danby's tired voice shuddered through my brain. 'I knew if she heard me out, she'd talk.'

Rowley gave me a stony look. 'Bullshit, Sophie. Not only is it a completely ineffective way to get someone to open up, it's harassment. I told you a week ago to leave that woman alone. And now I find out you've been back to the Milton estate to question her again.'

Rowley's high-pitched voice had earned him the ironic nickname of the Growler, but I knew better than to question his authority. He was a powerhouse editor who had overseen *The London Herald*'s transition from an also-ran to the third highest-selling newspaper in the country. A tough Yorkshireman, I knew from the moment I met him that I'd need to prove myself beyond the normal standard. Rowley despised family money and private education, both of which I had in spades. I knew my clipped accent grated on him, but I liked to think I'd earned his respect. I'd brought in more than my fair share of exclusives and it helped that I knew how to handle him: keep it short, sweet and never say no.

'Look, Mary Danby has been vocal with the press since then. She's gone on record to say The Met is scaling back its investigation. I just wanted to get a quote.'

Rowley's leather chair squeaked as he leaned back, his voice tight with sarcasm.

'And what quote did you get, besides *fuck off and leave me alone*?'

I sighed. 'Fine. I may have gone a bit overboard.'

'A bit?' Rowley's round bald scalp turned crimson. He slid on his tortoiseshell glasses and glanced at the piece of paper in front of him. 'It says here that you threatened to break down her door.'

A snort escaped. 'Break down her door? Have you seen the size of me?' I opened my mouth to speak again, then closed it when I saw the expression on Rowley's face. Instead I gazed out of the window. Thick clouds rolled across the sky over Hyde Park, building up to another downpour. Rowley's corner office overlooked the very edge of Kensington Palace, which really railed against his socialist sensibilities.

'One of the reasons I hired you is the talent you have for getting people to open up. You haven't been back at work long and this is the second complaint about your conduct.' Rowley's voice mellowed into a low whine. 'This isn't about Mary Danby, is it?'

I didn't want to see the pity in his eyes so I studied the framed pictures behind his desk. Rowley at Downing Street with David Cameron, at a Nato Summit with Angela Merkel, on the red carpet behind George Clooney. For all his ordinary, one-of-the-people spiel, Rowley was a sucker for the rich and famous.

'I need to go. I'm interviewing someone in Brixton in forty minutes.'

Rowley sighed. 'Sophie, what was the first thing I told you when you joined *The London Herald*?'

I looked him in the eye. 'Always know the line.'

'Exactly. The line is the truth. The line is what sells the story. Doesn't matter if you're writing fifty words, or five thousand. If you can't sum it up in one line, you haven't cracked it.' A shadow fell across Rowley's face. 'The line applies to more than just reporting. It applies to life. And when I look at you right now, Sophie, I can't see the line.'

'Philip –'

'I'm not finished. I know you've been through a difficult time, but I'm not running a charity. We are haemorrhaging money.' He yanked off his glasses and rubbed his eyes. 'Not just us: the *Mail*, *The Times*, the *Telegraph*, everyone. We've been lined up against a wall and shot. All that's left now is to see which of us bleeds out the last. Budgets have been slashed, readership is pitiful and we're being forced to evolve into digital wizards overnight. I spend more time considering page hits than Page One now. But that's the challenge: spend less, create more. We're pressing on into an uncertain future, delivering top-drawer journalism in myriad forms, and the readers who are still with us deserve our A-game. But where is *your* A-game, Sophie? Where is your line?'

He leaned forward, eyes hard, like varnished wood. 'The Sophie Kent I know would never have threatened a source. She would also know that coming to work hungover was a mug's game. You're talented. One of the best I've ever worked with. But you've lost your way, Sophie. You're a wordy, bloated overwritten piece of prose, bumbling from one sentence to the next with no structure, no *line*.'

I focused on my hands, not trusting myself to speak. I was staring down the barrel of grief so raw it felt as though it had fused into my bloodstream. Some days, I could actually taste it, and the only way to get rid of it was to drink something flammable. Other days, it was an anaesthetic sliding through my veins, numbing me from the inside out. But I couldn't tell Rowley how I felt. The newspaper industry was at war. He needed his soldiers firing on all cylinders.

'I'm sorry I let you down. You don't need to worry about me. I'm fine.' I kept my voice level but it sounded hollow, even to me.

Rowley folded his arms. 'You know what I think? You should have taken time off when it happened. Then I wouldn't have had to force delayed compassionate leave on you.' He sighed. 'I don't think a week was long enough.'

A memory of the long stretch of sharp-edged moments arrowed through me. 'Trust me, I'm better off here.'

'Not if you compromise the newspaper, you're not. The last thing I need is complaints from disgruntled civilians. You're lucky Mary Danby isn't pressing charges.'

The chair dug into my back and I moved forward. 'All she knew was that I was a reporter from *The London Herald*. How did she get my name?'

Rowley shuffled his papers with small, neat hands. 'No idea. Mack took the call. And took the sting out of her wrath, as it happens.' I rolled my eyes, earning myself another stern look from Rowley. 'He's worried about you. Thinks the murder beat is bad for your recovery. Reckons I should move you off the front line and into something less demanding. Lifestyle, or fashion.' The look on my face made the corners of Rowley's mouth twitch. 'If I don't see a change, I'll have no choice.'

I nodded briskly, my mind still on Mack.

'Anyway,' he sounded irritable all of a sudden, 'that's beside the point. I want you to send Mary Danby a handwritten note. Not on *Herald* stationery, in case she shops it elsewhere.' Rowley swung round to his computer screen, indicating our talk was over.

I was almost at the door when he spoke again. 'Don't be a martyr, Sophie. If you need more time, tell me. Three months isn't long when you're dealing with a family death.'

Harsh strip lights buzzed overhead as I sagged against the wall outside Rowley's office. The newsroom was alive with the discordant sounds of phones ringing and keyboards tapping. To my left, five-feet-high steel letters spelt out *THE LONDON*

*HERALD*. To my right, a wall of televisions flickered with rolling twenty-four-hour news. Banks of computers, two or three per person, sat on top of cluttered desks. Stacks of paper everywhere, proof that even in the digital age reporters relied on the tangible. I steered myself through the open-plan office, eyes firmly on the carpet and collapsed onto my chair.

My phone chimed with a text, interrupting my thoughts.

*Want to get a drink after work and talk about it?*

I stared at the screen, deliberating possible replies, but who was I kidding?

*Fine. Somewhere private.*

He replied with the name of a Soho bar I'd never heard of. I slammed my phone down on my desk. Then I grabbed my coat. Rowley, Mary Danby, Mack could wait.

I had somewhere to be.

# 3

She sat at our usual table, hunched over like a question mark.

I strode across the gloomy pub and slung my bag over the chair opposite. 'Sorry I'm late.'

Natalia Kotov stared at the space in front of her eyes. I put my hand on her shoulder and she jumped, spilling her drink.

'Oh, is you.' Morning light bled through the grimy, green window, giving the whites of her eyes a sickly tinge. The bruising on her face and wrist had disappeared, but my eyes were drawn to the invisible traces left behind. She slid a glass across the sticky table. 'Orange juice. Is OK?'

The pub was deserted except for two men in painters' overalls perched on barstools. They bowed their heads towards a portable radio that was bleating out horse-racing commentary. Their paint-speckled hands were wrapped around pints of beer, even though it was only 11 a.m.

I leaned back against the felt upholstery. It reeked of stale nicotine and sweat. 'So, are you ready for London Fashion Week?'

'My first show is Saturday. Bennett Turner. I have fitting tomorrow.' She gave a careless shrug of her shoulders, but I could tell by the lightness in her voice that she was excited.

'That's great. A few days ago you didn't have any bookings.'

'Things change fast.' Natalia fidgeted with the neck of her black sweater and bobbed her knee up and down. By now I was used to her jerky mannerisms, as though she was always on the verge of flight. But today they seemed more pronounced than usual.

'Have you spoken to your mum today?'

Natalia reached for her glass, took a long swig. 'Mamma is worried. Pyotr is sick. He has infection here.' She pointed to her chest.

A gentle *tap-tap-tap* made us look towards the window where rain was blurring the glass.

'Natalia, about yesterday . . . you left before we could properly talk.'

Her hand darted towards a china sugar bowl. She flipped it over, then began lining the sugar packets up in rows, separating them into colours, careful not to let their edges touch. I watched her for a while, remembering the first time we'd sat together at this table, the day after Jason Danby's murder.

Natalia had shown up looking as fragile as spun sugar. She barely lifted her eyes from the table; instead she'd arranged toothpicks into long, orderly lines. When I commented on it, she shrugged. 'I like tidy.' She told me how, back in Russia, she would fold the sheet corners on the mattress she shared with her brothers, until they were pristine. Her mother used to joke that Natalia was her little ghost-child. '*When you leave a room, milaya moya, it's as though no one was there.*'

We agreed to meet the next day, and we'd met every day since. I had a hunch our encounters would lead somewhere, to a revelation, an admission, a confession of sorts. Natalia was poised, old beyond her years, but a vein of vulnerability flowed through her, as though the child in her had yet to grow up. She touched lightly on her past; eyes softening when she spoke of her four younger brothers back in Ivanovo ('*Not a place where dreams come true*') and a mother who worked three jobs to put food on the table. When she was homesick, which was often, she wrapped herself in her mother's green woollen quilt, inhaling the sylvan scent of fir trees and pine needles. If she focused, she could hear the quiet hum of her mother's voice; a voice that grew softer with each passing winter.

Natalia's haunted eyes spoke of a difficult life, but she was quick to laugh. Her voice warmed when she spoke of her agent, Cat Ramsey, a woman she regarded as a second mother, and of her flatmate and fellow-model, Eva Kaminski. Occasionally I asked about the bruises she'd sported the first day we met, but Natalia always looked away.

'We need to talk about what you told me last time.'

'Why?' Patches of concealer had faded beneath Natalia's eyes, revealing skin the colour of claret. She raised her chin and gave me a defiant look.

A punter shuffled past, wafting a vinegary bleach smell towards us. I lowered my voice. 'Because we can do something about it.'

Natalia drained her glass. 'I need another. You want?'

I stood up. 'I'll get the next rou–'

'No!' Natalia's eyes widened. 'I buy.'

I stared after her, confused, as she trotted past a broken fruit machine and leaned over the bar. Her legs, wrapped in tight denim, were as thin as two pen lines. I sighed and opened my notebook to the page from yesterday. In the centre was one word, scrawled in blue ink and underlined. *Raped.*

Natalia returned clutching another drink and a packet of crisps. She tore at the foil, unleashing a sour oniony smell, and offered me one. I shook my head.

'It was a big step, sharing your secret with me.' Natalia crunched loudly on a crisp, not meeting my eye. 'Do you know the man who assaulted you?'

She lunged for her glass and gulped half of it down. Then she looked at her watch. 'Stupid thing. Is broken. You know time?'

I sighed. Natalia was like a star in a moonlit sky. To see her clearly, I had to shift my gaze, something I wasn't very good at lately.

I looked at my wrist. 'It's 11.30 a.m. Why?' Natalia rubbed at the watermark her glass had left on the table. 'Is everything OK? You seem distracted.'

'Sophie, I cannot tell you more.'

I closed my notebook. 'You know, I've lost count of the number of rape trials I've covered for *The London Herald*. Do you know what most convicted rapists have in common?' Natalia scrunched the empty crisp packet into a ball, her knuckles white. 'They're repeat offenders.' I caught her confused expression. 'I mean they raped lots of women. No one stopped them. Look, I don't want to pressure you. You don't owe anyone anything.

You have the right to keep this to yourself. But,' I leaned across the table and put my hand on hers, 'you also have a choice. You can speak out against this man. And I want you to know that if you do, I will be right beside you.'

Natalia pulled her hand away from mine and rubbed her middle finger with her thumb, distorting the butterfly tattoo. Her fingernails were bitten to the quick. She didn't lift her eyes. 'My career . . . it will be finished.'

'Because he works in fashion?'

She took another large gulp and looked at me with glazed eyes. 'Why *I* have to say something? Why not –' She stopped abruptly, running her teeth over her thumbnail.

'Last week, when I met you, those bruises. Was that him?' Natalia piled the sugar packets on top of one another, building a rickety tower. 'Is that when you were raped?' She flicked the corner of a sugar packet with a pale finger and the tower collapsed.

I rested my elbows on the table, fixing my eyes on her face. 'You know what, Natalia? I think your attacker picked on the wrong girl.' I squeezed her hand. 'You're here, you've done the hard part. I think his name is burning a hole in your tongue. All you have to do is speak.'

Natalia's hand twitched beneath mine. When she spoke, her voice was smaller than I'd ever heard it. 'After London, is Milan, then Paris. It must be secret.'

'You have my word. Give me a name, and we'll wait until the shows have finished before we do anything.'

Natalia drained her glass, wound a red scarf around her neck. She grabbed her cigarettes and gave me a rueful smile. 'I take a minute.'

'Do you want company?'

Natalia shook her head. 'You don't smoke. I be back. Then we talk.'

A chill wind blasted through the pub as Natalia opened the front door. I rested my head against the chair and closed my eyes, absorbing the sounds around me. The slide of glass across wood; the clink of empty bottles; the barman's wet cough. Alone again, my thoughts turned to Rowley and the disappointment in his eyes. He was right. I'd slipped. Lost focus. I was hanging on by a thread. And Rowley had seen straight through me.

The door slammed open and Natalia hurtled through, eyes wide.

'Hey, what's wro—'

'I have to go.'

I looked past her, towards the door. 'Did something happen?' Natalia's bag got caught under the table and she yanked it free, knocking herself off balance.

'Wait!' Frustration swept up my back and I grabbed Natalia's arm more forcefully than I intended. 'Think, Natalia. If you run, he wins. Is that what you want?'

'You think I want this?' Natalia's eyes flashed, like shards of glass in the sunlight. 'I have no choice.'

'I can help you.'

'No one can help me.'

Natalia crossed the pub in three long strides and was gone.

I half-rose from my chair, then sat down again. What was the point?

'Your girlfriend don't fancy you no more?' The bartender's gruff voice cut through my thoughts. 'Shame. We got used to your lady-dates round here.'

I hovered in the doorway of the bar, fidgeting with my umbrella strap, squinting into the darkness. Where the hell was he? Stained-glass table lamps glowed womb-red. The cocktail-laced air was sweet, the floor sticky. A loud throbbing from the speakers marched in time to my headache.

'Can I help you?' The waitress wore horn-rimmed glasses and a bored expression.

'I'm meeting someone.' I didn't want to say his name out loud. I pushed past a group of bearded hipsters who were drinking cocktails from jam jars. He was in a corner booth, leaning back against vinyl the colour of chopped liver. Bourbon, BlackBerry, navy suit (*'from Milan, custom-made'*), terracotta tan.

I slid into the bench opposite and saw his jaw unclench. 'Great choice, Mack.'

'Shut up, Kent. You didn't want to be seen, right?'

Two shots were lined up on the table. Mack pushed one towards me. I swallowed it without flinching. He watched me, running a long, bony finger round the top of his glass. He probably thought it was seductive. Everything Mack Winterson did had a studied air about it.

His BlackBerry vibrated on the table. 'I need to reply to this.'

Out of the corner of my eye I spotted a girl in a beanie hat and hot pants straddling a guy with greasy blond hair. He whispered something in her ear and she nodded. Then she climbed off his lap, pulled him towards a dark corner.

As Mack punched away at his keyboard, I caught the glint of gold around his finger. I threw back another shot, welcoming the burn.

'Steady, I don't want to have to carry you out of here.'

I said nothing. People have underestimated me my whole life. I don't care. As far as I'm concerned, it gives me the edge.

'Big deal, so you fucked up with Rowley. It won't be the last time that happens.'

Was that a threat? I couldn't think straight; the edges of my brain were starting to blur.

'I don't know what's happening to me.' I said it too quietly for Mack to hear, but part of me wished he had. I pushed my empty glass away. 'I need another drink. These aren't working.'

'Don't be so dramatic, Kent.' Mack signalled to the waitress for another round. 'Rowley gives every reporter the hairdryer treatment at some point. It was just your time.'

The insincerity was deafening. I wanted to point out that Rowley would never have known about Mary Danby if it weren't for him, but Mack already knew that. He pretended to support me, but we both knew the truth. He'd never forgiven me for making him look second-rate in front of Rowley. I hadn't been at *The London Herald* long when a man called Steve Wright, aka the Suffolk Strangler, embarked on a brutal campaign against prostitutes. Mack was let loose on the story but failed to bring home the bacon, so Rowley sent me instead. I scored an exclusive with one of the victims and it made the front page. I was rewarded with the metal plate from the printing plant, a memento all *Herald* reporters are given when their first front-page story is published. As I bounded back to my desk, I caught the scowl on Mack's face. Since then, our working relationship has been shaky, at best. But lately, there'd been a shift.

I squeezed out of the booth muttering something about the loo, and felt my way through a dark warren of corridors. Mercifully the bathroom was empty. I brushed a film of white powder off the toilet lid and sat down with my head in my hands.

*What am I doing?*

As News Editor, Mack was under extreme pressure from Rowley to boost circulation figures. He was a killer at playing the corporate game, and making the upper echelons believe he was the man for the job. But Mack wasn't a natural news hound. He was putting in sixteen-hour days with very little to show for it, and the stress was burning him out. He felt cornered, so he acted out. Took it out on those around him. Most of the staff thought he was a dick, but I understood. My life was hardly a bucket of rainbows, lately, and I recognised a fellow fuck-up. We didn't have to like each other to use one another as an escape. That's what I told myself the first time I unzipped his trousers in the deserted newsroom, anyway. Two months later, here we were. Same shit, different bar. Sharp, stabby small talk. Both knowing where the evening would end, neither happy about it.

Eventually, a sharp rapping on the door brought me back to the present.

'What the fuck are you doing in there? Some of us have gotta take a shit.'

I moved towards the mirror, smoothed down my silvery-blonde hair. I took a deep, steadying breath then stood up straight, as though an invisible force had zipped me up.

'I was about to file a Missing Persons Report.' Mack gave me a quizzical look, flicking the lid of his silver lighter open and shut. He slid another shot across the table. 'Chin up. I'm sure we can hold the fort until the great Sophie Kent climbs back onto her pedestal.' He went for breezy but his tight smile let him down.

I swallowed a last, stinging shot and wiped my mouth with the back of my hand. 'Let's go.'

As I swayed through the shadows, Mack put a bony hand on the small of my back. I flinched. Five more minutes and those shots would kick in.

Then he could touch me wherever he liked.

# 4

The air was thick and sour. Last night's vodka still coated the inside of my mouth. I lay there for a minute as fragments of the evening hovered on the edge of my brain, just out of reach. Slowly, I pushed myself up to sitting and waited for the spinning room to level out. It was still dark. I reached for my phone: 6.38 a.m.

I could make out the snoring mass beside me and the silhouette of a dressing table against the wall. The framed photos on top were illuminated by a sliver of light from a door to the hallway. Mack and a pretty brunette grinning in a snowstorm of confetti. We never really discussed his personal life but I'd heard a rumour that his wife had decided city life wasn't for her and promptly moved herself and the kids to Wiltshire. For the unpredictable life of a news editor, the ninety-minute commute was unthinkable, so Mack spent most weeknights in a tiny flat above a dry cleaner on Litchfield Street.

I scanned the room for my clothes, trying to avoid the other framed photo. Two little boys, both dark-haired, skinny-limbed copies of their father. I picked up my scattered clothes with the ease of a seasoned player, praying Mack wouldn't wake up.

I was halfway across the room when my phone chimed loudly. I grabbed it and scuttled into the bathroom, stubbing my toe in the process.

The pain was forgotten the moment I opened the text message. *The Rose Hotel. Room 538. She's dead.*

I didn't recognise the number.

*Who is this?*

I sat on the cold marble floor waiting for a response, but nothing came. The text could be a prank. Ever since the anonymous text apps hit the market, my daily interaction with nutters had increased tenfold. But what if it wasn't a prank? The Rose was only a few minutes away.

Hauling myself up, I splashed my face with icy water and rubbed the red gash where the pillow had imprinted on my forehead. Then I turned my knickers inside out, threw on yesterday's clothes and tiptoed across the bedroom. A newspaper lay on the doormat by the front door. I kicked it to one side, noting the date: 14 February. Happy fucking Valentine's Day.

The inky sky was turning indigo as I buried my chin in my scarf and crossed Shaftesbury Avenue. A line of red buses snaked along the street, their windows opaque with the hot, angry breath of people going nowhere fast. Rounding the corner into Old Compton Street, I paused by a tiny Vietnamese restaurant that smelled like feet. The Rose's gleaming brick facade was lit up by a row of spotlights; its green-and-white striped awnings rippled in the breeze. Fishing out my notebook, I scribbled down the number plate of every car I passed. The rule of thumb for any reporter? *Write everything down.* Random threads of information often weaved themselves into a complete tapestry down the line.

A portly doorman in a bottle-green overcoat smiled as he opened the door. I paused briefly, taking in the scene. The lobby's marble floor shone like an ice rink and amplified the tinkling of silver against china. Pink armchairs formed a circle in the middle and a shimmering chandelier hung from the ornate ceiling. A waft of buttered toast made my stomach growl. I kneeled down and pretended to get something out of my bag while scanning the lobby for anyone who looked shaken or upset. Always my first port of call; people let all kinds of information slip when they're in shock.

I couldn't see any evidence to suggest news had got out yet. If there was any news. The lack of police presence pointed towards the time-waster scenario, but it was hard to tell. A place like this wouldn't broadcast a scandal. And if someone was dead, the fact that hotel staff didn't know gave me hope. There was a chance the crime scene wasn't locked down.

'Can I help you?' A chiselled man behind the front desk looked up.

I smiled as widely as my hangover would permit. 'I'm fine, thanks.'

Act like you belong. Confidence gets you everywhere in this job. I strode past the mirrored bar to the stairs and hauled myself up the oak bannister. No one was guarding the landings. If police were here, it would only be uniform. No way would I have got this far if the Scene of Crime Officers had arrived. By the time I reached the fifth floor, my hangover was protesting loudly and I clung onto the bannister with sweaty palms to catch my breath.

In this quiet corner of the hotel, the street noise was muffled, as if the city had been gagged. A familiar crackle of a police radio drifted down the corridor on my right. I held my breath, cursing the deafening *thud-thud-thud* of my heart in my ears. The corridor was dimly lit; the thick emerald carpet soaked up what little light there was. I crept along until I reached where the corridor veered to the right and pressed my back against the wall.

'It's not ideal, but let's make the best of it.'

The voice was measured, with a pleasant lilt, and I unclenched my fists a fraction. Risking a peek round the corner, I spotted the back of Detective Chief Inspector Sam Durand's auburn head as he stooped in a hotel-room doorway, his six-foot-four frame filling the space. *What's he doing here?* CID weren't usually on the scene at this point. Still, it was good news. DCI Durand was one of the few police officers who had risen up the ranks without becoming a complete arsehole. Some were power-happy narcissists. Others were by-the-book guys, too straight to take a risk. But Durand was different. Razor-sharp, with an uncanny knack for reading people. And he wasn't afraid of getting his hands dirty. Thanks to the Leveson Inquiry, my drawer of CID business cards was about as useful as a bikini in a blizzard but, unlike many of his contemporaries, Durand didn't despise the press. He understood the point of a mutually beneficial relationship, particularly with me. I didn't care why he favoured me. I used it.

The nuances of my job boiled down to good, old-fashioned trust. '*Trust is like your virginity*,' Durand once told me. '*Once it's lost, you can never get it back.*' I took it as the warning shot he intended it to be. And I worked hard to ensure our trust remained intact. Including scratching his back every now and again.

Four years ago a hot-blooded Albanian immigrant called Ardit Dushku had waged a campaign against women in the Peckham area, sexually assaulting them before leaving them for dead. After victim number five, the police investigation, headed up by Detective Inspector Durand, pieced together a profile of the suspect, right down to the car he drove, which had been traced back to three of the crime scenes. I'd done the same, and had taken it one step further by tracking down his ex-wife and approaching her for an interview. When I arrived at a rundown bungalow by the side of the A3, my eye caught something on the driveway. A blue-and-yellow sticker with the words *Elbasani 1913* emblazoned across it. The edges were puckered, as if someone had tried very hard to peel it off. Later that day, I attended a press conference where DI Durand announced in front of thirty journalists that the suspect drove a silver Honda with an Albanian football sticker in the rear window. After he finished, I sought him out and quietly explained where he could find that sticker. In the trial, when Dushku pleaded insanity, the sticker was one of the incriminating pieces of evidence that proved he was of sound mind. A genuinely insane person wouldn't have had the foresight to dispose of the one thing that could identify his car. The sticker changed everything. Durand was promoted to DCI and my life got a whole lot easier. It helped that Durand thought I was a straight arrow. Which I was. Mostly.

'Lacey, secure the floor as far as the lifts. Here's a list of the occupied rooms. Start knocking them up. SOCOs should be here in ten.'

I pressed myself further into the wall as an officer stalked past wearing plastic shoe covers. A low murmur drifted from the room, then Durand's voice, softer this time. 'Someone needs to guard this corridor. Could you keep watch, Andrews?'

Moments later I heard a whooshing sound and took a peek. PC Doug Andrews was bent over, with his hands on his knees, exhaling loudly through his mouth. A shiver ran down my spine. He was a uniformed constable with more than two years in the field. He had seen his share of corpses.

*What is in that room?*

I pulled out my notebook and sketched a rough diagram of the floor plan. The long corridor I'd walked down had six rooms leading off it, then round the corner a shorter corridor with two further rooms, including 538. I made a note to get hold of the hotel guest log.

I glanced back down the corridor. Lacey would be back any second. I squared my shoulders and strolled round the corner, like I had every right to be there.

Andrews's eyes narrowed. 'How the hell did you get in?'

'I got lucky.'

He puffed out his chest in a clumsy attempt to reassert his manliness. He needn't have bothered. I'd been there enough times myself. It's rarely the sight of a body that makes you gag.

It's the smell. Cheap perfume splashed over rotting flesh. It clings to the mucus in your nose so that you can taste it for days afterwards.

I pulled out a box of mints and offered him one. 'Here, helps with the smell.' He eyed me suspiciously but shook one out of the box. I nodded towards the open door. 'That bad, huh?'

Andrews's lips pursed as he sucked greedily on the mint. 'You have no idea.'

PC Andrews was not my biggest fan. Our paths first crossed two years ago on his first-ever crime scene. A couple was shot dead in their Shepherd's Bush home, blood smeared over the walls, their dog's throat slit. I took one look at Andrews's ashen face and trembling hands guarding the crime scene and demanded he step aside. Mistaking me for a senior plain-clothed police officer, he let me under the blue-and-white tape. I lasted fifteen minutes before I was escorted out. Grinning, I introduced myself. Andrews was mortified and hadn't made the same mistake again.

'Can you confirm if the death is suspicious?' He glared at me. 'Where's your boss, anyway? How come Durand is catching this? This is Belgravia's jurisdiction.'

Andrews shrugged. 'He was in the area. Heard the callout and dropped by. Chief Inspector O'Byrne is downstairs with management. That OK with you?'

That didn't make sense. I wondered if Durand's appearance had anything to do with the new hotshot DCI who had been brought into the department. Rumour had it this guy was barely thirty, with an unbeaten track record.

'Come on, Doug. Give me the basics. Male, female, young, old? You know I'm going to find out anyway. Be a hero and help me out.' The corners of Andrews's mouth rose a fraction. 'Or we can play the guessing game until I get kicked out. It might pass the time until your stomach recovers.'

The corners dropped. 'When Lacey gets back it will be my pleasure to escort you out.'

'I'm going to make this easy for you. You don't have to say anything. Just nod if I'm right.'

Andrews rolled his eyes.

'The deceased is male.' I watched him closely but he gave nothing away. 'Female?' A ghost of a nod. 'Under forty?' Andrews nodded again. 'Under twenty-five?' Something flickered across his face. 'Overdose? Stabbing? Come on, I'm on a deadline. Who found the body?' I heard a cough from inside the room. 'What did Durand mean when he said "this isn't ideal"?' Andrews stared at a spot on the wall over my head. I'd have had more luck interrogating a plank of wood. 'I'll get out of your way, I promise. But give me something – *anything* – that means my trip isn't wasted.'

Andrews shifted his weight. I knew it was coming.

'There was some fashion do here last night. We think she was one of the models. It's hard to tell. She's . . .' He swallowed thickly, fighting to keep his face in check.

'Anything else? Method?'

Andrews shook his head. 'I wasn't in there long. Durand needed me out here.'

I smiled encouragingly, pretended I didn't know the real reason Durand sent him outside.

'She had a tattoo,' he added, almost to himself.

'A tattoo?' I scribbled it down in my notepad. 'Where?'

Andrews cleared his throat, snapping back into himself. 'Right here.' He pointed to the middle finger on his right hand. My pen stopped moving. 'The tattoo was upside down from where I was standing, but it looked like a butterfly.'

A chill spread through me. 'A blue butterfly?'

Andrews looked at me uncertainly. 'How did you –'

'Shit, shit, shit.' I slammed my fist against the wall and Andrews's eyes widened.

'You know her?'

'I need to speak to Durand. *Now.*'

Andrews nodded and ducked back along the corridor.

I sagged against the wall feeling sick. This couldn't be happening.

Durand stuck his head round the door and strode towards me, brow furrowed as he peeled off his latex gloves. His auburn hair had grown since I last saw him and hung limply over his collar. He always reminded me of a beaten-up Daniel Craig, but today he looked craggier than usual. You work on your inside sources until you're close enough to know what they ate for breakfast and what their wife gave them for Christmas. I knew Durand never ate breakfast and his wife had left him in November. I wasn't surprised to see the button of his grey jacket straining around his middle.

'Yes?' Durand knew I wouldn't ask for him directly unless it was important.

'I know who she is.'

His eyes, the colourless blue of marbles, flickered over my face but he didn't blink. 'I'm listening.'

'I need something in return.' Durand started to object but I cut him off. 'She has dark hair, a birthmark on her left thigh, and I'm betting you found a green woollen quilt somewhere in that room.' Durand looked startled. 'Sam, she was a source. I know all about her. Give me five minutes.'

Durand narrowed his eyes. 'I won't allow the crime scene to be contaminated. I don't care how well you knew her.'

'That's not what I meant.' I was damned if I was going to leave empty-handed. I pulled out my phone and handed it to him. 'A quick overview, a couple of snaps, anything you can get. And I'll give you a name and address, whatever you need.' And a head-start on your new DCI, I almost said.

Durand rubbed his eyes. He looked as though he hadn't slept for days.

'The SOCOs will be here any minute. Let's make this quick.' He took my phone and disappeared into the room.

I glanced over my shoulder. The consequences would be dire if either of us were caught. Drumming my fingers against my bag, I craned my neck, looking for signs of forced entry. The door hadn't been tampered with. I could picture Durand in the hotel room, auburn eyebrows pulled into a deep 'V'. He once explained to me that he always followed the left-hand wall round a crime scene. 'Like Hampton Court maze,' he explained. 'If you follow the left-hand wall, you get to the middle.' This technique ensured he didn't miss a thing, not the smallest blood spatter, nor footprint.

A few minutes later Durand reappeared, holding my phone between his thumb and forefinger. 'I won't insult you by explaining what will happen if anyone sees the images on your phone.'

I nodded, momentarily distracted by the cloying scent that clung to his suit. Not a corpse smell. Something else.

Durand led me round the corner away from prying eyes. I pulled up the photo folder on my phone with unsteady hands and studied the screen. Pale sunlight filtered through large windows, bathing the room in a ghostly light. A large, mirrored cabinet stood against green-flocked wallpaper, and on top, next to a vase of blue flowers, were five burned-out candles. I zoomed in on the label. *Rose Blossom*. That would explain the smell.

Durand peered at the screen over my shoulder. 'A couple of them were still burning when she was discovered this morning.'

'Travel candles. Expensive ones. Are they hers or were they already in the room? Only. . .'

'What?' Durand's voice was sharp.

'If they were hotel-issued, I doubt housekeeping would leave them on the glass cabinet. Candle bases get hot. They'd far more likely put them on that.' I pointed to a wooden dresser at the right of the frame.

I felt Durand shrug. 'Maybe she brought them with her.'

'Could the candles signify a ritual?'

'It's possible. The killer may have wanted to re-create some sort of romantic fantasy.' I didn't even react to the absurdity of that comment. Eight years on the newsdesk had taught me there was no limit to human depravity.

I swiped to the next picture. A green quilt flung over the arm of a powder-blue armchair and, on the seat, a pair of red-soled high heels. On the floor in front of the chair was a black hold-all with clothes spilling out of it. I studied the bedside table, a small mahogany unit with one drawer. On top was a telephone, a blank notepad and a glass containing an inch of clear liquid.

'Water?'

'Probably. It doesn't smell alcoholic.'

I zoomed in on the cluster of gems on the bedside table. 'Her jewellery is still there.'

'So is her purse. It seems the killer had no interest in taking anything from her.' He gave a wry smile. 'Apart from the obvious.'

Durand had taken a photograph through the crack in the bathroom door. Bottles and make-up brushes were scattered across honey-flecked marble.

The next photograph hit me, a jab under the ribs.

'Jesus Christ.'

The last time I'd had seen that butterfly tattoo, its blue wings had stood out against Natalia's milky-white skin like the veins on a Stilton cheese. Now those lifeless, twisted hands were the same bruisy colour. Fingers curled into ugly claws, as though reaching for salvation that never came.

She lay on her back. Her gold brocade dress hung low at the side exposing her ribs. The past week had taught me that each bone poking out of Natalia's body told a tale of denial and rejection. You could trace your fingertips over them like Braille and read her unhappy story. Blood had soaked through the ivory eiderdown beneath her lower half and I was grateful the dress hid whatever the killer did down there. I zoomed in on her face. The back of my throat burned as I took in the butchered mess. A small stub of nose was visible but nothing more. I forced my eyes downwards to the purple bruising on her throat. It was a couple of moments before I realised Natalia's hair had been hacked off into a cropped, boy's haircut.

Durand cleared his throat. I tore my eyes away from the photos and made a big show of returning my phone to my bag so he couldn't see how shaken I was.

I took a deep breath. 'Her name is Natalia Kotov. She's Russian. Moved to London last July to pursue modelling. She came here for a better life.'

Durand paused, letting that statement hang in the air. 'When did you last see her?'

'Nineteen hours ago.'

'Where?'

'The Goat in Boots on Brixton High Road.' I filled Durand in on how we met and he listened quietly, without interrupting.

'And you have no idea who her attacker is?'

I shook my head. 'She never identified him. But I believe he's in the fashion industry.'

'What makes you say that?'

'Just a hunch.'

Durand looked thoughtful. 'The timing is curious. Natalia is killed the day after she gets cold feet about ID'ing her rapist. If she kept quiet, why kill her?'

'Perhaps he couldn't trust her.'

'Or the rape had nothing to do with her murder.' Durand leaned against the wall and folded his arms. 'How did she seem to you yesterday?'

'Tense. But sources often get cold feet.' I gave Durand a wan smile and rubbed my eyes, feeling as if I was in a dream. 'I thought I'd give her a day or two and then try again.'

An image of Natalia's broken body smashed through my brain and my stomach heaved. 'What caused the bloodstain on the bed?'

'I won't know the details until the pathologist gets here, but it looks as if she's been mutilated. Her underwear is missing.' Durand's tone was matter-of-fact, but I detected an edge.

I shivered. 'It's a bold move, killing her in such a public place and not hiding the body. And it doesn't look like there are signs of forced entry. So, either she let her attacker in or he had a key.' I watched Durand closely but he knew better than to comment before the crime scene had been analysed. 'Who found her?'

Durand's phone rang. He frowned at the screen but ignored it. 'Housekeeper. Walked past this morning and noticed the door was open.'

'What do you mean "open"?'

Durand suddenly looked irritated. 'Open. Caught on the latch.'

I wondered who'd just called him. 'When will her name go public?'

'We'll release a statement in a few hours but be sensitive, Sophie. We haven't informed next of kin.'

I thought briefly of Natalia's mum; a survivor, a woman who'd endured enough hardship for one lifetime. 'I'll keep her name under the radar for now.' I didn't tell Durand that not naming Natalia worked in my favour. It gave me a head-start. I could pull together information without the competition getting in my way. But if Durand thought I was doing him a favour that worked for me too.

'Boss.' A warning shot rang down the corridor.

I slid my notepad into my bag, feeling as if the adrenaline had left my body.

Durand must have noticed. 'Are you OK?'

I shrugged. 'It's a shock. I only saw her yesterday.'

'That's not what I –'

'Yeah, I know.' I didn't meet his eye. 'I'm fine.'

Durand's shrewd gaze unsettled me. I strive to be a closed book, but he's one of the few people who can read me.

'Really? Because you look terrible.'

I snorted. 'You really know how to boost a girl's confidence.'

His eyes lingered on my face and I thought he was going to say something else. Instead, he turned away and disappeared into the room of death.

## 5

I stepped out of the lift and into the lobby, noticing a shift in atmosphere. The air was charged, a flame licking at the fuse. News had spread. Outside, reporters were being pushed back by police officers who had sealed the exits. I'd managed to slip through the net but I didn't have long. I sloped over to an ornate rosewood cabinet and pretended to inspect the jewellery on display, while reaching into my bag for my phone. I flicked on the video camera and, holding it close to me, filmed a 360-degree sweep of the lobby. Raising my gaze, I spotted two CCTV cameras, red lights blinking.

My shoes squeaked as I crossed the lobby to a heavy green door marked *Staff only*. I glanced over my shoulder, then pushed it open. A lanky waiter was wheeling a table along the corridor towards me.

I smiled brightly. 'I'm looking for the security room.'

'Third door on your left.' He nodded in the direction he'd come from. 'Roger's there.'

'Thank you.' I scuttled away before he could ask who I was. I opened the door a crack. A burly security guard with short, grey hair sat with his back to me. One meaty hand was wrapped around a chipped mug of tea, the other poised to turn the page of a car magazine. I slipped in and closed the door quickly.

He looked round in surprise and half-rose from the chair as if he was the one who'd made the mistake. 'Can I help you, madam?'

The room reeked of fried breakfast and BO. 'Roger, I'm Sophie Kent and I'm with *The London Herald*. I'm investigating the incident that happened here last night. Do you mind if I ask a couple of questions?'

He frowned, drawing together thick eyebrows, so dark they looked as if they'd been filled in with charcoal.

'How did you get in here?'

'I'll cut to the chase. I need to see last night's CCTV footage.' He gave me an incredulous look. 'I know. You can't, you'll lose your job. Here's the thing. You and I both know that images from that CCTV footage will be released to the press eventually. I'm asking for a head-start.'

Roger stood up. His body looked as though it was made out of building blocks.

He careened towards me and I ducked out of his reach, finding myself next to a corkboard covered with personal photos. Roger dressed in a plaid shirt with his arm round a petite, brunette woman I took to be his wife. Next to it was a photo of a teenage girl with Roger's heavy build, but her mother's delicate features and dark hair.

I had my angle.

'Listen, I know the girl who died.' I deliberately used the word *girl*, not *woman*. 'When I saw her yesterday, she was terrified. And now she's lying upstairs in a hotel suite bleeding out of her eyes.' An image of Natalia's mottled throat flashed across my eyes and I began to sweat. 'CID is conducting the investigation *their* way, which means thorough and slow. They'll interview every guest and member of staff. How long do you think that will take in a hotel this size? Meanwhile the killer is out there thinking he's got away with it.' I nodded towards the photo behind him. 'He's probably choosing his next victim and, by the looks of things, he likes them young, pretty and brunette. I am going to hunt down the monster who mutilated this girl with or without your help. But I'll get there much faster if you help me.'

Roger glared at me, a muscle pulsating under his eye. 'I'm eight months away from retirement. You're crazy if you think I'm going to risk it.' He rubbed a hand over his head and exhaled loudly. 'You know what, I need to take a leak. The bog is a few minutes' walk away and I drank a *lot* of coffee this morning so I could be in there some time.' He gave me a ghost of a wink and strolled out.

I threw myself into Roger's chair, wrinkling my nose as a cloud of BO engulfed me, and studied the CCTV screens on his desk. The main camera above the front door provided a wide-angle view of the lobby. A second was in the corner furthest from the entrance. I pulled up the last twenty-four hours' worth of footage. Then I plugged in a USB stick and hit *download*. A blue bar appeared on the screen moving at the pace of a winded snail. While I waited, I searched for the CCTV from the fifth floor. I couldn't find anything.

A faint whistle grew louder as Roger approached. The first camera footage hadn't finished downloading, let alone the second, but it was more than I could have hoped for. I ejected the USB stick and sprang away from the desk.

The door opened and Roger appeared, hoisting up the waistband of his trousers.

'You still here?' He lumbered across the tiny space and sat down heavily, resuming the position with one hand on his mug.

'Roger, hypothetically, if I wanted to get my hands on the CCTV footage from the fifth floor . . .'

'Aside from the fact that you're seriously pushing your luck, you couldn't. It doesn't exist.' He pointed a stout finger to a hotel floor plan that was pinned to the wall. 'We're in the process of updating our security system. The first three floors have cameras outside each lift and at the end of each corridor. But the top two floors haven't been completed.' He gave me a sharp look. 'Now if you'll excuse me.'

I slid my business card across the table and let myself out. Up ahead was a door bearing a neat, gold sign with black writing: *Housekeeping*. I pushed the door open and stuck my head round. The room was warm and smelled of freshly laundered linen. Housekeeping trolleys were lined up and I could just make out female voices above the drone of industrial-sized washing machines. I crept inside and saw two women sitting with their backs to me, wearing identical green dresses, their dark hair scraped back into tight buns. The one closest to me was folding towels, her slim hands moving on autopilot. The other, barrel-shaped with calves like a side of ham, had a pile of unfolded pillowcases beside her. I didn't need to speak Spanish to know they were upset.

I moved out of the shadows and the older lady swung round. Her face was carved with wrinkles but her hazel eyes were sharp. 'You lost, miss?'

I flashed my press card in front of her face, hoping it made me look more official. 'Could I ask you a couple of questions?' She shrugged. 'Do you know what happened to that girl last night?'

She threw her hands up in the air and babbled in Spanish, her eyes watering.

'Carlita, sshh, don't upset yourself.' The younger woman put a hand on the woman's thick shoulder, glaring at me. She was in her early twenties; tall and sullen and heavily made-up. Dark eyebrows pencilled on her high forehead, thick stripes of blusher on her narrow cheeks.

'Give her a break.' Her accent wasn't as thick as Carlita's. 'She found the girl.'

I nodded sympathetically. 'What time was this, ah . . .?'

'Sasha.'

She repeated my question in Spanish and Carlita looked at me warily. 'Around seven o'clock.' She pronounced it *seben*. 'The door is open and when I look inside, I see –' Her face crumpled like a dry tissue and my heart went out to her.

I inched towards them and took out my notepad. 'Did either of you have any contact with the girl?'

Carlita nodded. 'She call housekeeping when she arrive. She want a – how you say – steam?' She looked at Sasha for help.

'Steamer. Her dress was creased,' said Sasha impatiently. 'I took it to her around 6.30 p.m.'

'And you took the steamer to,' I looked down at my notebook, 'Room 538?'

Sasha thought for a moment. 'It was 340.'

I frowned. 'You're sure it was that room?'

'Yes, I remember because the light outside her room was broken and I had to report it.'

'Did she move rooms?' Carlita shrugged and her thick neck disappeared. I looked at Sasha. 'When you took the steamer to the girl, how did she seem?'

Sasha's eyes glittered. 'This going in the newspaper?'

'Only if you want it to.'

'She seemed, you know . . .' She mimed drinking from a glass.

'Drunk?'

'Her words sounded funny.'

I made a mental note to find out if Natalia had ordered anything from room service and, if so, who brought it to her.

'Would anyone have checked her minibar since then?'

Carlita hauled herself off the bench and shuffled over to a table and picked up a binder. 'No. Look, no one go inside her room. She had *Do Not Disturb* on door.'

She held the binder out for me to see. On the column marked *Turn Down*, next to room 340 were the letters *DND*. I pretended to look where her finger was pointing, while scanning the page lightning-quick for room 538. Again, the letters *DND*.

'Do you keep a log of which guests are in which rooms?'

Sasha shook her head. 'That's above our pay grade. We don't know names, we just clean the shit off their toilets.' Her smile stretched tight like a rubber band.

Carlita said something in Spanish and Sasha shrugged. 'You could try Dmitri on the front desk.' Her cheeks flushed at the mention of his name.

This was something I could use.

'You mean the hot guy I passed on the way in?' I leaned in towards her. 'How long have you been together?'

Sasha grinned. 'Almost two months. One day I found a note in my cubby asking me out for a drink. We went to a little Russian place round the corner. Forty-eight types of vodka. Dmitri showed me how to drink it the Russian way. *Na Zdorovie!*' She gave a high-pitched giggle.

'Could you persuade Dmitri to make a copy of the guest log?'

Sasha looked less certain of herself. 'I can try but I don't know ...' She glanced at Carlita. 'Do you have money? He might do it if you pay him.'

I sighed. 'I don't pay for information. People talk to me because they want to help. But if Dmitri feels uncomfortable putting himself on the line for this dead girl, that's his decision.'

'No, Dmitri is a good man. I will tell him it's important. He might do it for me.'

She smiled shyly. Dmitri must be something special. Sasha had gone from petulant to lovestruck in the blink of an eye.

I handed over my card. 'Call me as soon as you've spoken to Dmitri.'

As I pulled the door closed, Sasha was already reaching for her phone.

# 6

The first time I entered Premier News, I was fresh out of university, with a blunt fringe, strident views and a trouser suit that made me look forty-five. I dropped my bag at the security gate and had to scrabble around picking up loose change, lipglosses and a good-luck cactus from my brother, Tommy. I looked up to find a security guard beaming at me. His face was round as a button, with amber eyes and bright Tic Tac teeth. He ushered me over to a chair.

'First day?' He spoke slowly, his voice unspooling like honey off a spoon, with a hint of an Ethiopian lilt, even though I later found out he'd lived in London for more than twenty years.

'That obvious, huh?'

'Some of the most important people in the world have come through those doors and they all nervous when they hit the lobby. Something about this place.' He gave me a wink. 'Don't you forget, you's in good company.'

Eight years later, Joe Vassalo's black curls had thinned, his stoop deteriorated, but his smile was just as wide.

'Miss Sophie, you don't look so good. You getting sick?'

'I've had better mornings.' I rifled through my bag for my security pass, flicking him a smile. 'Rowley in yet?'

'It was still dark when he arrive this morning.' Joe grinned. 'You know what they say about the early bird –'

'Everybody hates them?'

Joe cackled and swiped me through the security gate. I click-ety-clacked across the marble lobby towards the lift, glancing up at the patch of grey sky through the glass ceiling five hundred feet above my head. The lobby's cathedral acoustics always made me feel both small and important at the same time. They pulled me upwards, made me walk taller. Even on a day such as today.

The lift doors opened on the eighth floor and I scurried over to News, an island of desks in the far corner by the window. I sat down heavily in my chair, my hangover intensifying as I was hit with a garlicky whiff from someone's lunch. I lay my cheek on my desk, waiting for the waves of nausea to pass. I needed to eat something but the thought turned my stomach.

My desk was virtually bare. No photos, no novelty desk toys, just a mug with the words *Don't Panic* printed on the side and a potted cactus. Not the same cactus Tommy bought – that had died after a month. Contrary to popular belief, cactae aren't that easy to keep alive. It didn't stop me replacing one each time it perished. I pressed my finger against a cactus needle until it pierced my skin. I felt nothing, even when a droplet of blood bubbled up.

Tommy had pricked his thumb on the cactus when he gave it to me. 'Christ, Sops. Ow!'

It was one of his more lucid days. He'd been staying with me for a week, ever since he showed up on my doorstep one bitter evening, stinking of the streets. It had been six months but, when the doorbell rang, I knew who it was. I opened the door to find Tommy shivering on the doormat; a beaten-up backpack, crammed full of God knows what, slung over his shoulder and a filthy sleeping bag secured to the top with a rusty bike clip.

He looked at me warily; his face the colour of chalk and eyes, once so clear and blue like mine, cloudy with toxins. 'Hi, Sops, any chance I can crash?'

I wrapped my arms tightly round him, burying my face in his navy parka, inhaling the grime and loneliness of the streets, until a tiny sob escaped; mine or his, I wasn't sure. It never got any easier. I pushed Tommy towards a hot shower, then laid clothes out for him. I'd taken to keeping men's clothes in a drawer for whenever Tommy showed up. He always took them gratefully but whenever he next appeared, with the exception of his parka, they were gone.

Tommy joined me in the kitchen wearing tracksuit bottoms and a T-shirt, looking almost himself again. He'd always been a slip of a thing. Five years my junior, he morphed from a child to an adult without really changing. His little freckled-egg face slimmed down, his silvery hair thickened and his voice deepened. But he only grew a couple of inches taller than me, then his body gave up. Our six-foot-one bully of a father took it as a personal slight, as though Tommy had chosen to stay small to spite him. He called Tommy 'Sparrow' and sneered that he had to run round the shower to get wet. Once, on holiday, I caught Tommy smearing suntan lotion in lines across his stomach, hoping the sun would darken his skin and create a shadowy six-pack.

As kids, we huddled under the duvet at our Surrey manor, Redcroft, where I read him Roald Dahl's tales of plucky children triumphing over wicked adults to gently instil in Tommy an alternative creed, where love and happiness were not defined by size and strength. But the less he grew, the baggier his clothes became, as though he was protecting himself with a fabric suit of armour.

Then, at thirteen, Tommy was packed off to boarding school and I couldn't look after him anymore. I begged my parents not to send him. Tommy was too delicate for the lofty dormitories and cruel rituals of boarding school. Even at that age, he woke up in soaked sheets.

My father warned me not to interfere. 'I'm doing Sparrow a favour. A ribbing will toughen him up. I learned that from your grandfather. Didn't do me any harm, did it?'

My mother didn't say anything at all. I always suspected that sending Tommy away was her idea. I was about to leave for Oxford University and, with Tommy gone, she could drift from room to room in a vapour of talc, devoting herself to gin-soaked nights playing bridge, before locking herself in her bedroom, turning up the record player and letting Rachmaninoff's nimble fingers play her to sleep.

That night, as I slid a mug of hot tea across the kitchen table, I noticed the bruised track marks running up the inside of

Tommy's arm. He caught me staring and hastily reached for his jumper.

'I'm trying, Sops, it was going well . . .' He cradled the mug between his small hands, looking down at the tea as if he couldn't believe it was real.

'Tomorrow, Tommy. You need sleep. The bed's made up.' His eyes flickered at the mention of bed and I wondered how long it had been since he'd slept in one. When I went to check on him later that evening he was fast asleep still wearing his clothes – old habits, I guessed. I hunkered down in my bedroom, mentally preparing myself for the gruelling days ahead.

'There you are!' Kate Fingersmith's chaotic brown curls appeared over the top of the desk divider, snapping me back to the present. 'God, you look shit.'

Kate was in her early forties and something of a mentor. She was tenacious, ballsy and her record for breaking news was legendary in the industry. She perched on my desk, enveloping me in a cloud of bergamot. Kate wore men's cologne; perfume made her feel 'frilly'.

She handed me a mug of coffee. 'Drink this. What have you been doing, Kent? Or should I say "whom"?'

I forced the memory of Tommy away. 'The tramp look is very Spring/Summer 2014. Which you would know if you ever bothered to read the fashion pages of our esteemed paper.' I took a sip, wincing as Kate's industrial-strength coffee hit my tastebuds. She drank so much of the stuff it was a wonder she didn't vibrate.

Kate gestured towards her outfit. 'Do I look as though I waste my time reading that drivel?'

She had a point. Kate's closet staples, baggy shirts and crumpled trousers, made her large frame look like a badly packed rucksack. 'There's more important stuff going on in the world. My piece on government corruption, for one. And who you were with last night.'

She gave me a sly look and I widened my eyes innocently. 'I have zero idea what you're referring to.'

Kate sighed. 'Where've you been anyway? Nutsack's been hovering around my desk looking for you.'

She meant Mack. Kate had secretly christened him Nutsack on a slow day in the newsroom, after deciding he walked 'like a man who'd been kicked in the nuts'.

I filled Kate in on what had gone down at The Rose. 'Natalia didn't want to open up to me in the first place, but I pushed and pushed and look what happened. I mean, *fuck*, Kate.'

Kate put her hand on my shoulder. 'You can't go down that road, my friend. Natalia knew the risks when she spoke to a reporter.'

I slammed the mug down on the table and two guys on the sports desk looked round. 'Bullshit, Kate. We have to protect our sources.' I squeezed my eyes shut. 'I should never have let her walk away yesterday.'

Kate gave me a long look. 'You know you're not responsible for everyone all the time.'

I knew what she was referring to but I refused to engage. 'I appreciate the concern but I'm fine.' I swivelled my chair back round to my computer.

'Where the hell have you been?' Mack appeared at my shoulder.

'She's been having a pedicure. Where do you think she's been?' Kate couldn't hide the scorn in her voice. As News Editor, Mack was technically her superior but Kate was far too experienced to take any crap from him.

'Sorry, I was about to fill you in.' I yawned loudly, then regretted it when I saw the look on Mack's face. 'I was on a murder scene at The Rose.'

'As your department head, I need to know where you are at all times.' He fixed me with a meaningful stare. The subtext wasn't lost on me. He was angry I bailed on him this morning.

'It all happened so fast,' I said, mumbling into my coffee mug.

'Oh, give her a break.' Kate stood up so she was at Mack's eye level. 'If there's a murder, you don't bugger about with office admin. *Sorry, Rowley, I missed that scoop because I was too busy cc'ing everyone in on my precise location.*' She roared with laughter. I glanced at Mack and saw he'd gone very still. 'Or better still, why don't you fix Sophie with a tracking device and save yourself the hassle.'

Mack glared at us, then hissed: 'I'll see you in conference.' He slunk away and I felt the air around me grow momentarily lighter.

Kate watched him leave, her face flushed with pleasure. 'Well, that was fun.'

She turned back to look at me. 'Speaking of conference, might I suggest you freshen up? You don't resemble a shining beacon of journalistic talent right now.'

I walked straight past the mirror, not wanting to see the evidence of last night etched into my face, and locked myself in a cubicle. This thing with Mack had to stop. Rowley frowned upon office relationships at the best of times (*'Don't shit where you eat, people'*), so God knows what he'd do if he found out about the affair. So far we'd got away with it, but Mack was teetering on the edge of a career nosedive. I couldn't trust him not to drag me down with him. It took two to tango, but only one would be labelled a 'slut'. And it wasn't the one with the penis.

A splash of water did little to sort my face out. I pinched my cheeks and rubbed the smudge of mascara under my eyes. My hair smelled like a fireman's armpit. I looked down at my grey Stella McCartney trouser suit. The expensive cut was doing its best but even a fifteen-hundred-pound suit looked as if it came from the clearance bin at Primark if you stopped hanging it up. I ran my fingernail over a small, crusty stain on top of my thigh and rifled through my bag for some gum. Then I stood back and gave myself the once-over. It would have to do.

'Shall we run through yesterday?'

Austin Lansdowne, *The London Herald*'s formidable Deputy Editor waved a copy of the previous day's edition in the air. I leaned against the wall of Conference Room Two, along with all the other second-tier reporters who weren't senior enough to warrant a seat at the oval table. The heating was on full blast and a few of the men had removed their jackets.

'Fuck's sake.' Kate fanned herself with her notebook on the chair in front of me. 'It's hotter than two hamsters farting in a sock.'

Someone near me stank of stale cigarettes and something else unpleasant that I couldn't put my finger on. I had a worrying thought it could be me. I shifted the weight in my feet as Austin began his daily critique of the news stories that hit the mark, and those that didn't. The European Union's plans to cut the speed limit to 60 mph on the M3 garnered the most online reader comments, followed by a sighting of the Kardashian clan on Bond Street. Austin rolled his eyes at the latter and earned a few sniggers from around the room. Rowley, sitting on his left, remained expressionless. He was careful to not scorn outwardly anything or anyone that caused a spike in readership.

Charlie Swift, the Business Editor, raised his eyebrows at me from across the room and I grinned. We'd been friends since the 2008 Christmas party: Charlie sweating in a Lycra Spiderman costume, me an irritable Tinkerbell. Over several vodka martinis, he confessed that his wife had recently died. Over the years, as the Tommy situation escalated, Charlie and I were often the last two in the office, using work as an excuse to avoid going home with our thoughts. Then Charlie met a pretty wedding planner from the Home Counties and didn't feel the need to hang around an empty office any longer. I was happy for him.

Austin finished talking and there was a pause.

Rowley cleared his throat. 'Today's edition. What has Page One potential at this stage?'

'It's got to be Operation Yew Tree and Dave Lee Travis,' said Spencer Storey, the City Editor. A murmur went round the room. The former Radio 1 DJ had just been sensationally cleared of assaulting ten women.

'An absolute catastrofuck,' said Austin, shaking his head.

Rowley nodded. 'Travis has another hearing on the 24th. I want someone live-blogging from the courthouse.'

I switched off as the discussion moved on to the new wave of English footballers who were filling the nation with hope ahead of the World Cup. Suddenly I realised everyone was staring at me.

'Sorry?'

Austin smirked. 'Would you care to enlighten us about your morning's activities? If it's not too much trouble, of course.'

I felt the colour rush to my cheeks. 'Uh, yes. An eighteen-year-old woman was killed last night. At The Rose Hotel.'

'Mmmm.' Austin was staring at his iPad only half listening.

I cleared my throat. 'Early reports suggest she was a model. London Fashion Week kicks off today so it's bound to bump up the interest level.'

'We're talking page three, at least. Fit model throttled in glitzy London hotel. It's sexy, it sells.' Mack's eyes shone desperately.

I stared at him, careful to keep my face neutral. 'That's one way of putting it.'

Rowley tapped his silver pen on his notepad. 'Any word on who she is?'

'Police haven't released her name but I know her. Her name is Natalia Kotov. She was my source on a potential story.'

'Which story?' Austin looked up.

I explained that Natalia and I had met the day before to discuss how to take the issue of her assault forward.

Austin snorted. 'Russian? She's got to be a hooker. What do we reckon: sex game gone wrong?'

I let the sniggers die down before responding. 'I need to find out whether Natalia was killed because of *who* she was or *what* she was.'

'What do you mean?' Rowley asked, watching me closely.

'Well, her face was hacked to bits. The killer symbolically destroyed her livelihood.' An image of the bloodstain on the bed resurfaced in my mind and I faltered. 'Or the motive could be more personal to Natalia.'

'What do we know about this girl?' Rowley scanned the room. 'Where's the bloody Fashion team?'

A timid hand went up from an assistant in oversized glasses. 'They're at the shows.'

'Well, when they appear, find out what they know about her.'

'Maybe she was killed because someone saw her talking to you.' Mack's voice was like ice. He clearly wasn't letting me get away with this morning's disappearing act. 'How hard did you push this girl?'

'That's enough, Mack.'

I threw a grateful look at Rowley. 'It's possible, yes. It's one of the avenues I'm investigating.'

'And what are the others?' Rowley asked.

'My priority is piecing together the hours between when I saw her and when she was murdered. I've already made some headway with the hotel staff and I know she's close to her agent. I'm going to Models International after this.'

'Ooh, do you need someone to hold your Dictaphone?' Rupert Brewster the Sports Editor batted his eyes at me.

'It's probably too early for any social media response to her death but I'll have a dig. Also, she had a flatmate who might let me snoop around their flat.'

Rowley nodded. 'Ask Pictures to start pulling off catwalk shots. Get something on the website in the next hour, then flesh it out for the print edition later today. There's no point peddling the personal angle until you have more to say. And keep her name off your first write-up. I don't want to do our competitors' work for them. OK, good.' He shifted his attention away from me and I exhaled slowly.

'Nice save, Kent,' Kate muttered. 'Next time take the nap after conference.'

Back at my desk, I downed painkillers with a swig of Kate's cold coffee, then typed out a story for the website. Once I got a thumbs-up from the web editor, I tweeted the link to my followers. Then I searched for Natalia's Facebook page. She didn't have one, but she did have a Twitter account. She posted her first tweet in July just after she moved to London.

*@N_Kotovofficial woooo luv London, u my best city!*

I scrolled through Natalia's feed. It was mostly lame chat-up lines and desperate shout-outs from male admirers. She'd racked up 15,432 followers but never responded to anyone. My eyes stopped on 16 August.

*@N_Kotovofficial Hey, u. Leave me alone. STOP.*

That was the last thing she ever tweeted. I scrolled back up, the black letters dancing in front of my tired eyes. There was nothing overly threatening in the lead up to her final tweet.

*@mr_sound I need you baby, I need you now*

*@Cityofbrides Looking for love?*

*@LyLaw what up bitch? See you at Givenchy!*

Even I knew that @LyLaw was Lydia Lawson, the notorious Brit model and tabloid darling. I clicked on the other two. The profile picture for @Mr_sound showed a teenage boy on a skateboard, skinny legs poking out the bottom of baggy shorts. His feed was full of exclamation marks and abbreviations I didn't understand but it didn't look particularly suspicious. And @Cityofbrides posted similar tweets to Natalia most days. I punched it into my search engine and a Russian dating website popped up. The tag line was *Beautiful, single Eastern European women looking for love.*

'Hey, Kate?' I stuck my head over the desk divider. 'When you covered that story about the Ukrainian woman who killed her Irish husband, did you ever come across a website called cityofbrides.rs?'

Kate stopped typing. 'Hang on.' I heard her rifling through her notebook. 'No. Why?'

'Could be nothing but a Russian dating service has been tweeting Natalia.'

'Yeah, I interviewed a woman who told me that agencies recruit potential brides via social media. They send out messages enticing them with money. You know, like in the olden days when your Hotmail inbox was full of penis enlargement emails.'

I raised my eyebrows. '*Yours* might have been.'

'Don't pretend you didn't get yours enlarged.'

I snorted and turned back to my screen. Did Natalia join this City of Brides website? I searched for her name but there were no matches.

I unscrewed a bottle of water and took a swig, then pulled up her most recent photo shoot: a fashion story in *W* magazine. Natalia was reclining on satin sheets, wearing nothing but a wig the colour of candyfloss and layers of neon chiffon. She gazed at the camera, eyes wide, lips parted, looking very Lolita-on-acid. The caption read: *photographs by Liam Crawford.*

A searing heat spread across the back of my neck. Liam was Fashion's *enfant-terrible* photographer and on–off boyfriend of Lydia Lawson. But that's not how I knew him. Liam and I were both at St Hugh's College, Oxford, before he dropped out to pursue photography, much to the anguish of the female population. I lost count of the conversations cut short by Liam's cheekbones entering the room. I refused to become one of the simpering masses and kept my distance. Until the night of the Keble Ball, when Liam flicked his eyes in my direction. A flash of that heated night lit up my memory. The bottle slipped out of my hand and clattered onto the desk.

I clicked on Instagram. The last photo Natalia had posted made me do a double-take. A slightly blurred selfie of Natalia and Lydia at the designer Leo Brand's party at The Rose the night she was killed. Underneath the photo she'd written: *#leobrand4eva #lylawurock*. Lydia pouted at the camera, her shoulder-length ebony hair falling across her eyes. Natalia was laughing with her head thrown back, her sharp features thrust into the spotlight. They looked like sisters. *The money shot*, I thought grimly. I copied the image into an email and sent it to the Picture Desk. So, Lydia was with Natalia the night she died. I needed to get to her fast, but that was easier said than done with London Fashion Week in full swing. A quick search revealed that Natalia and Lydia were both represented by the same agent, Cat Ramsey.

Kate was on the phone so I fired off an email.

If Nutsack asks, I'm at Models International. Don't wait up.

## 7

I stood outside the imposing glass doors of Models International and peered inside. The sleek lobby looked like a spread in an interiors magazine. A huge pendant light in the shape of a pyramid hung low over the orange reception desk. Poster-sized photographs of Models International's biggest names adorned the walls. Tammy French, Nadya Vodiova, Lydia Lawson. Even amongst the world's most beautiful women, Lydia dominated. Feline-shaped eyes the colour of expensive ink, set in an angular face with full lips. She was part Liz Taylor, part Angelina Jolie and as intimidating as hell. Something about her intense gaze made me shiver.

A striking black girl sat stiffly on the olive-green sofa with an unread magazine on her lap. She kept glancing at reception, where two women were chatting animatedly. One was girl-next-door pretty, the other edgier with custard-yellow hair. I looked up at the ragged clouds, willing the rain to stay away. I had to pick my moment.

Just then, a tribe of twenty-somethings approached the office, dressed in variations of slouchy harem pants, dark cable-knit sweaters and biker boots. A couple lingered outside to smoke and I held my phone to my ear, pretending I was on a call.

'I mean, it's fucked up.' A girl with ash-blonde hair sucked on her cigarette and the tip glowed neon against her black clothes. 'Dragon made me cancel her lunch with Christopher. I'm telling you, something's going down. She got a call, next thing I know she'd pulled the blinds.' She flicked her cigarette butt into a puddle. 'It's Fashion Week for Christ's sake. Like, crazy fucking busy. It blows.'

'Want my advice?' Her male companion ran a gloved hand over his shaved head. His ear was pierced with a miniature black tusk. 'If Dragon's having one of her moments, keep your head down or she'll knock it off.'

He pushed through the revolving door and I seized my moment. I slipped in behind them, thanking my tiny-person genes as I sailed past reception. I followed them into a large, open-plan office with concrete floors and exposed pipes running along the ceiling. In the centre, staff sat facing each other along walnut desks. I was momentarily thrown by the chaos in front of me. It made the newsroom feel like church.

'I've got Dominic on hold!' A willowy brunette screamed across the room. 'Joan is a no-show. What was her call time?'

A man with a peroxide quiff shot past trailing spicy aftershave. He had a mobile phone under his ear. 'Erdem's show has been pushed back. Check it's not going to clash with Serene's hair and make-up at Burberry.'

I assumed Cat Ramsey was senior enough to warrant her own office. The one closest to me was empty, but the office in the far corner had its horizontal blinds pulled down. I marched towards it, hoping everyone was so preoccupied they wouldn't notice me, and opened the door.

Cat was bent over her chair, rifling through her bag, her sleek blonde bob hiding her face. She looked up and I saw the sculpted face of a woman in her late forties or early fifties. It was hard to tell. Her skin was pulled tightly over her bones, giving her an expensive, Harley Street expression. Red lipstick only emphasised her pallor and her tall frame was hidden under a black tunic.

Cat frowned, her muscles not moving as much as they should for a woman her age. I took a moment to weigh up my approach. My job depends on my ability to decipher a person's state of mind bullet-quick. Nine times out of ten, they don't want to talk and so all I have is an intake of breath, an *eye-blink*, to assess their body language and decide how to proceed.

Something about Cat made me choose the direct approach. 'I'm sorry to barge in on you. I wanted to ask you about Natalia Kotov.'

'How do you know about – who are you?' Cat's voice emitted a don't-fuck-with-me tone, and there was an accent I couldn't place.

I kept my voice level. 'My name is Sophie Kent and I'm a reporter at *The London Herald*.' The shutters came down. 'Please, before you kick me out . . . I'm not looking for anything on the record. I just want to talk.'

Cat's eyes narrowed. 'What makes you think I have any interest in talking to the press?'

'If you hear me out, you'll understand. Please, it will only take a minute.'

She gave me a hard look, then said, 'A minute is all you have.'

I nodded and sat down in the chair opposite her desk. 'Natalia and I were working on a story together.'

Cat's bag was still on her lap and she gripped it tightly. 'I doubt that very much. Natalia wouldn't say boo to a goose, much less a reporter.'

'You're wrong. She was talking to me. Reluctantly at first, I'll admit, but we were getting somewhere.'

'What was the story about?'

I took a deep breath and explained how I met Natalia at her flat, describing her emotional state and the bruises all over her.

'And this was when?' Cat tried to sound nonchalant but I could hear the anxiety in her voice.

'Last week. I was worried about her so I stayed in touch.'

Cat looked at her watch. 'You're out of time.'

'Come on, Cat. I'm trying to help.'

'Are you?' Her voice was sharp. 'As far as I can see, you've muscled your way into my office to dig up dirt for your paper.'

Cat's reaction got under my skin and I was more direct than I intended to be. 'Did you know Natalia was raped?' To her credit Cat didn't flinch. 'What do you know about it?'

'I know that it's none of your business.'

'Wrong again. When Natalia met me yesterday, she agreed to identify her attacker, but something spooked her and she bailed. She was terrified, Cat. Then twelve hours later she was dead. I can't forgive myself for letting her walk away from me. So I can assure you, catching her rapist and her killer – whether they're the same person or not – is very much my business.'

Cat glared at me, then all of a sudden she put her head in her hands. 'God, I can't believe this is happening.'

I heard her sniff and handed her a tissue, seizing the fleeting chink in her armour. I continued more gently: 'Did Natalia tell you she'd been raped?'

Cat didn't look up. 'Not exactly, but I suspected something. She was using again . . .'

'You mean, drugs?'

Cat gave me a long look. 'This is off the record. I don't want you making her sound like a junkie in your paper. I've been looking after models long enough to know the signs. Dark circles under the eyes, extreme weight loss, oversleeping. I called Natalia into the office. It was a sweltering August afternoon, but Natalia showed up in a charcoal sweater and knee-high boots.' I thought about Tommy; he was always cold, no matter how warm the weather. 'She denied it at first. Said she just wasn't sleeping. I told her if she didn't get clean she'd be on the first plane back to Russia.'

I couldn't hide my scepticism. 'I thought drugs were pretty rife in the fashion industry.'

Cat's voice was pure ice. 'Not on my watch. I can't afford to be sentimental. Each year it's getting harder. More models competing for fewer gigs and for less money. I tell my girls, you're only as strong as your last job. Reputation is everything. Late nights, bad skin and ratty moods don't cut it in this climate. All I'm saying is that if a girl is showing signs, I nip it in the bud.'

'How?'

'Narcotics Anonymous, rehab, whatever. Depends how much I have invested in the girl. Natalia wasn't a big earner yet, she'd only been on the scene for five minutes. But I had high hopes for her. She was definitely a girl worth investing in. She had the current look – a wide-eyed androgynous vibe – but it was more than that. There was fragility to her beauty. Like she didn't know how stunning she was. The industry goes nuts for that sort of innocence.' Cat uncapped an Evian bottle and poured it into a glass. 'Sometimes a firm chat is all it takes. In other cases, well, it takes a little more persuasion. But they only get one chance to clean up or they're out.'

My coat was still on and the heat was making me sweat. I looked longingly at Cat's bottle of water. 'And did Natalia clean up?'

Cat's phone rang. She looked at the screen, gave a dramatic sigh, but didn't answer. 'At first, but she slipped. I was about to send her packing but I couldn't do it. Natalia was too special. So I got her into NA. I thought it was working. Excuse me.' Cat's phone rang again and she spun her chair round to take the call.

Cat's office was sleek and orderly, much like the woman herself. On the shelves behind her desk, framed magazine covers of her model clients were dotted with agency awards and trophies. One had two oars engraved on it along with a plaque: *Women's Single Sculls champion 2000*. A large whiteboard hung on the wall with what I presumed was the London Fashion Week schedule. Rows of columns were headed with each model's name. Under *Lydia Lawson*, someone had scrawled: *Jemima Snow, Berkeley*

*Square, Saturday 12:00.* Jemima Snow was a designer, a doyenne of the British fashion industry. I copied it down into my note-book. On the sideboard were two identical mirrored framed photographs of Cat and Lydia, arms round each other, with a gleaming Empire State Building in the background. A Post-it note stuck on one of the frames said: *Send to Lydia, 42 Sloane Gardens.*

Cat hung up the phone and saw me looking at the picture frames. 'A memento from New York Fashion Week. I had a copy made for Lydia.' She rubbed her eyes. I wasn't sure how long I had left.

'How did Natalia seem at Leo Brand's party?'

Cat seemed to choose her words carefully. 'A little out of sorts.'

'You mean . . .'

'Drunk, if I'm totally honest. I told her to pull herself together. Nathan Scott was taking photographs of the event. I didn't want him snapping Natalia making a scene.'

'Did she pull herself together?'

'I have no idea. My bloody mobile battery died. I had to go to the business centre to make a call. When I got back to the party Natalia had already left. I assumed she'd taken my advice and gone to bed. I went up to my room around 11.30 p.m. once the atmosphere ramped up a notch.' She gave a tight smile. 'I'm not much of a drinker. And I don't normally put myself up in expensive hotels, but I flew straight in from New York Fashion Week and was dead on my feet.'

'You must have been annoyed at Natalia's behaviour, after all the chances you'd given her?'

Cat sighed. 'I was more than annoyed. I was going to give her a piece of my mind today. Except, well . . .' Her chin wobbled and she looked away.

'How did you meet Natalia?'

Cat smoothed her hair down and leaned back in her chair. 'I take full credit for her. I go to Eastern Europe twice a year to scout for new faces. Last time I went off the beaten track to Ivanovo, a bone-chilling four-hour drive from Moscow.' She sipped her water, leaving a red smudge on the glass. 'I was on my way to a casting, in a taxi with a grizzly old driver who wore a fur hat, despite having the heat on full blast. We were stuck in a traffic jam and I looked out of the window and saw her. She was at the bus stop, sitting neatly with her hands in her lap, as though she was in the front row of a school photograph.' Cat tapped a fingernail against her glass. 'It's hard to define beauty. I've been doing this for a long time and I still couldn't explain it to you. But sometimes you get a feeling in the pit of your stomach. A flutter. Like you were destined to find that girl, that morning, on that street.'

Cat smiled her first genuine smile. 'Natalia was daydreaming and didn't notice me approach. Then she looked at me with those eyes and I was sold. She was vulnerable. She'd had a tough life.'

'How do you mean?'

'Oh, I don't know. It was as if she was running from something, or someone. Growing up poor in Ivanovo with its brutal winters, I mean, she was tougher than she looked but she struggled over here. You see it with girls who are scouted in poor areas. Some take to their new lives just fine, but others . . .' Cat stared into her glass.

I gave her a moment, then leaned forward in my chair. 'Do you know why Natalia stopped tweeting? Her account was still active but she never posted anything after 16 August.'

Cat sighed. 'No, and it was something I spoke to her about repeatedly. Our models are contractually obliged to use social media as much as possible. Brands look at models' Twitter followers before their portfolios nowadays. But Natalia was reluctant. I wondered if she was self-conscious about her English.'

'Do you have any idea why she ran out on me yesterday?'

Cat shook her head. 'No, and I don't know why she was in such a state last night. I've been going over it since the police called. I hadn't seen her for a week or so.' She checked the leather-bound diary on the desk in front of her. 'She flew to New York on 5 February for fittings, then she came back on the 9th because her schedule was free. I touched base with her a couple of times but she seemed fine. I wish she had come to me with whatever was bothering her.' Cat wiped her tearless eye with a red fingernail. 'I'm sorry. It's just that it's my job to take care of these girls.'

I shifted in my seat. My time was almost up.

'Do you know if Natalia signed up to a dating website that matches Eastern European women with British men?'

Cat looked surprised. 'You mean like those weird mail-order brides? I have no idea. God, I hope not.'

'One last thing. Do you have a number for Natalia's flatmate, Eva Kaminski?'

Cat arched an eyebrow. 'She's not one of my girls, but it's a company-wide policy not to give out our clients' contact details. Now, if you'll excuse me, I think you've had quite enough of my time.'

I pushed my business card across the desk. 'Could you give Eva my number? Please. I just want to talk. And if you think of anything else, I'd really appreciate your call.'

Cat studied my card. 'And none of this is going in the paper?'

'Not if you don't want it to. I meant what I said. You can trust me. I want to find out who killed Natalia and that's all. I'm not in the business of sensationalising stories. I leave that to the gutter press.'

The revolving door spat me out into the bracing cold. The air pressed down like a wet rug, and the sound of a nearby drill chomping through wet tarmac nearly split my head in two. An amber light glowed in the distance and I put a weary arm up to hail the cab.

'Bywater Street, please.' I sank into the leather seat and closed my eyes, while all around me the city protested noisily in the fading light.

# 8

The taxi pulled up outside a little enclave of pastel Victorian houses and I hurried up the steps to number 7. *Home*. I paused in the hallway listening to the faint ticking of the grandfather clock, inhaling the woody scent of oak floorboards warmed by radiators and the ghosts of suppers past. I kicked off my shoes and padded through to the kitchen. I switched on the TV, then turned it off again as my mind drifted. Marble-white neck. Piebald skin. Streaks of blood, lighter around the edges. Mangled flesh and Rose Blossom. I gulped down a glass of water, then sprinted to the bathroom. I only just made it. Hot, yellow bile poured out of me. I sank to the floor, squashed between the toilet and the wall, feeling sorry for myself.

I heard the front door open.

'Soph?' Poppy's voice, husky with a slight lisp.

'In here.' I had just finished rinsing my mouth out when my housemate's head poked round the door. The wet weather had blown her chestnut bob into straggly waves. Her face, angular with a strong nose, was offset by a pretty laughing mouth, as if she'd heard the punchline a second before everyone else.

She raised her eyebrows. 'Rough day?'

'Mmm.' I wiped my hands on the towel.

Poppy helped me into the kitchen, where I hoisted myself up onto the counter and watched her make tea. She was tall and big-boned but graceful.

'Last night I dreamed you moved to Albuquerque.' She pulled two mugs out of the cupboard, chuckling. 'You stuck your head round my bedroom door, all casual, and said the Albuquerque *Times* had offered you a job.'

I smiled in spite of myself. 'And you just let me go?'

'I told you to say hi to Walter White and went back to sleep. I need to stop watching *Breaking Bad*. Honestly, the other day someone asked me what I enjoyed cooking and my first thought was crystal meth. Here . . .' She pushed a mug of tea across the counter, watching me. 'You looked better in my dream. You weren't quite so . . . pukey and grey.'

'Albuquerque doesn't sound so bad right now.'

Poppy looked at me with wary eyes. 'You didn't come home last night.'

I took a sip. My throat was raw from vomiting and the hot tea burned. 'I swear to God. If our neighbour had the volume up any louder we could ditch our TV licence and use hers.'

Poppy sighed. 'Well, my day was pretty awesome, thanks for asking. That girl I slipped my number to on Saturday night just asked me on a date. And my deal is closing on the Fentonfleet case next week, which means the law firm is sending me to New York on Sunday.' I could see her studying me out of the corner of her eye. 'And to top it all off, the canteen served my favourite Sandwich of the Day: turkey cranberry.' She folded her arms. 'OK, now your turn.'

'I woke up, it sucked. Then it got worse.' I slid off the counter. 'I've got work to do.'

I was almost at the door when Poppy spoke. 'Soph, I'm here if you need me.'

I switched on my desk lamp and lowered the blinds, already regretting being such a bitch to Poppy. I pushed it to one side and sighed. After Tommy died I turned the third bedroom into an office, but hadn't got round to decorating it. All it housed at the moment was the mid-century desk I inherited from my great-aunt and a chair on wheels. The shelves were empty except for some well-thumbed books: Truman Capote's *Breakfast at Tiffany's*, the entire Sherlock Holmes collection (which I'd devoured by the age of thirteen) and reference books on police procedures and the British legal system. A corkboard was resting against the wall. I fished Natalia's headshot out of my bag and pinned it to the centre.

What Cat said about Natalia running away from something or someone back home made me realise how little I knew of her life before she moved to London. I took a fortifying sip of tea, then searched for the Russian telephone directory on my laptop and punched in her last name: Kotov, city: Ivanovo. Thirty-one names popped up. I checked my watch. Ivanovo was four hours ahead so it was two in the morning. And I had another problem.

I didn't speak Russian. Even if I managed to track down Natalia's family, I couldn't be sure they'd speak English. I couldn't do this alone. Scrolling through local news websites, I found an email address for a reporter called Mikhail Chernov at the *Ivanovo Post* and sent an email appealing for help.

Poppy clattered around the kitchen and I ignored my growling stomach. I plugged the USB stick containing The Rose's CCTV footage into my computer. A grainy image of the lobby flickered across my screen.

Thirty minutes later I was going cross-eyed. All I'd seen was the usual humdrum activity you'd expect from a busy London hotel. A family checking out surrounded by large suitcases, a man in a cap reading a newspaper in an armchair, a group of Japanese tourists returning from what was clearly the most successful shopping trip of all time. At 6.24 p.m. Natalia arrived, a small black holdall slung over her shoulder. She was at the desk for less than five minutes before disappearing into the lift. At 7.50 p.m., fashionable types started milling by the mirrored bar.

'Pops,' I shouted over my shoulder. 'Can I borrow you for a sec?'

Poppy stuck her head round the door, bringing with her a waft of lasagne.

'You know how your *Vogue* subscription and man-repelling shoes make you the most fashion-forward person I know?'

Poppy wiped her hands on her pyjama bottoms. 'You mean the *only* fashion-forward person you know.'

I smiled sweetly. 'I need your magical fashion powers. Can you ID the people on this tape?'

Poppy leaned over me and peered at the screen.

'That's Laurie Corona, the editor of *Vogue*. Check out her new cropped hairdo. Truly amazing.' Her voice was full of wonder and I smiled into my mug. 'And that's Daphne Leonard in the leather catsuit. She's married to Giles Thompson, the head of Sony, and only ever wears couture, even to the supermarket.' She paused. 'Not that she goes to the supermarket.'

'What about him?'

A man with a bleached-blond quiff was striding across the lobby. The flashlight from the photographer behind him lit up his silver suit.

Poppy folded her arms. 'You need to get out more. That's Amos Adler.' She looked exasperated when I shrugged. 'He's the editor of Stitched.com, the gossip website that makes my working day bearable.'

A familiar figure swaggered across the screen, wearing ripped jeans and a sweater emblazoned with the words: *More taste than money.*

Poppy sighed. 'God, if I was that way inclined, Liam Crawford would be top of my list.'

I cleared my throat.

At 8.16 p.m. the guest of honour, Leo Brand, arrived, polished and self-assured in a three-piece suit, with Lydia Lawson on his arm. Her black, sequinned dress shimmered and she leaned in close to Leo, flicking her glossy hair and laughing at something he'd said.

Then at 8.26 p.m. the lift doors opened and Natalia appeared, wearing the gold dress I'd seen her in this morning. Her face was partly obscured by a curtain of dark hair. She darted across the lobby, then stopped and glanced behind her. Darted, stopped, glanced. She repeated this three times.

'What's she doing?' Poppy leaned in close over my shoulder.

Each time Natalia paused, she jerked her head round. The final time, I zoomed in on her expression. My breath caught in my throat. She looked like a deer walking in front of a hunter's rifle. I rewound the tape to where Natalia began her strange dance across the lobby. What was she looking at?

At the bottom right of the screen the photographer moved in and out of the frame.

*The photographer.*

I rewound the tape.

'Pops, look.' The photographer was positioned behind Natalia, shooting in her direction. 'I wonder if he photographed whatever she's looking at?' I stretched my arms up over my head. My eyes felt dry and gritty.

'Shit! The lasagne.' Poppy rushed to the door. 'Be ready in ten.'

I was about to close my laptop when I noticed the man in the cap. He was still sitting in the same armchair with the newspaper on his lap, and the collar of his leather jacket obscuring his face. I checked the time. He'd been there for over two hours. I rewound the tape and sped through it again watching only him. In twenty minutes, he didn't turn the page of his newspaper once. At 10.45 p.m. he stood up and . . . I leaned forward. That was weird.

An email landed in my inbox from Charlie Swift.

Subject line: WTF?
Tink, check out this link (hey, that rhymes).
– Spidey

Charlie pasted a link to a story appearing in tomorrow's Business section about Kent Industries financing a five-billion-pound takeover of a steel company. It would put five thousand people out of a job. My father, Antony Kent, was quoted in the first paragraph:

> *My challenge was to turn Jenson Steel into a profitable company again. I've made some tough decisions and I stand by them. I'm proud to welcome Jenson Steel into the Kent Industries family.*

*What the fuck would you know about family?* The piece was accompanied by a photograph of my father staring bullishly at the camera. Eyebrows like silver bullets perched over penetrating blue eyes. Hair the unmistakeeable Kent silvery-blonde. His expensive suit barely contained his heavy frame. I slammed the lid of my laptop down and squeezed my eyes shut. Five minutes later I was pulling on my coat and heading for the door.

Poppy came out of the kitchen holding a wooden spoon. She saw what I was doing and sighed. 'Not again, Soph.'

But I was already closing the door behind me.

The rain stung my face as I stumbled along Lower Sloane Street, then over Chelsea Bridge and into Battersea Park. I pictured Natalia bleeding out of her eyes and ears as her body temperature plummeted. What had gone through her mind as the killer wrapped his hands round her throat? Did she struggle? At what point did she realise it was over? I inhaled the night air and a briny scent filled my lungs. I was half-soaked and shivering but I pushed forwards, joining the towpath.

How long did Tommy lie there, still warm, as the drugs shut down his organs? How long did it take his heart to stop beating? Suddenly I heard my father's voice, cold as steel. *Tommy is dead.*

The rain beat down but I was oblivious. All I could hear was my own ragged breathing. Then, almost without thinking, my footsteps slowed and eventually stopped. I'd always loved to walk but, ever since Tommy's death, my feet always found their way to the same place: the pink balustrades and twinkling lights of Albert Bridge. I leaned over the railings and stared into the shadows. When Tommy died, I regularly crawled down to the wasteland underneath the bridge to be near the place where he was last alive. I'd lie down amongst the rats and the stink, staring up at the same concrete beams Tommy saw, running my fingers through the same patchy grass he touched. Eventually an aggressive homeless guy told me to fuck off, so now I didn't venture further than the riverbank.

Since Tommy died, 128 days had passed and I was suffocating.

In the distance, a ferry disappeared under the bridge. I watched its green light bobbing like a firefly until it was swallowed up by the night.

# 9

*In 5 minutes.*

The text came through as I reached my desk. I'd barely slept, so I did what I always did when insomnia hit. I went to work.

At 5.30 a.m., the air was sharp, the streets still cloaked in night. Objects loomed into view under street lamps before being devoured by blackness. As I huddled by a wall on the chilly Tube station platform, I sent a text to general pathologist Dr David Sonoma. David was an early riser. He once told me it was hard to sleep peacefully after you'd had a four-year-old abuse victim splayed out on your table.

I peeled off my layers, nodding at the dregs of the night shift who were leaving for the day. I loved an empty newsroom. It was like a film set waiting to come to life. While I waited for David to call, I scanned my inbox. Mikhail Chernov had responded to say he would help track Natalia's family down; in return he wanted an additional reporting credit. I stood up to make tea when my phone rang.

'David. Thanks for calling.'

'Hello, Sophie.' He sounded tired. I could picture him in his office at St George's Hospital. Grey eyebrows that had a life of their own in an otherwise neat face, accentuated by small, rim-less glasses. David resembled a golf-and-*Gardener's-World* fan but I knew the truth. He got his rocks off at heavy metal gigs. I often got him tickets; a perk of the job. He said the music helped drown out the daily visual noise he was pummelled with. I understood. I know a police chief who unwinds by throwing racing cars round a track, and a crime reporter who does five triathlons a year. When you have front-row ticket to the horror show, a quick pint down the local doesn't quite cut it.

'What can you tell me about the brunette who came in yesterday?'

'You need to be more specific.'

*Christ.*

'Natalia Kotov, eighteen years old, killed at The Rose Hotel. I'm guessing she was strangled, judging by the bruising I saw on her neck.'

David didn't ask how I'd seen the bruising. I heard the sound of paper being shuffled. 'This is being released in a couple of hours. Can't you wait until then?'

'Can you wait for those Saxon tickets?'

He sighed. 'You're half right. She was throttled, not stran-gled, the difference being that the killer used his hands, not a ligature. She had bruising on both sides of the trachea and smaller bruises on the back of her neck, indicating her assailant was front-on.'

I scribbled down notes, balancing the phone between my ear and shoulder.

'Both her hyoid bone and larynx were fractured and the petechial haemorrhaging – sorry, the blood leakage into the white part of the eyeball – was severe. One of the worst cases I've seen. That, along with blood seepage from both eyes and ears indicates significant force was used.' He paused. 'Actually, that's an understatement. The killer broke all ten of her fingers, which is harder to do than it sounds. We're looking for someone strong and . . . determined.'

I stared down at my empty mug, wondering if a caffeine hit would have made this conversation easier.

'Often victims of asphyxia have broken fingernails, where they fight against their attacker's hands. The deceased's nails were unbroken. I tested for trace evidence but found none.' David coughed down the phone. 'Her bloodwork is still with the toxicologist but initial testing showed traces of Ritalin, a pyschostimulant most commonly used to treat Attention Deficit Hyperactivity Disorder. And I found significant levels of Gamma hydroxybutyrate in her system.'

My fingers were aching and my brain hurt. 'Plain English, David. What does that mean?'

He accepted the interruption graciously. 'She wasn't conscious when she was killed, which is some small mercy. GHB is a fast-acting central nervous system depressant. I imagine the killer used it to keep her docile.'

I leaned back in my chair. 'That makes sense. He chose a public setting. Couldn't risk her making a noise.' I gnawed a fingernail. 'Did he leave any marks?'

'No fingerprints on her body. Although I did find a very faint glove imprint – probably latex – underneath her left ear. Also, the killer is right-handed, the bruising is more pronounced on the left-hand side of her neck.'

'What about the damage to her face?'

'The incisions varied in length but were made with the same blade. The angle of the incisions isn't typical of a knife. It's my feeling that they were inflicted by the scissors he used to cut her hair. Probably your average kitchen scissors. Interestingly, the lack of blood loss indicates the killer slashed her face after she was dead.'

I let out a low whistle. He wasn't in a hurry then. The Rose was so public. Multiple potential witnesses and CCTV cameras all over the place. Either the killer was arrogant or stupid. I wasn't sure which was worse.

'Any idea about time of death?'

There was a pause as David put his hand over the receiver to talk to someone. 'Time of death is tricky to establish. Her low BMI and teeth enamel indicate an eating disorder, so the stomach contents weren't much use. But her body was in the latter stages of rigor mortis so I'd guess it happened somewhere between 9 p.m. and 3 a.m.'

I thought back to the bloodstained sheet and closed my eyes. 'Any sexual assault?'

David sounded almost apologetic. 'Not in the traditional sense. But she was sexually assaulted with an object that caused extensive internal damage.'

'What kind of object?'

'This is not to be printed. DCI Durand wants to use it as a control detail.' He cleared his throat. 'It was an eight-inch stick covered with thorns. The killer left it inside her. It's been sent off to Botany for testing but it looked like blackthorn to me. Sophie, I have to sign off. My 7.30 is here. Talk soon.'

I hung up in a daze and googled *blackthorn*. My eyes scanned the page.

*Blackthorn: the tree bears wicked long sharp thorns and small, delicate white flowers. Symbolism: inevitability of death, revenge.*

An image popped up of a thick woody branch bordered by long, angry spikes.

'I never had you down for a green fingers type.'

I spun round to find Kate looking at my computer screen.

'Want to hear something sick?' I filled her in on my conversation with Dr Sonoma.

Kate's eyes widened. 'That is fucked up. What kind of sicko rapes a woman with a tree branch? What, he couldn't get it up himself?'

I shuddered. 'Or maybe he's smart and didn't want to leave any trace of himself behind.' I sank down in my chair. 'He'd have had to carry a bag. Actually, that reminds me.' I rooted around in my bag for the USB stick. 'What do you make of this?'

I played the CCTV footage.

Kate grinned. 'I won't even ask how you got hold of that.'

I pointed to the screen. 'Watch the guy in the cap.'

We sped through the tape. The man stood up, slung his rucksack over one shoulder and disappeared behind the chair.

'Where did he go?' Kate leaned in close.

'Right. He doesn't go out the front door because you'd see him. He doesn't go into the lift because you'd see that too. I videoed the lobby on my phone and, believe me, there's nowhere obvious for him to go. But then I noticed this.'

I paused the tape at 10.46 p.m. On the left-hand wall hung an enormous framed painting of a dark landscape. The lobby chandelier was reflected in the glass, turning it into a sort of mirror. I zoomed in on the painting and ran the tape. We watched the man's reflection vanish into a door.

'OK, he goes through a door, so what?'

'Now look at this.' I handed Kate my phone and showed her the 360-degree panorama of the lobby. 'Where is that door?'

She squinted at the screen. 'I can't see it.'

'That's because it's been wallpapered over to blend in. Which means that door isn't meant for guests. So either the man in the cap is on staff, which is unlikely considering he's been sitting on his arse for two hours, or –'

'He's doing something he shouldn't.'

I printed off the clearest shot of his face, which admittedly wasn't great. My phone beeped. 'OK, I'm heading back to The Rose. The housekeeper has delivered the goods. I've got a hot date with dashing Dmitri.'

Kate stood up and yawned. 'What shall I tell Nutsack? He wants quotes from the Highgate Nursery parents. You know, the one they discovered was operating a brothel out of the top floor.'

I gave her a pleading look.

Kate sighed. 'Go on, Kate the Great will do it. In return you can slip the hot guy my number.'

Her cackle followed me all the way across the newsroom.

By the time I arrived at The Rose, the fine mist of rain had got under my skin and I was chilled to the bone. The only upside of the ten-minute walk was that I'd managed to get through to the photographer Nathan Scott, who agreed to see me at his Mayfair studio at 11 a.m.

Aside from the crackle in the air that always follows a tragedy, there was little else in the lobby to suggest a brutal murder had occurred thirty-six hours earlier. I glanced at the pink armchair, then at the wall behind it and saw the faint outline of a door, camouflaged by wallpaper. My pulse quickened as I strode across the lobby and ducked inside. I was in a narrow corridor, less opulent than the guest corridors and brightly lit. Three rooms ran along the right-hand side. The first was a storage cupboard filled with dusty cardboard boxes. The second door was an empty staffroom. I pushed open the third door and found myself at the bottom of a staircase. There were no CCTV cameras on the ground-floor level. I took the stairs two at a time, pausing on each landing looking for cameras. There weren't any. I reached the fifth floor and stopped. Ahead was a heavy, white door with the back-to-front words *Staff Only* printed on the glass panel. I'd completely lost my bearings. I stuck my head round the door.

Directly in front of me was room 538.


'Do you recognise him?' I was perched on the bench in the laundry room, watching Sasha pick the bubblegum varnish off her nails.

'I can't see his face.'

'It's the clearest picture I have. You said you were working that night. Is it possible you might have seen him?' Sasha flexed her fingers, assessing the damage to her nails, then shrugged. I tried to keep the irritation out of my voice. 'CCTV showed him entering the staff door in the lobby at 10.46 p.m. Were you anywhere near there?'

Sasha finally dragged her eyes away from her cuticles and looked at me. 'I had to take a bathrobe up to a room at the back of the hotel, so it was quicker to use the staff staircase. I think I did see a man coming down the stairs.'

'You think?'

She looked sheepish. 'I was distracted. Dmitri was behind him, with a rucksack. His shift finished at 9 p.m. I wasn't expecting to see him.'

'Can you remember anything about this man? His clothes? His bag? Distinguishing marks?'

Sasha screwed her face up. 'He was going so fast. Um, I don't know. Maybe his cap.'

'What about it?'

She frowned. 'It had a sort of patch on the front. Red or black. Or maybe red and black.'

'Did you get a look at his face?'

Sasha rolled her eyes. 'I told you, I wasn't looking at him.'

I slid the CCTV image into my bag. 'Thanks for seeing me again, Sasha.'

'Sure, no worries.' She studied her nails again, this time less convincingly. 'You going to meet Dmitri now? Tell him I said hi.'

I stamped my feet to keep warm while I waited in the alleyway behind The Rose Hotel. The drizzle had turned into sleet and it melted as it hit the tarmac.

A tall man dressed in a bottle-green uniform swaggered towards me. His hair was slicked back as if he'd just broken through the surface of a swimming pool. Sharp blue eyes and even sharper cheekbones.

'Dmitri?'

He nodded and pulled a brown envelope out of his jacket. 'No one must know.' His accent was the stuff of Hollywood villains. 'I'm only doing this because of Sasha.'

'Your girlfriend.'

Dmitri gave a hollow laugh. 'Is that what she told you?'

I rooted around in my bag for cigarettes and offered him one. My hands were so cold I couldn't work the lighter. Dmitri snatched it off me and lit a cigarette with long, thin fingers.

'Can you tell me anything about the incident on Thursday night?'

He exhaled, studying me through a long whistle of smoke. 'Sasha stays out of this from now on. She has a big mouth, she'll get in trouble.'

I batted the smoke away and nodded, wondering if it was Sasha he was protecting, or himself.

Dmitri leaned against the wall, flattening the filter of his cigarette between his thumb and forefinger. 'I didn't see anything. I was on front desk the whole time. It was a busy night.'

'That's not strictly true, is it? Sasha told me she saw you coming down the back staircase two hours after your shift ended.'

His eyes hardened. 'See what I tell you about her big mouth.'

'Why did you stick around?'

Dmitri shrugged. 'I had stuff to do.' He flicked his cigarette butt onto the ground and I reached into my pocket for another.

'Did you see Natalia?' He took the cigarette, looking at me blankly. 'The girl who was killed.'

Dmitri's mouth twisted into a leer. 'You don't forget a woman who looks like that. She left the party at around 10 p.m. Her dress pulled high up over her. . .' He made a circular shape with his hands and wiggled his eyebrows up and down.

'Did you see anyone follow her?'

'Nope.' He swivelled his head round and looked along the alleyway with a bored expression. 'I need to get back.'

I fished the CCTV image out of my bag. 'Did you see this man on Thursday night?' Dmitri glanced at the piece of paper and shook his head. 'Really? He sat in your lobby for two hours.'

'It was a busy night.'

'And according to Sasha this man was walking down the back staircase a few feet ahead of you later that night.' He took a couple of steps away from me and I put my hand on his arm to stop him. 'Dmitri, exposing liars is what I do. I read body language the same way you read cheap porn, and you're fidgeting like a pig in a slaughterhouse.' I fixed him with a glare and folded my arms. 'You barely looked at the photo, so you'll take another look. Then you'll tell me where you were after your shift ended. Because if you don't, I will make it my life's mission to find out and, believe me, you do not want that shit on your plate.'

Dmitri slammed his fist against the wall and muttered something under his breath. 'I was with a woman. A hotel guest.' He ran a hand over his hair, then wiped the gel on his suit. 'Whenever she stays at The Rose I meet with her.'

'For money?'

His eyes were mocking. 'Why? You putting this in your story?'

'What about Sasha?'

'What about her?'

I waited for him to show a hint of remorse but the bored expression was back. Except . . . 'You sneaked me the hotel log as a favour to Sasha because you feel guilty.'

Dmitri peered down his sharp nose at me. The wind had turned it red. 'I feel nothing. For any of them.'

'I'm going to need her name.'

'Who?'

'The hotel guest. To check you're not lying to me again.' I couldn't keep the disgust out of my voice. Dmitri heard it but didn't seem to care.

'Sadie Long. Her details are in the log. Be careful, she's married to a billionaire. I doubt she'll want this made public.'

'And this man?' I thrust the piece of paper under his nose again.

Dmitri took one last exaggerated look. 'I didn't see him.' He flung his cigarette butt onto the tarmac and ground it in with the heel of his boot. 'Are we done? I don't want my boss to find me out here talking to the press.' He hissed the last word between tight lips and didn't wait for an answer. I watched his broad back disappear down the alleyway, feeling a wave of pity for Sasha.

# 10

Half an hour later I was struggling to catch my breath in the lobby of a smart townhouse on Dover Street. A candle the size of a fire extinguisher was spitting out a sickly scent that made me want to gag. A chic woman with pale, cappuccino-froth hair beckoned me over to her desk. Her cream tweed jacket and pearl clip-on earrings reminded me of my mother. Before she stopped getting dressed in the morning.

'Go straight down the hallway. You won't have long, though. Mr Scott has to leave in fifteen minutes.'

I padded along a plush corridor with burgundy damask walls and gold light fittings, until I reached a studded black door.

'Sophie Kent, how charming to meet you.' Nathan Scott spoke like old money, but looked very much like new. He had the over-amped physique of a man who knew his way round a steroid bottle. Chunky gold bracelets adorned his wrists. Skin the colour of rust, and dark hair slicked back. He motioned towards the purple velvet chair by his desk.

'This place is like the Palace of Versailles –' I glanced up at the huge photographs of naked male and female torsos on the wall – 'well, if Madonna had designed it.'

Nathan laughed and rolled up the arm of his tight grey T-shirt. 'You have an eye for design, darling. The P of V was exactly the look I was going for. I don't have a proper studio. I move with the fashion crowd. I'm a nomad, a drifter. I capture the young and the beautiful. Then I return here to my sanctuary.' He waved his hand with a flourish. 'Hadley Summerville did it. The man is a genius. Do you know this desk is an *exact* replica of the one Louis the Fourteenth had in his private chambers?' He slid his large hands lovingly across the surface and I pressed my lips together, trying not to laugh.

'I wondered if I might ask you some questions about the murder at The Rose the other night.'

Nathan's face darkened. 'What a terrible affair on what was such a wonderful evening. Do you know Leo Brand? Dear Leo. Fabulous that the Fashion Council is honouring him at last. What that man has done for women's silhouettes is simply astonishing. He should be knighted.' He pushed a button on the wall behind his desk. Moments later the door opened and the lady on reception appeared. 'Margot, darling, I'm *parched*. Could you put the kettle on?'

I opened my notebook on my lap. 'You were the official photographer at Leo Brand's party. Did you see Natalia Kotov that night?'

He sighed. 'I stare at people all night long but I don't *see* them, if that makes sense. I'm too busy shooting, trying to cover every base and every face. I'm afraid I don't remember her at all.'

'Have you been doing this long?'

'Oh, all my life. I'm from the sort of family that expects one to suit up and run a FTSE100, but photography is all I've ever wanted to do.'

'How come you photograph parties rather than magazines or fashion campaigns?' I was genuinely interested but when I saw a shadow pass across his face I realised I'd offended him.

'Any chump with a camera can shoot in a studio with light-boxes and backdrops and teams of assistants. There's great heritage in reportage photos. Lord Snowdon, Slim Aarons, Norman Parkinson. I imagine no one asked them why they didn't aim higher.'

I shifted in my chair. 'That's not what I said.'

Nathan rose from his seat and glided over to a wall of shelves. 'The real challenge is to shoot today's stars on the hoof. There's no time to prepare; you work with what you have.' He pulled a binder off the shelf and returned to his seat. 'Take the photos from Thursday night . . .' He spun the binder round in my direction. 'I may shoot digitally but I'm old-school, my dear. I love the feel of paper between my fingers. Costs me a fortune to print them all, but I need to see the real thing. Only then do I know if it's a keeper.'

I leaned forward to look.

'That's Cecily Press, the newest nymphet on the music block. Irish, I think. And there's Diana Lewis, pretty slip of a thing. Not sure what she does for a living but who cares with those peach-blossom cheeks!'

'Wow, these are amazing.' And I meant it. Nathan's pictures crackled with energy. They made me want to climb in and join the party.

'Thank you.' His voice was thick with pleasure. 'The trick is to disappear. You want them at their most natural. And it helps that I never take a bad photo,' he added, grinning.

The door opened and Margot appeared with a silver tray. She walked like a geisha, all the while gazing at Nathan with heart-struck-schoolgirl eyes. Margot placed a cup and saucer on the desk in front of me. I thanked her and her small pink mouth curved up into a smile.

'Dear woman. Isn't she fabulous?' Nathan's eyes shone as Margot shuffled out of the room. 'And you should see her daughter. She came in the other day, a dazzling bundle of sunlight. All long brown limbs and golden skin. I'm desperate to photograph her but Margot won't let me. Says she's too young. I'm hoping to persuade her. Very few people make it into my personal collection.' He gestured at the photographs on the walls. 'But when I have a subject in my sights, I don't let go.' He paused, his eyes travelling over me. 'Would you consider being photographed?'

'Naked?'

'Don't be shy, Miss Kent. The body is Nature's masterpiece.'

Nathan's laser-beam gaze unnerved me, flattered me. I knew he was being inappropriate, but he was so charismatic that part of me didn't want him to stop. I coughed, embarrassed, and my overly perfumed Earl Grey went down the wrong way.

Nathan grinned as I pulled the binder towards me. The photographs from Thursday night were time-stamped. I pulled my chair in closer to Nathan's desk. I knew from the CCTV footage that Natalia had crossed the lobby at 8.26 p.m. I turned the page and, in the background of a shot of two blondes clinking champagne flutes, I caught a glimpse of Natalia's gold dress.

'How long have you been at *The London Herald*, my dear?'

I tore my eyes away from the binder. 'Eight years.'

His eyebrows arched. 'My goodness, you don't look old enough. What were you when you started? Child labour?' He leaned forward in his chair. 'Do you know darling Molly?'

It was hard to avoid the Fashion Director, Molly Simpson. Tall and reedy, she sported an uneven black bob that looked as if the hairstylist started on it, and then got called away. Her signature look involved anything pink, shiny or covered in feathers. Rumour had it she was desperate to move into magazines, but no one took her seriously enough to offer her an editorship. So she was destined to haunt the newsroom resembling a demented liquorice allsort.

'Molly is a dear friend of mine. She used to stay in my apartment during Paris Fashion Week. A shoebox of a place but, my, did we have fun.'

'You lived in Paris?'

He waved a hand in the air. '*Bien sûr!* Paris, Florence, Venice, Brussels. You name it I've lived there. I'm quite the travelling minstrel.'

'Where do you live now?'

Something flickered across Nathan's face. 'Well, in truth, my dear, I'm between places. I had a small financial upset – a bad investment, shall we say – that meant I had to sell my little place on Marylebone High Street. Things are on the up but, right now, I'm staying here.' He pointed to the plum-coloured daybed behind me.

'You sleep in your office?'

'It's only temporary, darling. And who wouldn't want to sleep in the Palace of Versailles, right?' Nathan winked and sipped his tea.

The gold-plated telephone on his desk rang and he pounced on it.

'Yes, darling? Well, can't you tell him I'm busy?' A dramatic sigh. 'Fine, I'm coming.' He slammed the receiver down, and gave me an apologetic look. 'Sorry, my dear. I have to go deal with something. Sit tight, I'll be right back.'

Nathan swept out in a fog of sandalwood and I pulled the binder towards me. In the next shot, Nathan had moved position and was shooting from behind Natalia towards the mirrored bar. She was in the centre of the photograph, her stride shortening as she slowed down. I knew what was coming. In the next photograph Natalia was slightly out of focus. Her dark hair fell around her face, hiding her expression. But I recognised the rigid stance, the unnatural angle of her head. What was she looking at? At first, all I could see was a blur of faces in the background. In the next photo, the background sharpened.

I was looking directly at Liam Crawford.

I froze for the briefest of moments, then grabbed my phone and began snapping Nathan's photos. Footsteps approached, along with the muffled sound of Nathan calling out to Margot. The door handle creaked and I sprang back into the chair.

'Do forgive me, darling.' Nathan flounced over to a walnut dresser, opened a drawer and began piling camera equipment into a leather holdall. 'I'm afraid our time is up. Duty calls. I have a date with the bold and the beautiful at Berkeley Square.'

My ears pricked up. 'Jemima Snow?'

'The very same.' He was only half listening, his eyes scanning the room for something. 'Where's my jacket? Margot!' His voice made the walls shake.

I gathered my things, wondering how I could keep him talking. 'I'm going to Jemima Snow too.'

The door opened and Margot shuffled through, clutching a battered leather jacket.

'Margot, you angel.' Nathan kissed her cheek, then turned to me. 'Well, you must allow me to escort you there.' He held the door open for me, turning back as he wrapped a silk scarf around his neck. 'Margot, darling, if Laura calls, tell her I'll meet her at Browns at 6 p.m.' Then he turned to me. 'Ready?'

Over his shoulder I watched Margot put her hand to her cheek, to the spot where Nathan had kissed her.

Nathan pelted down Dover Street as if he was a groom late to the church. 'Goodness me, this weather is frightful.'

He stopped suddenly by a silver Rolls Royce and I slammed into the back of him.

'This is your car?' I asked, rubbing my head.

'Isn't she a beauty? Vintage – 1984. She corners like she's on rails.' He patted the roof as he spoke, a smile spreading across his face.

'Wouldn't it be quicker to walk to Berkeley Square?'

Nathan gasped. 'Walk? Are you mad?' I slid into the passenger seat, laughing.

'Now, let's hope she starts.' He turned the key in the ignition and the engine purred into life. 'The show starts at midday, which means we're already late.'

I looked at my watch. 'But it's only 11.45 a.m.'

Nathan snorted. 'Darling, everyone knows the real show occurs *off* the catwalk.'

'Do you mind if we talk about Thursday night? Did you see anything suspicious?'

Nathan opened the window a crack. 'Sorry, I know it's arctic in here, but the windows will steam up.' I burrowed deeper inside my scarf. Nathan's mode of transport might look the part, but there was a very real chance we would freeze to death.

'Hmmm, anything suspicious.' He turned sharply into Berkeley Street, narrowly missing a pedestrian. 'Not that I can recall. There was a delightful moment with Lydia Lawson. Some tipsy actress ricocheted into her and Cat Ramsey. I managed to stop Cat falling flat on her face.' He lowered his voice, even though it was only the two of us in his car. 'And, darling, that's no mean feat. T-i-m-b-e-r! Lydia flounced off in a huff. I would love to have captured the murderous expression on her face.' Nathan's face fell. 'Sorry, darling, wrong choice of word. But the night only got worse for Lydia. I caught her having a blazing row with her ex.'

'Liam Crawford?'

Nathan nodded. 'A real piece of work. They were out by the loo just after dinner wrapped.'

I wiped the condensation off the window to get my bearings. 'Any idea what they were fighting about?'

'I couldn't hear what they were saying but Liam was furious. Then Natalia staggered over to them, which only made it worse. I didn't venture closer. Trust me, you don't want to get on the wrong side of La Lawson! Or Liam Crawford,' he added. 'Anyway, didn't see much more after that. My camera died on me. Well, the flash. I had to whizz out to grab a spare from my office.'

Nathan reverse-parked into a disabled spot on the north side of Berkeley Square. He fumbled around in the glove box, then threw a blue disabled badge onto the dashboard.

'Is that real?'

He turned off the engine and winked. 'OK, my darling. This is where we part ways. But I do hope our paths cross again, you delightful creature.' He grasped my hand between his, slung the camera strap over his neck, and he was gone.

## 11

Traffic was almost at a standstill. The fashion elite streamed out of SUVs and made their way towards a white domed marquee that rose from the grass, looking like a half-sunk spaceship. Some were dressed for the chilly conditions; others tottered along icy pavements in five-inch heels and bare legs. An Asian woman peacocked for the cameras in a tutu and shiny purple cap. A pack of photographers roared towards a petite redhead, cameras raised, as though their lives depended on it.

I paused by a group of women whose black-clad spiky limbs reminded me of spiders. Leaning against a tree, I pulled a pair of Louboutins out of my bag, slicked on some red lipstick and mussed up my hair. Next to me, a tribe of blondes, decked out in clashing prints, chattered on their phones.

'Yah, sub-zero temperatures, darling. Jemima better not be running late. I will *die.*'

'Did you see the front row at Aria Gold? Pitiful. How many shows are you doing today? I have nine. It's only midday and my feet are *killing* me.'

A man with bleached hair and silver biker boots was being interviewed by a Vogue.com reporter. I recognised him from the CCTV footage: Amos Adler. Suddenly, former catwalk star Chloe Buchanan emerged from a blacked-out Mercedes, wearing a trench coat and thigh-high boots, and the Vogue.com reporter scampered away. A flash of annoyance blew across Amos's face.

I sidled up to him. 'Don't you hate it when that happens?' He gave me a quick once-over, disappointment pulling down the corners of his mouth at the sight of my MaxMara suit. 'I don't know what they see in her anyway. Isn't she about fifty?'

Amos shuddered. 'Did you see the size of the old bag? Someone pulled the ripcord on her. What is it with fat girls and belts?' He turned towards Chloe and raised his voice. 'A belt only cinches your waist if you have a waist to begin with, love.'

I watched Chloe preen for the cameras. She was a size ten, at most.

'Can I just say I'm a huge fan of your website.'

Amos straightened his skinny, grey tie. 'Four million hits this month. *And* I've been approached to take over the Hollywood slot on *Good Morning London*. Amazeballs, huh?'

'Well, you are the most connected man in town. How do you dig up so much dirt on people?'

He looked past me, momentarily distracted. 'That would be telling, doll.'

'Speaking of which . . .' I lowered my voice. 'Weren't you at The Rose the other night when all that drama went down?'

Amos nodded. 'What. A. Shocker. Poor girl.'

'Any idea who'd want to hurt her?'

'My money's on Lydia Lawson. Bitch gotta slap down the rivals, amiright?' His green eyes twinkled. 'Just kidding. Lydia ended up at the club, DreamBox, with me so she's home and dry.' Amos strutted off, cackling to himself.

I shifted my attention to the marquee entrance. A flame-haired woman in leopard-print trousers was on the door, clutching a clipboard. I hobbled round the marquee searching for a weak spot, my feet already protesting to the four-inch heels. Round the back, standing guard at a small doorway, was a man with pink hair and a neon-green sweater printed with the words *Kiss the boys and make them cry*. I watched as he struck a pose and took a selfie with his phone. On a hunch, I logged on to Twitter and typed in *#jemimasnow*. Sure enough, his grinning photo was already there. I rolled my eyes. Sometimes it was too easy. I clicked on his details. *Matt Brent: junior assistant at Jemima Snow. Forgive the haters. Beauty IS skin deep.*

Squaring my shoulders, I marched over to him, adopting my best don't-fuck-with-me voice. 'Matt Brent?'

He looked startled. 'Yeah?'

'You're needed at the front entrance. Anna Wintour is arriving. The crowd is out of control.'

He looked puzzled. 'But I'm not supposed to leave my post.'

'I'd hurry if I were you. The leopard-print door bitch is on the warpath.'

The colour left his face and he scuttled away.

I ducked into the backstage area and was dazzled by the full force of a fashion show on countdown. An area the size of two tennis courts was filled with rows of brightly lit mirrors on makeshift tables. At each mirror, a team of make-up artists and hairstylists fussed over individual models, shouting to be heard over the shriek of hairdryers and deafening music. Models who were waiting their turn passed the time reading or scrolling through their phones. Others were nearing the final stages: hair scraped into severe topknots, lips painted stop-sign red, eyebrows hidden by a thick layer of foundation. A TV reporter was interviewing a famous Brazilian model, and photographers darted about. I craned my neck, trying to spot Nathan, but it was impossible to see anything through the smog of hairspray.

I spied Lydia Lawson, arm extended, pouting for a selfie.

Some models look freakish in real life. The girl sitting next to Lydia wasn't what you'd call attractive, with her narrow face and large protruding ears. Even Natalia, with her gappy teeth and wide-set eyes, had looked a bit Planet Mars. But Lydia's face looked as though it had been assembled in a CGI lab. Only a slight overbite stopped her face from descending into cartoon-perfection territory.

I cleared my throat. 'Lydia?'

She arched a perfect eyebrow at me in the mirror. 'Yes?'

'I need a minute of your time. It's about Natalia Kotov.'

Lydia gave me a withering look. 'Who's asking?'

As usual, introducing myself provoked a look of disgust. 'Listen,' I said hastily. 'Natalia and I were working together on a story. I saw her the day before she died.'

The hairstylist shoved me out of the way. 'Move it or I'm calling security.'

I ignored her, standing my ground. 'Please, Lydia, give me five minutes after the show.'

Lydia rolled her eyes. 'Do you have any fucking clue how crazy my day is?'

I thought back to the schedule I'd seen in Cat's office. 'I know you have nothing else for a while after this. I wouldn't ask if it wasn't important.' In the distance, I spotted the door bitch scanning the backstage area, teeth bared like a rabid dog.

Lydia huffed. 'I barely knew Natalia.'

'That's not true. She often spoke about you.' Lydia's expression softened a fraction and I went for the jugular. 'The last time I saw Natalia she was terrified. I can't help thinking if I'd been there for her, she might still be alive. I don't think I'm the only one who feels guilty.'

Out the corner of my eye, I could see the door bitch charging towards me. I instinctively shifted onto the balls of my feet, regretting my shoe change. It would be hard to make a quick getaway in heels.

Lydia waved the glowering hairstylist away. 'The last thing I need is more drama. Go to Danny's café on the corner of Albermarle and Stafford Street. I'll be there as soon as I can.'

Danny was a walrus-shaped man with a moustache like a smudge of paint. He slid a muddy tea across the counter and I sat down next to a group of builders, thinking back to Lydia's parting shot. Ever since she was discovered in Topshop three years ago, drama had followed her around as if she was a dog on heat. At first she could do no wrong. High-profile ad campaigns and magazine covers flowed thick and fast, but her true power lay online. Thanks to her goofy personality, Lydia was a social media sensation. Eight million Twitter and Instagram followers hung on her every selfie. But her fans, dubbed the La-Las, had started to turn on their idol. They'd grown tired of her diva antics and exhausting on–off relationship with Liam Crawford. I wasn't surprised when Liam bagged a supermodel. Or when his career took off. But success went to his head. Always on the volatile end of the spectrum, Liam's temper became a loaded gun. Soon after they started dating, Lydia was photographed with a black eye. She claimed she tripped, but the public wasn't convinced. Soon after, Liam was arrested for punching a journalist twice his size outside a bar in Hackney. The guy's nasal bone crushed his skull and he was in hospital for a fortnight.

Liam and Lydia's breakup last September had sent Lydia into a mile-high bender that ended in a scrap with a fellow first-class passenger. The photographs of her being marched off the plane in handcuffs went viral. A gossip columnist nicknamed her Loony Lawson and the tabloids revelled in her transformation from fashion catnip to kryptonite. A few loyal industry insiders still backed her, but the majority had deemed her damaged goods. It seemed there was such a thing as bad publicity.

I sipped my tea and drew out the brown envelope Dmitri had given me. I was looking for the name of the person who had originally checked into room 538. I frowned as my eyes landed on a name I recognised.

A cold breeze hit the back of my neck and I saw Danny jump to attention. 'Welcome back, Miss Lydia. I bring you a green tea.'

The builders fell silent as Lydia, dressed in red jeans and a fur jacket, carved her way through the café and sat down.

I raised my eyebrows. 'Green tea?'

'Danny stocks it for me. I've been coming here for years.' Lydia's voice was expensive; each clipped vowel spoke of lacrosse matches and trust funds. She unwound her scarf and her slender neck rose like a tapered candle from her jacket collar. 'I come here to be anonymous. Danny's clientele doesn't read *Vogue*. Although they do read the tabloids, so I should probably find somewhere else to hide.'

The café's fluorescent strip lights drew attention to the fine spray of spots on Lydia's chin and the dark circles beneath her midnight-blue eyes. Even so, she looked luminous.

I smiled. 'I appreciate you meeting me.'

Lydia threw back her long, dark hair and gave me a haughty look. 'I'm not staying long.'

The chill wind didn't intimidate me in the slightest. I opened my notebook. 'Had you seen much of Natalia lately?'

Danny waddled over and set a mug down in front of Lydia, then backed away, eyes shining.

Lydia tapped a long fingernail against the china. 'As I said, my schedule has been crazy.' She glanced past me at the table of builders and arched an eyebrow. 'Seen something interesting, boys?' Their embarrassed laughter fluttered through the air, then fell flat. 'I saw Natalia at the Fashion Council lunch at Somerset House.'

'When was this?'

'About ten days ago. We were on different tables. I was next to the CEO of NovTel. The sponsor.' She rolled her eyes.

'So the next time you saw Natalia was at Leo Brand's party?'
Lydia nodded. 'How did she seem?'

'Like she had everything to lose. Did you see her dress? Cat
really outdid herself.'

'What do you mean?'

'You think Natalia chose that dress herself?' Lydia's beautiful
mouth twisted into a smirk. 'Oh no, honey. Those parties are all
about making an impression. Agencies bring in at least twenty-
five new faces every season. There's only space for so many, so
you do the maths. Models get one or two seasons to make a
splash or . . .' Lydia mimed cutting her throat.

'Was Natalia making a splash?'

Lydia yawned without bothering to cover her mouth. 'Who
knows? Sometimes there's buzz around a girl but, for some
reason, the stars don't align. Do you remember Ella King? She
walked at Prada, McQueen *and* Marc Jacobs last season. Then
this season, nothing. One minute you're the Face To Watch, the
next you're sitting at home looking in the mirror wondering
what the fuck happened.'

The sharpness in her voice pierced the air and I shifted awkwardly in my chair. 'Can you tell me about the night Natalia died?'

'I barely saw her. I had my own crap going on.'

I remembered what Nathan had seen. 'You mean your fight
with Liam?'

Lydia bristled. 'How do you know about that?'

'What did you fight about?'

'None of your fucking business.'

'OK.' I held my hands up to placate her. 'Did you speak to
Natalia that night?'

'Only once. Just after I arrived with Leo. Darling Leo. *He* hasn't jumped on the Lydia-bashing bandwagon.'

I bit down on my frustration. Lydia had a way of making all my questions about herself. I steered her back on topic. 'What did you talk to Natalia about?'

Lydia picked an invisible thread off her shoulder. 'Nothing much. Our schedules, really. Well, mine. Hers wasn't exactly full.' I held my tongue. It didn't sound as though Lydia's would be full for much longer. 'She was alone at the bar so I went over to say hi. I'm not the bitch everyone makes me out to be. Sometimes I take a new girl under my wing.'

'New girls like Natalia?'

Lydia gave a beatific smile that didn't quite reach her eyes. 'Well, why not? She reminded me of myself when I first started out. And she was young too.'

'Eighteen.'

Lydia snorted into her mug and a wisp of steam rose upwards. '*Sure*, eighteen.'

I rifled through my notebook and pulled out Natalia's composite card, which contained her vital statistics. 'It says here she's eighteen.'

Lydia gave me a withering look. 'Honey, just because it's written in black and white doesn't mean it's true. You're a journalist, you should know that.'

I ignored the barb and studied the card. Natalia gazed hungrily at the lens. Needles of dread prickled my skin. 'So, how old was she?'

Lydia glanced at Natalia's photo and shrugged. 'Who knows? Fourteen, fifteen? Designers and casting directors want fresh faces. And by "fresh", I mean "young". Except the industry's upped its standards, so now they can't openly use girls who are barely into puberty.' Lydia smiled sweetly and gripped her mug with tight, white knuckles. 'Agencies get round it by lying about their models' ages. Just one of the many ways they manipulate us.'

My mind fizzed. Natalia was a minor? Would her rapist have known? Would he have cared?

'Still, I shouldn't complain because it works both ways. Lying about your age can keep you in the game longer. I know a girl who's been nineteen for five seasons.' I raised my eyebrows and Lydia folded her arms. 'Don't judge, honey. In this industry, you're over the hill at twenty-five. Let me ask you this: if you go to the supermarket to buy some milk, which bottle are you going to buy, the one that goes off tomorrow or one that goes off next week?'

I shoved Natalia's card in the back of my notebook, burying her face where I couldn't see it. 'Did you see much of Natalia at Leo's party?'

'It was hard to miss her. She was hammered.'

'Was it unusual for Natalia to drink so much?'

'How should I know? Maybe she needed Dutch courage. Those fashion dos can be intimidating when you're starting out. You're rubbing shoulders with people who can make or break your career. But I will say this: she didn't do herself any favours getting drunk. It was unprofessional.'

Something struck me while Lydia was talking. 'If Natalia was such a fresh face, why did Models International fork out on a hotel room for her when she lived in London anyway?'

'You don't think rookies get paid actual money, do you?' Lydia drained her mug, her eyes glittering. 'A handbag here, a night in a luxury hotel there. But nothing to help pay your rent, *silly*, not until you start making cold, hard cash for your agency.' She glanced at the oversized Rolex on her wrist and sighed. 'We need to wrap this up or I'll be late for my next appointment. Loony Lawson can't keep the world waiting.' Lydia wore her bitterness like an expensive coat.

'I have another question.'

'Well, it will have to wait.'

I leaned forward. 'Did you know Natalia was raped? I think it was someone in the fashion industry.'

Shock spread across Lydia's face like a handprint after a slap. She half-rose from her chair. 'I have to –'

I put a hand out to stop her. 'Lydia, please. Do you know who raped her?'

Lydia glared at me then, in one swift movement, she collapsed on the chair and covered her face with her hands. She stayed in that position so long that I started to worry I'd blown the interview.

Eventually she spoke, her voice barely audible. 'It's the oldest tale in the book.'

'What is?'

'Naive young girls desperate for success. Perverted men in positions of power.' She stared down at the table. 'What do you think goes on behind the scenes? Natalia's not the only –'

'Lydia, are you saying something happened to –'

She cut me off with a sharp look. 'I don't know who raped Natalia. We weren't that close. And it's hardly the sort of thing she would broadcast, especially if her attacker was important.'

'But you must have some idea.'

If Lydia heard the desperation in my voice, she ignored it. 'Honey, if you think I'm going to name names and pile more shit on my career, you're more stupid than you look.'

I tried to stay calm. 'Men in positions of power? Designers, casting directors?' I paused, watching her closely. 'Or photographers. Such as, I don't know, Liam Crawford?'

'Liam?' Lydia gave a brittle laugh but a trace of fear clouded her eyes. 'He's a complete bastard but he wouldn't harm anyone.'

'Not according to the rumours.'

'What did you say?'

I lowered my voice. 'Liam has quite the temper, doesn't he? And he's notorious for sleeping with the models he shoots. Say Natalia put up a fight, can you hand on heart say Liam wouldn't have pushed it?'

'How should I know? It was hard enough to keep up with his sexual conquests when we were together.' Lydia bent down to fiddle with her boot buckle, hiding her face in the process.

'Lydia, has Liam done something bad? Is that why you fought at the party?'

'You know what? Fuck. You.' She gathered up her things. 'I should never have come. You reporters are all the same. You know fuck all.'

I shot to the edge of my seat. 'I know three things, Lydia. One: Natalia's rape is a strong motive for her murder and the police suspect Natalia's rapist was someone in the fashion industry. Two: your ex, Liam Crawford, aka the ticking time-bomb with a sideline in domestic-violence rumours, was at The Rose the night she was killed.' I thought back to Natalia's terrified expression on the CCTV footage. 'Even if Liam is innocent, how do you think his track record will play out in the press? He doesn't have many friends on Fleet Street, not after the stunt he pulled last year. He and, by default, *you* will be living under a microscope. You think your career is in a shit-spiral now, wait until your on/off lover is the prime suspect in a murder inquiry.'

My outburst stopped Lydia in her tracks.

'And the third thing?'

I looked Lydia directly in the eye. 'Three: you're here. In spite of your crazy-arse schedule and your claim that you didn't know Natalia well. You're sitting in a greasy café in the middle of London Fashion Week when you have a thousand other places to be. That says to me you care. So, for Christ's sake, Lydia, *help me.*'

My words hung in the air. Out of the corner of my eye, I saw the builders looking at us with interest.

All of a sudden, the sharp angles of Lydia's face melted. 'I honestly don't know who raped Natalia.'

'Can you think of anyone who may have wanted to hurt her?'

Lydia sighed. 'She once mentioned an old boyfriend. Some guy back in Russia. She didn't say much but I got the impression she'd had a lucky escape. Romanced her with his fists, if you catch my drift.'

This was news to me. 'Did she tell you anything about him? His name? Where he lived?'

'No. Only that she was scared to go home. I think she would have done anything to make it as a model here. Including letting her rapist get away with it, if she thought it would help.'

We sat in silence for a moment, then I closed my notebook. 'Do you know if Natalia had ADHD?'

Lydia frowned. 'She never said. Why?'

'The drug used to treat it was found in her bloodstream.'

Lydia held my gaze for a beat too long. 'I need to go.'

As she stood up, Danny shuffled over. 'No charge, Miss Lydia! We see you soon, I hope.'

Lydia's smile was a sliver of sunlight on a rainy day, all the more beautiful for its unexpectedness. Then her face darkened and she stalked out of the café, leaving a trail of stares in her wake.

## 12

Over the past decade, Shoreditch's soaring property prices had brought in a new breed of young professionals, high on sugary cocktails and shit cocaine. But while E1's crack dens and dive bars had become galleries and artisanal coffee shops, not every inch had been gentrified. The end-of-terrace house in front of me looked Dickensian in the flat, wintery light. Decades of pollution blighted the Victorian brickwork as though it were a beautiful woman gone to seed. I skirted a yellow skip, brimming with rubbish, and pushed open the shabby black door.

A large desk stood on a black-and-white Herringbone rug. Dozens of white roses filled a square vase and their fragrance mingled with the woody scent of the fire burning in the grate. A tall woman with brown hair down to her waist was reaching up to place a book on the shelf.

'Can I help you?' Small eyes, like two cigarette burns in a blanket, peeped out beneath a wispy fringe.

I cleared my throat. 'I'm with *The London Herald* and I have a few questions for Liam Crawford.'

Her smile faltered. 'Do you have an appointment?'

'I don't, but he'll want to hear what I have to say.'

'Wait here and I'll ask.'

A large photograph hung behind the desk. A naked woman lying in the surf, her glistening body arched towards the sun. I closed my eyes, suddenly nervous about seeing Liam after all these years.

'He can spare five minutes.' The woman's voice pulled me back from the sun's warmth. 'Up the stairs to your right.'

Music drifted through an open door at the end of the landing. *Wise men say, only fools rush in.*

I hoped it wasn't an omen.

Giant pillars ran down the centre of the studio, rising to a vaulted ceiling thirty feet above the floor. Liam was bent over a laptop at the far end. My foot caught on a lightbox and I landed with a crash that echoed round the studio.

'Fuck.'

A hand reached out to me, but I ignored it and pulled myself up.

'Good trip?'

I glanced up to the half-smile I remembered. Liam had barely changed. A slim build and effeminate face, the kind Shakespeare would have cast to play his heroine. Perfect cheekbones and finely curved lips, hooded eyes the colour of faded denim. A woman's face reconfigured as a man's. The effect was strangely intoxicating.

Liam frowned. 'Hey, I know you.'

I brushed myself off and managed a tight smile. 'Sophie Kent. We were at Oxford together. Briefly,' I added.

'Sophie Kent.' Liam's lips pulled into a lazy grin. 'Keble Ball, right?' He spoke slowly, and his voice, deep and melodic with a hint of Cockney, took me back to Oxford.

'I wasn't sure you'd remember.'

'You don't forget a night like that.' He looked me up and down, then cleared his throat. '*The London Herald*. You've done well for yourself.'

I waved a hand round the vast studio. 'Likewise.'

Liam pulled a navy sweater over his head. 'Alice said you have questions?' He gestured to a spot next to him at the desk, but I moved to the opposite side.

'You were at Leo Brand's party the night Natalia Kotov was murdered.' It was a statement not a question, but Liam answered it.

'Another night, another "celebration" of British talent.' He mimed quote marks in the air.

'You didn't want to go?'

'Fancy dos aren't really my thing. I'm more at home with the rats, not that you'd know about that, duchess.'

I heard the tease in his voice and inched backwards, as though to distance myself from him. 'So why did you go?'

Liam shrugged. 'I do as I'm told. All part of the rehabilitation. Making amends after the *encounter* with one of your lot last year.'

'Did you see Natalia at the party?'

'I was gone by 9 p.m. Stayed just long enough to press the flesh with the right people.'

'That's not what I asked.'

Liam bristled at my tone. 'I may have seen her in the crowd. But I left early. Hit the hay. I'd had a long day shooting for Burberry. And, before you ask, no one saw me.'

I could tell by the way he fidgeted with his cuff that he was lying, but I needed to know why before I showed my hand. I turned the page of my notebook and pretended to read something I'd written. 'A witness told me he saw you fighting with Lydia –'

'What's that got to do with anything?' There was an edge to his voice.

'I'm covering my bases.'

Liam drummed his fingers against the desk and I spotted the tattoo on his wrist: *Be the Change.* A memory stirred in me like dry leaves. My fingers tracing those blue letters on his hot skin. I shook the memory from my head. 'What were you fighting about?'

'I dunno.'

'Liam, it was two nights ago.'

'I know, right?' He smacked his hand against his head, his voice taking on a mocking tone that I didn't appreciate.

'How well did you know her?'

'Lydia?'

'Natalia.'

'I shot her a couple of times.'

'And what did you think of her?'

'You want the truth?' Liam ran a hand through his hair. 'She took a lot of directing. I don't think she was ready.'

'Can you tell me about this shoot?' I pushed the image from *W* magazine across the desk.

Liam frowned. 'Wasn't an easy shot to get. Natalia took far longer than the other girls. Don't get me wrong, she had something about her. Eyes like velvet, and you see the way her jawline hits the light?' He reached across me to trace the picture and I caught a musky scent that wasn't unpleasant. 'But she lay there, a sack of spuds, for the first ten minutes. Still, she warmed up. They always do.' The corner of his mouth twitched.

'For Christ's sake, Liam. This isn't a joke. Did Natalia seem unhappy to you?'

'I wasn't paid to be her therapist. That shoot was a big deal for me. Ten pages in *W* is a game-changer.'

'Was it your idea to shoot her in that position, wearing basically nothing?'

Liam cocked his head to one side. 'I don't expect you to understand, duchess. No offence but you never were the high-fashion type. I had a brief and we ran with it on the day. I think she looks beautiful.'

'And young.'

'*How beautiful is youth! How bright it gleams with its illusions, aspirations, dreams!*' He grinned. 'Longfellow.'

Talking to Liam was like drifting along a flat, sun-soaked river in a rowboat, knowing that Niagara Falls was round the bend.

'You said you photographed Natalia twice. What was the other time?'

Liam reached for his laptop. '*Dazed and Confused*. We shot it three weeks ago but I doubt it will run.'

'Why not?'

'See for yourself.' He spun his laptop round. My mouth went dry.

The image showed Natalia lying on the carpeted floor of a luxurious bedroom. Her face was the colour of chalk, her eyes glassy, a ring of purple around her neck. Sheer underwear revealed nipples, small as buttons, and a dark smudge of hair between her legs. My eyes landed on the object on the floor beside her. I sagged against the desk as ugly memories I'd tried to bury blazed through my mind. 'Are you kidding me?'

Liam's voice was soft. 'What are the chances, right?'

'A noose? What was the fucking brief for this story?'

'It's not as bad as it looks. The idea was to explore celebrity culture. Nudity has lost its shock value. Well, what if the woman in the photo was dead? Would you still flick past without noticing?' He paced away from the desk, then turned round. 'Anyway, *Dazed* won't run this now. Or maybe they will. It might shift a few extra copies. How's that for fucked-up celebrity culture?' He slammed his laptop closed.

'How did Natalia feel about the concept?'

'She did the shoot, didn't she?'

'Do you know how old she was, Liam?'

A flash of irritation registered on his face. 'I just shoot who they send me.'

'What if I told you she wasn't legal?' Liam's shoulders shrugged and didn't fully release. 'Did you sleep with her?'

He whipped his head round. 'What kind of question is that?'

'Answer it.'

'Why? Are you jealous?'

I almost slapped him. 'Did you know that *sack of spuds* was sexually assaulted by someone in the fashion industry last summer? By someone important enough to do damage to her career if she reported him. You're pretty important nowadays, Liam.'

The colour drained from Liam's face. 'What the fuck? Do you honestly think I'm capable of that?'

'You're plenty capable of photographing naked, vulnerable minors in provocative poses. Your moral compass is fucked, Liam. It always was.'

There was no sign of the famous Crawford charm now. The pupils of his eyes shrank down into pinpricks. Liam barrelled towards me, but I stood my ground.

'The same witness who saw you fighting with Lydia, also saw you threaten Natalia. What did they have on you, Liam? Did Natalia tell Lydia you raped her? Is that why you killed her?'

Liam paused, struggling to get his emotions under control. Then he leaned in close, his voice velvet-soft. 'Fuck off, Sophie.'

I stepped towards him, towards the heated air between us, catching him by surprise. 'You think this is bad, wait until the gutter press starts hounding you. You think they'll care if you're innocent? As far as they're concerned, you're a woman-beating Lothario who has it coming. You don't even have an alibi. Wake up, Liam. You'll be thrown to the wolves.'

A phone rang. Liam didn't move. He clenched his jaw so hard, his cheeks turned white. 'I didn't fucking kill her.'

'So prove it by helping me figure out who did.'

Liam glared at me, then all of a sudden the fire left his eyes and he turned back to his laptop. 'I'm a big boy. I'll take my chances.'

I counted to ten but he didn't turn round.

I was halfway down the alleyway when I heard footsteps.

'Wait!' It was the brunette from Liam's studio. 'Liam will kill me if he knows I'm telling you this, but I was on that *Dazed* shoot.'

'It's Alice, right? You were listening to our conversation?' Alice looked down, twisting a silver ring around her finger. I turned away from the wind to face her. 'Go on.'

'Natalia was weird on the shoot. She was nervous, like *really* nervous.'

I shrugged. 'She was shy.'

Alice wrapped her arms around herself. Her skin was already puckered with goosebumps. 'That's not what I mean. Look, Liam can get any woman to open up and perform. It's his thing.' I detected a trace of bitterness in her tone. 'But Natalia was different. She froze any time Liam went near her.'

'Do you know why?'

Alice coiled a long strand of hair round her finger, a strange look on her face. 'I couldn't really say.'

The wind stung my ears. 'Alice, I don't have time for this. If there's something you want to say, just say it.'

She sighed. 'Don't let the charm fool you. Liam's not what he seems.' She glanced over her shoulder. 'I have to get back. He'll notice I'm gone.'

'Why are you telling me this?'

'Natalia was sweet. She didn't deserve what happened to her.'

Alice grabbed the business card I held out, then sprinted back to the studio. I watched the door close, wondering what to make of her. Generally, the more eager the source, the less you could trust them. Alice might have received a shitty pay rise from Liam, or been dumped by him for all I knew. Everyone had an agenda. But she was right about one thing.

Liam was hiding something.

London's streets were dark and glistening. I tramped home along the King's Road, past the Saturday night revelry drifting out of steam-soaked bars. On a particularly screwed-up day on the job,

I used to welcome the rain. It washed the dirt away, ready for a new day. Since Tommy died, the sky could cry itself dry and London would never be clean again.

I'd just collapsed on the sofa when my phone beeped with a press release from the the Met. *Subject line: Appeal following murder at The Rose Hotel, CCTV image available.* I logged on to my laptop and pulled up an image of a man in a dark jacket leaving the back entrance of the hotel. He had a cap pulled low over his face. Was it the same man I'd seen on the CCTV footage last night? It was hard to tell.

The grandfather clock chimed nine o'clock and I switched on the news. A plane had gone down in Malaysia, killing all 398 people on board. I shuddered. I'd covered enough plane crashes to turn me into a twitching wreck any time I had to fly. The third item was Natalia's murder. I turned up the volume.

'*The body of the Russian woman found dead at The Rose Hotel in London has been identified as the model Natalia Kotov.*' The CCTV screen grab appeared. '*Police are appealing to the public to come forward with any information on this man, who was seen leaving the back entrance of the hotel at 10.20 p.m.*' The newsreader mentioned the small memorial service being held at St Mary's, Holborn, in the morning.

I switched off the TV and padded through to the kitchen. There was leftover fish pie in the fridge with a note that read *Eat me!* stuck on top. I turned the oven on, my heart swelling with love for Poppy. But then my phone beeped with another email. One that made my stomach drop into my feet.

It was from my father.

When can we meet? I need to talk to you. AK

Cold and blunt, like the man himself. I paced round the kitchen while I formulated my response. In the end, all I could manage was one word.

Monday?

His response came a moment later.

8 p.m. L'ondine. AK

Two days away.

The wind whistled through gaps in the windowpane like an overwrought horror movie.

# 13

I woke up to some news.

Rachel Foster, a twenty-four-year-old sales manager, had given an interview to the *Star*, identifying the man in the Met's CCTV image. She'd been at a client dinner and had taken a shortcut down the alleyway behind The Rose when a man crashed into her, knocking her handbag to the ground. He didn't apologise, didn't even break his step, but she caught a glimpse of his face in the half-light of the hotel's security light.

Liam Crawford.

I leaped out of bed and ran to the shower. How would I explain to Rowley that I'd missed the scoop? Turns out, I didn't need to. An email landed in my inbox less than a minute later.

Why aren't we breaking this story? Pull your finger out or I'll find someone else who's up to the job.

I thrashed out an apology, fumbled into a black trouser suit and raced out of the door.

St Mary's, Holborn, was a small, rundown church that sagged between two office blocks on Boswell Street. Police had erected barriers along the pavement to keep the press and public away and a sizeable crowd had turned up to gawk. I turned my back against the wind and dialled Durand's number.

He picked up after two rings. 'Good morning.' His voice sounded unnaturally formal; a sign that he had company.

'Not a good time?'

'Bear with me.' Durand put his hand over the receiver and I heard muffled voices. Then he was back. 'What can I do for you?'

The winter sun was so weak, it was as if a hologram of the sun hung in the leaden sky. I sheltered against a wall, wishing I'd worn a coat.

'Is Crawford being questioned?'

'I believe he's in the building.'

'Is he talking?'

'I can't comment.' There was a pause. 'So, the *Star* broke the story.'

I rolled my eyes. 'Don't rub it in. Crawford lied to my face yesterday.'

'Men like Crawford have a talent for pulling the wool over people's eyes.'

'Do you think he did it?' Durand didn't answer. I sighed. 'I'm really up shit creek with my editor. Can you give me something? You know I'll beg if you ask.'

Durand laughed, a sound that always warmed me, then lowered his voice. 'A small tidbit to cheer you up. Forensics lifted some fingerprints off Natalia's hotel doorhandle. So far we've managed to eliminate everyone we know to have entered her room. And there's no match in our system either. The housekeeper cleaned Natalia's room at 2.30 p.m. and remembers wiping the doorhandle, so whoever the prints belong to entered the room after that.'

'The prints aren't Crawford's, though.'

Durand sighed. 'That would be too easy. But it doesn't rule him out.' I remembered what the coroner said about the latex imprint on Natalia's neck. The killer wore gloves. 'Hotel rooms are notoriously tricky. Too much footfall. It takes time to eliminate all the traces and prints Forensics uncover.'

I was starting to lose the feeling in my toes. 'What can I use?'

'Nothing, yet. If those fingerprints do belong to the killer, we don't want to alert him to his mistake.' Durand's voice took on the formal edge from earlier. 'I have to go. Let's touch base soon.'

The crowd outside the church had swelled and, as I pushed my way to the front, I spotted a tall figure with a familiar mop of blond curls. I tapped him on the arm.

Aiden Isaac's grey eyes brightened. 'Soph! How's it going?'

We had worked together as junior reporters at *The London Herald*, before Aiden decided his skin was too thin and his stomach too weak to pound the streets looking for trouble. He left to pursue a more upscale experience at a weekly gossip magazine. Now the extent of the dirt under his fingernails was identifying which reality-TV star was cheating on his wife.

Aiden shivered dramatically. 'Darling, isn't this vile? We're packed out here like vultures. Fatlobes has decided she *must* have frontline colour to go with our piece on dead models.'

Fatlobes was Aiden's notoriously tricky editor, Liz Brent – wildly unpopular thanks to her catatonic inability to make a decision under pressure. A lifetime's passion for enormous dangling earrings had stretched her earlobes beyond recognition. Hence the nickname.

Aiden lowered his voice. 'She's already written the cover line. *Messed-up models: young, beautiful – and dead.* It's so not my bag but, you know, in this climate one must make oneself indispensable.' He beamed. 'I'm so glad you're here. Apparently Lydia Lawson is on her way. *Squeal.*'

Poor Natalia was being sidelined at her own memorial service. 'Who's gone in?'

'Hardly anyone. It's t-r-a-g-i-c. A waif arrived a few minutes ago wearing a short red kilt. To a memorial service!'

I glanced past Aiden. 'I need to get inside that church.'

A mixture of shock and admiration registered on his face. 'Darling, you *wouldn't.* You're shameless. How will you get past the barriers?'

At that moment an SUV pulled up outside the church. The driver opened the door and Cat Ramsey stepped out, her mouth set in a grim line. Lydia Lawson appeared behind her, in a black figure-hugging dress and a glossy pout. Her dark hair fell in thick waves, her face hidden behind oversized sunglasses.

The crowd surged forward and I lost my footing. Aiden propped me up.

'Do you want to sit on my shoulders, Dopey?'

'Very funny.'

Cat propelled Lydia towards the church entrance. I managed to squeeze through a gap between two barriers just as they reached me.

'Lydia, it's Sophie Kent!' Lydia looked round. 'Please, Lydia. I want to pay my respects to Natalia in person but I can't get through because I'm press. Can you help?'

Cat tugged at her arm. 'Lydia, I really don't think –'

Lydia cut her off. 'Natalia would have wanted Sophie here.'

I paused in the church doorway, risking a quick look back at the throng of reporters. In the middle of a sea of envious faces stood Aiden, giving me a wide grin and a double thumbs-up.

'My God, that was awful.' Lydia paused by the font and removed her glasses to reveal puffy eyes. Up close, I could see a thick line along her jaw where she hadn't blended her foundation. 'Those bloodsuckers. They're wrong about Liam. He came back to the hotel to –'

'That's enough, Lydia. *She's* press too.' Cat gave me a cold look, then led Lydia to the front of the church.

Despite the interest outside, the church was almost empty. London Fashion Week was keeping the style crowd busy, and clearly Natalia hadn't made many friends. As I slipped into a pew near the back, I recognised a couple of Models International employees chatting merrily away. Did Cat make them come to bump up the numbers?

A few rows behind them sat a solitary figure in a red coat. Her long, honey-blonde hair dipped behind the back of the seat and, when she turned to look at the stained-glass window, she revealed a pretty profile. Was she Natalia's flatmate, Eva Kaminski?

The organist began to play 'Ave Maria' and a vicar appeared in the doorway at the side of the altar. He was about to step up into the pulpit, but changed his mind when he saw the size of the congregation. He shuffled to the front of the altar and cleared his throat.

'Dearly beloved, we are gathered here today to remember the tragically short life of one of God's brightest angels, Natalia Kotov. As difficult as it is for us to comprehend, know this: the Lord Almighty had a reason for calling Natalia to his side.'

I rolled my eyes. How could he put a positive spin on Natalia's fate? She wasn't swept up to heaven on a fluffy, white cloud. What happened to her was savage. It was hypocritical to pretend otherwise. I'd seen too many senseless horrors to believe there was a God. Only six weeks ago I'd covered the brutal killing of a sweet-tempered Indian man who worked eighteen-hour days to keep his corner shop afloat. He was stabbed eight times in the chest by a group of smashed-up teenagers who enjoyed themselves so much, they forgot to take the money from the till when they left. People often ask if my job hardens me; whether I become desensitised to news. The answer is the opposite. I care more every day that passes.

My phone buzzed in my bag and I took a surreptitious look at the text, then wished I hadn't. It was from Mack.

*I'm staying in London tonight. Join me.*

The closing bars of 'He Who Would Valiant Be' floated through the air and the Models International crew filed to the back of the church. Lydia reapplied her lipstick and plumped her hair ready for the cameras. Cat hung back looking at her phone and I sidled over.

'Thanks for letting me say goodbye.'

'Well, as Lydia said, you were trying to help Natalia.'

'There's something I've been meaning to ask you about the night she died.' I fiddled with the belt buckle on my coat. It didn't feel good questioning a source at a memorial service, and the curl of Cat's lip told me she agreed. 'Why did you swap rooms with Natalia at The Rose?'

Cat slid her phone into her clutch bag and sighed. 'Because she asked me to. She rang me, crying, to say she couldn't stay in her room. She wouldn't tell me why and I didn't have the energy. The hotel was full so the easiest solution was to swap with her.'

'And you have no idea what scared her?'

Cat shook her head. 'I wish I did.'

'Did anyone else know she moved rooms?'

Cat was momentarily distracted by Lydia cursing loudly as her heel got stuck between two flagstones. 'No idea. Why?'

'Because the killer knew which room to find her in.'

A light went on in Cat's eyes. 'Shit, I hadn't thought of that.'

'Cat, are we standing here all day or are we making my exit?' Lydia leaned against the font, pouting. Cat gave her dress a quick brush-down. Then Lydia slid on her dark glasses, thrust her shoulders back and strode out into the spotlight.

When I turned round, the blonde girl was swinging her bag over her shoulder. Her short skirt was wildly inappropriate for a memorial service but something about her awkward, teenage gait told me she wasn't trying to stand out. I lingered, pretending to gather my things.

When she reached me, I put my hand out to shake hers. 'Eva?' She looked at me with large eyes the colour of a hot, August sky. 'I'm Sophie Kent.'

A flicker of recognition swept across Eva's face. She shook my hand. Her skin felt dry and papery. 'You're the reporter who was helping Natalia.'

'Not hard enough, as it turned out.' It was difficult to keep the bitterness out of my voice.

Eva zipped up her red coat. 'Still, you tried.'

'Eva, do you have time for coffee?'

She looked at her watch. 'I have a casting at twelve o'clock and have to go home to change. You can come with me? It's New Cross.'

Number 32 Milton Way. How could I forget?

# 14

Eva kicked off her shoes. 'Do you want coffee?'

I nodded. The flat looked the same, except for the thin, red blanket covering the sofa and the smattering of photographs tacked onto the fridge. Frost blurred the windows and a peaty, damp smell hung in the air. I put my hand to the radiator. 'Doesn't your heating work?'

Eva shrugged. 'Sometimes. A man came to look at it.'

'Your English is very good.'

Eva moved gracefully round the kitchen. As she reached up to grab two mugs from a cupboard, her jumper lifted to reveal a very pronounced hip bone. 'My pappa is British so I grew up speaking it. I moved here in June. Lived here with Anya, until she went to Tokyo.'

'Anya's a model too?'

'*Was* a model.' Eva's hand wobbled as she tipped spoonfuls of coffee into the mugs. 'She got fat. On purpose, I think. Anya hated Tokyo but couldn't afford the flight back to Kosovo. Her Japanese agency made her sign an agreement saying she'd forfeit her contract if she gained more than a centimetre around her waist. So she ate like a pig and, bingo, home sweet home.' She gave a throaty laugh.

I raised my eyebrows. 'It's that strict?'

Eva shrugged. 'Depends who you're signed with. British agencies are better at disguising it. I've been asked to *tone up* and *get in shape*. Whatever phrase they use, we all know what they mean.' She handed me a mug and I winced as the heat scorched my frozen skin. 'Models International shaved a centimetre off my hips and waist for my composite card. If a client expects those measurements, you can't show up any larger. Better to be skinny than sorry.'

Eva talked quickly, her words running into each other. I parked myself on the sofa, digesting what she said. I didn't know which was worse, the industry's passive-aggressive control techniques or Eva's cheerful acceptance of them.

She caught my horrified expression and laughed. 'Look, no one ever said it was easy. You do what you need to do. Before my trip to Toyko last month, I spent a fortnight on celery and green juice and managed to book a couple of magazine shoots.' Her voice swelled with pride. 'Tokyo sucks but it's where you go to earn cash. Especially if you're young and blonde. It's not *Vogue*, but I have to clear my debt somehow.'

'Your debt?' I thought back to what Lydia said about agencies not paying real money.

Eva perched on the sofa and blew the steam across her coffee mug. 'My agency paid for my visa and my flight from Russia. Plus my test shoot and composite card. And my rent, of course.

It's expensive. Most models owe their agency a few thousand pounds before they even book a job.'

I set my mug down on the table and took out my notebook. 'Was Natalia in debt?'

Eva jumped up from the sofa. 'Sorry, I didn't ask if you wanted sugar in your coffee.'

'No thanks.' I frowned, watching as she dumped three sugars into her mug. She stirred her coffee but didn't return to the sofa. 'How come you weren't at Leo Brand's party?'

Eva leaned against the counter, cradling her mug between porcelain-white hands. 'The agency picks which models to invite. Natalia did a couple of magazine shoots. And she'd been optioned for three shows so she was obviously impressing them.' Something about her tone was off. Was it jealousy . . . or something else?

I tucked my legs underneath me to keep warm. 'How well did you know Natalia?'

Eva gazed out of the window, the corners of her pretty mouth pulled tight, as if she didn't trust herself to speak. 'We lived together for three months.'

I waited for her to continue, but she just sipped her coffee. 'Did she ever confide in you?'

Eva didn't meet my eye; all the warmth and openness of earlier had evaporated.

I stood up and moved across to the window, yesterday's downpours forgotten as the sun shone low in the cruel blue sky. I pressed my hand against the glass and thought back to the day I'd looked out at Jason Danby's body. I'd been right to worry about Natalia. If only I'd known then the danger she was in.

'Natalia talked about her family all the time. I felt as if I knew her brothers. Pyotr, Viktor, Nikolay and what was the eldest called?'

'Roman.' I heard Eva sigh. 'Every month Natalia sent money to her mamma. It was the first time little Pyotr was bought anything new. Everything else was handed down from his brothers. Her mamma posted her a photo. You should have seen Natalia's face. It lit her up inside.'

'She must have been doing pretty well if she was able to send money to her mother.'

Eva shrugged, then dumped her mug in the sink. 'I need to get ready for my casting.'

I put a hand out to stop her, even though she was on the other side of the room. 'Please, Eva.'

She didn't move. When she spoke, her voice was barely more than a whisper. 'Natalia was ... complicated. She was dealing with a lot of stuff.'

'What kind of stuff?' Had Natalia told Eva she was raped?

Eva turned to face me, her eyes brimming with tears. 'Coming to London was a fresh start for Natalia. But things happened to her here that ...' She tailed off, staring at the floor.

I took a step towards her, then hesitated. 'I know Natalia was raped.' Eva pulled her cardigan more tightly around herself, not catching my eye. 'Do you know anything about it?'

'No.'

'She never mentioned it to you?' Eva shook her head and I swallowed my frustration. 'Look, I feel as though I'm missing something here. What aren't you telling me?'

Eva stared into the space between us, as though we were on opposite sides of a pane of glass. 'I used to hear her screams through the wall. She had terrible nightmares. Then, all of a sudden, no more screams. One day I went through her bag to find a lipstick she'd borrowed and I found some pills. She said they helped her sleep. But she took so many, she couldn't wake up so she started taking stuff for that too.'

'Cocaine?'

Eva shrugged. 'Cocaine, speed, whatever. You don't have to look hard in this business. I tried talking to her about it but she got mad. Then she overslept and missed an important casting. Her agent, Cat, was furious. I heard her yelling down the phone. Natalia was terrified. She thought she was being sent home.'

'What happened?'

Eva plaited her hair as she spoke. 'Cat booked her into NA. Told her if she didn't get clean, she'd be dropped. Natalia went every Monday morning to a place on Shelby Street. It helped at first.'

'But she relapsed?'

Eva wrapped her arms round herself. 'Like I said, Natalia was complicated.'

A thought struck me. 'Do you know if Natalia was taking drugs for ADHD?'

Eva's eyes flitted across my face and settled on the floor. 'Ritalin is an appetite suppressant. It's an old industry trick.'

That's why Lydia and Cat were cagey when I asked. I leaned my forehead against the window. An old lady was watering flowers on her balcony in the high-rise block opposite. Tiny brushstrokes of pink and violet against a canvas of concrete. I looked back at Eva. 'Did Natalia ever mention an ex-boyfriend? A man she knew in Russia?'

The tension in Eva's jaw melted as we changed topic. 'Yeah, a couple of times. He was a drug dealer in her hometown. Had a thing for young girls, although I don't think he knew quite how young Natalia was. Caused that scar on her eyebrow. Pushed her down the stairs one night when she tried to go out with friends.'

'Did she tell you his name?'

Eva screwed up her face. 'I don't know. We never really discussed him. Even here, he had some kind of hold over her.'

'Why, what did she say?'

'It wasn't what she said. It was an impression I got. The way her voice grew smaller the few times she mentioned him. As if he could hear her. I asked her about him but she wasn't big on sharing. Sometimes keeping your feelings inside is the only way to survive.'

Eva didn't meet my eye and I got the impression she wasn't just talking about her flatmate.

Suddenly she checked her watch and rolled her eyes. 'Shit, I'm going to be late. I really need to change. Ever since my agent, Laura, caught me at an appointment in a romper suit and cowboy boots, she makes me go into the office for a pre-casting outfit check.' She pulled her plait into a bun and laughed. 'There was an upside, though. She took me to Topshop and bought me a load of new clothes. Out of my future earnings, of course,' she added.

I stood up. 'Would you mind if I took a quick look at Natalia's bedroom while you're changing?'

She pointed at a door to the right of the kitchenette. 'Be my guest.'

Natalia's bedroom was small and dank. A bare lightbulb hung from the ceiling and the nicotine-coloured walls pressed in on me as I stood in the middle, looking round. The single bed had already been stripped, indicating the room had been searched by police. They would have taken anything of interest but it was still worth a look.

A pile of magazines stood against the wall. I turned my head sideways and read their spines: *Vogue*, *Elle*, *Glamour*. Two pairs of earrings lay in a small, blue dish. I opened the wardrobe door, unleashing a faint waft of citrus and mothballs, and ran my hand along Natalia's clothes. Dark denim, baggy T-shirts, oversized sweaters. I brushed the soft fabric of the flowery skirt she'd worn the day I met her.

The memory made me light-headed and I sank onto the bed. Being surrounded by Natalia's things, the minutiae of her life, weighed me down with sadness. I stared at the scuffed crate that served as a makeshift bedside table. On it was a half-used tube of hand cream, a Russian dictionary and a picture frame. I leaned across and picked it up.

It was a photograph of Natalia and her brothers, bundled up in coats on a snowy street. Natalia's face was soft and doughy, and she held baby Pyotr on her hip. Five identical pairs of blue eyes gazed at the camera. The casual intimacy, the love and warmth, caught in my throat like a fishhook.

'She looks so happy there.' I jumped as Eva appeared at my shoulder. She'd changed into leather trousers and a green parka.

I cleared my throat. 'Where was it taken?'

'Ivanovo. She was about eleven. Look at Pyotr's dimples. Couldn't you just eat him?'

'Do you know Ivanovo?'

Eva shuddered. 'I know of it. It's a bit of a backwater. I don't blame her for escaping the City of Brides.'

I stared at Eva. 'What did you say?'

'What, City of Brides? When they shut Ivanovo's textile factories, the female workers never left. Women still outnumber men two to one. Someone nicknamed it City of Brides and it stuck.' She must have noticed my expression. 'Did I say something wrong?'

Natalia's Twitter account: The daily tweets from @Cityofbrides.

It couldn't be a coincidence, could it?


Jasdeep Chopra was a quiet, tidy man who trudged to work at *The London Herald* IT department every day in the same polyester suit; a packed lunch tucked under his arm. While colleagues progressed up the career ladder, Jasdeep sat in his small, windowless office on the seventh floor in a state of rapture. He didn't want more money or responsibility. The higher he climbed, the further away he'd be from the coalface. Jasdeep *loved* technology. He once told me that the sight of an elegant sequence of computer code gave him goosebumps.

His office light was off and I swore as I remembered it was Sunday. I was about to leave when I heard a clatter from inside. Jasdeep was hunched over his computer.

'Sophie!' Switching on his Anglepoise lamp, he gestured for me to sit in the chair opposite his desk. 'Just move those files. What brings you to the Bunker?'

I squeezed into the chair, my knees touching his desk, and unwound my scarf. I'd sprinted from the Tube station and beads of sweat trickled down my back.

'It's a Twitter handle. I can't identify the sender. It might be nothing . . .'

'But it might be something.' He grinned, and the bluish light of his computer screen made his teeth look absurdly white. I explained the background and Jasdeep nodded. 'OK, let's see what we're dealing with.'

He tapped at his keyboard and I glanced at the sign on the wall behind his head. Swirly black writing spelled out *No stone unturned*. I smiled. Jasdeep's dogged determinism had got me out of a scrape before.

Two years ago, I had interviewed Aimee Waters, a twenty-eight-year-old lobbyist who was campaigning for better treatment of rape victims. Not everyone thought she was right. An internet troll going by the anonymous Twitter handle @ll32 sent her a litany of threats and Aimee, being a smart woman, reported him to the police. In my report, I called him *a poisonous coward* and @ll32 found a new target: me.

For three days my phone pinged intermittently with abuse, but police couldn't track him. Then @ll32 made a fatal error. He upgraded his mobile phone and forgot to hide his IP address. Jasdeep found the chink in his armour. When police knocked on the door of unemployed computer repairman,

Eric Simpson, twenty-four hours later, he was smoking a joint in bed. His mum, Julie, was horrified to find out her university graduate son was moonlighting as a misogynistic Twitter troll. 'All that time I thought he was on his computer looking for a job,' she had told me sadly. When Jasdeep brushed off my thanks, I realised his motive wasn't rescuing me; it was solving the problem.

Jasdeep leaned back in his chair and rubbed his eyes. 'You're right, it's a fake account. And it's a good one. I can't trace the sender from these public tweets but there's always a chance they sent Natalia a Direct Message. The more messages I see, the greater the odds of cracking it.'

I knew where this was going.

Jasdeep lowered his voice. 'How badly do you want this, Sophie?'

The portable heater under his desk belched warm, stale air and my toes felt clammy in my socks. After the phone-hacking scandal, we were walking on eggshells, no longer able to get into places we shouldn't. Mostly it was a good thing. Until moments like this. But with Mack and Rowley breathing down my neck, I couldn't afford any missteps.

'More than you know, Jas, but I won't be able to do much if I'm in jail.' I smiled weakly. 'Don't worry. I'll figure something out. Thanks. And say hi to Sameera for me.'

He didn't reply. I was almost at the door when a *tap-tap-tap* made me turn back. Jasdeep's eyes were fixed on the screen, his fingers flying.

*I can smell her on me.*

*On my skin, my hands, embedded in the seams of my shirt.*

*The cold night air vibrates through the trees. My hands close around the masking tape, but I hesitate. She isn't likely to make a sound. Not tonight.*

*My shoes glide on the sodden leaves. I kneel down beside the girl and my knees sink into the mud. She is on her stomach, still as a stunned calf. Her skin glows in the moonlight. Milky and pure. Except for the marks. Like notches on a bedpost, every bruise is a memory. Every scar, a flash of ecstasy. I slide off her pink trainers. The girl's slender feet are ice in my hands. I run my fingers up the soft fuzz of her legs, feel the heat of her young body through my gloves. I slip the polka-dot nightie up over her shoulders. I want to see every inch of her.*

*A rustle in the bushes behind me. Out of the corner of my eye, I spy my companion, head low, back turned.*

*I clear my throat. 'Come closer, you're missing the show.'*

*Hesitant footsteps, a sharp breath. A pair of cool, blue eyes meet mine.*

*'That's better.'*

*A whimper draws my eyes down again. The sound ignites my blood. I twist the girl onto her back. Her breath is high in her chest, her wet mouth struggles to form words.*

*I bend down, her voice grazes my ear. 'I . . . forgive you.'*

*She gazes up at me through swollen eyelids. Defiant. Judging. Who the fuck does she think she is? I don't need her forgiveness. This is her fault. Not mine.*

*My daddy's rank, whisky-laced voice in my head.*

You deserve it. You deserve it. You deserve it.

*I close my eyes. Feel him panting behind me. My small, six-year-old hands leave sweat marks on the headboard.*

*The blackness descends. I breathe. Savour the moment. I squeeze her white throat. Gently at first, then harder. Her pulse thrashes against my fingers.*

*It's over too quickly. I bring my hands to my face and inhale deeply. I can still smell her on me. Only now she's mixed with something sweeter.*

*It's a moment before I realize, it's the scent of death.*

# 15

The following morning I took a deep breath outside the stucco-fronted building on Shelby Street, and pushed memories of the last Narcotics Anonymous meeting I'd attended out of my mind. I couldn't afford to fall apart, not when I'd disappointed Rowley for the second time in five days. Squaring my shoulders, I strode down the corridor and through the door marked 4C.

The morning sun was out, but the grimy window drained the cobalt sky of all its colour, casting a gloomy light over the room. Slate-grey walls jarred with colourful posters and their upbeat shouty slogans: *You are not alone! Trust in miracles!* Although rows of chairs had been lined up in the centre, knots of people huddled around the edge, their shoulders hunched over, as though the air above them, thickened with broken promises, pressed down until they couldn't move. Even now, I wanted to believe they could help themselves.

But faith was a weakness. Tommy's death had taught me that.

'Time to get started, people.' A booming voice cut through my thoughts. I slid into a seat in the back row as a large, bearded man in a grey polo-neck lumbered towards the lectern. 'For those who don't know me, I'm Sean. I run the group. Welcome.

Do we have any new members here today?' I shrank down in my seat. 'OK, who wants to start?'

A man in the second row raised his hand, then shuffled to the front of the room, his skinny frame swamped in baggy jeans and an oversized Adidas sweatshirt. Something about the shrunken, apologetic way he carried himself reminded me of Tommy.

Looking back, that scorching August day was the last time I allowed myself to hope Tommy could get better. He'd done his usual and turned up at my house unannounced. After a good night's sleep, Tommy stared down at his breakfast and told me he wanted to get help. By the time he showered, I'd found the nearest NA meeting, printed off the details and left them on the kitchen table.

'Will you come with me, Sops?' Tommy's eyes were troubled as he looked at the piece of paper.

Two days later, I ducked out of work mid-afternoon and held Tommy's arm as we walked up the steps of St Luke's Church in Chelsea. It was a disaster from the start. Tommy fiddled with the frayed edges of his parka and tapped his scuffed boots on the stone floor. He asked to leave twice but I put a firm hand on his leg. Five minutes in, just as a pasty woman called Sally broke down in tears, Tommy bolted. He was silent on the walk to the Tube station and I went back to work more worried than ever. When I arrived home that evening, Tommy was gone, but not before he'd cleaned out the spare cash I kept in a box under my bed. It was the first time he'd stolen from me and my heart broke.

All of a sudden, the flat grey air around me shimmered, as though displaced by Tommy's presence. I heard his voice, low and urgent. '*Sops, let's go.*' My heart began to race and tiny coloured lights flashed in front of my eyes. I gripped the seat of my chair with damp hands. A white-haired man a few seats down looked over and mouthed 'You OK?'

I forced myself to nod back. My head felt heavy but my arms felt lighter than air. I looked down to check they were still there. My mind whirled. My heart slammed in my chest. I closed my eyes and Natalia's terrified face burned into the darkness behind my eyelids, then morphed into Tommy's face, smiling, then not smiling, then crying, then sobbing, his mouth all twisted and sad like it was the day he was sent away to school.

I stifled a sob. People glanced round and I pretended to cough. Breathing deeply, I focused on the back of the man in front of me, on the dandruff that looked as if a bag of flour had burst over his brown, tweed shoulders. Slowly, I felt control ease itself back into my body.

The kid in the Adidas sweatshirt mumbled to a close and Sean half-rose from his seat. 'Who wants to go next?'

At first no one moved, then a figure dressed all in black marched to the front, head lowered, shoulders rigid, as though she were battling through gale-force winds. She had short dark hair and a heavily made-up face, with vast sweeps of eyeliner that, ironically, made her look younger.

'My name is Violet and I'm an addict.' She had the gravelly voice of a die-hard smoker.

'Hi, Violet.' The room replied in flat unison.

'Most weeks are dark when you're in recovery, but this one was the ninth circle of hell. My mate got killed. You might have seen it on the news. Some of you might know her; she came to this meeting a few times.' I sat up a little straighter, momentarily distracted from thoughts of Tommy. 'It makes you think, right? She fought her demons. Tried to clean up. And then some fuck kills her. All that struggle. All that *effort*. And she winds up dead in a hotel room.' She ran a hand through her hair and it stuck up in angry, black spikes. 'It's bullshit. They tell us we have bright futures ahead of us. If we stay strong, good things will come our way. But the way I look at it is, you don't know what ten-tonne load of shit is about to hit your fan. So, what's the point?' Violet spat the last word out, her top lip curling into a sneer.

The room was silent, poised, waiting for her to continue. Violet took a long, shaky breath. 'That's what I told myself, anyway. As I racked up a line on Saturday night. Cut, scrape, cut, scrape. I was dizzy at the sight of it. My powdery salvation. I could already taste it at the back of my throat. But as I shoved the tenner up my nose, it hit me.' She gave a hollow laugh that sounded like pebbles dropping in a bucket. 'My mate got killed and I made it all about *me*. I used her death as permission to get high. And that ain't fair.' Violet swatted a tear away, leaving a sooty smudge on her cheek. 'There ain't no answers in a rolled-up tenner. There ain't no answers full stop. It's too late for her, but you know what, maybe it's not too late for me. I'm *alive*. Against all the odds, here I fucking am. And I owe it to her not to . . . not to . . .' Violet wiped her nose with the back of her hand.

Her voice cracked but she stuck her chin out and glared at us. 'I owe it to her not to fall apart.'

Violet paused for a moment, then stomped back to her seat. As the group broke into quiet applause, Sean moved towards Violet, but she recoiled from him.

I fidgeted in my chair as Sean gave a final speech full of life-affirming soundbites that had me wondering whether recovering addicts ever stopped talking like self-help pamphlets. Then the meeting ended and I scanned the room for Violet. I spotted her next to a long table laid out with coffee. The last thing my post-panic-attack system needed was caffeine, but I sidled over to pour myself a cup, swearing under my breath as I spilt scalding liquid over my wrist.

'I almost poured the whole bloody pot over myself the first time I came.' Violet blew into her mug and then inhaled sharply. 'Ahhhh, caffeine. The closest I get to a hit these days.' She leaned against the table and raised her eyebrows. 'First time?'

'Uh, second.'

'You have that look about you.'

I finished mopping up my mess and held out my hand. 'I'm Sophie.'

'Nice to meet you.' Violet's hands were ice-cold.

I took a sip of watery coffee and shuddered.

Violet grinned. 'Yeah, the coffee sucks. They don't make it strong in case the buzz sets us off. Weak willpower, weak coffee. They should put that on a sign above the door.'

'How long have you been coming to NA?'

She chewed a fingernail. 'This one? A few months. I was down at Dellis Street but it got too crowded. The bigger the meeting, the more nutjobs there are.' She smiled sweetly, revealing small, pointed teeth. 'Not that I'm judging or anything but that place was *full* of 'em. The final straw was when one guy confessed to me he fantasised about killing his parents. He'd actually planned it step by step. Said he'd wait till they were asleep then slit their throats. Apparently it was the most effective way to knock 'em both off together without one raising the alarm.' Violet sipped her coffee. 'He was only sixteen.'

'Christ.' I ran my fingernail along the polystyrene cup, wondering how to broach the subject. 'I'm sorry about your friend.'

Violet's dark eyes clouded over. 'I hope they catch the bastard and hang him up by his nuts.'

'Had you known her long?'

'Few months. It's hard to make friends at NA. You'll find out. Half the group is one hit away from a nuclear breakdown and the other is drowning in a pool of "me". A bunch of fuck-ups all in one room.'

A couple of people drifted over, including the kid in the Adidas sweater and I lowered my voice. 'How bad was your friend's addiction?'

Violet gave me a cool look. 'Why are you so interested?'

I looked down at my hands and shrugged. 'No reason, I just . . .'

'What are you in for anyway? Coke? You're too la-di-da for meth. Molly? I doubt it.' Violet looked me up and down, then her eyes hardened. 'Why are you really here?'

I shifted awkwardly, wished I'd told her who I was from the start. Lying to an addict is a mug's game; they know every trick in the book. I cleared my throat. 'Actually I'm a reporter.'

Violet's eyes narrowed. 'What the fuck?'

'My name is Sophie Kent and I'm looking into Natalia Kotov's murder. I'm trying to figure out who killed her.' The corners of Violet's mouth twisted and I thought about pushing it but, on the off-chance she didn't report me, I wanted to leave the door open for another go. It's amazing how often people talk once they have a chance to calm down. 'You're right. I'm sorry. I came here today for answers. Natalia was a friend. I know how you feel –'

'You know how I feel?' Violet wheeled towards me and the heat in her eyes made me take a step back. 'You? With your posh voice and your fancy suit? I bet you've never hung out in a room like this, have you? Amongst people who didn't go to fancy schools and end up in cushy jobs.'

'Wait a sec—'

'You're preying on a bunch of losers to *sell papers*. Don't pretend otherwise. It's a fucking insult. To me, to Natalia, to every person in this room.'

Violet's words grated my skin, scraping off my composure in thin flakes. 'You know nothing about me, Violet. Coming here might be misguided. But I took that risk because I want to help. Question my methods, but never question my motive. I care more deeply than you know.'

Violet gave a thin laugh and all the emotion bubbling inside me boiled over and oozed out as though I were made of cracked glass.

'In your speech, you asked what the point is. The point is *saving* each other. When someone has been swallowed up by darkness, it's yanking them back into the light. And if we're too late, we save the next person, then the next. We never stop.' I crumpled the empty cup between my hands and threw it on the table. 'You get it, Violet. Deep down, you get it. You had the note in your hand, the coke on the table, but you turned away.' I stared up at the ceiling as tears threatened to spill over.

'Who was it?' Her voice was flat. 'I saw you earlier, struggling to get through the door. I figured you were a first-timer, psyching yourself up, but if you ain't an addict, there's only one other explanation. You lost an addict. All this saving people stuff, it's not just about Natalia, is it? So, who died?'

I was scared to open my mouth, scared of what might come out if I let it. My tears blurred Violet's features and I couldn't read her expression. 'My brother, Tommy . . . he didn't have your strength and the darkness stole him from me. I think the darkness has taken me too.' A sob escaped, and I bent over the table taking ragged breaths.

There was a pause. 'Like I said, a room full of fuck-ups.' Violet slung her bag over her shoulder and grabbed my arm. 'Come on, let's get out of here.'

We walked in silence past a parade of rundown shops. The vinegary scent of a fish-and-chip shop mingled with fatty smells wafting out of the fried-chicken place next door. We reached a small triangle of grass and Violet led me over to a bench.

'I live round the corner. Opposite the Co-op, above the Sun-Do. It's a Chinese restaurant,' she said, when I looked blank. 'Handy, really, because I can't cook. Although I sometimes wonder if I'm going to start shitting spring rolls.'

I smiled. It felt good to be outside, even if the cold air pinched my fingers and toes. 'I'm sorry I didn't tell you who I was in there. When I'm on a story I get tunnel-vision and forget to behave like a human being.'

Violet kicked the grass with her boot. 'What happened to your brother?'

I leaned back against the bench, shaking my head. Every single detail about the day Tommy died was carved into my brain. But I never told anyone. It was as if speaking the words aloud would preserve the memory, wrap it in velvet and bury it in a pocket of my soul.

Violet registered my silence and I felt her shrug. 'Don't matter. I shouldn't have asked.'

The wintery sun ducked behind a cloud, then reappeared and suddenly I felt the words in my throat. 'It was October. A Wednesday.' I stared down at my gloves and took a deep breath.

That day, I'd rushed over to Earl's Court after a woman's body was discovered in a basement flat in Nevern Square. It was an apparent suicide but you could never be sure. When I arrived at the expensive, red-brick building, my first question to the officer on duty was whether the suicide could have been an accident.

'Not unless she accidentally took off all her clothes, climbed into a bin, then stabbed herself in the stomach,' he said.

Jennifer Lyle was a neat freak. Even in death, she couldn't bear the thought of anyone having to clear up after her. On 9 October, Lyle left her office where she worked as an upmarket travel agent, came home to her one-bedroom flat and sat down to write three letters. One to her friends, one to her boss and one to the police. She wrote that, ever since her parents were killed in a plane crash the year before, she was living in a world with no light. Lyle sealed the envelopes, then stripped naked, climbed into a large black dustbin and stabbed herself with a serrated knife.

The story was so bizarre that when I heard my phone ring and saw it was Tommy, I hit *cancel*. We hadn't spoken since he'd stolen from me, and I wasn't in the mood. I knew what he was going to say. Tommy would tell me how sorry he was, how he wanted to get clean. I would inch open my heart and let in a sliver of hope, telling myself that *this* time it would work. Then he'd decide real life was too hard and slink off to the nearest crack den to disappear, leaving my heart in tatters. So, when Tommy called again ten minutes later, I put my phone on silent. Only Tommy wasn't ringing to apologise.

He was ringing to say goodbye.

By the time I got home at midnight, Tommy had phoned six times. But I was too exhausted to return his calls. The following morning, I woke at dawn and went for a walk along the river. I couldn't shake the tragedy of Jennifer Lyle. The shiny brass knocker on her front door, the neat window boxes filled with blousy hydrangeas. How could a woman who'd taken such obvious pleasures in her home be filled with such despair that her only salvation was folding herself up in a bin and bleeding to death? I didn't look at my phone again until I'd showered the strangeness off. Only then did I see the text from my father: *Call me.* His phone rang three times and, by the time he picked up, I knew in my heart what he was going to say.

*Tommy is dead.* Three words, spoken so matter-of-factly he could have been talking about the weather. I waited for the catch in my father's voice, the trace of emotion, but it never came. Neither of us spoke. I couldn't breathe. Then my mind detached from my body and I floated upwards so that I was looking down on myself, shivering in a towel in my bedroom.

'He was found under Albert Bridge this morning.' My father cleared his throat. 'Overdosed.'

I wanted to tell my father that Tommy couldn't be dead because he'd been calling me and I was about to call him back, and it must be another junkie's body that had washed up on the banks of the Thames.

'Let's not pretend this is a surprise. Tommy never even got out of the starter blocks.' His voice softened a fraction. 'He's at peace now, Sophie. It's the most we could hope for. I'm in Tokyo for the next few days but my secretary is handling the funeral plans.'

My father hung up and I floated higher and higher until the woman below me was a tiny blue dot. I watched her sink to the floor.

Violet put a cold hand on my arm. 'I'm sorry, Sophie.'

I touched my wet cheek and smiled ruefully. 'I haven't told anyone that. The part about me ignoring Tommy's calls.' I twisted my coat button round and round. 'In *Breakfast at Tiffany's* Holly Golightly calls it the Mean Reds. You're afraid, but you don't know what you're afraid of. Protecting Tommy filled me up like helium in a balloon. It kept me afloat. But I turned my back on him when he needed me most. And the guilt? Well, that's the meanest red of all.'

We sat in silence, watching a flock of pigeons peck at the grass in front of us.

Eventually I sighed. 'Do you mind if I ask you about Natalia?'

Violet shrugged. 'What do you want to know?'

'Did she ever say anything to you that might lead us to her killer? Anyone she hung out with? Any boyfriends?'

Violet leaned back, rested her boot on the bench. 'Definitely no boyfriend. She used to say how hard it was to meet decent men in London. She thought they were all flash. I was like, *Listen love, maybe they are at them fashion parties you go to but the men round here certainly ain't.*'

I thought about the man who raped her. 'Did she seem scared of anyone?'

There was a pause. 'If I tell you this, I don't want my name in the paper.' I nodded, my heart starting to beat faster. 'Natalia was being stalked. Some Russian bloke who followed her to London.'

'Her ex-boyfriend was *here*?'

Violet nodded. 'Not sure if she used the word *ex-boyfriend*, but he was definitely someone from back home. He kept appearing all around London. He left blue flowers to show he'd been watching. On her doormat, in her gym bag, even in her bedroom once. She was a wreck.'

My mind raced. 'Blue flowers?'

'They were symbolic, she said. Something to do with the part of Russia they were both from. The stress really got to her, and she started self-medicating. I told her she should report him but she was too scared.' Violet looked down at her hands. 'She wasn't the first woman to fall for a violent man.'

I clung on to the arm of the bench, tethering myself to something solid. 'Can you remember the last time Natalia saw him?'

'It was really recent. Uh...' Violet scrunched her face up like a fist, then she sat bolt upright. 'It was the same day that black kid got killed with an axe on her estate. She was proper messed up about it.'

I stared at Violet, my brain taking a second to piece it together. Natalia's stalker was there the day Jason Danby was murdered? How far behind him had I been? No wonder Natalia was so upset.

The sun disappeared behind a pillow of cloud and I hugged my coat around myself. 'Have you told the police what you know?'

I felt Violet stiffen. 'I called that number, the one on the news.'

I closed my eyes. Thousands of people called those helplines. It would be ages before the police managed to sift through all the information.

Violet seemed to read my mind. 'I ain't talking to them. Me and the filth don't have the best relationship.'

I heard the edge in her voice and handed over my business card. 'If you change your mind or if you think of anything else, call me.'

Violet took it and stood up. 'Nice to meet you, Sophie Kent. Keep on saving.' She made a peace sign with her fingers. 'And I'm sorry. About your brother.'

Violet strode across the grass, the heavy tread of her boots scattering the pigeons as though she were Moses parting the Red Sea.

My phone trilled in my pocket and I pulled it out with raw hands, still reeling from Violet's bombshell.

'That slimy bugger Liam Crawford has been released.' Rowley's whiny voice cut straight through me. 'I want a quote from him for tonight's edition. I don't care how you get it, just get it.'

He rang off and I dialled a number.

'Liam Crawford Studios.'

'Alice, it's Sophie Kent from *The London Herald*. We met on Saturday. Is Liam there?'

'He's not shown up yet. Not since,' she lowered her voice, 'he was arrested. What a shocker. Do you know why he went back to the hotel that night? Stitched.com is saying it's got something to do with Lydia. Is that true? Do you think they're back together? I mean –'

'Alice,' I didn't have time for this, 'do you know where I could find Liam?'

'At the bottom of a whisky bottle, I imagine. Try his apartment.'

'Which would be?'

'Number 47, Block B, Sandalwood Close, Islington. But don't tell him I told you that. And if you see him, find out if he and Lydia are back together.'

I fished around in my bag for my Oyster card. 'Why do you care, Alice?'

There was a pause. 'No reason.'

I was almost at the Tube when I realised what had been bugging me about the blue flowers Violet mentioned. I'd seen blue flowers very recently. On top of the mirrored cabinet, next to the candles.

In room 538.

# 16

An army of council blocks stretched upwards, like giant concrete needles piercing the heavy, woollen clouds. A dense smell of sewage hung in the air. Other than a plastic bag dancing in the wind, the estate was still, deserted. I scanned the buildings, then shuddered as my foot sank through a brown puddle. I found the communal front door to Block B and was about to ring Liam's bell when I changed my mind. The less warning he had that I was here, the better. I sat down on a brick wall and pulled out my phone, trying to ignore the icy gunk seeping into my sock. I'd received another text from Mack, asking to go for a 'drink' after work. I really needed to end things, but not by text. Mack could wait. I dialled Eva's number. When she didn't pick up, I left a message warning her to be on the lookout for Natalia's ex-boyfriend.

Just then, a baggy-clothed kid darted out of the building. I caught the door, scampered up to the fourth floor and rang Liam's doorbell.

Footsteps approached and a shadow passed across the peephole. I held my breath.

'I thought I told you to fuck off.'

'I'm just here to talk. Can I come in?' I stepped back from the peephole.

There was a pause, then the door opened. 'How did you find me?' The soft hallway lighting hit Liam's sharp cheekbones, carving shadows across his face. Dark circles ringed his eyes, but the irises were Tiffany-box blue.

'I'm a reporter. It's what I do.'

'This is reporting, is it? Harassing people in their homes?' He leaned against the door frame and a faint, slow smile spread across his lips. 'All that class and money, duchess, and look at you now. Down in the gutter with the rest of us.'

'The gutter's fine. It's closer to the action.' I ignored the tug in my stomach, opened my notebook. 'Would you care to comment on what happened at the police station earlier?'

Liam gave me a cool look. 'What do you think?'

'Can you explain why you lied to police about returning to The Rose?' His jaw tightened and I braced myself for a slammed door. 'If there's a reasonable explanation for why you lied about your alibi, now would be the time to reveal it.'

'Is that right, duchess? Unless I'm mistaken, no one's charged me yet.'

'Do I need to explain to you how trial by press works?'

Liam's eyes slid over me. 'You know, ever since you turned up at my studio, I can't stop thinking about that night.'

I rolled my eyes. 'Liam, that was ten years ago.'

'You left before I woke up.'

'I had some place to be.'

'At 4 a.m.?'

'You knew the time?'

'I wasn't really asleep.'

I shivered as a slice of cold wind struck the back of my neck. I wasn't about to get sucked in. 'You know what's interesting, Liam? A witness saw you having words with both Lydia and Natalia after dinner. I didn't put the pieces together before, but you told me you left at 9 p.m. Dinner didn't start until then. That means your fight with Lydia occurred after you returned to The Rose.' A strand of hair blew across my face and I pushed it behind my ear. 'Why did you go back to speak to her?'

Liam's mouth twitched. 'No comment.'

'You were halfway home but you cycled all the way back. It must have been important. Something you couldn't say over the phone.'

'I said no comment.'

'Was it about Natalia? Is that why she came over to break up the fight?'

The mention of Natalia snuffed out all the warmth in Liam's face. His voice took on a hard edge. 'No. Fucking. Comment.'

I knew I should stop, regroup and find a different approach but the words swelled in my mouth. 'Did Lydia know you raped Natalia? Did she threaten to expose you? Why else would you lie about going back to The Rose?' Liam glared at me, his eyes like the barrels of a handgun. 'Do you see what I'm getting at, Liam? Even if you're innocent, none of this adds up. And staying silent only makes you look more guilty.' A loaded, angry stare stretched between us. Eventually, I sighed. 'I saw Lydia yesterday at Natalia's memorial. She thinks the police are wrong about you.'

Liam exhaled slowly and leaned against the wall. 'She's a smart girl.'

'Is she smart? It's not the first time she's covered for you with the police.' An image of Lydia's famous black eye flashed through my mind. 'You threatened her at Leo Brand's party, you lied about your alibi, God knows you weren't boyfriend-of-the-year material. And yet, on the two occasions I've talked to Lydia, she won't hear a word against you. So, is she smart?' I paused, watching him closely. 'Or is she scared?'

'For fuck's sake.' Liam slammed his fist into the wall. The sound made me jump. 'That's what you think? That Lydia's scared of me?'

I stared at the spot on the wall where his fist made contact. 'Can you blame her? You broke her heart publicly. And now she's acting as if she's too frightened to speak out.'

Liam pushed himself off the wall and ran a hand through his hair. 'You think I broke *her* heart? Let me tell you this: Lydia isn't the victim she makes out.'

'What do you mean?'

Liam stared through me, as though I were invisible. 'She's a difficult woman to love. A beautiful, impenetrable fortress.'

I narrowed my eyes. It annoyed me when a man labelled a woman *difficult*, absolving himself of responsibility.

'If Lydia has put up barriers, whose fault is that? Ever since you got together, she's been torn apart by the press. Maybe sharing your toxic limelight forced her to toughen up.'

Liam gave a hollow laugh. 'Yeah, well, certain shades of limelight can ruin a girl's complexion.'

'If Lydia isn't the innocent in all this, why keep quiet? People want to believe you're guilty. If you explain why you lied about your alibi, it might help.'

Liam inched closer, his gaze on me hot as a bare hand. 'You know what, Lois Lane? This might be hard for you to understand but I care about Lydia. I won't air our dirty laundry in public. If that screws me over, then so be it.'

I stepped backwards, removing myself from the rapidly shrinking space between us. 'Can you be sure Lydia would do the same for you?'

'You're missing the point. People are going to believe what they want. So, why bother?'

I could feel the truth slipping away from me like quicksilver. 'This is going nowhere, is it?'

'You tell me.'

'Liam –'

'I know, I'm sorry. I just . . .' He held his hands up. 'Why do you care so much whether I talk?'

I remembered the edge in Rowley's voice. *I don't care how you get the quote, just get it.* 'Because I don't want to see an innocent man crucified in the press.'

'How can you be so sure I'm innocent?'

'Who says I'm sure?'

A soundless storm swelled in the doorway. When I spoke, my voice was calm. 'I asked you this once before, Liam, and I'm asking you again: did you kill Natalia Kotov?'

Liam leaned in close, his breath sweet and hot on my ear. 'If you still need to ask me that, then you're right. This is going nowhere.' He bent down to kiss my cheek. 'See you around, duchess.'

The door closed. I stared at the chipped blue paint, willing my feet to move. Screw Liam. It was all an act. He was messing with my radar. For what? For kicks? Because he had something to hide? As I ran down the stairs, my foot squelched in my shoe.

And Liam's kiss burned a hole in my cheek.

I raced along Kensington High Street towards *The London Herald*, already writing the Liam update in my head. The office block was a lit firework against the black sky and I sprinted into its welcoming heat. Skating into the lift, I flexed my fingers to get the blood flow going. Just as the doors closed, a bony hand appeared.

'Kent, what a pleasant surprise.' Mack brought with him a sour waft of alcohol. I gave a tight smile and hit the button for the eighth floor. 'So you're not replying to my texts now?'

I unbuttoned my coat and sighed. 'Mack, I don't have time for this.'

His dark eyes narrowed into slits. 'I thought you'd say that.' He reached across me, lightning quick, and pulled the red *Stop* button. The lift juddered to a halt.

'What are you doing?'

'We're going to talk, Kent.' Mack raised his arm along the wall by my head, trapping me in the corner. 'About us.'

I ducked away from him and pressed my back against the wall. 'Don't be ridiculous. You can't trap me in a lift. Look,' I ran my eyes over his crooked tie and creased suit. 'I'm sorry. You're right, we do need to discuss it. But not here. Let's –'

'We're not going anywhere.'

I yanked my flimsy shield of a bag in front of my body. 'OK, you want to talk? Let's talk. This has to stop. You're married, for Christ's sake. And I'm a mess –'

'I know that, Kent. I see the late nights and the mornings after, the five cups of coffee it takes before you can even log on to your computer. You don't eat. You don't laugh. Half the time I look over at your desk, you're staring at nothing. Your work is shoddy, you're missing things a retarded work-experience kid would pick up, and you look homeless.' The expression on my face made him pause and his voice softened. 'I see you, Kent.'

I couldn't look Mack in the eye. Instead I focused on the over-gelled strand of hair that had glued itself to his forehead. 'I appreciate the concern. More than you know. But I can't handle this anymore. I'm fighting fires on all fronts.' I couldn't tell Mack the truth. That I felt nothing, for him, for anyone. I wasn't fighting fires. I was arming an arsonist with kerosene.

*Throw another barrel on the fire. Watch your life burn.*

But sleeping with your married boss only got you so far. And it wasn't fair on him. 'I can't live each day wondering if we're going to be found out.'

'I need you, Kent.'

Up close, I could see the desperation in Mack's eyes. Not love, or even lust. *Despair.* Something shifted. I put a hand on his arm.

'Think, Mack. If things go tits-up at the paper, you need something to fall back on. You have a family. A chance at the happy-ever-after. But that's at risk all the time we're fucking around. So, go home. Be happy.'

The words sounded ridiculous. Who the hell was I to give advice on how to be happy? Exhausted, I reached out to press the *Stop* button, but Mack swayed towards me, loosening his tie. When he spoke his voice was soft. 'What if I choose you?'

The sharp edge of shame needled through me. 'You won't. Because you're smarter than that. Listen to yourself, Mack. You think I'm the answer, but I'm not. We can't make each other happy. What we have is . . . co-dependence. Cheap hotel rooms. Pity fucks.' I regretted the phrase the moment I saw the hurt in his eyes. 'I'm sorry, I didn't mean –'

'Fuck you, Kent,' he said softly. 'If that's all this is to you, then fuck you.' I watched as he drew himself up, and ran a shaky hand over his face. 'Saint Sophie, crusader of truth, fighting evil, one sentence at a time. You should be careful about burning bridges.' He started to move away, then changed his mind.

Before I could move, Mack was on me like a fallen tree. The heat of his hands burned through my shirt. His lips on mine, rough and painful; his acid breath filling my mouth. Without stopping to think, I pulled my knee up sharply between his legs. Mack folded over in pain.

'Shit, Mack. I'm sorry. Are you –'

He slammed the *Stop* button and the lift swept upwards.

Still wincing, Mack smoothed his hair and straightened his tie. 'You've made your point, Kent.'

The doors opened and I turned towards the jet of cool air. 'Go home to your wife. One of us should get a shot at happiness.'

Kate's fingers clattered across her keyboard and she didn't look up as I reached my desk. 'I heard Growler tore a strip off you for missing the Liam story.'

'Mmmm.' I sat down, feeling momentarily winded. I couldn't shake the hurt look on Mack's face. I already knew he would make me pay for it. *Throw another barrel on the fire. Watch your life burn.*

I checked my emails. Mikhail Chernov had responded to say he'd tracked Natalia's mother down, but she didn't want to talk. I glanced at the time on my computer screen. Three hours until dinner with my father. Dread corkscrewed through my veins. First Liam, then Mack and now my father. I tossed my notebook onto my desk and massaged my temples, attempting to soften the sharp edges of a headache.

Ours was always a fractured relationship. Affection had been in short supply in Antony Kent's childhood. His own father had steel running through his veins, so he grew up equating emotion with weakness. My father did his duty in the marital bed but that was as far as his parental responsibility stretched. No sports days or school plays. No steadying hands or words of encouragement. He'd pass Tommy and I in the long corridors at Redcroft without making eye contact, let alone speaking to us. My father was in Tokyo when I got my A-level results, and read about my four As in the weekly newsletter his secretary compiled to keep him up to speed with family news. Instead of calling, he sent me a text. Pathetically I saved it in my phone, as though it were sent by God himself.

The irony is that other kids were jealous of my life. They were charmed by the airy grandeur of Redcroft where gossamer-thin Georgian windows turned sunlight into rainbows; where staff served gin cocktails on the terrace, and we spent long, lazy days baking by the swimming pool. A weaker person might say they would have traded in all that luxury for a loving father.

While my peers basked in parental applause, I was busy taking care of myself. I was bright but studied hard, and my grades carried me to the gleaming spires of Oxford and a first-class degree. My degree, my job, my money, my life. Everything I did, I did for me.

And Tommy.

Tommy took our mother's emotional distance harder than our father's. Twenty years falling short of Antony Kent's expectations had broken her. She floated around Redcroft, tethered to the earth by the highball she clutched in her right hand. When I was little, I used to hide behind the pool-house and watch the sun glinting off the pearls around her neck as she swam. She was so slight, her strokes barely made a ripple on the water's surface. I could handle her indifference, but Tommy couldn't. She acted like he wasn't there. So I became Tommy's mother and his father. I took care of the freckle-faced boy, and the wounded, angry man he became. Until I couldn't take care of him anymore.

The sound of my phone ringing jolted me out of my thoughts.

'Hello?'

'Is that Sophie Kent?'

'Eva? Hello. Did you get my message about Natalia's ex?'

'I did.'

I frowned. 'You sound . . . what's wrong?'

There was a pause. 'I just saw him.'

I sat up straighter in my chair. 'Where?'

'I got back from a casting five minutes ago and he was on the other side of the road.'

I chewed the end of my pen. 'Is he still out there?'

'I can't see him.'

'Eva, call the police, just to be –'

'No police!' The sharpness in her voice caught me by surprise. 'I'm sure it's nothing. I just thought you should know.'

The line went dead.

Why was Natalia's ex-boyfriend following Eva? Why was he still in London? Did he have unfinished business? I stared down at my keyboard as sinister thoughts hijacked my brain, and noticed the edge of a brown envelope poking out. It was marked *Sophie Kent, PRIVATE.*

Intrigued, I cut it open and emptied the contents onto my desk. A Post-it note had been stuck on the front of an A4 page. I read the scrawled handwriting:

*Don't look if you don't want to. No stone unturned.*

I laid the pieces of paper face down on my desk. What had Jasdeep done? I glanced over my shoulder. Kate was on the phone; Mack was nowhere to be seen. I hesitated, fingers tingling. Then I slid the pages back into the envelope and stuck it in my drawer.

'Sophie!' It was Spencer Storey, the City Editor. 'I need an ETA on your Crawford copy. We're moving it to page three.'

I raised my head. 'Ten minutes, fifteen tops.'

Spencer grunted in response and I turned back to my computer screen. My fingers hovered over the keyboard, then my eyes flicked towards my drawer. Who was I kidding? I yanked it open and grabbed the envelope before I could change my mind.

The first page was a printout of all the direct messages @cityofbrides had sent to Natalia's private Twitter inbox. Individually they sounded innocuous, but the sheer volume was compelling. The last one was sent on 11 February, six days ago: *@Cityofbrides @N_Kotovofficial Don't ignore love. You'll regret it. Forever.*

My hands slowly turned over the second page. On it was an address. *84 Cautley Avenue, Clapham.*

Underneath Jasdeep had typed:

*IP address came from this location. Sender: Alexei Bortnik.*

# 17

I lingered outside L'ondine, breathing in the brittle night air. Liam's piece had taken longer than I anticipated and then I'd wasted forty-five minutes doing a fruitless background search on Alexei Bortnik. By the time I'd emailed Mikhail Chernov asking for help, it was almost 8 p.m. and I'd raced over to Mayfair in a blind panic.

I ducked inside, into the candlelight and warm scent of log fire and freshly baked bread.

'Welcome, Miss Kent, your father is waiting.' The whippet-thin maitre'd stepped forward to take my coat but I shook my head. I wouldn't be staying long. He led me through the hushed, wood-panelled restaurant and stopped by a corner table. My father sat alone, like a freshly carved ice sculpture; his face chiselled into razor-sharp edges, a severe parting in his white-blonde hair.

He gave me a sharp look. 'You're late.'

I slid onto the velvet chair, flinching as my knee brushed against his. 'I got caught up at work.'

'You look tired.'

'It's been a long day.'

My father raised his hand an inch off the table and a dark-haired waiter glided over. 'Albert, two sirloins, rare, and two glasses of the Argentinian Malbec. And not the '87 I had last week, far too young. Bring the '65.' My father slid his frameless glasses into his blazer pocket. 'The steaks are hung for fifteen months. As the blood drains, the muscles relax, which makes for a far more tender cut. But it must be rare. To cook it any longer would be sacrilege.'

I nodded, wondering how I was going to manage an entire steak with no saliva in my mouth. 'Are you going to tell me why I'm here?'

My father unfolded his napkin and dropped it onto his lap. 'How are things at the newspaper?'

'Fine.'

He raised his eyebrows. 'Really? The latest circulation figures are dismal. It must be demoralising to work so hard, for so little.'

Albert poured red wine into my father's glass. He tasted it without taking his eyes off my face, then nodded curtly. Albert filled my glass and I grabbed it gratefully.

'Don't gulp, Sophie. Where are your manners?'

Reluctantly I put my glass down, watching as my father ran his hand over the white tablecloth. As a girl, I always imagined his skin to be cold and hard, like the bonnet of his steel-grey Jaguar.

'A smart person in your shoes would be looking for an exit strategy.' His BlackBerry vibrated on the table and he turned it face down. 'The goalposts are changing. It's all about the 360-experience. Print, web, mobile, television, social media.'

He waved a dismissive hand. 'But I probably don't need to tell you that.'

I raised my glass to my lips and allowed the warmth to spread through me. 'What's your point?'

'Where will you be in two years' time? Five years? Ten?'

'Why do you suddenly care what I'm doing with my life?'

My father leaned forward and steepled his fingers together. 'Humour me, Sophie. What's your goal?'

'My goal?' A dull ache pressed behind my eyes, and it felt as though a lump of clay had settled in my stomach. 'I want to report the news. I don't care how I do it. The platform doesn't matter. What matters is the story, the truth. And consequences. Holding people accountable for what they've done.' I looked him in the eye as I said the last part.

'Any idiot with a smartphone can report the news, so where does that leave you?' My father tilted the blade of his knife and the reflection of the candle flame danced across its surface. 'What is *The London Herald*'s readership?'

A waiter set a plate down in front of me. The wet, meaty smell turned my stomach. 'You wouldn't have come here without doing your research, so you tell me.'

'It stands at 1,700,000.' A smile spread across his lips as he cut a sliver of steak. 'Readership is falling by nearly ten per cent year on year; advertising revenue is declining by fifteen per cent. How long do you think Premier News can sustain it? The business model no longer works.' He dabbed the corner of his mouth with his napkin. 'Do you know how much Premier News makes from digital advertising a year?'

I shrugged, the lump of clay in my stomach hardening.

'Put it this way: you're on borrowed time. So, I'll ask you again. What's your goal?'

I pushed my food around, not meeting his eye. 'Why do you care?'

'Don't be petulant, Sophie. It's weak and unbecoming.'

I took a fortifying sip of wine and shifted forward in my chair. 'You're missing the bigger picture. It's not about number-crunching. Methods are changing, yes, but the stories remain the same. Murder, war, oppression, revolution. People will never tire of reading about human struggle. The world is getting smaller. It's a cliché to say knowledge is power, but that's exactly what it is. It doesn't matter *how* we know about gun crime in South London, or protests in the Middle East, or sex-trafficking in Namibia. The point is we know. And if we know, we can do something about it.'

I glanced down. My fingernails had left miniature crescent moons in the tablecloth.

'You say any idiot with a smartphone can report the news. To call them idiots is both narrow-minded and patronising. Technology has given everyone a voice. And, for good or bad, they're using that voice. They feel part of something – a greater cause, humankind, whatever you want to call it. You're wrong if you think technology is my enemy. It's my friend. If I can reach a wider audience, if I can make people care about things that matter, how can it be anything other than good? News is evolving so fast it's like trying to nail a lightning bolt to a brick wall. But if I can play some small role, if I can inform an over-saturated, over-stimulated public, that is goal enough for me.' I leaned back against the chair and lunged for my wine.

A skeleton of a smile spread across my father's thin lips. 'I see you've lost none of the Kent spirit. But I don't agree with everything you've said. There are finite options for someone in your position. At some point, the bubble will burst.'

I stabbed my fork into a morsel of steak. 'So, you're here to discuss the future of journalism?'

My father cleared his throat. 'Actually, I'm here to offer you a job.' My fork froze mid-air. 'I've been following your career. You're talented, Sophie. You're tenacious, fearless and resourceful. Good qualities in a reporter, but great qualities in a Head of Digital Media.'

My fork clattered onto my plate. My father had been following my career? He thought I was talented? The compliments were tiny grenades, burrowing deep inside me. 'You don't own a media company.'

My father pushed his cutlery together. 'Let's say I'm in the process of acquiring one. I need someone to head up the digital department. Someone I trust. Someone who has knowledge of the news industry and isn't afraid of pushing it into unchartered territory.'

I eyed him suspiciously. I had no experience of digital media strategies and my father knew that. 'What makes you think I would work for you?'

'Because you've chained yourself to a sinking ship and I'm offering you a lifeboat. And a six-figure salary, with a bonus. You talk a good game about changing the world, Sophie, but are you willing to act on it?'

My father was cold and ruthless, but he was also shrewd. If I allied myself with him, I would have more power and influence than I could have dreamed. A genuine chance to nail that light-ning bolt to the wall.

On the table beside us, an elderly lady in mint-green cash-mere leaned across the table and took the hand of her male companion. The double-breasted jacket hung off his frail frame and the patchwork of lines across his face was softened by the candlelight. The tenderness of the moment caught me off-guard.

'Do you know it's three months ago this week that Tommy died?' My father held my gaze for a moment, then glanced down at the table, silent. 'What, we can't even talk about him now?'

'Talking won't bring him back.'

'That's your attitude to everything. God forbid we should ever discuss anything in this family. Bury it deep. Hope it will go away. That's what you did with Tommy, Dad. Well, it worked. You got your wish. He went away.' My father flinched. 'You may be a king in the world of percentages and profit-margins but, in real life, all that empathy you lack makes you a shitty person, and an even shittier father.' The stem of my wine glass slipped between my clammy hands. 'Tommy was flawed but he was your son –'

'Enough.' My father's voice was fringed and sharp. 'You're not the only one who lost Tommy. I'm not here to explain myself. I came to offer you a job, which I see now is a mistake. I took you for someone smart and ambitious. But if you can't get over the whole Tommy thing –'

'*The whole Tommy thing?*' My words came out in a strangled heap. 'You talk about him as though he was a problem to be fixed. Your son – your flesh and blood – killed himself.' Tears melted through my eyes. 'Poor, sweet Tommy, who had only goodness in him until you stamped it out. He chose to end his life, because of you. You failed him. You failed all of us.' My words weren't fair, but it was too late to take them back. I twisted the napkin with hot, angry hands and let the tears fall noisily into my lap. 'Where have you been since he died? I needed you, Dad. I still need you.'

A sound escaped from my father's mouth. It sounded suspiciously like a sob. I stared at him, amazed. Watched as he pressed his lips together, battling his emotions. It was almost enough to make me reach for his hand. But then the crack in his armour sealed shut.

He folded his napkin and calmly placed it on the table. 'I didn't come here to fight you, Sophie. So go ahead, live your life your way. Be average, be unexceptional, be ordinary. But don't come crying to me when your world implodes.'

'It's already imploded!' My words hissed out in a half-scream, half-sob. I was dizzy with hate and grief and fury and regret. I couldn't breathe. Stumbling out into the cold, unforgiving night, I collapsed against a building.

Then I pounded my fists against the brick wall until they bled.

It's easy to disappear if you're a crime reporter. The all-consuming nature of the job protects you. You climb inside it, build yourself a cosy little home filled with darkness, and burrow deep until you're nestled amongst the rubble of other people's sorrow. Then, just like that, you vanish.

When I surfaced from Sloane Square Tube Station, to the sight of flashing police lights, my heart lifted. Whatever drama was unfolding would help me forget my father, and Tommy, and Mack. It was only when I glanced up at the street name that my happiness turned into something else.

Sloane Gardens. *Lydia's street.*

I squinted into the blackness and saw two police officers surrounding a figure on the pavement. I hurried towards them.

'What are you punks going to do, handcuff me again?'

I faltered as I recognised the voice. 'Liam?'

One of the police officers looked round. 'You know this man, miss?'

I ignored him. 'Liam, what's going on?'

Liam lurched towards me, a sneer curling his lips. He was horribly drunk. 'Why don't you ask her?' He nodded behind him, towards a front door that was open a crack.

The other police officer grabbed his arm. 'Come on, Crawford. It's time you left.'

'Areyoufuckingdeaf? She's not pressing charges.'

'Do you want to sleep this off at the station?'

'Fuck off. I'm not going back to that place.'

'If you don't move, Crawford, we'll arrest you for disturbing the peace.'

Liam raised his arms in the air. 'Fucking fine then. I'll go.'

The police officer gave him a cool look. 'There's a taxi rank over there. I suggest you ask the cab driver nicely if he'll take you home.'

Liam stumbled forward and ricocheted off some steps. 'Fuck.'

I ran towards him. 'Liam, are you –'

'What do you want from me?' Liam wheeled round and the look on his face burned straight through me. 'Why is it that every time I turn round, you're there, duchess? Don't you have someone else to harass?' He staggered off towards the square, like a kid who'd overdone the carousel.

I turned back to the police officers. 'What happened?'

The one nearest to me shrugged. 'He's a bloody liability, but there's nothing we can do without her say-so.' He slid into the car and slammed the door.

I watched the tail lights disappear, then ran up Lydia's steps. 'Lydia, are you OK?'

'Please, just leave me alone.' Her voice sounded small and sad.

'Is there anyone I can call for you? Are you hurt?'

The door opened another inch. Lydia's hair was scraped into a topknot, her almond-shaped eyes were pink and puffy, but even in grey tracksuit bottoms and an old T-shirt she looked achingly beautiful.

She thrust her face forward. 'See, Liam didn't hit me. He did nothing wrong.'

Under the bright porch-light I could see signs of strain on her face. 'Just because Liam didn't leave a mark doesn't mean he did nothing wrong. What happened?'

Lydia stared down at her bare feet. 'A row. It was hardly anything.'

'That can't be right. The police –'

'I didn't call them. It must have been my neighbour. Meddling bitch. Honestly, we weren't even that loud.'

As she talked, a curtain twitched in next-door's window.

'Are you sure you're OK?'

Lydia nodded, not meeting my eye. 'I need to go. Big day tomorrow at the shows.'

The door closed and her footsteps faded. I hesitated, then ran next door and pressed the buzzer.

'Yes?' A woman's clipped tone came over the intercom.

'I'm sorry to bother you, I'm a reporter with *The London Herald*.'

'I have nothing to say.'

'I understand your reluctance. But whatever happened next door was serious enough for someone to call the police. If it was you, it was very sensible.' There was a pause. 'Your neighbour looks shaken but she's not pressing charges. Do you agree with her decision?'

Silence. I didn't move until the door opened. A slender woman in her sixties, with a small, ferret face and sharp, darting eyes, stood in the hallway in stockinged feet. 'I'm not in the habit of speaking to reporters.'

'I understand. And I appreciate you sparing the time.' I took out my notebook. 'Did you call the police?'

The woman sniffed. 'I don't regret it.'

'Did you hear what they were fighting about?'

She pursed her lips. 'Are you suggesting I'm an eavesdropper?'

'I only mean, if they were shouting loudly, did you happen to overhear?'

She folded her arms. 'I couldn't make out the actual words. But, my goodness, the noise. I heard something smash against the wall and, well, I've read the newspapers. I know what sort of man he is.' She glanced towards Lydia's door and lowered her voice. 'I thought he might hurt her.'

'You did the right thing, Mrs . . .?'

'Smythe.' She frowned. 'I don't want my name in your newspaper. Heavens no. I shall sue.'

I suppressed a smile. 'I won't use your name. Can you remember anything else? What time did Liam arrive?'

She thought for a moment. 'About an hour ago. I was just settling in to watch *Newsnight* and I heard a man shouting on the street. I looked out of the window and it was *him*.'

'What was he shouting?'

'No idea, he was drunk. But then he pressed his face against her front door and whispered something over and over. I heard him apologise.' She fiddled with a bangle on her wrist. 'He said something about drapes.'

'Drapes?' Fear fluttered through me. 'Mrs Smythe, could Liam have said the word *rape*?'

She shrugged her thin shoulders. 'I suppose so. As I said, he was very drunk. I was amazed Lydia let him inside. Fifteen minutes later I heard loud shouts, then a scream, and something smashed, so I dialled 999.'

I closed my notebook and handed her my card. 'Thank goodness you did. You might have saved Lydia's life tonight.' It was a bit much, I'll admit, but Mrs Smythe drew herself up an inch taller. 'If you remember anything else or if you see anything important, you have my number.'

It wasn't until I fell into bed an hour later that I noticed my knuckles were crusted with blood. I lay there, heart thudding in my ears, willing sleep to come.

But it never did.

# 18

By the time the buttery sun rose above the rooftops, my body was rigid with exhaustion. I dragged myself into a scalding shower and out of the front door where the cold morning air slapped me awake. Shuffling up the King's Road, everything seemed detached and far away, as though I were looking at the world through the wrong end of a telescope.

I passed the end of Sloane Gardens on my way to the Tube station and glanced along the tree-lined street. A throng of paparazzi loitered on Lydia's steps, their collective breath thawing the air in white streams. I recognised a large figure leaning against the railings, smoking a roll-up. It was Jurassic Jones, so called because he chased celebrities with the ferocity of a T-Rex hunting lunch. JJ had been in my speed-dial for years. Paps made great sources; they were sharp-nosed with loose morals, a crime reporter's dream date.

JJ glanced up from his camera screen as I approached. 'Come to slum it with the guttersnipes, Sophie?'

I laughed and pulled the collar of my coat up. 'Any action yet?'

JJ swung the camera strap over his neck and sighed. 'S-l-o-w. A snooty blonde arrived twenty minutes ago.' He held his camera out and I saw Cat Ramsey, wearing dark glasses and a grim expression on her tight face. 'They're bunkering down but Lydia's doing Burberry at eleven so she'll be out of there in an hour, tops. She's got to get to Somerset House and the traffic is grid-locked. Indiana is in town for the Brits and the streets are teaming with girls on heat.'

I frowned. 'Indiana?'

He flicked his cigarette onto the ground. 'Boy band. Sounds like five colicky babies howling in a bath. But they're bigger than One Direction, so it's ker-ching for anyone who snaps them.'

My phone beeped and I moved away from JJ, shielding the screen from the sun's glare. It was a text from Eva.

*He is outside again.*

A bad feeling coiled in my stomach. That was two sightings in two days. What did Alexei Bortnik want with Eva?

Suddenly a loud shout went up. In the distance, Lydia's door opened and the paparazzi fell on a figure leaving the house. I glimpsed a blonde head, pushing herself through the fireworks of flashbulbs with surprising grace for a woman her size. At first the paparazzi followed, but they gave up once they realised Cat wasn't going to break.

When she spotted me, a shadow passed across her face. 'I might have guessed you'd be here.'

'I was just passing, actually. Saw the paps.'

Cat glanced over her shoulder. 'I hope they freeze to death.'

I slid my phone into my pocket. 'How is Lydia?'

'No comment.'

'Come on, Cat. I saw her last night. She was a mess after that fight with Liam.'

Cat's eyes flashed. 'Don't mention that man's name to me. Honestly, if you knew what it took to get Lydia back in favour with everyone. And now she's refusing to get out of bed. Christopher at Burberry will go ape-shit when Lydia doesn't show. It's career suicide. I give up.'

I watched her storm down the street to the taxi rank. Then I drew out my phone and dialled Durand.

He picked up on the third ring, sounding distracted. 'Yes?'

'Good morning to you too.'

'Sophie, I'm snowed. What do you want?'

I was taken aback by his tone. Still, it had been five days since Natalia was killed and he was no closer to formally charging a suspect. 'I'm just ringing for an update on those fingerprints.' I thought about Eva's text. 'And also to tell you that –'

'I can't speak to you.'

I put a hand over my ear as a siren wailed past. 'Shall I try you later?'

There was a pause. 'Listen, you should know that something's going on at *The London Herald*. I had word this morning that you're being investigated.'

I stopped in my tracks. 'What?'

'I can't risk anyone finding out we're talking.'

'Where did you hear this?'

'I can't say.'

'Sam, this is bullshit. I'm fine.'

'*Are* you fine?' I could hear the concern in his voice. 'This is serious. You need to get your ducks in a row.'

He rang off and I resisted the urge to smash my phone against the wall. I didn't even get the chance to tell Durand about Alexei Bortnik.

My phone pinged with an email from Mikhail Chernov.

Hello Sophie, I find Alexei Bortnik in small newspaper. He is arrested three years ago for burglary with guns. No charged. People here say he is criminal. But he has friends in a high place. The newspaper is showing a photograph of him.

*Mikhail*

I huddled against the wall and opened the attachment. My eyes glossed over the Russian text and landed on a small black-and-white photograph of a dark-haired man. Thick stubble coated his face and both ears were pierced with studs. He glared at the camera with the air of a man who was used to getting away with it. I dialled Eva's number with raw fingers.

'Hello?' She sounded out of breath.

'It's Sophie. I need you to do something for me.'

Eva gave me her email address and I forwarded the newspaper article to her.

'Is he still there?'

'Yes, I just went to buy milk and when I got back he was waiting for me. He ran towards me but I managed to get inside the lift before him.'

'Did you get a look at his face?' A bus roared past me, kicking up rainwater. I raised my voice. 'Eva, can you hear me?'

'Just about. He had a cap on so I couldn't see him that clearly.'

'A cap?'

'Black, with a red football on the front.' I paced up and down along the pavement outside the Tube station. Sasha had said the mysterious man at The Rose wore a cap with a red patch on the front. Was Alexei at the hotel that night? 'He started to say something but I shouted that I was calling the police.'

My heart sank as I pictured Eva's flimsy plywood door. 'And have you? Called the police?'

'No police, I told you. I just told him that to make him leave. Hang on, your email's arrived.' There was a pause. She sounded alarmed 'Yes, that's him. Oh my God. What does he want?'

I tried to keep the panic out of my voice. 'Eva, Alexei Bortnik is dangerous. Hang up and call 999.'

'I can't call them.'

'Why not?'

'I can't ... wait, he's leaving. He's running along Highland Road.'

Where was he going? Was Eva's threat enough to send him underground again?

'If you won't call the police, I will.'

I hung up. The cold made my fingers feel leaden and I struggled to dial Durand's number. One of my rules was never to do the police's job for them. I didn't work for them, I worked for the press. But that rule didn't apply if someone's life was in jeopardy.

It went to voicemail.

'I know you don't want to hear from me, but this is important. Natalia's ex-boyfriend is a Russian criminal and he's been stalking her for months. I have a source placing him at The Rose the night she was killed. He's moving on to her flatmate,

Eva. If you get this message, his name is Alexei Bortnik and the address is 84 Cautley Avenue, Clapham. I'm going there now.'

I hung up and broke into a run.

Leaning against the black railings, I studied the large, Edwardian house in front of me. I hadn't expected Alexei's address to be so upscale. A box-hedge bordered the front garden, and rosemary and lavender bushes filled the wet air with their aromatic scent. The metallic sounds of a builder's drill, and scaffolding poles clashing against each other, rang through the air.

Had I beaten Alexei here? Innocent or guilty, I wanted his story. And it would be impossible, once he was arrested. I crunched up the gravel path, my heart rattling in my chest. I rang the bell, but there was no answer, so I counted to ten and rang again. Still nothing. I put my ear against the door. All quiet.

I craned my neck and saw the hallway light on in one of the neighbours' houses. I scooted round and pressed the buzzer. Moments later a blonde woman opened the door, with a bawling baby on her hip.

'Yes?'

I held up the photo of Alexei. 'I'm sorry to bother you. I'm looking for this man. Do you recognise him?'

The baby stuffed a tiny fist in its mouth, and the howl became a whimper.

'That's Lev's cousin. He's been staying next door for a while. We complained about the noise. No children,' she gave me an exasperated look, 'and they party late.'

'Have you ever spoken to him?'

The baby's cries kicked up a gear and she swayed back and forth. 'Do you mind if I ask what this is about?'

I smiled. 'Of course. I'm sorry. My name is Sophie Kent and I'm a reporter with *The London Herald*. I'm investigating a story and believe this man could be connected in some way.'

Her eyes widened. 'What kind of story?'

There was no point frightening her. 'I can't say at this stage. I was hoping to speak to the cousin. Do you know when he'll be back?'

She shrugged. 'Lev's at a tech conference but he told us his cousin was leaving soon. The house has been pretty quiet. I hoped he'd already gone.' She smiled tightly. 'Not that I have a problem with Russians. But Rafferty isn't the best sleeper, and the blaring techno doesn't help.'

I handed her my card, just as it started to rain. 'If you see him again would you give me a call? I'd really appreciate it.'

I hurried down the path, and spotted a café on the corner opposite. Rain beat down and bounced violently back up from waterlogged pavements. People pressed into doorways marvelling at the sight. A man in a dark suit broke cover, zigzagging down the street; a flimsy newspaper over his head providing scant shelter.

My shoulder collided with something hard. As I turned, I caught a glimpse of a pierced ear and a shadow of stubble disappearing up the gravel path. I stared after him, debating what to do. A light went on in an upstairs room.

I needed a second to regroup. I ran to the café and ducked inside just as a low boom of thunder shook the windows. Fumbling with my phone, I dialled Durand's number. He didn't pick up.

'Can I help you?' A skinny waitress in a pink-striped apron raised her eyebrows.

I opened my mouth to speak but a sight across the street made the sound die in my mouth. The front door opened and Alexei appeared with large holdall over his shoulder.

Without stopping to think, I hurtled through the café door. Silver needles of rain stabbed my face, blinding me, but I could just make out Alexei across the street. If I hurried, I could cut him off. I stepped off the curb and a car railed past, honking its horn, and soaking my feet in icy water. As I jumped out of the way, I skidded on a wet leaf. Pain sliced through my ankle. Alexei was twenty feet away and approaching fast. I had to stop him.

'Alexei!' His head snapped up but he didn't slow down. 'I need to speak to you. My name is –'

'Get out of my way.' He shoved me roughly to the side, and a spasm of pain shot through my leg.

'Wait!' I ran past him, blocking him off. The driving rain drowned out my voice. 'I need to ask you about Natalia Kotov.'

Alexei stopped in his tracks. 'What did you say?' His voice was coarse, crushing, like rocks smashing together.

The wind blew a sheet of rain into my face and I shielded my eyes with my hand. 'I know you're Natalia's ex-boyfriend. Your Twitter handle is @cityofbrides. I know you were at The Rose the night she was killed –'

There was a low growl and Alexei spun round to face me. Rainwater flowed down the narrow contours of his face and off the end of his sharp nose. His black eyes dug into mine as if they were spikes.

My heart was in my throat. 'I know you were following her. Please, I just want to ask you –'

Alexei took a step towards me. 'You know many things, Sophie Kent?'

'How do you know my name?'

'I know many things too.'

'Look, I'm not the police. I don't have any hold over you. I just want to ask you some questions. If you're innocent, what have you got to hide?'

Alexei inched closer and his mouth twisted into an ugly smile. 'I watched you and her. In that pub. I was there, watching, the first day you knocked on her door. She should never have opened her fucking mouth.'

'Why did you follow her to London?'

'Because she ran from me. I loved her so much I could crush her skull between my hands. I tried to make her see how much I loved her but she wouldn't listen.'

'You scared her, Alexei. I know about the blue flowers. I saw them at the hotel. You were stalking her –'

'I was protecting her, you bitch.'

Two brick walls loomed in the corners of my eyes. With a stab of fear, I realised Alexei had edged me into an alleyway. 'Is that why you went to The Rose that night? To protect her?'

Something flickered across his face. 'And why would I tell you that, Sophie Kent?' He spat my name out as if it were poison on his tongue.

I had to keep him talking. 'Because you loved her. I don't think you're a bad person.'

'Wrong again. I am the very worst kind of person.' Alexei backed me further into the alleyway. My legs came into contact with something hard. I stumbled and hit the ground. 'Get up, bitch.' Alexei was so close that I could smell stale cigarettes and his unwashed clothes. I dragged myself off the ground and held my hands up to protect myself. Rain dripped down my face and seeped into my clothes.

The noise eased and I looked up to find we were standing underneath an iron fire escape. Alexei's hands gripped my shoulders and he slammed me against the wall. I looked past him to the mouth of the alleyway, but the bins hid us from view. 'Expecting someone?' His eyes were mocking.

I shivered with fear and forced myself to look at his face. 'Why are you following Eva?'

Alexei's eyes hardened. 'Don't mention that bitch. If it weren't for her . . .' His grip tightened and I cried out. 'You should have left her alone. If people hadn't tried to keep us apart, Natalia would still be alive. I told her bad things would happen to people.'

I opened my mouth to speak but Alexei clamped a large, wet hand over my face. Struggling to breathe, I scrabbled at his hand. 'The police . . . are on . . . their way.'

Alexei gripped my neck, his eyes bristling with menace. The skin on his hand was velcro-rough and my pulse thrashed against it. I met his gaze and the savagery in his eyes forced my stomach to the floor. Something sharp grazed my neck.

Alexei put his mouth beside my ear. 'This is your fault. I would have left you alone if you hadn't come looking for me.' I squeezed my eyes shut.

'Drop the knife, Bortnik.'

A voice rang out, loud and clear. I opened my eyes and saw Durand halfway between us and the alley entrance. His face was calm, but I heard the edge in his voice.

Alexei growled, and pushed the knife against my skin. White-hot pain speared through me.

'Bortnik, I'm warning you. I have a team of officers here. You do not want this woman's death on your record. Drop the knife.'

My vision blurred. I couldn't breathe. Over Alexei's shoulder, shapes edged towards us. I stopped struggling and went limp, trusting Durand to do his job.

Alexei's eyes burned into mine and he pressed harder against me.

Then he let go, and my knees gave way.

The shapes descended and I was distantly aware of Alexei being thrown against a wall and handcuffed.

Durand crouched down beside me and gripped my shoulder as I gulped down lungfuls of icy air.

'You took your time.'

Durand shouted over his shoulder. 'Waters, call an ambulance.'

I pushed myself up to sitting. 'I don't need an ambulance.'

Durand gave me a stern look. Then he pulled me onto my feet. 'Let me have a look.' His jaw tightened as his eyes flickered over my neck. His voice was tight with anger. 'What were you thinking?'

I shrugged. 'I wanted the exclusive. And you were ignoring me.'

'And the story is worth risking your life for?'

The coldness in his face made me feel like crying. 'Not now, Sam.'

He looked as though he was going to say something else, then he held out a large, warm hand. 'Let's get you out of the rain.'

As he led me towards the flashing blue lights, I saw Alexei being pushed into the back of a police car. 'Can I come with you?'

'Absolutely not.'

'But –' I clenched my fists. 'If it wasn't for me you wouldn't have found Alexei Bortnik. And now you've made your arrest, you're shutting me out?'

Durand looked over my head and signalled to an officer behind me. 'Thank you for your help. I'm grateful. But this doesn't change our situation. I will call you when we have news, I promise.' He put a hand on my shoulder and guided me out of the alleyway. 'Officer Waters will drive you home. Or to the hospital. You should get checked out, Sophie.'

He held the car door open. I gave him a scathing look, then slid inside.

Officer Waters, a neat-looking woman with a chestnut plait, turned round. 'Where to, Miss Kent?'

I tried to lift my wrist to look at my watch but I couldn't summon the energy. 'What time is it?'

'Almost two thirty.'

I looked down at my sodden clothes, my trembling hands and my swollen ankle. 'Take me to *The London Herald*.'

# 19

Kate hung up the phone. 'Christ, what happened to you?'

I limped towards the desk. 'Turns out Natalia's ex-boyfriend isn't my biggest fan.'

'You're soaked through. Do you have a change of clothes?'

I shook my head numbly and she disappeared behind the desk divider. 'Here, these will be enormous on you but at least they're dry.' She held up a pair of navy trousers and a creased white blouse. 'Go and change. I'll make tea. Although you look as though you need something stronger. Should you even be here?'

I shrugged. 'Where else would I go?'

Kate nodded. She got it.

I hobbled to the bathroom and stared at myself in the mirror. My hair hugged my head like a swimming cap, and sooty streaks of mascara ran down my cheeks. Alexei's stench clung to me. Inching down my shirt collar, I winced at the cuts on my neck. Then I peeled off my wet clothes and stood under the hand-dryer until my puckered skin turned pink. Kate's clothes drowned me, but I rolled up the sleeves and trouser-legs, grateful that they smelled of her cologne, and not Alexei.

By the time I got back to my desk, Kate was nowhere to be seen. She'd left a mug of tea for me and I cradled it between trembling hands, willing the warmth to spread through me. I had to keep busy. I left a message on Eva's phone, informing her that Alexei was in custody, and asking if she'd give me an official interview. I'd already tweeted Alexei's arrest from the back of the police car, although I didn't mention the role I played in becoming his next victim. Rowley would want that for the print edition. When I pulled up my Twitter feed to check my responses, something caught my eye. #Modelmeltdown was trending. So was #loonylawson. I clicked on Lydia's Twitter page. She had posted a video an hour ago. It had already gone viral.

I clicked on the link with a heavy heart. The video showed Lydia in bed naked, one arm outstretched above her holding the camera. She was drunk, or high, or both. Her almond-shaped eyes were glassy and her lips moved as she gazed into the lens. In the background, bottles of pills lay scattered across her bedside table. It took me a moment to realise she was singing; her voice wavered, like a ribbon of smoke.

'She'll cut you with her smile, then laugh as you bleed.' I could only make out snatches of lyrics before Lydia appeared to pass out.

Forty-five seconds of sweet agony. I replayed it three times and each time Lydia looked more unhinged. If she was teetering on the edge of career suicide, this video surely meant sudden death. It had already been retweeted 450,000 times. *What was she thinking?* I logged on to Stitched.com. Amos Adler's headline jumped out: *BREAKING NEWS Has Loony Lawson Lost It For Good?*

I pictured Cat pacing in her office, phone under one ear, spinning this story with everything she had.

'No, darling. She's *fine*. Suffering with exhaustion. Between you and me Lydia works *too* hard. That's why we're scaling back her London Fashion Week appearances.'

Suddenly my phone rang. 'Yes?'

'Do you have half an hour?' Durand's deep voice poured balm into my troubled head.

'That depends.'

'Come to the station. You need to see something.'

I sat up straighter. 'I'm invited to the party now, am I?'

I heard the smile in his voice. 'You can drop that attitude. I've had to pull every string going to get you in here.'

There was something different about Durand's voice.

'Has Alexei Bortnik confessed?' I reached for my coat, but it was soaking wet so I left it on the back of my chair.

'I'll fill you in when you get here. And Sophie?'

'Yes?'

'Use the back entrance.'

I shivered in the back of the taxi, counting down the minutes on my phone, as though staring at those plump little digits would block out the white noise of the city around me. Alexei was in custody. Eva was safe. But Lydia was a walking disaster-zone. I dialled Cat's number.

'If you're ringing for a quote about that video, you can fuck off.'

I smiled in spite of myself. 'I want to know if Lydia is OK.'

'Does she look OK to you?'

'How bad is it?'

'It's a fucking PR disaster. Three more designers have cancelled their contracts and her campaign with Maybelline is about to go down the toilet. I have a conference call with them in an hour and I know they're going to pull the plug.' I heard street noise in the background, as though Cat had walked outside. 'She needs to lie low, get her shit together and make a comeback next season. It worked for Kate Moss.'

I leaned my head against the window. 'Cat, I meant how bad is *Lydia*?'

There was a pause. Her frosty tone thawed a fraction. 'I've never seen her like this before. I don't know what to do. Look, I have to go. I've got a stinking migraine. I'm going to check if she's OK on my way home. I mean, honestly. As if Fashion Week isn't crazy enough.'

Ten minutes later, the taxi pulled up outside New Scotland Yard, and Durand met me at the door. He glanced at my clothes.

'Did you shrink in the rain?' The wind whipped my hair into a frenzy and I put a hand up to flatten it. He noticed me limping. 'I take it you didn't get checked out by a doctor?'

'What do you think?'

He shook his head. 'You are the most stubborn woman I've ever met.'

The bottom of my trousers dragged along the carpet as we made our way through the warren of corridors. Durand stopped outside a white door marked *Property Stores*.

'Seriously?'

'My way of saying thank you,' he said, pushing open the door.

The room was large and stuffy and smelled of old cardboard. I hovered by the edge, looking along the endless rows of shelves that held plastic containers, each marked with a number. I wanted to ask Durand about our conversation earlier. I needed to know who was spreading malicious gossip about me. But he strode over to a square table in the centre, where a box marked *419* was waiting, and I was back in the room, mind on the game. Durand handed me a pair of latex gloves and I watched as he unlocked the container and pulled out a battered, brown notebook.

'This was in Alexei's bag.'

The corners of the notebook curled upwards and the cover was distended where too many bits of paper had been stuffed inside. I peeled off the elastic band, anticipation rippling through me.

Page after page was filled with photographs of Natalia. Instagram and catwalk photos, old pictures of her in Russia. He'd defaced the *W* magazine photograph with crude illustrations: a penis between her legs, a knife sticking out of her breasts. Creepiest of all were the photographs Alexei had taken without Natalia's knowledge. Her on the phone outside Green Park Tube Station, leaving a newsagent's holding a can of Coke. One was taken on the top deck of a bus, showing the back of her head three rows in front of him.

I whistled. 'What a nutter.'

Alexei had scrawled Russian words in scratchy blue pen in every available inch of white space. 'Do we know what he's written yet?'

Durand leaned against the table and folded his arms. 'He won't tell us. But a translator is working on it.'

'Has he confessed?'

A shadow fell across Durand's face. 'He originally claimed he went to the hotel to talk to Natalia, but changed his mind and left. When we revealed his prints were on her door-handle, he changed his story. He's now saying he opened the door, stuck his head round but she was already dead so he ran.' Durand cleared his throat. 'There's one more thing.' The catch in his voice made me look up. 'Alexei's prints match something else.'

He crossed the room in three strides and returned with a large plastic bag.

'Recognise this?'

I felt the air leave my chest. 'That's not – but –' I peered into the bag. The axe-head was still crusted with Jason Danby's blood. My brain struggled to piece it together. 'I don't understand.'

'Alexei went to Milton estate that day to see Natalia. Evidently he didn't appreciate the way their conversation ended so he took it out on Jason Danby when he left.'

I stared at him uncomprehendingly. 'That's *it*? That's why Danby was killed?'

Durand heard the hysteria in my voice and moved towards me. 'Alexei is a despicable man. When I told him Danby was only fourteen he laughed.'

I sank against the table. 'Christ, it's all so . . . meaningless.' I plucked at the edge of my glove. 'So you knew about Alexei?'

Durand shrugged. 'We knew someone was sending Natalia threatening messages, but the IT team hadn't tracked down the sender. A couple of her friends mentioned an ex-boyfriend in their statements and Interpol gave us a name. We were almost there but your meddling got us there quicker.' Durand's face grew serious. 'Sophie, you have to be more careful. Men like Alexei Bortnik don't play games.'

I bristled. 'Neither do I.'

'I know that.' Durand cocked his head to one side. 'But you are five inches tall.'

I met his gaze and a laugh bubbled up in my throat. '*Six* inches, you idiot.' I glanced down at the notebook and a thought struck me. 'Was this the only notebook you found?'

Durand nodded. 'Why?'

'If Alexei is stalking Eva, shouldn't there be photographs of her somewhere?'

Durand crossed the room to the window so I couldn't see his face. 'So far, nothing has turned up.'

'If he killed Natalia, why risk staying in London and getting caught?'

Durand faced me and opened his mouth to speak, when his phone rang.

He glanced at the screen. 'I have to take this.'

I stared down at the notebook, at the photographs of Natalia plastered across the page. Instinctively, I raised a hand to my neck.

'Thanks for letting me know. I'll be there shortly.' Durand hung up and a smile spread across his face.

'What is it?'

'Just had confirmation. Bortnik's prints match the ones we lifted from Natalia's bathroom door. And his shoe fits the imprints we found on her carpet.' Durand drew himself up and squared his shoulders. 'We've got him.'

I rifled through my desk drawer for a first-aid kit. I knew my ankle wasn't broken but I bandaged and elevated it to be on the safe side. Since leaving Durand, the nagging feeling had got worse. Why hadn't Alexei put his gloves on before he touched Natalia's hotel door, when he was so careful not to leave any traces of himself on her body? And why kill her at The Rose? He'd been to her flat; he knew where she lived. Why kill her somewhere so public?

The fever of exhaustion spread through me. Only the fact that Alexei was in custody kept me going. Finally, justice for Jason Danby. Security for Eva. And, who knew, maybe Durand was right and he would confess to Natalia's murder. These thoughts were tiny sparks that electrified my nerve endings and jump-started my fingers. I pulled my keyboard towards me.

'Good afternoon, Sophie.' A brisk voice interrupted my flow. 'Mr Rowley has asked to see you in his office.'

Rowley's elderly secretary, Cheryl, stood over my desk, clasping her papery hands in front of her.

'Sophie, did you hear what I said?' She peered down at me through glasses that made her eyeballs appear twice the size. There was a tiny brown splatter on her lavender cardigan. 'Are you quite well?'

'I'll be right there.'

Cheryl didn't move. 'I'll wait.'

I hauled myself off the chair and limped across the office in the slipstream of Cheryl's scent: talcum powder and Imperial Leather soap. She smelled just like my grandmother; but my grandmother was small and round and full of laughter. In eight years, I'd never heard Cheryl laugh.

She knocked sharply on Rowley's door, then stood back to let me past, her eyes following me until I was safely inside.

Rowley was flanked by Mack and a woman I didn't recognise. 'What happened to your foot?'

I sank onto the chair opposite his desk. 'It's a long story.'

'This is Helena Schriver from HR.' I gave her a nod, then glanced at Mack. He wouldn't meet my eye.

Rowley rested his elbows on the desk, his voice more pinched than usual. 'Less than a week ago, you sat in that chair and told me you'd get your act together. But this morning I received some very distressing news about your conduct.' I stared at him, dread pooling in my stomach. 'Could you explain how you came by the address of a man called,' he glanced at the piece of paper in front of him, 'Alexei Bortnik?'

I frowned. 'Where did you –'

'Answer the question.' Rowley's voice was sharp.

I fiddled with the button on my blouse; my tongue felt heavy in my mouth. 'I can't tell you.'

Rowley's cheeks sagged with disappointment. 'I thought you might say that.'

He glanced at Helena and she cleared her throat. 'Sophie, did you pressure someone in the IT department to hack into a dead woman's phone?'

I looked at them incredulously. 'Do you know that Alexei Bortnik is in custody? He just confessed to killing Jason Danby. What's more, Forensics can place him in Natalia's hotel room the night she was killed. She was his ex-girlfriend, the one he was stalking right up until she was strangled.' I gripped the arms of the chair and made an effort to slow my words. 'This morning I confronted Alexei in Clapham and he assaulted me.' I yanked down my collar, exposing the cuts on my neck. Rowley's eyes widened. 'Because I joined the dots, Jason Danby's killer is off the streets. Natalia's flatmate is safe. And you're querying my methods?'

'Your methods are illegal.' It was the first time Mack had spoken and I barely recognised his voice. It was flat and small.

'Are you kidding me?'

Helena coughed. 'Who hacked into Natalia's phone? Give us a name and you won't bear the full brunt of this investigation.'

'The . . . investigation?'

Rowley cleared his throat. 'As you know, *The London Herald* has a zero-tolerance policy towards phone-hacking.' He leaned forward and I saw a flicker of sympathy in his eyes. 'Now, please, Sophie. Who assisted you?'

I craned my neck to look at the pieces of paper in front of Rowley. It was the document Jasdeep had sent me, the document I'd hidden in my desk, minus the Post-it note he'd scribbled absolving me of responsibility. 'Where did you get that?'

Rowley gave an exasperated sigh. Mack sloped over to the window. I didn't need to see his face to understand what was going on. He knew me well enough to know that I would never reveal a source. I sighed and looked out over the expanse of Hyde Park. An enormous oak tree lurched back and forth in the strong winds. The great battering had ripped the leaves from its branches, and yet the trunk remained solid and unyielding. It would take more than these gales to bring it down.

'I take full responsibility for what happened. It was a calculated risk. If I hadn't done it, Alexei Bortnik would still be out there. I had a target in sight. It's not the same as hacking into a celebrity's phone to break a kiss-and-tell story, and if you can't see the difference, then I'm wasting my time.'

Mack started to speak but Rowley shushed him. 'The ends don't justify the means anymore, Sophie. If you don't know where to draw the line, you don't belong at *The London Herald*. You committed a crime. I cannot – I *will not* – allow you to put this newspaper in jeopardy.' He paused and I felt the blood drain from my face. 'You leave me no choice but to fire you. Please gather your things and leave immediately.'

My eyes burned with tears but I refused to break down in front of them. I mustered all the dignity I could and I limped out.

I collapsed onto my chair, numb with shock. What had I done? Rowley was right: I broke the law. I didn't ask Jasdeep to hack into Natalia's phone, but it was my decision to read what he found. But there was a difference between hacking for good and hacking for bad. This wasn't a celebrity kiss-and-tell. It was in the public's interest to rid the streets of Alexei Bortnik. I was the good guy, right? I stared down at my desk. I didn't know anymore. I had to get out of the office. I couldn't breathe. I grabbed my wet coat and hobbled to the lift.

'Sophie, wait.' Mack appeared beside me, looking pale. 'I never meant –'

'What did you think was going to happen? That Rowley would shake my hand and congratulate me for breaking the law? I fucked up and, as my boss, you had every right to call me out on it. But we both know why you did it.' Rage fizzed inside me; I couldn't get the words out. 'I knew screwing you would cost me, I just didn't know how much.'

Mack stole towards me. 'I warned you about burning bridges.'

'You think that was me burning my bridges? Try this.' I slapped him hard across the face. 'You may have convinced Rowley that you're a competent news editor, but everyone round here knows the truth. You couldn't break a story if it landed on your dick. No wonder your wife won't sleep with you. You clearly don't satisfy her, you sure as hell didn't satisfy me. So, if this is what it takes to make you feel like a man, be my fucking guest.'

The last thing I saw as the lift doors closed was Mack's shocked expression and a bright red stain spreading across his cheek.

The wind beat against me, ripping the hot tears from my cheeks. I leaned my full weight into it as I crossed the street to Hyde Park. I stumbled across wet grass, with no idea where I was going. Eventually, my feet stopped under a large horse-chestnut tree and, before I knew it, my arms were wrapped round the trunk, clinging on as the wind roared around me. And there was another sound. Faint at first, then louder. A wail, carried away by the wind, then rolling back towards me.

With a start, I realised the sound was coming from me.

I sank to the ground and rested my head on the scratchy bark. I was so tired. Tired of pretending to be strong. Tired of fighting everyone. In the days after Tommy died, when I couldn't move for all the hurt inside me, *The London Herald* was my lighthouse in the dark. But I was naive. My job couldn't save me. Nothing could.

All of a sudden, I became aware of a buzzing in my pocket. I ignored it, but it persisted.

I held the phone to my ear. 'Yes?' My voice sounded as weak as a lamb's bleat.

'Is that Sophie Kent?'

'Who is this?'

'Mrs Smythe. We met last night. I'm Lydia Lawson's neighbour.'

She said something but the wind drowned it out. I pressed a frozen hand over my ear. 'What did you say?'

'Where are you, my dear? You sound as though you're in a wind tunnel.' I sat up, wincing as pain burst through my stiff legs. 'You said to ring you. I don't know what to do. Lydia was very displeased with me for calling the police last night. I . . . and it sounded . . . once . . . check.'

'I can't hear you. Can you speak up?'

Mrs Smythe raised her voice. 'There was a crash next door. Just now. I saw Liam running away from Lydia's apartment. I'm afraid to bother her if it's nothing, but I really think someone ought to check on her.'

A violent gust of wind shook my core and I closed my eyes.

'Sophie? Are you still there?'

'Give me fifteen minutes.'

I trekked back through the park to the taxi rank on Kensington Road. The taxi driver gave me an odd look in his rear-view mirror and I glared back. Screw him. Screw everyone. I'd swing by Lydia's house, get a door slammed in my face, then I'd crawl into bed and sleep for the rest of my life.

Ten minutes later we arrived at 42 Sloane Gardens. I threw the cabbie a tenner and swore as my ankle buckled on the curb, sending me crashing into a silver car. A dustbin rolled towards me, carried by the wind, its contents skating across the pavement.

Lydia's front door was open a few inches. I groped around in the hallway and found the light switch. 'Lydia? Are you OK?'

I edged past the glass console table, past the vase of wilting flowers that filled the air with their heavy scent, and through a door on the left. I flipped on the lights and found myself in a large sitting room with dove-grey walls and a corniced ceiling. A large photograph of Lydia hung over the fireplace. I poked my head round the door of a small, marble kitchen and padded round to the stairs. A brass coat-stand lay sprawled across the mosaic tiles. I stepped over the umbrellas and bags.

'Lydia, it's Sophie. I'm sorry to barge in but your front door was open.'

The silence pressed heavily against my eardrums. Sighing, I leaned against the bannister and hauled myself upwards, pain splintering through my ankle. The landing was cloaked in darkness. I put a hand out to steady myself and staggered towards a chink of light coming from a door up ahead.

The floral scent was even stronger up here. It took me four steps to realise it wasn't the wilting flowers I could smell. It was something else. Something I'd smelled before. I reached out and pushed the door open.

The smell of blood hit my face like a punch.

# 20

The scene flew at me in fragments through the candlelight. Splayed legs. Bloodstained camisole. Slashed hair. The rusty odour tasted like coins on the tongue. Vomit swelled in my throat. I forced myself to focus on the reflection of tiny candle flames fizzing and dancing in the brass bedposts.

I dug around in my bag with clumsy hands and snapped on latex gloves and shoe covers. My ragged breath was loud in my ears. I flipped the switch but the bulb had blown, so I felt for my torch and limped across the room. My fingers were almost at the pulse point on Lydia's neck when the torch beam fell on her face. Red-veined, bulging eyes stared straight through me. Her skin reminded me of the scored flesh on an uncooked joint of pork.

Swallowing hard, I reached instead for her wrist, shivering as my fingers closed around spongy flesh. No pulse, but her skin was slightly warm. She hadn't been dead long. I glanced over my shoulder. Could the killer still be here?

I shrugged the thought away and slid the light over Lydia's body, down to the sticky red mess between her legs. I glanced at the candles. Rose Blossom, same brand. I punched out a quick text to the photographer, Ned Mason. Outside a driver leaned on his horn, but the sound was muffled by the heavy gold curtains drawn across the bay window. My finger hovered over Durand's phone number, then scrolled to another name, and hit *dial*.

'What do you want?'

I flinched at Rowley's tone. 'I have an exclusive for you.'

I heard a thwack in the background, then a cheer. Rowley was watching cricket in his office. 'Sophie, the fact you're calling me mere hours after I fired you only reaffirms my belief that –'

'Lydia Lawson is dead.'

'What?'

'Lydia Lawson is –'

'How do you know?'

'I'm standing next to her body.'

Rowley switched off the TV. 'Start at the beginning.'

I ran through the details, shining my torch over Lydia's bedroom at the same time. Plates crusted with food littered the carpet, along with overflowing ashtrays and empty KitKat wrappers. Clothes flopped out of open drawers like they'd made a half-baked bid for freedom. I crouched down next to Lydia's bed where a row of cigarette burns dotted the carpet. I shone the torch under her bed. Two Smirnoff vodka bottles, both empty.

'You said her killer was in custody.' Rowley's nasally voice sounded higher than usual.

'Well, either Alexei Bortnik can shape-shift or he's not our guy.'

Rowley was silent and I could picture him leaning back in his leather chair, assessing his options. I knew better than to hurry him.

Eventually he spoke. 'What are you proposing?'

I gripped the phone more tightly. 'Either I hang up and call Ted at the *Mirror*. Or you reinstate me and I write the story of the decade for *The London Herald*.' It was a bit much. I was already regretting *story of the decade* but Rowley didn't pull me up on it, which showed how distracted he was.

'Sophie, you broke the law. There are consequences.'

'So give me an official warning. Do whatever's necessary, but please,' my voice wobbled for the first time, 'let me come back. Philip, you don't know how sorry I am about the way things have turned out. You were right. About my judgement, about everything.' I took a deep breath, not wanting him to hear the desperation building in my chest. 'The past few months have been . . . I let you down. I let Natalia down too. I should have realised the danger she was in. I should have stopped this man before he got to Lydia.'

I caught my reflection in Lydia's full-length mirror. My hair hung in wet ribbons around my pale face, but my eyes were bright. 'You told me to find my line, Philip. This is my chance, but I need your help. I don't want to write this story for anyone else. *The London Herald* is . . .' My voice died as I caught sight of a figure in the mirror behind me. 'Shit.'

'Sophie?' Rowley's voice was sharp. 'What is it?'

I spun round, then cried out with relief when I realised it was just a black dress hanging on the wardrobe door. 'False alarm.'

I waited, not daring to breathe.

'Right, this is what's going to happen. You'll write this for *The London Herald* as a freelance reporter.'

'But –'

'No, Sophie.' Rowley's voice hardened. 'You don't get to waltz back in. Not after the stunt you pulled. Reporters have to earn their right to a seat at my table.' I opened my mouth to speak, then closed it. 'I'm opening a back door. Use it wisely. Now, let's talk logistics. We need to get a photographer to you ASAP.'

'Ned Mason's already on his way.'

'I'll ignore the fact you instructed a *London Herald* photographer before speaking to me. Now, call the police. I don't want them filing a complaint against us for obstructing justice. You can't write up the first report, not given the circumstances.' Rowley was right. I was part of the story now. 'Feed everything through to Kate. She's, wait, where is she?' Rowley raised his voice. 'Where the hell is Kate Fingersmith?' Someone must have responded. 'She's at a press conference. Police are announcing Alexei Bortnik's confession. Expect a call from her soon.'

'What about Mack?'

'Forget Mack. Deal with Kate. When you're done, file two hundred and fifty words and stick a teaser on the end that there's more to come tomorrow. And tweet the living crap out of it.' His voice swelled with adrenaline. 'I want *The London Herald* to own this story. We need to give the killer a name. Something that sticks in people's heads.'

I stared down at Lydia's mangled body and felt a shiver of self-loathing. A nickname would glorify the killer. But my career was hanging by a thread and I wasn't in a position to argue. I ignored the fact that Lydia's body was still warm and ran through options. 'Uh, the Model Maimer, the London Strangler, the Fashion Slasher, the –'

'The last one. It's punchy. Right, I'll brief the team this end. Molly and her Fashion lot can pull together a puff piece on Lydia's career. Christ, we don't have long. Hang up and call the police. And, for God's sake, don't tell them you called me first. And don't let them intimidate –'

'Philip, I know what I'm doing.'

Rowley exhaled loudly. 'Go find your line.'

He hung up and my shoulders dropped. I couldn't believe I'd pulled that off.

My eyes jerked towards the black dress on the wardrobe. Its sequins shimmered in the candlelight. Where had I seen it before? It took a few seconds before I realised it was the dress Lydia wore to Leo Brand's party. The night Natalia was murdered. A coincidence that it was hanging there? A message? The sweet air was making my eyes sting and I rubbed them with the heel of my hand. I limped over to a framed picture on the wall; a magazine cutting from *Vogue*'s September 2010 issue, with the headline: *Why We've All Gone La-la for LyLaw*. Above it was a candid photograph of Lydia at Milan Fashion Week. She was mid-stride, head turned back to the camera, tongue sticking out, energy radiating from every pore. What a difference four years made. Fun-loving fashion darling to self-obsessed tabloid fodder to . . . I glanced at the bed and sighed heavily.

It was time to make the next call.

'Have you already left?' Durand sounded busy.

'Sorry?'

'The press conference. I couldn't see – hang on.' A chorus of voices rose in the background. 'No more questions. We'll update you.' He gave an exasperated sigh. 'Why aren't you here? Got somewhere more important to be?'

I heard the tease in his voice and cleared my throat. 'I was fired.'

Silence. 'Are you OK?'

It warmed me that Durand's first question was about my welfare. I turned my head just as a coppery waft hit the back of my throat. The words slipped out like a sneeze. 'Lydia Lawson's dead.'

'What?' Durand lowered his voice. 'How do you –'

'I'm at her house: 42 Sloane Gardens. Fuck, Sam. It's –'

'I need to call it in.' His voice was flat. 'Don't touch anything. I'm on my way.'

The phone clicked and I was alone. I tasted metal and dabbed my mouth. I'd chewed through my lower lip.

I stuffed the torch into my bag, grabbed my phone, then photographed as much of the scene as I could. The only sound was the rustle of my shoe covers sliding across the carpet. I snapped the threadbare stuffed elephant on the armchair, next to a gold cushion stitched with the words *All you need is love (& piles of £££)*. The kind of details that make a reporter's copy sing.

Satisfied, I hobbled towards the door. The air on the landing smelled as fresh as a mountainside in comparison to Lydia's room; I gulped a couple of lungfuls to steady myself. Then I staggered downstairs to take more pictures, glad to be back in the light. Aside from the upturned coat stand, the house was much tidier down here. In the sitting room, a few framed photographs stood on the shelves. Lydia backstage with an older couple that I took to be her parents; with Cat Ramsey in New York, in the photograph I'd seen in Cat's office; on the beach with . . . I moved closer. Lydia was dressed in skimpy bikini bottoms and nothing else. Her body was pressed against Liam's chest and he was frowning at something behind the photographer.

Suddenly an icy blue light flashed across the room and I heard multiple car doors slam. Without stopping to think, I limped up to Lydia's bedroom. I wanted to be there when Durand saw her body.

'Sophie?'

'Up here.' Footsteps creaked up the stairs and Durand's large frame appeared in the doorway. He had changed into a navy suit for the press conference and his auburn hair was wet from the rain. His eyes darted past me and his jaw tightened.

'How long have you been here?'

Durand didn't need to know I'd negotiated a career comeback and helped myself to photographs of the crime scene. 'Not long.'

Durand glanced at my gloves and shoe covers. 'The SOCOs will be here any second. I . . .' He pulled his torch out and ran the light round the room, pausing on Lydia's face and the blood between her legs. I watched him struggle to get his face under control. 'How did you get in?'

'Front door was open.' I explained what had happened. Durand's eyes hardened when I mentioned Liam fleeing the scene. He patted his jacket, then pulled out his phone and turned away from me.

My hands were sweating inside my gloves. I tried to breathe shallowly. The smell was turning my stomach.

If Durand hadn't crossed one arm under the other and pointed his torch downwards, I would never have spotted the sliver of silver beneath the chest of drawers. I pulled out my torch and inched forward. I could just about make out the edge of a scissor-blade. Next to it lay something round and purple and . . .

I crouched down, squinting. 'Jesus.'

A hand on my shoulder. Durand's voice floated towards me from the end of a tunnel. 'You need to give a statement. PC Waters is –' He saw the look on my face. 'What's wrong?'

I pointed at the carpet beneath the chest of drawers. Durand kneeled down, then swore under his breath.

Eventually I spoke, my voice strained. 'I thought there was more blood than last time.'

Durand strode over to Lydia and angled his torch towards her chest. He lifted up her camisole.

'He cut off her nipple?' Saliva pooled in my mouth and I swallowed it away. 'Why did he leave it here? Isn't the point of a trophy that you take it with you? And is it odd that he left the scissors behind?'

Durand's jaw was working. 'We don't know the scissors belong to the killer.'

I raised my eyebrows but didn't press him. 'Something or someone disturbed him. He left in a hurry.'

Mrs Smythe's words came back to me and I shivered.

Durand noticed. 'A team has been dispatched to bring Crawford in. But, as much as I dislike the man, we mustn't jump to conclusions. And we mustn't automatically assume this is the work of a serial killer.'

I wheeled round to face him. 'Seriously? You don't think it's the same killer?'

Durand sighed. 'I don't think anything until Forensics have done their job. Who's to say this isn't a copycat killer? A great amount of detail from Natalia's murder was reported in the press.'

I cleared my throat. 'One detail wasn't reported, though, was it?'

Durand's eyes slid towards the blood-soaked eiderdown, and his face sagged.

I frowned. 'That's weird . . .'

'What?'

'In the Twitter video, Lydia was in bed. But, look, now she's on top of it and the bed's been made.'

Voices drifted up the stairs. Durand drew himself up and put a hand on my shoulder. 'Time to go.'

I followed him towards the door, then cast my eyes back towards Lydia's mutilated corpse. Britain's most notorious model would be stripped, prodded and examined. Then she would be photographed, one last time.

Back down in the hallway, I sidestepped a Scene of Crime Officer who was laying stepping plates along the carpet and made my way towards the door. My path was blocked by the neat, brunette police officer who'd given me a lift to *The London Herald*.

'Sophie,' she gave a quick smile, 'I need to speak to you before you leave.' I followed her into Lydia's sitting room to give my statement. When I finished, PC Waters handed me a document to sign. 'Can you write down your contact details, DCI Durand is bound to need them.' I didn't mention Durand had my number on speed dial.

I slipped through the front door, stumbling in my haste to get out. The air was cold and solid, like inhaling sheet ice.

'Sophie!' Ned Mason was on the wrong side of the police tape, his bulky frame silhouetted against a streetlight. 'Bloody Northern Line was jammed.'

I trudged over to him. 'They've shut the scene down anyway.'

Ned gave me a once-over and frowned. 'You all right, love?'

'Never better.'

Ned unclipped his lens cap. 'I've missed the preamble, but Rowley will want a shot of the body leaving the building.' He gave me another look. 'You should get yourself home.'

The chill wind burrowed inside my bones and my ankle burned, but I limped past Sloane Square Tube Station. I needed to walk off the stench of death. I got as far as Cadogan Gardens when my phone rang. I yanked my glove off to answer it.

'You have more lives than a sodding cat.' Kate cackled down the phone. 'Growler told me about Lydia Lawson. Fuck me. I'm primed and ready and the web team is standing by.'

I shuffled along the King's Road, filling Kate in. She went silent when I revealed what was underneath the chest of drawers. 'Don't be specific. Police are using it as another control detail.'

'Growler's got the Fashion team working on Lydia's style highs and lows. I've sent a stringer to doorstep her neighbours and we're trying to reach the Fashion Council. Tomorrow is the last day of London Fashion Week so they're bound to be jittery. Once I've filed, I'll head over to the police station to see if I can get an update on Liam's status.'

My heart lifted as I spied my front steps. 'I'll get my copy to you within the hour. Keep me posted on Crawford.'

I pulled the front door closed behind me, locking the city out.

# 21

I woke up after a thick blank sleep and reached for my phone. News of Lydia's murder had gone stratospheric. The shocked public were reacting all over social media: #RIPLyLaw was trending at number one; #fashionslasher was number two. Designers and fashion editors, most of whom had turned their backs on Lydia, were posting iconic photographs and saccharine tributes. Stitched.com's homepage displayed a black border and a gallery of Lydia's greatest hits. I rolled my eyes at the headline: *A Tearful Farewell To Our Favourite Icon.* Written by the man who had devoted four gleeful pages to Lydia's mental breakdown yesterday.

Milan and Paris Fashion Councils had released statements to say they were tightening up security ahead of their shows. Damian Anderson, Chair of the Fashion Council, announced that London Fashion Week would go on, and that each show would observe a minute's silence in honour of the victims. I propped myself up on my pillows and switched on *BBC Breakfast*. A bronzed news reporter, with eyebrows like two scribbles, was in front of the Models International office.

*Police are still questioning photographer Liam Crawford, who was seen fleeing the scene at five o'clock.*

*Lydia's body was discovered* by London Herald *reporter, Sophie Kent.*

I dropped the phone as my photograph flashed up on the screen. It was the byline shot I'd had taken a couple of years ago, the one where I looked about eight. I checked *The London Herald* website; my piece had been retweeted 649,000 times.

*Despite the increased security measures issued by the Fashion Council and the Metropolitan Police, some model agencies have pulled their clients from the final day of London Fashion Week.*

I switched the TV off but could still hear it coming through the walls from my neighbour's house. I listened to my voicemails. Nine messages from radio and television news channels inviting me on to their shows. My gruesome discovery had turned me into a minor celebrity. I deleted the messages. My loyalty lay with *The London Herald*.

Even though I had no office to go to, I showered and dressed in a charcoal trouser suit. Kate had sent me a text late last night to say Liam and Alexei were both being held, and I knew the coroner, David Sonoma, wouldn't be ready to talk until the end of the day. I made tea, then shuffled through to my office and pinned a photograph of Lydia next to Natalia. Two heart-shaped faces. Two pairs of blue eyes. Two heads of glossy black hair. What was the link between them, other than the fact they were models? Or *was* that the link? I pinned other names to the board. Liam Crawford, Alexei Bortnik, Dmitri, Cat Ramsey,

Leo Brand, Nathan Scott, even Mrs Smythe. Then I used different colour threads to link them – red for suspect, green for witness, blue for acquaintance, yellow for alibi, black for motive. Afterwards I sat back and stared. The tangle of coloured threads resembled a map of the London Underground.

I only had two suspects. Alexei had a strong motive for Natalia's murder but the tightest of alibis for Lydia's. Liam had access to both women, but what was his motive? I clinked my fingernails against my mug. Was there a third suspect?

A sudden bang made me jump. It was my letterbox slamming shut. I wandered into the hallway to find a padded envelope on the doormat. Inside was an unmarked USB stick, no note or anything to suggest what was on it. Frowning, I strode into my office and plugged it in.

Then I ran to the toilet to throw up.

'I don't think I should be talking to you.' Cat's assistant, Isabel Baker, ran her raspberry tongue over the silver stud in her lip. From where I stood, I could see Cat's tired face, paused mid-blink on her computer screen.

'I really need to speak to her. Do you know when she'll be in?'

'When she has a migraine she's usually out of action for twenty-four hours. But, given the circumstances . . . I'll tell her you dropped by.' She turned her chair pointedly towards the computer and ran a hand through her Lucozade-coloured hair. 'I don't mean to be rude but if I don't get yesterday's Maybelline Skype call transcribed, she'll kill me.'

Isabel played the video and I turned away, pretending to read something on my phone. An American voice: 'You know we love Lydia. But she's making it kinda hard to back her right now. Joseph and I think she's too high-risk.'

Cat's Botox-filled face didn't move. 'Marc, you need to have faith. Lydia is the poster-girl for her generation. *Your consumers.* And they're about to witness the ultimate comeback.' The sun must have emerged at that point because light flooded the room and flashed on a mirror on the shelf in the background. It was the photograph of Cat and Lydia in New York. The corner of the frame was missing.

The man cleared his throat. 'I understand your position but I'm afraid –'

An email alert popped up on Isabel's screen and she pressed *pause*. 'Shit, she's here.'

I looked round. 'Where?'

Isabel nodded towards her screen. 'Alessandra on reception always gives me a thirty-second warning.'

Cat swept across the room in a furry black coat and sunglasses, her lips tightened into a thin line.

Isabel jumped up, her voice bright and fake. 'Good morning. I wasn't sure if you'd be – um, can I get you anything?'

'Ibuprofen. And coffee.' Cat turned towards me and I cleared my throat.

'I'm sorry to barge in . . . again. It's urgent.'

Cat stared at me for a moment, then she nodded. 'Five minutes.'

Once we were in her office, Cat raised a large, manicured hand and gestured for me to sit. Then she thumped her bag onto her desk and sat down, without removing her sunglasses.

'I need to show you something.' I rooted around in my bag and pulled out the USB stick. 'This is the reason Lydia has been such a lunatic these past few months. Someone put it through my letterbox this morning.'

Cat removed her sunglasses and fixed her flinty eyes on my face. Then she held her hand out for the USB stick. A blank video screen appeared on her computer. I leaned over her and pressed *play*.

The video showed Lydia on a bed, on all fours, wearing a black-lace bra, her dark hair pulled over one shoulder. An overweight man with a pixellated face was penetrating her from behind, his stomach rippling like jelly with each thrust. The video cut to Lydia, naked with her wrists and ankles bound, being forced to perform oral sex on a different pixellated man. The next showed a tangle of limbs; in the centre was Lydia, spread-eagled, eyes glazed, being mauled by three pairs of hands. Two of the men gave a high-five over her limp body and, even though I'd watched it twice, nausea rose in my throat. I fast-forwarded the tape to where a man was leaving a pile of cash next to Lydia's slumped body. Then it cut to a different man doing the same thing, then another.

I pressed *pause*. 'You get the idea.'

We sat in silence.

Eventually I cleared my throat. 'I'm not sure how long this has been going on.'

Cat took a deep, shaky breath. 'I'd say from the length of her hair in the first clip that it's been a year, at least.'

I pulled out my notebook. 'I've been running through possibilities on my way over here. It's got to be a prostitute ring. Lydia can't have known she was being filmed. My guess is that she was being blackmailed.'

There was a knock at the door and Isabel appeared with a Starbucks coffee and a box of painkillers. Cat yanked the screen round, and dismissed her with a cold look.

I waited until the door closed. 'What if this . . . this sex ring is bigger than Lydia? What if Natalia was being blackmailed too?' Cat popped two orange tablets out of the packet and swigged them down with coffee. 'If Natalia was involved, it's the link we've been looking for. A motive.' Thoughts whistled through my brain. 'Shit, don't you see? Both Natalia and Lydia met with me in the past week. We weren't discussing the sex ring, but what if the person behind it didn't know that and got spooked. What if he silenced them before they could expose him.'

Cat cradled her cup between her hands. 'The police never found a blackmail tape at Natalia's.' A note of hostility crept into her voice. If two of Cat's clients were caught up in a sordid sex racket, she was the sort of woman who would take it as a personal failing.

I doodled on my notepad, as a thought began to take shape in my mind. 'You know, something's been bothering me about Natalia's hotel room. There was mess. Clothes scattered round the room, toiletries dumped over the bathroom counter. Not the sort of mess that would bother most people, but Natalia was a neat freak.' I dug my pen into my pad. 'She was drunk, and drugged, so maybe she didn't care. But,' I looked up, 'what if the killer was looking for something?'

Cat sat up a little straighter. 'A USB stick?'

I shrugged. 'If I was blackmailing someone, I'd want to remove the evidence before I killed them.' Cat's phone rang and she ignored it. 'We need to ask around. The sex ring needs exposing, even if it is a coincidence.'

'Do you think it's a coincidence?'

I shook my head. 'The timing is too suspicious. It won't be easy getting people to talk. Whoever's behind this has delivered the ultimate warning shot. Can you put feelers out?'

'What about the police?'

'What about them?'

'Do we tell them?'

'Who's to say they don't already know? Perhaps whoever sent me the USB stick sent a copy to the police.' I sighed. 'I don't want to do their job for them, but the other women involved in the sex ring could be in real danger. He's already killed two of them.' Cat gripped the desk more tightly. 'I know it's bad for business, but we can't pretend it isn't happening. A few lost contracts are a small price to pay for exposing the monster behind this.'

Cat nodded briskly, her voice distant. 'I wonder if anyone else has seen this footage?'

I thought for a moment. 'Liam?'

'It could explain their recent arguments.'

*Certain shades of limelight wreck a girl's complexion.* Liam said it to me on Monday and I hadn't picked up on it. Now I remembered it was a line from *Breakfast at Tiffany's*. Spoken by Holly Golightly, the high-class call girl. *He knows.*

'Do you think Liam is involved somehow?' I asked.

Cat leaned her chin against her hand. 'Who knows what he's capable of?' Cat shivered. 'I can't believe this is happening again.'

Cat had said the same thing the first time I'd sat in her office. I studied her face. Concealer was wedged in the lines around her mouth. A haze of white dotted her hairline where she hadn't brushed out the dry shampoo.

I leaned forward in my chair. 'Who else had access to Natalia and Lydia?'

'Besides me, you mean?' Cat gave a thin laugh. 'The list is endless. Photographers, make-up artists, casting directors, assistants. And that's without the cranky fans.'

'But the killer knew exactly where to find them.'

'What I want to know is, who are the men in that video?' Cat threw a quick glance to her computer screen.

I nodded. 'They're rich if they can afford to do those ... things to a supermodel. If we could track one or two down ...' I scribbled a note on my pad, without meeting Cat's eye. I knew we had a snowball's chance in hell of succeeding. The wealthier the man, the more invisible he is. 'Why did Lydia get involved in the first place? She was successful. Why risk everything for some extra cash? I could almost, *almost,* understand a rookie such as Natalia getting sucked in. But Lydia? It doesn't make sense.'

Cat clasped her hands on the desk. 'There are things you don't know about Lydia. She was complicated. One of those kids who had everything handed to them on a plate. The looks, the charm, the support. Her parents doted on her. Never told her no. The fashion industry fell at her feet. You know what happens to those girls? They take it for granted. And they push and push until someone tells them to stop. You won't know this because I'm good at my job, but Lydia was arrested for shoplifting last year.

Walked off a shoot wearing a £40,000 diamond necklace. Not long after she and Liam broke up, I think it was. She has all the money in the world. Could have bought a necklace three times that price, but she chose to steal it. What does that tell you?'

'So the sex . . . she didn't do it for the money, she did it for kicks?'

Cat nodded. 'Girls like Lydia, they're always after the next thrill. Normal rules don't apply. And they're used to people cleaning up their mess.'

I shifted in my chair. 'Cat, if I don't break this story, someone else will. You need to prepare yourself. The industry is going to be pulled apart; your agency will be put under the microscope.'

Cat folded her arms, as though to protect herself. 'Once people know what Lydia was going through, they'll see she wasn't a bad person. It might teach them to be less judgemental in future.'

I frowned. 'There's something else, though, isn't there? He loses his power, once the secret's out. Perhaps it will help other young, vulnerable models to think twice before they get caught up in something like this.'

Cat ejected the USB stick and was about to hand it over, when she paused. 'I'm happy to help you, Sophie, but I have one condition. I don't want my name in the newspaper.'

'But, Cat –'

'Take it or leave it.'

I took the USB stick. 'You have my word.'

I opened the door and clusters of eavesdroppers dispersed like startled woodlice. The last thing I heard was Cat yelling at Isabel to hold her calls.

He smiles at me, and I'm transported back to those heavenly nights, ripe with pain.

I didn't think I'd see him again. But somehow, through the black, the dirt, the muck, we found each other. And now I'm awake, for the first time since . . . her.

There she is, reflected in the dark whirlpools of his eyes. The way she was at the beginning. Pink and pure, before we carved her open.

The memory sets my skin off. I shiver. He blinks, feels it too.

Lightning snaps at the window. The girl is on the bed, twitching, drowsy, drugged. Her skin calls to me. She is a blank canvas. I'm itching to colour her in.

The candlelight dances across her downy limbs. He dips towards her, and the air thickens and slows. Tiny hairs bristle along her lily-white stomach. My fingers buzz inside my gloves as I watch him feed on her body. Soon, it will be my turn. We will share her until there's nothing left. Just like we used to.

He climbs off her. Catches his breath. Catches my eye. The years melt away. All twenty of them. I count them off in my head. Slowing down time.

The bed is red and wet. The blade feels light in my hand. I run it gently across her forehead, her nose, her quivering mouth, then drop it onto the pillow. Not yet, my pretty.

She moans, a clotted sound through parted lips. The blood twists in my veins.

He leans forward, urging me on. The air fizzes with promise. I take a long, golden breath.

Then I reach for her throat.

# 22

Dark, swollen clouds pressed down. It was going to snow. The media had dubbed it the Big Freeze 2.0, after last year's Big Freeze, which entailed a centimetre of snow that melted by mid-afternoon. *All fart, and no shit*, as Rowley liked to say.

By the time I got home, I'd called Durand to sound him out about the sex tape. Turned out my hunch was right; he'd received the same USB stick that morning. Then I updated Kate and left a message on Eva's phone, asking her to call me urgently. I had to find out if she was involved.

We didn't have long to break the story. Every good reporter has inside sources in the police force so chances were, this would leak. But Rowley wouldn't go for a hatchet job. Even in the current climate. He never printed a story until it was backed up by three sources. I had the sex tape; a quote from Durand would be two. I needed a third.

I tapped my fingers against the flagstone floor and closed my eyes. The image of Lydia's limp body being pawed by meaty hands seared itself across my eyelids. This story would send an already hysterical public into an orbit of melodrama. Lydia's tape would become a global water-cooler conversation, crunched into soundbites, screengrabs, tweets and blog posts. It would taint Lydia's image forever.

I couldn't let it cloud my head. My job wasn't to pick and choose who and what I wrote about. My job was to report the facts.

I jumped as my phone rang.

'Just got out of conference.' Kate was eating something. 'Growler's head nearly fell off when he heard about the sex tape.'

I took a scalding sip of tea and burned my mouth. 'Fuck.'

'Quite. Look, Growler wants to run the story, but says you need more people on the record. All we have at the moment is that tape and it doesn't actually prove there's a sex ring. Do you have any idea who put it through your letterbox?'

'None at all.' I spun my chair round to face the corkboard. 'What does Mack think?'

Kate coughed. 'Mack's not here.'

'Where is he?'

Kate lowered her voice. 'He's asked for some time off. Something's happened. The newsroom's buzzing with rumours.' An image of Mack's desperate, bloodshot eyes flashed up in front of me and I frowned. 'Anyway, a lot of people are in favour of running with what we have. *The London Herald* is leading the pack for once and they reckon if we don't break this, someone else will.'

'They have a point.'

'So, you'd better come up with two more sources, pronto. I'm sending a bike for the USB stick. Growler wants to see it with his own eyes.'

'We need to trace the men in the video –'

'Rahid's working on it.' Rahid was a junior member of the team.

'Give me this afternoon to put something together.'

'Will do. And Soph?'

'Yeah?'

'Great scoop, girl.'


I clicked on the Models International website and painstakingly went through all two hundred female models, tracking down their social media pages, and messaging them directly to ask if they'd be willing to talk. Then I badgered my hotel contacts for their guest records. I was looking for patterns. If this sex ring was operating out of London hotels, someone must know something.

By the time I'd finished, the sky had darkened and the windows were blurred with frost. I stretched my arms over my head, my stomach growling. I hadn't eaten since breakfast. I grabbed a few crackers from my stash in the bottom drawer, then dialled Durand.

I cut straight to the chase. 'I'm writing up the sex ring story.'

'I thought you'd been fired.'

'Didn't you hear? I discovered a supermodel's body. My stock's gone up. Can you give me a quote?'

Durand sighed. 'Is this running tomorrow?'

'Doubt it. I need more witnesses. Why?'

'I'd love to have a shot at this before mass hysteria sets in.'

I squared my shoulders. 'My piece might encourage women to speak out.' There was a crumb of truth in that, but we both knew the bottom line was breaking the story before anyone else.

'OK, we're taking the contents of that tape very seriously. Prostitution and blackmail are illegal, and we will punish whoever is responsible.'

'Any idea who that is yet?'

'I'm not in a position to comment.'

I heard the strain in Durand's voice. Two murders, a serial killer and now a possible sex ring involving wealthy businessmen. Any one of those stories was a dynamite front-pager, and Durand was dealing with them simultaneously.

'Can we talk about the crime scene?'

'What about it?'

'The killer didn't break in.' I didn't phrase it as a question because I knew Durand wouldn't answer it. 'Either he had a key, or Lydia knew him and let him in.'

'It's one of the possible explanations.'

'What other explanations are there?' I played dumb to keep him talking and Durand fell for it.

'The killer could be someone Lydia didn't know but let in anyway. An electrician, someone checking the gas meter. We have teams doing door-to-door, retracing Lydia's steps, checking phone records, you name it.'

'Did you get anything from the crime scene?'

There was a pause. 'This is off record. Forensics lifted a partial print from the scissors and we're checking it against the database. That's not to appear in print. I don't want the killer to know.'

I took a sip of water before asking my next question. 'Can you give me anything on Crawford?'

Durand's silky voice hardened. 'He's still being questioned.'

'You've detained him for almost twenty-four hours. You'll have to release him soon if you're not charging him.'

'Thanks for the tip, Columbo.'

He hung up, and I spun my chair towards the window. A flurry of snow was falling and it was eerily silent. I reached for my leather contacts book. Amy Kaufman was a criminal profiler and one of the smartest women I'd ever met. A former criminal lawyer, she grew disillusioned after defending too many questionable characters and retrained as a psychiatrist. We first worked together three years ago, when the second-division footballer, Lawrence Pope, went missing: #findpope became a global Twitter sensation and police focused their efforts on tracking down a kidnapping gang. Amy researched Pope's medical history, his social media and his friends' testimonies, and eventually asked police to locate a person who was anonymously posting Bible quotations on Pope's Twitter feed. Police traced the sender all the way to a rundown hotel in Ipswich. When the police knocked on the door, Pope thought it was room service come to restock his minibar. Turned out he couldn't cope with the pressures of professional football and faked his own disappearance. He never realised it would blow up the way it did. Pope's new plan was to swallow a bottle of painkillers, and then slip into a hot bath. He was just waiting for reinforcements. Without Amy Kaufman, I'm sure the police would have found Pope. But I doubt they would have found him in time.

Amy picked up immediately. 'I had a feeling you'd call.'

I smiled. 'How are you?'

'I think the more pressing question is: how are you? You had quite the adventure last night.'

I curled my legs underneath me. 'I need to talk to someone about . . . what I saw.'

Amy's voice was soft. 'Perfectly natural to want to make sense of a gruesome crime scene.'

'Is it possible to make sense of it?'

'Even killers have a behavioural pattern. You just have to reason the same way they reason. Give me the details and I'll give you a ballpark theory.'

I went through the two crime scenes in as much detail as I could.

Amy cleared her throat. 'What I'm about to tell you is surface-level stuff. I haven't had access to the investigation records, the crime scene, witness statements.'

'I understand.'

'There are many interesting factors at play here. The first murder took place in a hotel, a public place; the second occurred in the victim's home in a busy area. And they took place only days apart. All this implies a supreme level of confidence. The fact the killer is able to adapt the location means he is intelligent. From what you've told me, the murders are very well planned, and he left no fingerprints or traces behind.'

I flicked my pen against my notebook. 'What about the damage he inflicts?'

'It's in line with someone who feels he has been rejected by women in the past. He feels inferior. It's no coincidence that he's chosen models – women that society holds up as an ideal of beauty. Both times he's destroyed their faces. In Lydia's case, mutilating her breast could be a cheap thrill, or it could mean he intends to increase the violence each time he kills.'

I drew in a breath. 'What do you make of the blackthorn branch?'

'It could signify his impotence. Or his perceived impotence. He can't perform for these women, so he rapes them with an object. The rape itself is a form of orgasm for him.'

I stared down at my hands, trying to process my thoughts. 'Why does he allow them to be unconscious?'

Amy paused. 'My guess is that the fantasy is so strong in his mind, he doesn't need them to play along. He just needs a vessel. The fact that the victims look so similar means they are conforming to his fantasy woman. And that's the other thing. The bodies aren't left in a haphazard manner. In both cases, the bed is made, the victims are dressed, candles are lit. None of those things happened by accident. The visual impact matters to him. When a killer leaves the victim face-up, it indicates he feels no shame.'

I wandered over to the window. Snow was settling on rooftops like a layer of gauze.

'In my view you're looking for a highly intelligent, socially adjusted sexual sadist. Possibly someone the victims knew. The most useful piece of advice I can give you is this: murdering the country's most famous model takes nerves of steel, and a calm hand. He's killed before.'

I pulled the keyboard towards me and searched for *model* and *strangled*. I read about the British model, Jessica Parker, who was killed in Tokyo in 2007. I vaguely remembered the case. A Japanese computer technician lured Parker to his car and strangled her with his belt. He was later executed. I kept scrolling. An American model, Brittany Weiser, was strangled by her boyfriend in Detroit in 2004. A Brazilian model, Alessandra Garcia, was strangled by an ex-fiancé in 2002. British model, Amanda Barnes, was strangled by her stepfather in 1994. My eyes were starting to glaze over and I was about to take a break when I spotted a photograph of Amanda Barnes. I grabbed the headshots of Lydia and Natalia that were pinned on my board and held them up. Cut-glass cheekbones, almond-shaped eyes, shoulder-length black hair. The three women looked like sisters.

I searched for *Amanda Barnes murder* but nothing in the national press appeared. A piece in the *Liverpool Echo* popped up.

*The body of a sixteen-year-old girl was found in the wooded area just outside of Formby at 7.30 a.m. yesterday morning. Initial reports suggest the girl – who has been identified as model Amanda Barnes – was strangled. Her best friend, Melissa Wakefield, told police that Amanda left the Old Oak pub at around 9.30 p.m. the night before. Merseyside Police are appealing for witnesses.*

The next mention was dated 23 March 1994.

*Michael Farrow, forty-eight, has been arrested on suspicion of murdering his stepdaughter, Amanda Barnes. Police uncovered evidence in the shed at the bottom of her garden*

*that indicated Amanda was being sexually abused by*
*Farrow. Detective Inspector Fred Weatherly is describing*
*this as a 'significant breakthrough'.*

Then 25 March 1994:

*At 9.38 this morning suspect Michael Farrow, forty-eight,*
*was found dead in his cell at St Anne Street Police Station. It's*
*reported that he hanged himself with his belt while waiting to*
*be questioned. Police are continuing their investigation into*
*Amanda's murder, but have stated that the evidence against*
*Michael Farrow was overwhelming and believe his suicide is*
*a strong indication of his guilt.*

It took a moment for the information to sink in. Amanda was
killed in February 1994, exactly twenty years ago. A flush of
adrenaline swept through me, but I forced myself to take a step
back. A model who resembled Natalia and Lydia was sexually
abused and strangled two decades ago. Amanda's killer committed suicide. It was a dead end. And yet, as I stared at Amanda's
heart-shaped face, something stirred inside me.

I dug out the contact details for Liverpool Prison and left
a message on the press officer's voicemail. Then I pulled up
Facebook and searched for *Melissa Wakefield Liverpool*. Three
accounts popped up, but only one was born before 1995. I fired
off a message, pretending I was writing a tribute piece to long-
forgotten murder victims. The naff angle made me wince, but it
was the sort of thing that garnered a response.

I drummed my fingers on the desk. Then I clicked on the Merseyside Police website and pulled up the list of current police officers serving the area. DI Fred Weatherly wasn't there, but I found a tiny news story stating he'd retired and now volunteered at Victim Support. I found his direct line and dialled.

'Victim Support, Fred speaking.' His voice was warm and friendly, but when I explained who I was, there was a frosty pause. 'That was a long time ago.'

'Do you remember the case?'

'I remember all my cases.'

'I'm working on a double-murder investigation in London. Two models have been –'

'I read the papers.'

'Look, this is a long shot, but I've noticed some similarities between the current murders and the murder of Amanda Barnes.'

'What similarities?'

'Amanda was killed February 1994. Natalia Kotov and Lydia Lawson were killed in the same month two decades later. All three women were sexually assaulted and strangled. They looked alike, I mean *really* alike.' I tailed off, waiting for him to laugh, or make a sarcastic comment, but his voice was surprisingly kind.

'I don't think I need to point out that your theory is a bit thin.'

'Can you humour me? I've only just started looking into it. And the press coverage is slight.'

'You need to do your homework, love. There was a much bigger story coming out of Liverpool around then. The name James Bulger mean anything to you?'

*Of course.* The toddler who was tortured and left to die on a train track by two young boys. No wonder Amanda's murder slipped through the cracks.

'Can you give me any more details on the abuse angle?'

'Trust me, you don't want to know. It's not a sight I'll forget in a hurry. The marks on her body . . .' Weatherly coughed wetly down the phone, 'It had been going on for some time. Not just sexual abuse either. She was covered in cuts, bruises and cigarette burns. Poor kid. What we found in the garden shed . . .'

'Shame he never got his day in court.'

'Stringing him up from the rafters was too good for him.' Weatherley's voice took on a hard edge. 'Farrow was a real piece of work. Blank eyes, like marbles. I only questioned him once before he died, but he told me Amanda was a prick tease and led him on. Had a real temper on him. Turns out he went through the foster system and was heavily abused as a kid. There was a string of sexual assault accusations littering his record, but he was never convicted. Victims were too scared to testify so he got away with it.' Weatherly sounded disgusted.

'Were there any other suspects?'

Weatherley paused. 'It was an open-and-shut case with regards to evidence. Farrow's semen was all over her; and the footprints we found on the scene matched his size nine boots –'

'You remember his shoe size?'

'As I said, I remember all my cases.'

'So why did you hesitate? When I asked about another suspect.'

'Look, you have to understand, we were under the microscope. The Bulger case was taking all of our resources. And Farrow was guilty, that I'm sure of.' He sighed. 'We found another trace. Semen, on the mattress in the shed. But the Forensic who collected the sample was wet behind the ears. It was contaminated before we could properly identify it. I was all for expanding the investigation, but then Farrow committed suicide and my SIO, well, you know . . .'

'He needed support elsewhere, yeah, I get it.' I pressed my forehead against the window as disappointment crashed over me.

'Farrow wasn't around to ask, and Amanda's mum wasn't much use.' Weatherly paused. 'This wasn't in the newspapers because the guv didn't want it known, but Amanda's mum was there when it happened. He made her watch.'

'She watched her own daughter being murdered?'

'You can imagine the state she was in. She was so terrified of him, she could barely speak by the time we got to her. A shell of a woman. I imagine she spent the next decade in therapy. At least, I hope she did.'

'I don't suppose you kept any notes from Amanda's case?'

'The wife made me move the boxes up to the attic when we did the extension, but they're up there somewhere.'

I crossed my fingers. 'Fred, is there any way I can persuade you to dig them out? I can come and look at them in person if you don't want to let them out of your sight.'

I heard the smile in his voice. 'Even I've heard of a scanner. I'll have a dig around. Give me an excuse to look over my past. But, I'm warning you, don't get your hopes up.'

## 23

My phone woke me up. It was like surfacing through treacle. I forced my arm out from under the covers. The text was from Eva.

*Can we meet? Bench on the Embankment, by Waterloo Bridge.*

It had just gone 6 a.m. I yanked my covers off and dressed quickly, pulling on a thick sweater and fur-lined boots. I grabbed my coat, then closed the front door quietly, recoiling as the freezing air blasted my face.

Twenty minutes later I fled the stale warmth of the Tube and hurried along Embankment. The Thames slithered alongside like a fat grey snake and I could taste the salt on the wind. Up ahead a figure in a periwinkle hat sat huddled on a bench. Her face was hidden but I recognised the awkward posture and long golden hair. I sat down beside Eva and waited for her to speak.

'You can see everything from this bench: The London Eye, Big Ben, Westminster. Even now I have to pinch myself that I'm here.' She gave a shy pink smile. 'I always dreamed of being a princess. Now I live near Prince Harry. What are my chances, do you think? It would make my mamma and pappa very happy. We could all live in a palace together.'

A jogger zipped past, steaming the air with his hot, wet breath.

When he was far enough away, Eva cleared her throat. 'So, Alexei Bortnik didn't kill Natalia.'

I stared down at the dirt. 'Alexei is a killer, just not her killer.'

Eva yanked a silver pendant over the top of her black polo neck and began twisting it around her gloved finger. 'I still hear her, you know. In our apartment. Every time a door slams, or someone laughs outside. Last night I heard her screaming through the walls.'

The frozen bench seeped through my coat. I couldn't wait any longer. 'Eva, did you know Lydia was being blackmailed?' A flock of crows landed; their bright caws drowned me out. Eva picked up a smooth round stone and lobbed it at them. The flock exploded into the air.

'I'm getting a new flatmate. Iman something. From Nairobi.' She tilted her head up to the sky, and closed her eyes. 'She's moving in Monday.'

I reached out and squeezed her bony fingers. She whipped her eyes open and stared down at my hand.

'Eva, I need your help. I think Lydia was caught up in –'

'The Juliets.'

I frowned. 'The –'

'Juliets. The sex ring. That's what you're talking about, right?'

The cold air had numbed my face. I struggled to form the words. 'Who told you about it?'

'Who do you think?'

I pulled out my tape recorder. A risky move, but Rowley would kill me if I didn't get our conversation on the record. 'Do you mind? I won't use your name. Just pretend it isn't there.'

Eva's eyes darted from the device to my face. Then she shrugged and wiped her nose with the back of her hand. 'Natalia came home trashed. It was Bonfire Night. I remember because I watched the fireworks on Clapham Common. It wasn't long after she started those NA meetings. I'd had enough of her mood swings, plus,' she smiled sheepishly, 'I'd eaten nothing but apple slices for two days. Told her if she wasn't going to take it seriously, she should give someone else a chance.'

'What did she say?' The wind burned pink roses onto Eva's cheeks and she stared straight ahead, seeing something behind her eyes.

'I was so stupid.'

'What do you mean?'

Eva shrugged. The friendliness of earlier had evaporated; it had happened in her flat the other day. The sudden change unsettled me. A surge of questions bubbled in my head, but I forced myself to order them.

'Was Natalia being blackmailed by the sex . . . the Juliets?' Eva gave a quick nod, without taking her eyes off the river. 'What exactly did she tell you?'

Eva flicked her thigh with her finger. 'It's an exclusive club. Only the most beautiful models are chosen. It's a way to clear your debt and meet influential men at the same time.' Eva's fingernail snapped hard against denim. 'That's how Natalia sold it to me, anyway. When she recruited me.'

I stared at her. 'Natalia recruited you?'

Eva's fingers stilled, then she tucked her legs beneath her and shook out her long hair. 'I thought she was doing me a favour, letting me in on a secret. The agency had fronted me thousands of pounds and I wasn't making enough to pay them back. I didn't want to be sent back to Russia. Prince Harry, remember?' She gave a pinched-lip smile. 'I figured I'd do it a couple of times, then get out. But when I tried to leave . . .'

'They blackmailed you?' The bench dug into my back. 'Why is it called the Juliets?'

Eva shrugged. 'Who knows? I assumed it was after Shakespeare's heroine. Beautiful, and underage,' she added, with a wry smile.

'But Natalia can't have known how twisted the Juliets were before she recruited you.'

Eva gave a bitter laugh. 'That little bitch knew everything. The blackmail, the fetishes, the beatings.' She yanked her gloves off and pressed the skin on the back of her hand with slender fingers. 'I was her escape route.'

'What do you mean?'

'The Juliets have a rule. No one is allowed to leave until they've found a girl to replace them.' A riverboat slid into view, pushing through the muddy water like a lazy worm. 'The Juliets make you do things that . . . each time you're forced to do something worse. Something you'd rather die than let the world see. Then they send a tape of you doing it. Eventually you start to feel worthless, as though you deserve it. I was desperate to tell someone, but I didn't want the tape to go on the internet. And then Natalia was killed . . .'

'That's why you refused to call the police when you noticed Alexei Bortnik hanging around.'

Eva nodded, fumbling with a cigarette packet. 'He showed up the day after you came to my flat. I thought the Juliets had found out and sent someone to scare me.'

A dull ache was spreading across my frozen fingertips and I curled my hands into fists. 'Did you know Lydia was a Juliet too?'

Eva inhaled deeply and the tip of her cigarette burned coral. A gust of wind blew a heavy waft of sewage across the river towards us and I covered my nose with my glove.

'When I was sent the tape, I was so mad. I confronted Natalia. At first she played dumb, but I could tell she was lying. Eventually she admitted she was in deep too.'

'When was this?'

'Late November, I think. She told me Lydia recruited her in August when she wanted to get out. It's a perverted chain letter. The Juliets break you, then dangle a carrot and offer you a way out.'

'Have you managed to get out?'

Eva ignored me, and exhaled a ribbon of smoke. 'The Juliets don't want you after a while anyway. Once you become too damaged, your innocence fades and you're not as valuable to them.'

'So if Natalia and Lydia both recruited someone, that means they no longer worked for the Juliets.'

A wisp of blonde hair blew across Eva's face and she brushed it away. 'Natalia told me that the Juliets never let Lydia go. She made too much money for them.' She flashed a wry smile. 'I know, shocking. Filthy pimps don't keep their word.'

'But why would the Juliets kill Natalia and Lydia? Why not just release their tapes?'

Eva tossed her cigarette onto the ground and squashed it with the heel of her boot. 'I have no idea. Maybe it was warning signal to the rest of us. Maybe they were worried the tapes would lead police to them.'

Suddenly Eva folded over and burst into tears.

I laid my hand on her quivering shoulders. 'I'm so sorry, Eva.'

'I didn't want to return to Russia a failure.' The words punched through her sobs. 'I figured this would buy me some time. But the clients, they're not normal. One guy urinated in my mouth. Another could only orgasm if I cried out in pain, so he punched me over and over in the ribs during sex. It was as if they were competing with each other for a sick crown.' Tears ran down Eva's face, turning it black with mascara, like tiny lumps of coal. 'By the time I became a Juliet, clients were no longer allowed to hit girls in the face. So they were asked to be discreet. One man had a fetish for the smell of burned skin. He used to stub cigarettes out on me.' She thrust her hand in my face. The delicate skin between her fingers was puckered and red.

I looked away. An image of Lydia's famous black eye flashed into my mind. Maybe Liam had told the truth, after all. 'Didn't anyone notice the marks on you?'

Eva dragged her fingers across her cheeks, wiping away the tears. 'You get good at hiding them. Still,' she shook another cigarette out of the packet, but didn't light it, 'I almost miss the days when my biggest fear was a leaked sex tape.'

'Can we put this on the record? If so, I need details. How does the sex ring operate?'

Eva sucked on her unlit cigarette and slumped down lower on the bench. 'When a client books you, you get sent a Burn Notice on your phone, telling you where to be and when.' A Burn Notice was a self-destructing text app. 'It also lists a number to call in case you get a last-minute job and can't make the appointment. That number changes each time.'

'Did you ever save any of those numbers?'

Eva shook her head. 'They told me to destroy them.'

'Who are the clients?'

'Middle Eastern, Asian, Russian. I never knew their real names and I never recognised anyone.'

'Where did these appointments take place?'

'Hotel rooms, mainly. The key would be in an envelope half-tucked under the door. Once I discovered they were filming the sessions, I tried to hide my face but it's not easy when you don't know where the camera is.'

'How much do clients pay?'

Eva bit down on the tip of her index finger. 'Depends how long the client books you for, what he wants to do to you. The minimum is a grand. The most I've ever got is five grand.' She dug her teeth in deeper. 'Three guys with a suffocation fetish.' I forced myself to move briskly past the incoming image. 'That night, I called the number they gave me.'

'Who answered?'

'It went to voicemail. I left a message saying I wanted out. The following day I received a package with the USB stick.'

'Was there a note?'

Eva stretched her arms out above her. Then she dropped them into her lap with a sigh. 'I did whatever they told me after that.'

I cursed as I noticed the battery light flashing on my tape recorder. 'Which hotels do they use?'

Eva bent forward to light her cigarette and took a long drag. 'The Parker, The Chateau, The Palace –'

'The Rose?'

Eva shrugged. 'I never met a client there but it's possible.'

I remembered Natalia's odd behaviour the night she was killed. The drinking, the terrified glances over her shoulder, wanting to swap rooms. 'Could Natalia have been meeting a client the night she was killed?'

Eva sighed. 'As far as I knew, Natalia no longer worked for the Juliets. She'd recruited me, remember. Then again, we weren't exactly speaking. Things were . . . difficult between us. I couldn't forgive her for getting me involved.'

I chewed my bottom lip as another thought struck me. 'Do you think Natalia's rape is linked to the Juliets?'

Eva stared down at the ground. 'Before you're booked, the man in charge vets you. To check you'll do as you're told. I was blindfolded and taken somewhere cold and damp. I didn't see his face. He drugged me, then . . .' Eva paused, took a sharp breath. 'He used things on me, whispered *you're nothing*, over and over. There was someone else, helping, I think. It's still hazy.' Eva squeezed her cigarette between her thumb and forefinger, 'Like I say, I wasn't really conscious for most of it . . .'

I swallowed thickly. 'You didn't get a glimpse of his face?' Eva's eyes flittered once to mine, then dropped to the ground. 'Come on, Eva. If you're not going to give me his name, why did you ask to meet?' She flicked her cigarette into the dirt, but didn't answer. 'You know, the last time I saw Natalia alive, she was about to tell me who raped her. But then she ducked out for a cigarette.' I frowned. 'The Juliets must have known she was meeting me that day. How did they . . .'

Eva's gaze shifted to the river and she curled a long strand of hair around her finger. Her voice was whisper-soft. 'I was so mad at her. I thought if I got on their good side . . .'

I felt my jaw slide downwards. 'You told them Natalia was meeting a reporter?'

'I-I never thought they would kill her. I –'

'Is that why you're here? Because you feel guilty?' Eva yanked out a cluster of hairs, then opened her hand. The golden threads writhed in the air, then disappeared. The realisation hit me. 'Did you send me Lydia's sex tape?'

'It's not safe for me . . . Natalia and Lydia both spoke to you and now they're dead. The Juliets are watching me, I know it. I owed it to Natalia to point you in the right direction but I can't . . .' She staggered off the bench, towards the river.

'Eva, wait!' I raced after her. She stopped by the railings and leaned over. 'You need to call the police.'

Eva turned to face me, an odd smile on her face. 'We've been through this before.'

'The police can help you.'

Eva's clear blue eyes stared directly into mine. 'No one can help me.'

Déjà vu crashed over me like an icy wave. *No one can help me.* That was the last thing Natalia had said to me and, eight hours later, she was dead.

# 24

Over the years, the tiny news-stand outside Sloane Square Tube Station has become my industry touchstone. A reporter can't tell how good they are until they see what the competition has brought to the table. And that table is the news-stand. It's your battlefield, your arena, your sink or swim. It's not the place to play coy. It's balls-to-the-wall-show-'em-what-you-got. Shout loud, offer big. Force people to part with their cash.

As I paused on that arctic corner, still reeling from Eva's interview, it struck me that the line between news and entertainment was barely a line anymore. The *Sun*'s front page showed a paparazzi shot of Lydia arriving at Natalia's memorial service under the headline: *2 More Days To Live*. The *Mirror* ran with a grid made up of Models International headshots and the headline: *Who's Next?* A weekly style glossy had managed to find the sartorial spin with the cover line: *RIP LyLaw: The Most Stylish Funeral Ever?*

This wasn't news; it was hysteria. Peddled by editors and lapped up by consumers. Lydia's behaviour over the past year showed a deeply troubled woman, but who really cared? Her tabloid-friendly meltdowns shifted papers and increased website traffic. Her misery was good for business. Her death was even better.

By the time I was cocooned inside my house, I had dealt with my fleeting existential crisis and got to work.

Throwing myself into my office chair, my fingers flew across the keyboard. I reread my copy, tweaked it, then sent it to Kate.

Ten minutes later, she called. 'Fuck me. You're sure this is watertight?'

'One hundred per cent. But I can't name her, so don't even ask.'

Kate sighed. 'I wish we had longer on this before everyone else joined the race. Rahid's not getting anywhere with the men on that tape. Rowley wants to run all this past the legal team. I'll let you know when it's going live.'

I made another cup of tea and by the time I got back to my desk, Amanda Barnes's best friend, Melissa Wakefield, had responded.

*Leaving work in a min. U can call.*

I switched on my tape recorder and dialled.

'Sophie?' A thin, shrill voice like a budgerigar's cheep. 'I've never spoken to a real reporter before. I haven't been able to concentrate since I got your message. I don't know how much help I can be.'

I smiled brightly so Melissa would hear it in my voice. 'That's what all my interviewees are saying, but it's amazing how many things come back to you once you start talking. Let's start with an easy one. Do you still live in Liverpool?'

'No, I moved to Huddersfield years ago. I studied at the university and met my hubby-to-be in a pub. Well, I couldn't see myself going back to Liverpool so I just stayed. Got a job in a travel agency, except that went bust, so I got a job as a receptionist at the dentist on the High Street, been there for around, let's see, six and a half years. And –'

'Thanks, Melissa, that's perfect. Do you mind if I ask you about the night Amanda Barnes died?'

'Is this going in the newspaper?'

'Is that OK with you?'

'Yes, but can you use my new name? Melissa Wakefield-Channing. I hyphenated it.' She sounded pleased with herself. 'I want people to know I'm married. My husband is Dave Channing, he's an electrician. Second in command of the company now.' There was a pause. 'I don't suppose you can add that bit in?'

'It depends how much space I have.' I cleared my throat. 'I really want to get a sense of Amanda across in this piece. What was she like?'

'That depends on when you're talking about. Before Mands' stepdad came on the scene she was the best. Beautiful, funny, smart. The kind of girl you'd hate if she wasn't so nice. I was three years younger but we lived on the same street. Bonded over New Kids on the Block and Jimmy Hunt. Jimmy was the year above Mands, curly brown hair and eyes you could melt in. Mands and I kept a log in the back of our school jotters called The Hunt Hunt, we'd write down every time we saw him and where. A bit sad, really, now I come to think of it, but we were only young. Anyhow, sorry, what was the question? Oh yes, Mands.'

Melissa took a quick breath and I relaxed into my chair. 'She was the real deal. A bit awkward about her height, she was already five foot ten at thirteen. But she grew into it, you know? By the time we were in the third year she had men dancing circles round her. Everyone fancied her. She once got eleven

Valentine's cards in one year. From actual boys, she didn't even need to send any to herself.' A pause. 'Not that I ever did that. But anyway, none of us were surprised when she got a modelling contract.'

'Was Amanda comfortable with the attention?'

'Are you kidding me? She loved it. Especially the male attention. I'm not saying she was a slag or anything, but she wasn't exactly at home reading the Bible on Saturday nights.'

'Did she have a boyfriend?'

Melissa gave an undignified snort. 'Mands wasn't the type to commit. A lot of them fell in love with her. But Mands never got serious with anyone. We used to joke the poor bastards should form the AA group – Amanda Anonymous. If Facebook was around back then, there would have been a page devoted to it. She drove men wild.'

'Men like Michael Farrow?' There was a pause.

'Yes.' Melissa didn't elaborate. I waited, and eventually she sighed. 'When Mands' stepdad came on the scene, she changed. Started dressing differently, covering herself up. Stopped wearing make-up. It got worse just before she died. She lopped all her hair off. Told me she needed a new look to make it in London. But now I wonder if she was trying to make herself look less attractive.'

The hairs on the back of my neck started to prick up. 'Amanda had short hair when she was murdered?'

'The irony is that the uglier she tried to make herself, the more modelling jobs she got. She had a real future in front of her.'

'Did you have any idea she was being abused?'

Melissa's voice grew cagey. 'I haven't thought about this for a long time. Her stepdad was the kind of man you tried to forget.'

'Can you describe him?'

'He was very quiet-natured, but he had an intensity about him. He never raised his voice or anything, but you did what he said.'

'But she didn't tell you what he was doing to her?'

'No.' There was an edge to Melissa's voice. I was losing her. I changed tack.

'Tell me about Amanda's mum.'

A bus roared past and Melissa paused. 'She was a bit odd. Distant. But then it all came out . . . what he did to her. Not surprising that she shut down, really. I felt sorry for her, after it happened. She lost everything.'

I wondered if Melissa knew the full extent of what Amanda's mum went through. 'What happened to her?'

'She moved away not long after Mands' death. Couldn't handle it. I mean, could you? The guilt. Christ.'

'Did you ever doubt that Michael killed Amanda?'

'Not for a second.'

'Why do you think he killed himself?'

'He was scared of prison, probably. Criminals don't love paedophiles, do they? Anyway, Michael was a total creep. Do you know, when the police searched his stuff, they found a cuttings file full of Amanda's modelling photographs. Her face had been scratched out in every one. Literally scratched out with a pair of scissors. Talk about creepy.'

I stared up at the ceiling, my mind working overtime. Amanda's face was scratched out with scissors. Another coincidence?

But Michael Farrow was dead. So, who was the link? I thought about what DI Weatherley had said.

'Melissa, do you know if anyone else was involved in Amanda's abuse? Or anyone else who might have wanted to hurt Amanda, besides Michael Farrow?'

'As I said, there were a few dented egos. But nothing that would lead to her murder. I mean, occasionally it got dark . . . Not long before she died, I was over at hers studying and a man turned up. Amanda freaked out, looked like she'd seen a ghost. Told me I had to leave straight away. I asked what was wrong but she wouldn't tell me.'

'Did you get a look at him?'

Melissa exhaled loudly. 'No, sorry. I can't remember much about it, to be honest. I mentioned it to her mum.'

'Amanda never told you his name?'

'John someone.' Amanda exhaled loudly, chewing the words over in her mouth. 'She let it slip, then told me never to tell anyone. Said he was a friend of her stepdad's.' Melissa laughed suddenly. 'You know what, though. I kept a diary back then. Unlike Amanda I wasn't popular. Spent my life scribbling in my diary, convinced I was the next Adrian Mole. I've still got them somewhere. I'll have a look.'

'Thanks, Melissa. That would be great.'

'You know, I often wonder what would have become of Amanda if she'd lived. She'd probably be on the cover of *Vogue*, and on to her fourth husband by now.'

I scooted over to the corkboard, thanking the universe for creating a Melissa-shaped chatterbox, and pinned Amanda's headshot next to Lydia's. I stuck Michael Farrow's name next to it. Then a blank scrap of paper with a question mark that represented the as-yet non-existent person linking the three murders. I massaged my temples. I couldn't go to Rowley yet. This wasn't even a skeleton of a theory.

I tried David Sonoma again. This time he picked up.

'Sorry I didn't get back to you yesterday.' David Sonoma sighed. 'I'm still writing up the report.'

'What are the highlights?'

'Manual strangulation marks are consistent with those found on Natalia's neck. As are the contusions on Lydia's face, which were made post-mortem. All ten fingers were broken, her hair was cut, and she was object raped with the same item.'

'What about time of death?'

'Rigor mortis wasn't very far along so I'd say it wasn't long before you found her body. Somewhere between four and six o'clock. She had traces of Xanax in her system but that's consistent with the drugs found in her house. And I gather she seemed under the influence of drugs earlier in the day. So my daughter tells me, anyway. I'm not one for social media. Like Natalia, she was also drugged with GHB, so I doubt she was conscious when it happened.'

'What about the . . . body part I found?'

David cleared his throat. 'The killer cut round the areola of her left breast and removed her nipple. The scissors found on the scene are the right size and shape to have caused the lacerations on her face, but . . .' his voice tailed off.

'What is it?'

A pause. 'The lacerations aren't consistent with the last victim. The cuts are deeper on the right-hand side of her face, indicating a left-hander held the knife.'

'Could the killer have used his other hand?'

'Possibly. But unlikely. There's something else too. Blood splatters on Lydia's chest and stomach indicate she was naked when she was killed. Which means the killer dressed her afterwards. Do you know how hard it is to dress a dead body?'

The hairs on my neck starting to rise. 'What are you saying, David?'

'I don't think he's working alone.'

I stared at the phone. Two killers. Eva was right when she said someone else was involved in her assault. I was about to call Durand when my phone rang again.

'Hello? Sophie?' A husky voice scratched my ear like a blunt razor. 'It's Violet. We met at the NA meeting on Monday. I need to talk to you.'

'Sure, go ahead.' I was scribbling down notes, only half-listening.

'Not on the phone. Can we meet?'

'Is this about Natalia? I'm on a deadline now, but I could meet you first thing tomorrow.'

'I think you're gonna want to see me tonight.' A pause. 'It's not about Natalia.'

The catch in her voice made my fingers tighten round the phone. 'What is it?'

'It's Tommy.'

## 25

I took another slug of red wine and stared at the door. The softly lit pub was warm, but I was chilled to the bone. I covered the fifteen-minute walk to the Enterprise pub in Pimlico in eight minutes, all the while darting along the dark streets in my mind.

The door opened and I held my breath, but it was just a group of gilet-clad men with ruddy cheeks. The pub was packed. Raucous laughter rolled off the walls. The sound of happy people returning to the fold after a long, dry January. I swirled my glass around, staring at the crimson whirlpool.

'Oof, it's fucking freezing out there.' Violet threw herself into the chair opposite, plucked the glass from my fingers and took a large gulp.

It took a moment for me to realise what she'd done. 'Wait, Violet, should you be –'

'Drinking?' Violet arched an eyebrow. 'Booze was never the problem.' She unzipped her puffa jacket and yanked off her woolly hat. Her short, black hair lay flat and unwashed. 'This makes a nice change from my local. Someone got bottled last week. They still haven't cleaned the blood off the fruit machine.' I slid my wine glass across the table towards her. 'You don't want it?'

I shook my head. 'I'd rather hear what you have to say.'

Violet took another sip and I noticed her hands were trembling. Her kohl-rimmed eyes snapped towards mine, then she looked away. She leaned both elbows on the table. 'My dad brought me to Chelsea once. When I was eight. To look at the Christmas lights in Sloane Square. The trees glittered like diamonds; it was fucking Narnia.' Violet chewed the skin around her fingernail. She had words scribbled across the back of her hand but I couldn't make them out. 'Afterwards, he took me for a hot chocolate at a posh French café. Even the chocolate tasted rich.' She shifted back in her chair and fixed her eyes on my face. 'Six months later he was gone.'

'Gone where?'

'I woke up one day and he'd fucked off. Mum said he'd run off with Lycra Leslie, the perky aerobics instructor who lived on our street. Leslie was married to a wet wipe called Norm and, according to Mum, she and Dad buggered off into the night like a couple of lovesick teenagers. We moved house soon after. Mum couldn't hack the memories.' A pink-faced man with a stubby nose and no chin caught the edge of Violet's chair. 'Fucking watch yourself, mate.' He opened his mouth to respond, then changed his mind when he saw the ferocious look on Violet's face.

'I was eight and my heart was broken. I loved my dad. Kept wondering if I could have done anything to make him stay. If I'd been a better daughter would he have left me? If I'd stopped giving Mum grief over my homework, or not got told off in Miss Capron's class, if I'd done all them things, would he have thought twice about leaving me behind?'

A loud smash, then jeers to my left. A braying Sloane had dropped his pint, much to the delight of his friends. I leaned in closer to Violet. 'Did you ever see him again?'

Violet picked a thread off her maroon jumper and sighed. 'A year later, I found out the truth from an older kid at school. My dad did have a fling with Lycra Leslie but Norm caught them at it. Pulled out a carving knife and stabbed them both in the chest.' Violet gave a small shrug. 'Turns out Norm wasn't such a wet wipe, after all.'

I stared at Violet in horror, trying to formulate a response. A grin spread across her face. 'So I get home and ask Mum. She don't even try to deny it. Stands there, in the kitchen, in her crabby old apron and says she told me Dad ran off because she thought I was too young to know he was murdered fifty feet from our house.' Violet leaned forward. 'You want to hear the truth? I was relieved. He didn't choose to leave me behind. I could have done all the homework in the world, and Norm would still have killed my dad.'

Violet leaned back in her chair and gave me a defiant look. Everything about her screamed aggression. The butch hair, the Goth wardrobe, the don't-fuck-with-me glare. I didn't buy it.

'Why are you telling me this?'

Violet shrugged. 'I want you to know that finding out something bad can sometimes be a good thing.'

My insides started to knit themselves together. 'What do you mean?'

Violet drained her glass, then stood up. 'I'm going to get another–'

'Violet!' I grabbed her hand and yanked her down. 'What's going on?'

Violet rubbed both hands through her hair and exhaled loudly. 'Look, I've been killing myself the past couple of days. Wondering whether to tell you. Why fuck with someone's head, right? Except,' she picked up the empty glass and drained it anyway, 'if it was me, I'd want to know.'

I slammed my hand down on the table and Violet looked me in the eye.

'Tommy didn't kill himself. He was murdered.'

When I was eight years old, I started having turns. I called them my 'funnies'. I would shut down, switch off, blank out for two or three minutes. It felt as if I'd been scooped up and sealed inside a glass box. The world was shut out, or I was shut in. My vision clouded over. Sounds were muffled. I couldn't move. I'd sit frozen until the funny passed and I came round.

Of course, my mother thought I was doing it for attention and ignored me, until I had a funny while riding my pony and almost broke my back. The specialist diagnosed me with mild epilepsy and prescribed gloopy brown medicine that tasted like cabbages. It did the trick. No more glass boxes.

Except. Every so often, a strange dreaminess enveloped me and flooded my brain with light. I always fought the feeling because I didn't know where it would take me. As I stared at Violet, the feeling brushed past me, chiffon grazing skin. For a moment I gave myself to it. Closed my eyes, leaned against the wall of my glass box, the world around me blurred. Until something cold closed around my hand, pulling me upwards, back into the noise, into the light. I looked down and saw Violet's pen-scrawled hand wrapped around mine.

'Sophie? Can you hear me?' Violet gave me a long look, then stood up. 'We can't do this sober, wait there.' She elbowed her way to the front of the bar and returned with a tray of amber shots. 'Start drinking.'

I threw one back, wincing as the whisky hit the back of my throat. Then I reached for the next. I waved my hand at her to continue.

Violet necked a shot. 'It was Damo who told me. Remember the skinny kid in the Adidas sweatshirt? He overheard your name, then later when you told me about Tommy. Turns out they used to crash in the same spot under Albert Bridge.'

Violet shifted in her seat and downed another shot. 'That night something woke Damo up. He has no idea what time it was, but it was late enough that the traffic over the bridge had died away. He sat up and saw two figures crouching over Tommy and . . .' Violet tailed off and stared mournfully towards the door.

'Tell me, Violet.' The words came out jagged and clipped, like they were from someone else's mouth.

Violet took a deep breath and rested both elbows on the table. 'He heard Tommy struggling, says it sounded as if he had something stuffed in his mouth. Damo said two figures held him down. It was over pretty quickly. Damo hid behind the bush until the men left, then crawled over to Tommy. He was already dead. There was a syringe in his right hand.'

'Damo just lay there the whole time. He didn't try to help?'

'Come off it, Sophie.' Violet's nostrils flared. 'One homeless druggie against two killers. What would you have done?'

I sagged against the chair. I knew Violet was right, but it was easier to focus on Damo. 'He could have told someone. Reported it. Christ, it was three months ago.'

'Who the fuck would he have told? The police? Don't be stupid. You think they'd listen to a tramp? And even if they did, you don't think they have more important things on their plate than a dead homeless guy? Damo had no idea that Tommy was from such a rich family. He did what he needed to do to survive. Buried it and moved on. Look, sleeping rough is . . . I don't tell many people this but I've been there. You have two things on your mind: survival, and your next hit. You're an animal.'

Violet's nose had started to run and when she wiped it on the back of her hand, the snot smudged the ink. 'Except Damo couldn't move on. Tommy's last moments haunted him. He managed to get himself into a shelter, and then into a programme, and he's been clean for six weeks. He wanted to tell someone but didn't know where to start. He couldn't believe it when you mentioned Tommy. He came to the meeting yesterday morning and asked me about you. When I told you were a reporter, his face crumpled.' Violet's husky voice softened. 'Tommy told him all about you. Called you his guardian angel.' She dug around in her pocket. 'The night Tommy died, Damo took something from his jacket. Wanted something to remember him by.'

I knew what it was, even before Violet opened her hand. A badge, an orange cartoon bear with a heart on his white tummy.

My vision blurred with tears, but I smiled. 'Tenderheart Bear. Do you remember the Care Bears? Tommy and I used to watch the show as kids.' My hand shook as I took the badge from Violet and pressed its dulled edges into my palm. The whisky was starting to muddle my brain, and my words felt slow and treacly. 'I bought that badge with my pocket money. Gave it to Tommy and told him that no matter what happened, or what our parents told him, he was to remember he had a heart to end all hearts. And that would be enough to see him through.' An image of Tommy's solemn face as he wrapped his little hand around the bear punched me in the heart. 'Fucking hell.'

I leaped back from the table. I'd only just stumbled outside when I bent over and vomited an arc of hot brown liquid. It bounced off the pavement and splattered my shoes.

'Shit, Sophie, are you –'

I held up a shaky hand. Tears streamed down my face. 'I'm so fucking angry.' But my voice didn't sound angry. It sounded sad.

Violet handed me my coat and bag. 'Damo isn't to blame. Look, he's volunteering at a rehab centre in Dusseldorf for two weeks, but he told me he'd be happy to speak to you when he's back. You know what this means? Tommy wasn't looking for a way out. His death had nothing to do with you.'

'He was murdered, Violet,' I said flatly. 'Isn't that worse?'

'Depends on how you define worse. I'd take revenge over guilt any day. You're a reporter, ain't you? You must be able to figure out who was behind this.'

My phone rang in my pocket and I pulled it out. 'Yes?'

'Where are you?' Kate sounded breathless.

'Pimlico.'

'I'm at the police station. Liam's just been released. Durand is spitting. No one is supposed to know. I overheard them talking.'

I leaned against the wall and ran a sweaty palm across my forehead. 'Has he left yet?'

'He's ducking out the back door. There's a mob out front. I've never seen anything –'

My brain started to kick in. 'I'm nearer his place than you are. I'll go.'

I turned to Violet, opened my mouth to speak, to thank her, but couldn't form the words. Instead I pulled her into a fierce hug that made my eyes water.

*It's easy to disappear when you're a crime reporter.* I hit the Tube station steps hard and made the train with seconds to spare.

And, just like that, I vanished.

# 26

I took the steps up to Liam's flat two at a time and pressed my ear against his door. A curtain of marijuana drifted along the concrete corridor and my stomach heaved. I leaned over the railings, inhaling the sharp, night air. *Where the fuck is he?* Images cannonballed through my brain. Shadows creeping up on Tommy. Stifling his screams. Forcing a poisoned needle into his skinny arm.

I breathed out, turning the black air smoky-white. Pulling Tommy's Tenderheart badge out of my pocket, I kissed it. Then I unfastened the pin and jabbed it into my thumb. I didn't stop pushing until blood dribbled out. I dug my thumb in my mouth and sucked. The hot, metallic taste took me back to Lydia's bedroom. Fuck. *Something bad is going to happen.* I needed a clear head to see Liam. The whisky had lit the fuse on my anger. It was as if I'd been plugged into an electrical socket for too long. My mind was knife-sharp, invincible, cruel. My skin tingled. I wanted to hurt someone. Hurt someone else, to stop the hurt inside. *Something bad is going to happen.*

I gripped the icy railing and squeezed my eyes shut. I'd almost made my mind up to leave, when I spotted a cyclist pulling up to the curb. The figure dragged the bike into the lift and disappeared.

I shoved Tommy's badge into my pocket just as the lift doors slid open. Liam's eyes were on the ground and, for a moment, all I could hear was the gentle click-click-click of his bike wheels. I squared my shoulders and stuck my chin out, then changed my mind. Barefaced aggression wouldn't get me through his door.

I lowered my chin and peered up at Liam through my lashes. 'Welcome home.'

Liam looked up, stopped, frowned. 'You have got to be kidding me.' His skin was pale, with a veil of stubble that hadn't been there three days ago. Hooded eyes ringed with purple. Sunken cheeks that made his cheekbones jut out so far, they looked like elbows.

'Can I come in?'

'Why?'

'Because it's three degrees.'

Liam gave me a long look, patted the pockets of his jacket for his keys, then skated straight past me. He hesitated for a moment at his front door, then ducked inside. He wasn't inviting me in. As the door began to swing shut, I lurched towards it. 'Please.'

Liam heard my voice crack and his hand shot out to catch the door. 'What's wrong?'

'I just want to . . .' My voice rose high and shrill.

Liam frowned and moved towards me. 'Sophie?'

I felt the hot, wet threat of tears and dug my teeth into the inside of my cheek. I lurched backwards, away from Liam, away from the story. My swollen thumb throbbed in my pocket. Had

Tommy's arm swelled when the needle pierced his milky skin? How many seconds did he lie there knowing he was dying? Saliva pooled in my mouth. My jaw tingled. I knew what was coming. Clamping my hand over my face, I hurtled past Liam, into his flat. I bashed open the first door I came to, barely registering the blunt pain as my knees made contact with tiles. I crawled to the toilet and threw up. Pain seared behind my eyeballs. My stomach roiled. When I opened my eyes, Liam was holding out a glass of water. I took a sip. It tasted of boiled sweets.

Liam sat down on the side of the bath, picking at the cuff of his red-plaid shirt. He pushed his dark hair off his face. It curled over to one side like a breaking wave. 'That part of your pitch?'

I leaned my head against the cold porcelain. 'Well, you haven't told me to fuck off yet.'

'Give me a chance.'

I hauled myself up and looked in the mirror. The bruised skin under my eyes was dotted with red pinpricks. I ran my tongue over my teeth. 'Got any toothpaste?'

Liam chucked me a grey washbag, then left me to it. I brushed my teeth, then did my best to flatten my knotted hair. I took a deep breath and opened the door. As I shuffled along the hallway, floorboards, like shiny black piano keys, creaked beneath my shoes. I followed the sound of ice plinking against glass and found myself in a small sitting room that smelled of coffee and sandalwood. Shutters covered the long, low window. A wall of shelves was crammed with books; glossy photography bibles peppered with literature's heavyweights: Dickens, Joyce, Eliot. I paused by an enormous oak table, too large for the small room, and ran my hand along the grain. Through a gap in the door on my left I spotted a stainless-steel kitchen, with flagstone flooring and the same overpriced double-width cooker I had at home. 'This is really –'

'Not what you were expecting.' Liam hovered by the kitchen door, thumb hooked into his belt-loop. 'Yeah, I get that a lot. You sticking with water?' He gestured towards the tumbler of amber liquid in his hand.

'I'll have what you're having.' It was a bad idea, but I was in the mood for bad ideas.

Liam shrugged, and poured me a glass. Then he gestured for me to join him on the leather sofa. I perched on the opposite end and took a large slug. The whisky slid around my empty stomach, but the hit zipped me up, straightened my back, hardened my voice.

I glanced at the bike propped against the wall behind the sofa. 'What's with that?'

Liam swirled his drink around his glass and held it up to the light. 'Haven't driven a car for fifteen years. Not since I wrapped my car round a lamp post.'

'That wasn't very smart.'

A ghost of a smile. 'Spent three months in hospital. Came out like Robocop.' He patted his left leg.

I threw back another mouthful and stared at the blue neon light behind Liam's head that spelled out the words: *Rage against the dying of the light.* I drained my glass, then gave him a brittle smile. 'Got any more?'

'Haven't you had enough?'

I ignored him. Moved to the drinks cabinet and poured myself a large measure. 'Lived here long?'

Liam watched me closely, his brow furrowed. 'Since we moved from Manchester, when I was a kid. When my parents died I had enough cash to buy it from the council. I did it up a bit. My sisters think I'm crazy but I love it here. Happy memories.'

*Of course.* Liam's parents died in a plane crash shortly before we all went up to Oxford. The moon-eyed female population couldn't pass that particular trinket round without misting up at the thought of Liam and his cheekbones enduring so much suffering. The memory made me roll my eyes, which Liam obviously mistook for my reaction to his parents' death.

His face darkened. 'Are you going to tell me what's going on?'

'You first.'

'What do you want to know?'

'Tell me about Lydia.'

'I heard you found her body.'

'Must have just missed you.' I muttered it into my glass but could tell by the way Liam stiffened that he'd heard. 'I thought you were supposed to be lying low, working on your public image.' I set the glass down and slipped off my coat. 'What were you doing at Lydia's?'

'I've already told the police everything I know.'

'How gallant of you.'

Liam emptied his glass, then sauntered over to where I was standing to refill it. It was the closest we'd been since he kissed me. I stood my ground. The whisky was melting my insides. They felt fluid. My whole body felt dangerously untethered.

Liam paused, staring into his glass. For a second I thought he was going to close the gap, but he wandered over to the window and pulled open the shutters. The crescent moon hung in the night sky like a freshly shaped fingernail. Liam rolled his head round in circles. I could see the tension in his shoulders from here.

'If I tell you what happened, will you explain why you're acting like a lunatic tonight?' I nodded, not trusting myself to speak. 'I was in my studio all day Tuesday, working on my edit for a magazine. Alice interrupted me to ask if I'd seen Lydia's meltdown on Twitter.' He took a breath. 'I called Lydia straight away but she didn't answer. The video . . . she looked . . . I needed to get out of there, get some air. So I grabbed my coat and took off.'

'Where did you go?'

'I walked around for a while.'

'For how long?'

'An hour or so. I wasn't feeling particularly charitable towards Lydia after our fight on Monday night. But that video . . .' I pressed my thumb against the corner of the drinks cabinet, watching the back of Liam's head. 'I'd made up my mind to leave her alone. Me bowling up to her gaff would only feed the drama. That's what she wanted. But then,' Liam turned round to face me, 'she sent me a text.' He drew his mobile out of his pocket and held it out to me.

The text was sent at 3.58 p.m.

*I need to see you. I'm in trouble.*

'After that video, I was genuinely worried about her. I thought she might try something stupid. So I jumped on the Tube. Got to

Lydia's around five. The front door was open. There was a storm, and I wondered if the wind had somehow blown the door off the latch. I called out her name, but there was no sound. I . . .' Liam leaned his head back against the window and closed his eyes. 'I went upstairs and she was . . .'

I shuddered as the memory of Lydia's scored, sticky flesh flashed through my mind.

Liam's eyes snapped open. 'I've had two run-ins this week with the police. Lydia was . . . there was nothing I could do for her. I panicked. Fell down the stairs, nearly broke my neck trying to get out of there.'

I watched the torment play out on his face with a sense of detachment, clinking my fingernail against my glass. 'Innocent people don't run.'

Liam slammed his glass down on the window sill, his voice strained. 'Sometimes they do, duchess.'

For a moment, we stood on opposite sides of the room, like two repelling magnets. Was Liam telling the truth? I studied his face. The corners of his mouth tugged downwards, his eyes burned with emotion. He was unravelling in front of me. But was it part of the act? These murders were staged, brutal, violent. They required a steely stomach. David Sonoma's words rang through my head: *I don't think he's working alone.* The thought made me reach for my glass.

Liam gave me a cool look. 'I really think you should stop.'

'It irritates you when women don't do what you say.'

'What are you talking about?'

I waved the glass around; whisky dripped over the side. I licked it off my fingers. 'You're used to being in control. You don't like it when women defy you.'

Liam ran a hand through his hair, his face hardening. 'What the fuck is wrong with you tonight?'

The whisky was beginning to screw with my brain. I tried to order them. Natalia and Lydia were both scared of Liam. Why? What hold did he have over them? Was he involved in the Juliets?

'Did Lydia betray you? Or did you betray her?' I looked him in the eye. 'I know about Lydia's sex tape.'

Liam's hand closed tightly around his glass. 'How the fuck –'

'I've seen it. That gives you a pretty strong motive, right? You find out your girlfriend is cheating on you with other men. *For money.* You want revenge. Unless you were the one black-mailing her.'

'Blackmailing her?'

'The tape, you fuck. The blackmail tape.' When Liam still looked blank, I slapped my palm against my forehead. 'Do I really need to spell it out?' The alcohol started to knead the corners of my vision. My words were sticking to my mouth. 'That tape was insurance. To keep Lydia quiet. To keep her working.' The colour drained from Liam's face and he sank back against the window.

I arched an eyebrow. 'I take it you didn't know. How much *do* you know?'

Liam staggered over to the sofa. 'I knew Lydia was being paid for sex. I'd heard a rumour months ago but didn't believe it. Then Lydia saw me flirting with an assistant at Leo Brand's party. Took me to one side and told me that I was an arsehole, that she never loved me and that she ... well, that she'd been earning money all the way through our relationship. I couldn't believe it. I fled the party. But on the way home I saw red and went back to confront her.'

Liam raked his hands over his face. 'Lydia told me it was none of my business. Laughed at me, in fact. Told me I was weak for still caring. Then a package arrived for me on Monday. A USB stick. It was one thing her telling me, but seeing it. Jesus.' Liam's voice caught and I felt a brief surge of compassion for him. 'I sank a bottle of Scotch, then bombed round to her house. She refused to let me in. I was sorry I'd ever fallen for her. Yelled it out over and over. When I told Lydia I'd seen the tape, she opened the door.'

A memory rippled across the surface of my brain. Mrs Smythe's words: *He whispered something over and over. Something about a drape.* I'd assumed the word Mrs Smythe heard was *rape*. But could it have been *tape*?

'I knew Lydia was spiralling but I didn't realise quite how much. I was drunk enough to wonder if Lydia had sent me the tape herself.' He gave a thin laugh when he saw my expression. 'You don't know Lydia. It's the kind of sick game she played. For all I knew, she wanted me to see her with those men. But she swore she never sent me the tape. When I asked why she'd let herself be filmed, she lobbed a picture at my head; it was lucky I ducked. When the police arrived, Lydia begged me not to mention the tape, or anything about the sex ring. I figured she didn't need the press getting hold of it. And, well,' Liam drained his glass, 'I didn't want the world finding out Lydia had been cheating on me the whole time. So I agreed to stay quiet.'

I eyed him suspiciously. 'If you're telling the truth, why wouldn't she tell you about the blackmail? I mean, you'd seen the tape. Why hide it?'

'Fuck knows.' Liam covered his face with his hands. When he looked up it was as though every single torment he'd suffered the past week had taken a chisel and carved its mark into his face. 'So, Lydia really wanted out?'

I nodded. 'She wasn't the only one. Natalia too. And there are more.' Liam's jaw slid downwards. 'The sex ring films models doing sordid things, then when they want to stop, they blackmail them.'

'Fucking hell.' Liam pushed himself off the sofa and staggered towards the drinks cabinet. The decanter rattled against his glass. He took a slug, then wiped his mouth with the back of his hand. 'Is that why they were killed?'

I didn't answer. A thought shoved through my foggy brain. 'How come the police didn't ask you about the sex ring? They've known about it since this morning.'

Liam stared at me, then shrugged. 'Maybe they already know who's behind it.'

*Or maybe they're building a case against you.* I glanced towards the window and shivered.

Liam gave me an odd look. 'Sophie, what's wrong? You seem weird.'

He reached out and brushed my cheek. For a moment, the room spun.

I reeled backwards. 'That part of *your* pitch, Liam?'

'What the fuck –'

'I've listened to you all evening. You talk a good game, but the point I keep coming back to is this: Natalia and Lydia were scared of you.' I rocked from one foot to the other, as adrenaline and booze coursed through my veins. I felt like a firework that had shot up into the sky and was about to explode. 'Both were being blackmailed to keep quiet, both were spotted talking to the press, and both were murdered. I mean, humour me here.'

A muscle tightened in Liam's jaw but his gaze was steady. 'Do you think I'm guilty?'

'I think you're guilty of being a grade-A dick.' The comment was ridiculous. A snort escaped, then another. Suddenly I was laughing.

'What the fuck is wrong with you?'

'Everyone I talk to dies.' I wiped my eyes as laughter caught in my throat. 'You'd better watch yourself. Unless you're the killer, in which case I'm screwed.'

Liam gripped my shoulders, forcing me to look at him. 'What is going on?'

I could feel tears melting out the corner of my eyes. 'It hurts, doesn't it? When someone is taken from you. Did you love Lydia? Did you really love her?'

'Sophie, I –'

'And you couldn't save her. That blows. Of course, you could have killed Lydia, and Natalia, in which case you're a fucking liar and –'

Liam grabbed the back of my hair and pulled my face up towards his. 'Sophie, if you don't tell me what's going on, I'll –'

'Kill me? That what you said to the others?' Liam flinched and I laughed in his face. 'I found out tonight my brother was murdered. He overdosed three months ago. Except, he didn't overdose. He was killed.'

'What?'

I shook my head, tried to wrench myself away, but Liam wouldn't let go. 'Get the fuck away from me.' I slammed into his chest, catching him by surprise. He dropped his hands and took a step back. The air thickened and pulsed and matched the throbbing between my legs.

It hit me like a falling axe. I charged at Liam, shoved him onto the sofa. Straddled him. Slid my tongue across his. Liam pulled back and looked up at me with eyes, large and blue, pools of ink. 'Sophie, wait –'

But I couldn't wait. The images were coming thick and fast. Ripped skin. Mottled throats. Glassy eyes. Sharp things: scissors, thorns, needles. I squeezed my eyes shut, slammed my mouth into his. Stubble clawed at my chin. My lips burned, but I pushed harder. My hands were on Liam's shirt, his chest, his belt. When he didn't respond, I ripped open my blouse, yanked down my bra and pressed his hands against me. Liam buried his head in my neck and I heard a moan. Then he was tearing at my clothes, flipping me underneath him. He groped around for my knickers, but I batted his hand away, snapped the fabric to one side.

His breath was hot on my face. 'Are you sure you –'

I wrapped one hand round the back of his head, moved the other down my body to where he was hesitating, guided him in.

Natalia, Lydia, Tommy. The images slackened, slowed, stopped. And then there was nothing.

I kissed the tattoo on Liam's wrist and swung myself up to sitting, peeling my body away from the leather sofa. I felt Liam's eyes on me. The air around us smelled dark, wet, like a cave. I reached across Liam, grabbed his glass and took a swig. He pulled me towards him, licking the whisky from my lips. I fumbled with my bra strap, staring down at the floor. The brazenness leaked out of me, along with the stickiness between my legs. My eyes landed on a photograph of Liam and Lydia at a red-carpet event. Lydia's silver dress fell in pools of iridescent light at her feet. Behind her, Liam, in a navy suit, glared at the camera.

'Where was that taken?'

'Last year's Met Ball.' A shudder ran through me as Liam's lips brushed my neck. 'Your skin smells of honey.' He dug his teeth into my bare shoulder and my eyes fluttered closed. 'Your brother. I'm sorry. What happened?'

I tried to stand, but Liam pulled me back down.

'I need to go.'

'*She flees from me, that sometime did me seek, With naked foot, stalking in my chamber.*'

'What's that supposed to mean?'

'It wouldn't be the first time you've fucked me and run.' I gave a thin laugh and Liam leaned back against the sofa. 'So, it's OK when you're the one asking questions.'

I wrapped my blouse around me. 'That's my job.'

'Is sleeping with me part of the job too?'

My hand made contact with his face before I could stop myself. Liam shoved me to one side and stood up. Buckled his jeans. Padded into the kitchen. I heard the coffee machine spurt and bubble.

He returned with two mugs and sat down beside me. 'You're so tightly wound, Sophie. You always were.' My hand shook as I lifted the mug to my mouth. Liam's voice dropped to a whisper. 'I know why you left, that night in Oxford. You had no faith in me. You still don't.'

'You're pissed at me because I didn't stick around to get dumped?'

'I'm pissed because you never gave me a chance.'

The coffee chased all the lightness away and I felt clumsy and irritable. 'You'd better watch your back, Liam.'

'I'd rather watch yours.' He ran a finger across my shoulders, sending tingles all the way through me.

I pushed him away. 'I'm serious, you fuck. They're building a case against you. Just because you've been released . . .'

Liam crossed one leg over the other and sighed. 'You know what they think? That Lydia was my intended victim and I killed Natalia first to make it look as though it was a serial killer. They even think I sent that text to myself from Lydia's phone. Eat your heart out, Fred West.'

I turned to face Liam just as he adjusted his smile. I shivered and slipped away from him. 'I really do have to go.'

I was slipping on my shoes when Liam came up behind me. He stopped inches away, as if there was an invisible force field between us. 'The sex ring. You're not running the story, are you?'

I sighed, but didn't turn round. 'What do you think?'

Liam pressed himself against me. 'It will blow her reputation out of the water.'

I spun round to face him. 'Keeping it secret is letting them win. It's letting her killer win. Nothing can bring Lydia back, but we can show the world the choices she had to make. And anyway,' I fell back on every reporter's most hackneyed explanation, 'the story might encourage other victims to come forward.'

Liam gave me a cool look, then drifted over to the oak table and grabbed his phone. 'I'm calling you a cab.'

Five minutes later, Liam walked me to the front door. When he bent down to kiss me goodbye, his lashes felt like tiny spiders crawling on my cheek.

## 27

A loud thumping noise pulled me out of the cloudy seconds between sleeping and waking, and I crashed to the surface. It was a few seconds before I twigged the thumping noise was my pulse. I lay there waiting for my heart rate to slow, but it didn't. I forced myself into the shower. Hot water flooded the soreness between my legs. My cheeks burned with memory. I yanked the temperature dial round to cold and let the icy water wash me clean.

*Tommy was murdered.* Three small words that filled my head with noise. I sat down on the bath and let the words swirl around me, curious to know where they'd take me. Violet was right. As twisted as it sounded, I did feel a sense of relief knowing that Tommy hadn't chosen to die.

I got dressed, bolted down a bowl of cereal, then switched on the news. The acid colours and shrill voices sharpened my hangover, so I turned it off. The Juliets story still hadn't run, which meant Rowley wasn't confident it was watertight. I reached for my phone to update Kate about the two-killer bombshell and spotted a text from Melissa. *Hi, Sophie! Found diary! Man who turned up at Mands' house was called Bairstow. John Bairstow. Melissa (W-C)*

I chucked my bowl in the sink and wandered through to my office.

I searched for John Bairstow online, but nothing obvious came up. On a hunch, I called Detective Inspector Rob Birch. Rob was short and wiry, with black hair and a grin that belonged on a more handsome face. We first met face down on a pavement in Hackney, following an explosion in a block of flats that catapulted us fifteen feet into the air. I fractured my wrist but considered it a small price to pay for an intro to a decent inside source.

Rob didn't ask why I was searching for John Bairstow, and I didn't tell him. It took less than a minute for him to find a match.

'Yeah, there's a John Bairstow who was convicted of rape in March 1988. Served four years at HMP Liverpool.' Adrenaline rocketed through my veins. 'Looks like the victim was seventeen-year-old Ariel Butters from Kent, but before you ask, no, I can't give out her details.'

I thanked Rob and hung up. A quick search on the electoral roll gave me her address in Edenbridge.

Forty-five minutes later I was sitting in a South West train carriage that stank of burgers and BO. As the train slipped out of Victoria Station, my phone pinged with an email from DI Weatherly. I whipped open my laptop and clicked on the attachment. He hadn't just scanned his notes, he'd included local newspaper cuttings, statements, post-mortem photos and crime-scene photos. I slurped my muddy tea and opened the crime-scene photos.

Amanda Barnes was on her stomach, her head and shoulders hidden under a thick hedgerow. Her feet were bare; her pink trainers lay next to her. Amanda's polka-dot nightdress had ridden up above her hips. The next photo cropped into her hands, half buried in the leaves.

I bit down on the polystyrene cup and moved on to the post-mortem photographs. The hedgerow had sliced Amanda's face to ribbons and one eye was half closed in a lazy wink. Her throat was dotted with red marks, like smears of strawberry jam. The detail shots showed faded bruises around her wrists, cigarette burns on her breasts, her shoulders, her neck. The report stated cause of death was asphyxiation. Traces of Preludin were found in her system, but friends stated Amanda was taking it to lose weight.

I scrolled through the rest of the case files. Pages and pages of statements: Amanda's distraught mother, Clare; Melissa Wakefield-Channing and three other schoolfriends testified to Michael Farrow's obsession with his stepdaughter and the change in Amanda's behaviour. There was a statement from the last teacher to see Amanda alive and from the jogger who discovered Amanda's body.

Then there were photographs of the evidence collected. Michael Farrow's white Nike trainers caked with mud. A small brown envelope containing pictures of Amanda at different ages, all with her face scratched out. The caption read: *exhibit H found under floorboards in suspect's bedroom*. Next to it, scribbled in red pen were the words: *scratches on A's face linked to scratched photos?* At one stage, Weatherly had entertained the theory that Amanda's cuts weren't accidental. Nowhere in the report was there any mention of John Bairstow.

As the train pulled into Redhill Station my phone rang. 'Yes?'

'What happened with Liam?' Mack's voice rumbled down the phone.

My cheeks flared. 'What do you mean?'

'Did you get a quote?'

'I . . . I thought I was dealing with Kate on this.'

'Kate's busy. Did you get Liam on board or not?'

I rested my head against the window as the train jerked forward. When I slapped Mack round the face, I didn't actually think I'd have to work with him again. 'He wouldn't go on the record.'

The conductor's tinny voice came over the tannoy, announcing the next station. 'Where the hell are you?' I filled Mack in with all the energy of a flat Coke, knowing he wouldn't go for it. 'What's this got to do with the Juliets?'

I opened my mouth to make up some bullshit, to buy myself time, but what was the point? 'Possibly nothing. I don't know yet.'

'Kent, we're up to our eyes in this story. Rahid is drawing a blank with the pixellated perverts on that tape, and no hotel employees are talking. We need more evidence or Legal won't let us run the story.'

I glimpsed a flash of white as the train sailed through frost-covered fields, and felt myself grow heavy with doubt. 'I have a hunch, Mack. There are too many coincidences.'

'Amanda's killer committed suicide. It's a dead end. But what would I know, I'm the idiot who couldn't break a story if it landed on my dick, right?'

'Mack –'

'Don't you think you should be doing as you're told, given your latest fuck-up? Whatever Rowley told you, I still run this team . . .'

I tuned him out and scrolled back through the crime-scene photos. Amanda's slim feet, the leaves caught on her nightdress, the tiny white buds on the branches of the hedgerow. I zoomed into the photograph. White flowers, black jagged branches, long dark thorns. My breath caught in my throat.

Amanda Barnes was hidden under a blackthorn tree.

The taxi wound its way through identikit streets that were named after Shakespearean characters: Ophelia Drive, Hamlet Close, Viola Crescent. The developer must have hoped they would lend grandeur to the housing estate, but it still resembled a cheap film set.

Number 10 Oberon Way stood at the end of a deserted cul-de-sac. A plain two-up, two-down with a fuzz of lawn and a wind chime hanging over the front door. I told the taxi to wait, then rang the doorbell – a synthesised Big Ben chime – and rehearsed my pitch. A curtain twitched, then the door swung open, revealing an overweight woman in stonewashed jeans and a shapeless grey shirt, clutching a phone to her chest. A pretty face that was on the turn. Large hazel eyes marred by bags; a jawline that was heading south and straggly blonde hair that had long grown past its happy length.

'Are you Ariel Butters?'

She chewed her lip, smearing pearly pink lipstick across her teeth. 'Who wants to know?'

'My name is Sophie Kent. I'm a reporter with *The London Herald*. I want to ask a few questions about John Bairstow.'

Ariel frowned and the deep lines almost split her brow in two. She lowered her voice into the phone. 'Rach, I'm going to have to call you back.'

I followed her into the kitchen and noticed her surreptitiously wipe off her lipstick with her palm. A lemony smell in the air. A scatter of voices from the retro radio in the corner. A mop languishing against the fridge.

'Ignore the floor. I've got to start again.' She gestured with a bloated hand towards a trail of small, black footprints. 'Bloody cat.'

Ariel's shoes clacked across the kitchen floor. I was startled to see she was wearing fluffy marabou heels. A shoe that screams peroxide curls, fast glamour and vintage Hollywood. She caught me staring and kicked them off, where they settled like pink clouds on the wet linoleum.

She didn't invite me to sit, but I did anyway. I wanted to make it harder for her to throw me out. 'Thanks for seeing me. I'm –'

'Look, I only invited you in because my neighbour is a nosy cow and I didn't want to say this on the doorstep. I can't tell you anything about John Bairstow. That part of my life is over.' She thumped down onto the chair opposite and folded her arms.

'I understand it must be difficult.'

'No, you don't.' No malice, no rudeness, just telling it like it is. 'Sorry, but you have to go. My boys will be home from school soon.'

I spotted a framed photograph of Ariel with a bearded man and two teenage boys, who'd inherited their mum's overbite. 'Handsome kids. They giving the girls grief yet?'

A ghost of a smile. 'And then some. I can't keep up with their love lives. You got kids?'

I shook my head. 'No, but I had a teenage brother once.'

'Then you know. Boys. They're a different species.'

The smile caught on my lips. Tommy never broke any hearts, unless you count mine.

'That photo was taken on our Canary Island cruise last month.' Ariel's voice was soft and low with an Estuary twang. 'Rained the whole week. Two thousand depressed tourists bobbing about in a sardine tin. Wasn't my idea of fun but Miles thought it would be good for . . .' She sighed heavily.

My bag was on my lap, my hand inside ready to pull out my tape recorder. I let it go. 'Ariel, I just need two minutes of your time. Please, hear me out.'

She rubbed her lower lip with a finger, erasing more traces of lipstick. It was the only make-up she'd been wearing and, without it, her face looked bare and hard. 'There's no point. Nothing you can say will make me talk.'

The hunch in Ariel's shoulders, the way she avoided my eye, reminded me of Natalia. A subconscious effort to take up as little room as possible. Common in rape victims. Even victims who'd been raped decades ago, apparently.

'Where did you say you worked again?'

'*The London Herald*.'

'Your name . . . it's familiar. Wait, it's coming back to me. I saw you on telly. You found Lydia Lawson.' I didn't speak; let her piece it together. 'Hang on, that's not why you're here, is it? Did he have something to do with . . .' Ariel scratched her eyebrow. Her hand was trembling.

*It's a dead end.* Mack's words gnawed at my nerves. I had to prove him wrong. But bolshie wouldn't get Ariel to open up. I leaned in and softened my voice.

'Honestly? I don't know if John Bairstow is involved. I'm chasing a lead. It could be nothing but . . .' I shrugged, and clasped my hands in my lap, waiting for her move.

Ariel fiddled with her collar and stared up at the vintage print that was tacked to the wall above the table. A signpost that said *Rat race* one way and *Beach* the other. I resisted the urge to speak, to push, to do anything other than show I was a sympathetic listener with time on my hands.

Suddenly Ariel jumped up and dragged a stool over towards the cupboards. She clambered up, reached on top of the cupboard, then hopped down clutching a pack of Marlboro Lights.

'I don't smoke but . . .' She lit a cigarette and opened the back door, shooing the smoke outside. 'Miles'll kill me if he smells it. We're giving up together. Last time he cracked first and I gave him hell.'

I smiled. 'Take your time.'

'My therapist warned me about this. Told me the past is never buried. It'll revisit me in many forms. I didn't think she meant a reporter. I had years of therapy. Some of it even helped. Not as much as Miles did. When he came along, a year after . . . it happened, I grabbed onto him with both hands.'

I pulled my coat around me. Ariel, in her bare feet, didn't seem to notice the icy draught. 'How did you two meet?'

'In a bar. Not exactly fairytale stuff, but, well, it was a fairytale to me. I was in a bad way, but he saved me.' Ariel took a long drag, then exhaled the smoke out of the back door, where the wind blasted it straight back in. Unless Miles was an idiot, Ariel's secret wouldn't be safe for long. 'Did everything I could to make myself as ugly as possible. Which took some doing.' A shy smile. 'You should have seen me back then. I know you shouldn't toot your own horn but . . . Here.' Ariel opened a drawer behind her and handed me a tatty red photo album.

I flicked through pages torn from magazines and catalogues, barely recognising the face staring out at me. It was crafted from sunlight; a golden fringe, mocha skin and kitten-round eyes speckled gold. It was a moment before I properly registered what I was looking at, and I kept my voice neutral.

'You were a model?'

'*Just Seventeen* called me the new Bridget Bardot. Bet you'd never guess that was me.' I opened my mouth to object but Ariel waved her cigarette around, wafting more smoke into the kitchen. 'I chose a different path. My looks brought me nothing but trouble. When Miles came along I hitched a ride out of that world. Focused on building a family. To tell the truth, it was a relief. Not caring what I looked like. Every pound I gained, the stronger I became. Said goodbye to the weak girl I once was, the one who allowed herself to . . .' She stared down at the ground, chewed her fingernail. Then she turned her face towards me, raised her chin. 'Miles gets it. Says I'm beautiful anyway. Even without all the pretty. Who needs it, right?'

My eyes flicked towards her marabou heels, then to the pearly smudge above her top lip. Ariel still indulged in pretty, but only when she thought no one else could see. The thought made my insides tight with anger.

'You weren't weak.'

'Sorry?'

'Back then. You stood up for yourself. You sent a guilty man to jail.' Ariel, leaning on the door frame, flinched, but didn't look away. 'You put your neck on the line; you reported the attack, and, let's face it, not many women get that far. Then you went public, endured a trial; you succeeded. So, no, you weren't weak. I'd say you were pretty heroic.'

Ariel stubbed her cigarette out on the doorstep and hid the evidence in the outdoor bin. Then she padded over to the counter, put the kettle on and switched off the radio. Without the noise, the air felt charged, electric. The way it always does when a source is about to turn.

'What exactly do you want to know?'

Heart thumping, I reached into my bag and pulled out the tape recorder. 'The sex offender I'm looking for is a very specific type. The more detail I have, the better. Can you tell me where it happened?'

Ariel was facing the wall. I heard her exhale slowly. 'A catalogue shoot in Chislehurst.'

'John was on the shoot?'

'He was the photographer. Tall and bald. Round glasses. You know, the Harry Potter kind.' Ariel shoved a hand into her pocket. 'I'd only been modelling for a few months and was nervous. John was nice; told me he'd chosen me personally because he knew I had something special. When I was done, he suggested I hang at the house until it was time to catch my train. Said he wanted to teach me about lighting and angles.'

Ariel grabbed two mugs and dumped a heap of sugar into hers. 'For a while we just talked. I was flattered he took an interest. Then he told me the natural light was better upstairs.'

I left space for Ariel to continue, but a taut silence stretched through the room. The kettle boiled, but she didn't move.

I took all the emotion out of my voice for the next question. It was important to pull Ariel back from the edge. 'The man I'm looking for . . . the evidence shows he struggles to perform sexually. He has to be creative during his attacks. Does this sound like John Bairstow to you?'

Ariel closed her eyes. A hint of a nod. This time I waited.

'At first I fought back. He wasn't overly strong. But he clamped a pillow over my face. I thought I was going to suffocate. I won't forget the pain. He used a bottle, then he . . . he finished himself off all over me. I lay there, frozen, as he buckled up his belt. Before he left, he told me he'd filmed the whole thing. Said he'd edit it in a way that made me look as if I was gagging for it. He'd send the tape to my boyfriend.'

Ariel opened her eyes and gazed over my head. 'I felt sure my mum would notice. I couldn't sit down for two days. It took me three to confess. Mum marched me straight to the police station. I'd stashed my clothes at the bottom of my laundry basket so there was plenty of evidence and the bruising on my, you know, proved it was rape. I felt disgusting. He told me

I was nothing. Over and over, during the attack. And you know what? He was right.'

Eva's attacker had said the same thing.

I shifted forward in my chair. 'Do you know what happened to John? After prison, I mean.'

'I tried to move on with my life. Never looked back.' The corners of her mouth dropped. 'Well, almost never.'

She walked me to the door, her face tight and worn, and held out a cold hand. 'He was confident, had a certain way about him. That's why I didn't see it coming. I never doubted there were others. He was too good.'

I nodded and pushed my card into her hand. Then I charged towards the waiting taxi, the wind chime tinkling behind me.

## 28

I hopped off the Tube at Embankment Station. I needed to clear my head. John Bairstow had filmed himself sexually assaulting a model, then tried to blackmail her with the evidence. That definitely sounded like the sort of pervert who could go on to set up the Juliets. Then there was the fact he showed up at Amanda's house the week before she died. And the fact Amanda was hidden under a blackthorn tree. With each step, I became surer of myself. I pulled out my phone and texted Rowley: *Big developments, we need to talk.*

The sun was dipping behind the city horizon, turning the sky into a patchwork of pinks. It was one of those miraculous February sunsets that comes out of nowhere, providing sustenance to winter-weary souls. By the time I reached Lambeth Bridge, fire had burned to coal and the spectacle was over. I trudged up Vauxhall Bridge Road, lost in thought, when my phone rang.

'Soph, we're running a theory this end.' Kate sounded breathless. 'We've been through the shots of Leo Brand's party at The Rose and can track Lydia's movements through the pictures. But there's a hole. After she fights with Liam, she disappears.'

I frowned. 'Yeah, she went to DreamBox with Amos.'

'No, before that, because she reappears in the photos again later on. She argues with Liam, when he returns to the hotel, then she goes AWOL for at least an hour.'

'What are you thinking?'

'What if she was working the night of the party? What if she vanished upstairs to meet a client? It's a long shot because she's not on hotel CCTV as far as we can tell –'

'But if she was working for the Juliets that night, they'd know how to sneak her upstairs without being seen.'

I stood on the street corner as the traffic belted past me. Could that be why Liam went back to confront Lydia? He was trying to stop her from meeting a client. And when his pleas fell on deaf ears, he stormed off into the night. Behind me, a lorry driver leaned on his horn and I jumped.

'I wonder if she was filmed. Someone would have needed to set up a camera in the room beforehand, then take it down again.'

Out of nowhere, Sasha's voice filled my head. *I was distracted. Dmitri was behind him, with a rucksack.*

'What are you thinking? Inside help?'

'I'll ring you back.'

I tore towards Pimlico Station, almost knocking a woman into the path of a bus. Yelling out my apologies, I raced underground.

I found him in the alleyway behind the hotel, smoking a cigarette. 'Your colleague said you'd be here.'

Dmitri frowned and blew out a twist of smoke. 'You again.'

I pulled out my notebook with ice-cold hands. 'I need to ask you a couple more questions.'

'I already told police everything I know.'

'Not everything.'

A thin smile stretched across Dmitri's pale face, a knife-mark in uncooked pastry. 'I was with Sadie Long, remember? I couldn't have killed Natalia.'

'You weren't with Sadie that whole time, were you?' Dmitri flicked his cigarette butt onto the ground and gave me a cool look. 'Does the name the Juliets mean anything to you?'

Dmitri stuck his chin out and jammed his hands in his pockets.

'It's a high-class escort service operating out of London's top hotels. Only, it's not just an escort service, the person in charge is blackmailing the women. Secretly filming them and threatening to expose them if they ever try to leave.' Dmitri flicked his finger against the wall. 'My bet is this person would have needed inside help. I've been thinking about your movements that night. About how Sasha saw you on the backstairs that evening carrying a bag. Sadie confirmed you were with her until 11 p.m., which would have given you fifteen minutes to make a quick pit stop. If I take this to my contact at the Met, I bet CCTV footage from that day will show you taking that rucksack into a guest room.'

Dmitri's lip curled and he pushed himself off the wall. 'You can't prove what was in that bag.' He started to walk away and I grabbed his arm. 'I wouldn't do that if I were you.'

Dmitri raised his eyebrows. 'And why not?'

'Your papers are good forgeries, I'll give you that.' Dmitri froze. 'You know how long it would take for me to alert Immigration? You'd be deported. As well as being charged for aiding and abetting a criminal.' Dmitri's shoulders tensed, but he didn't turn round. 'The man I'm looking for isn't just blackmailing these women. I think he's a killer.'

Dmitri froze. When he turned round, the light had gone from his eyes. He sagged against the wall. 'I didn't know about the blackmail.'

'What happened?'

Dmitri pulled a cigarette out of his pocket and lit it. 'He called me six months ago. Said he needed help. All I had to do was rig up the video camera, then take it down the next morning and leave it in a safety-deposit box. I'd get a cut of the fee. Made a few hundred quid each time. It was enough to supplement the shit I'm paid here.' He took another drag and stamped his feet.

'And you did it the night Natalia was killed?'

Dmitri nodded. 'He wanted to film Lydia Lawson.'

'I need a name.'

'He never told me his name.'

I pulled out my phone. 'You've got five seconds before I'm calling Immigration.'

'I'm sorry. I had no idea it would go that far. When Natalia was killed, I wondered if it was him. I was too scared to say anything. But,' Dmitri inhaled deeply, eyes on the phone, 'I thought if the press knew, they could dig around.'

I stared at him. 'You sent me the text the morning after she died?'

'I didn't think you'd be on my case so much. Turns out I picked the wrong reporter.' He laughed thinly. 'I'm telling the truth. I don't know his name. But I spotted him once, picking the camera up. And he was at that fashion party the night Natalia was killed.'

A blonde head poked round the wall. 'Dmitri? Where have you been? Front desk is overrun.'

I leaned in close and put my hand on his arm. 'What does he look like?'

Dmitri glanced down at my arm. 'I'm better off taking my chances with Immigration.' He flicked his cigarette onto the ground and sauntered away.

I slammed my hand against the wall in frustration, just as my phone beeped. It was a text from Rowley. *Get here as quick as you can. – R*

I strode across the newsroom, shaking off people's stares.

Kate launched into a tuneless rendition of 'I Will Survive' when she saw me.

'Shut up, you idiot.' I grinned, slipping off my coat.

'Seriously, what's your secret?'

I shrugged. 'Don't take no for an answer.'

Kate pretended to scribble it down on a Post-it note. '*Don't take no for an answer.*' She gave me a quick once-over, her hazel eyes narrowing. 'You look a damn sight better than the last time I saw you.'

'You mean the crippled-drowned-rat look wasn't working for me?'

Kate grabbed her notebook. 'Growler's waiting.'

We stopped outside Rowley's door and Kate tucked a corner of her creased blouse into her skirt. 'Right, *let's get this party started.*'

We filed through the door, and I took a deep breath, feeling suddenly unsure of myself. Cheryl was fussing over Rowley's desk, setting down a cafetière, clearing a pile of newspapers, straightening his mouse mat. Rowley waved her away with a small hand and gave me a curt nod.

'Philip.' I looked him in the eye, then sat down beside Mack. On a normal afternoon, when most of the newsroom had slung their jackets over chairbacks, Mack's suit was immaculate. But today his shirt was half untucked and he wasn't wearing a tie. When I sat down beside him, he leaned back, crossing an ankle over his knee, a scowl on his face.

Rowley poured coffee into his *London Herald* mug and looked at me. 'You said there were developments.'

I took a quick breath. I had one shot at this and I didn't want to screw it up. 'I don't think this murder case begins with Natalia Kotov. I think it begins twenty years ago, with the murder of a sixteen-year-old model called Amanda Barnes.' I waited for a flicker of recognition to appear on Rowley's face, but nothing happened. So, Mack hadn't bothered to fill him in on my theory. 'Amanda was strangled in a wooded area two miles away from her home in February 1994.' I held up a photograph of Amanda and passed it to Rowley. 'Remind you of anyone?' Rowley's steel-grey eyes widened a fraction. 'Amanda was killed by her stepfather, Michael Farrow, who committed suicide in custody. So far, a dead end, right?' I sneaked a defiant look at Mack, but he looked away.

'But, get this, a week before Amanda died, a convicted rapist called John Bairstow was seen at her house. This morning I interviewed his victim, Ariel Butters. She told me he filmed the attack and tried to blackmail her. She also said that while John was raping her, he said the phrase *you are nothing* over and over. Another source who is involved in the Juliets told me that she was raped by the man in charge and he used that exact phrase.'

Mack coughed loudly, then held his hands up in mock apology. I ignored him and focused on Rowley. 'An ex-copper who worked the Amanda Barnes case told me there was DNA evidence of a second abuser, but the sample was never identified. There's a fighting chance it belonged to John Bairstow.'

Rowley tapped his pen on the edge of the desk. 'Where's John Bairstow now?'

I leaned back in my chair. 'That's the question. Police have no forwarding information for him, he's ex-directory and there's no evidence he changed his name.'

'It's a bit of a stretch, isn't it?' Mack's voice was calm but the tightness around his eyes told me he was holding back in front of Rowley.

I gave him a cool look. 'You don't think it's worth investigating? Two models who look like Amanda are sexually abused and strangled exactly twenty years later. Natalia and Lydia both had their hair cut off into the style Amanda sported when she was murdered.' I opened my laptop and slid it across Rowley's desk. 'This is a post-mortem photograph of Amanda. Look at her face. Bad shape, right? Natalia and Lydia's faces were also slashed to pieces. I think the killer is re-enacting Amanda's murder.' I paused, gauging their expressions, not wanting to show all my cards at once.

'Wouldn't the police have already looked into Amanda Barnes?' Kate sounded apologetic. 'I mean, if you found the similarities between –'

'I was lucky. I doubt the similarities would show up on the Police National Computer.' I clicked on another attachment and swung my computer round to face them, ready to play my trump card. 'We know Natalia and Lydia were both sexually assaulted with a blackthorn branch. Check out this crime-scene photograph from 1994. See where Amanda's hidden? That's a blackthorn tree. Those thorns caused the lacerations on her face.' Rowley and Kate were leaning forward in their chairs; even Mack looked interested. 'The blackthorn tree wasn't mentioned in the press. So the only people who knew about it were Michael Farrow, the police, someone Michael told, or someone who saw him kill Amanda. Michael is dead, so unless someone on the police force has switched sides, it's got to be one of the last two. I think Michael and John were friends and they both abused Amanda as part of a sordid sex game. If we find John Bairstow, my bet is we find the man behind the Juliets, and our serial killer.'

Rowley sipped his coffee thoughtfully. 'What's his motive?'

'He gets wind that two of the models are talking to the press and decides to silence them. When he does it, he imitates Amanda's murder. It's what he's fantasised about all these years.'

'And by some coincidence the two models who were spotted talking to you just happened to look like Amanda. Give me a break.' Mack had a point.

'There is another option.' Kate rested her forearms on Rowley's desk. 'Police got the wrong man. Michael Farrow didn't kill Amanda. Maybe this Bairstow guy killed her.'

I pushed my hair behind my ear and nodded. 'The thought's crossed my mind, but the evidence against Farrow was irrefutable. His semen was all over Amanda's clothes and the footprints found around her body matched his shoes. Plus, there are loads of state-ments from friends talking about how obsessed he was with his stepdaughter. He was a nutter. He abused Amanda's mum, then made her watch him kill Amanda.'

Kate whistled. 'Where's the mum now?'

'I'm working on it.'

Rowley paused, then steepled his fingers together. 'Let's talk about the holes.'

I sighed. 'Well, motive, clearly. I'd always assumed Natalia and Lydia were killed because they talked to the press. But once you factor in Amanda Barnes . . .' I shrugged. 'And then there's the second person. Both the coroner and my Juliets source think another person is involved, but I have no idea who, or why, unless it's just another crony who joins in for the ride. The stakes are raised each time, hence the escalating violence. But my biggest hole is the twenty-year gap. If the killings are linked to Amanda, why wait two decades to murder again?'

Rowley poured more coffee and nursed the mug between his hands. 'What leads have you got on John Bairstow?'

I explained what Dmitri had told me. Kate was doodling on her pad, but she looked up.

'Did he give you a name?'

'No, but it all ties in with your theory on Lydia. I think Liam Crawford found out what Lydia was about to do, which is why he went back to the hotel to confront her.'

Rowley cleared his throat. 'Am I the only one who can see what's right in front of us?' We all looked at him, perplexed. 'What if Liam wasn't stopping Lydia? What if he was forcing her to go through with it?' There was a pause. Rowley pushed his mug to one side, leaning forward in his chair. 'Look, Liam knew Lydia was a prostitute. He admitted that to you, Sophie. He told you someone sent him Lydia's sex tape anonymously, but he could have lied about that. Once he realised you were on to the Juliets he had to change his story.'

I breathed slowly, forcing my voice to stay calm. 'But Liam would have been twelve when Amanda was killed. He couldn't be linked to her.'

'Couldn't he? Where did he grow up? Plenty of kids witness traumatic things that stay with them. Or even if he isn't directly linked to Amanda, isn't it possible that Liam is the second person? You said yourself that Natalia and Lydia were scared of Liam. Plus his alibis have always been suspect, and he knew both victims. Let me tell you, I've been doing this a long time, and often the most straightforward theory is the right one.'

I looked out of the window at the expanse of Hyde Park. The oak trees stood silent and still, like vast timber towers. 'If Liam's involved, why has he been released?'

'There's a thing called evidence, Kent.' Mack's voice cut straight through me. 'Perhaps they don't have enough to charge Liam yet.'

I thought back to my conversation with Durand. Forensics had lifted a print off the scissors. Surely if it matched Liam's, he would be in custody.

Kate swivelled round to face me, frowning. 'How did Liam seem last night?'

I dug my nails into my palms. 'He was upset when he found out Lydia was being blackmailed.'

'Or was he upset you found out Lydia was being blackmailed?' asked Rowley.

I stared down at the nail marks on my hand.

Rowley cleared his throat. 'OK, here's what we're going to do. The Amanda Barnes link is compelling, I grant you. But it needs more digging. Right now, my concern is that we're going to lose our Juliets exclusive. According to Rahid, one of the hotel employees let slip that another paper asked him the same questions. So, do we have enough to run it?'

Kate flipped through her notebook. 'We have Sophie's source on record giving us background colour to the Juliets. This source ties the sex ring to Lydia and Natalia. We've seen the sex tape ourselves. Rahid has got quotes from two hotel employees who suspect their guest rooms were used for such activity, and Jasdeep is looking into whether the sex tapes have appeared online.'

Rowley slammed his hand on the table, his eyes shining with adrenaline and caffeine. 'I want this pulled together by seven. That will give the lawyers one last chance to look over it before we go to press.'

I looked up, startled. 'For tomorrow's edition? But it's Lydia's funeral.'

Mack stretched his arms over his head and yawned. 'Didn't you hear what our esteemed editor said? We're going to lose the exclusive.'

I looked desperately at Kate. 'We're breaking the story that Lydia was a prostitute the day she's buried?'

Kate shrugged and stared down at her notepad.

Rowley pushed up his shirtsleeves. 'Sophie, keep tracking John Bairstow and see what turns up. But the Juliets copy is the priority. Flesh the story out with Kate. Let's see where we are in an hour.'

We trooped out into the corridor and Mack pushed past me. Kate opened her mouth to say something, but I dodged her and ran after Mack.

'Why didn't you tell Rowley about Amanda Barnes?'

'I didn't have a chance. I was busy. We're all fucking busy. We're a reporter down, remember?'

'Well, whose fault is that?'

Mack clenched his jaw and I braced myself for the verbal punch. Instead, he leaned heavily against the wall. 'She left me, Kent. Rachel fucking left me.'

'What?'

'She found the text messages I sent you. The other day . . . in the lift. She'd just called. She's taken the kids to her parents. I've fucked everything up.' Mack's voice wavered and he rubbed his eyes with the heels of his hands.

I reached out to put a hand on his arm, but stopped myself. I didn't know who was watching. 'I don't know what to say.'

'I never meant for you to lose your job. I thought you'd just get a warning,' he finished lamely.

'Does Rowley know?'

'He knows Rachel's gone, but not why.' When Mack finally looked at me, his eyes were wet and pink and full of sadness. 'So much for the happy-ever-after.'

By the time Rowley was happy with the copy and pictures, it was pitch-black and too late to think about dinner. Not that I could have stomached food anyway. Mack's news had affected me more than I was letting on. I'd spent the past twenty-four hours wishing all sorts of horrors on him. Now that justice had been served, why did I feel so sad? I sighed, turning my thoughts to the other Bad Choice in my life: Liam Crawford. I couldn't shake Rowley's theory. Could Liam have been lying to me this whole time? My fingers itched; I couldn't settle. I dialled Durand.

'Yes?'

'Well, if it isn't my favourite detective.' I waited for Durand to speak, but he didn't. 'I'm just calling to shoot the breeze, catch up, discuss the theory that the killer has an accomplice –'

'That's classified information.'

Durand's sharp tone threw me. 'I know but –'

'Classified. Anything else?'

I frowned. Was he worried he'd get in trouble for talking to me? 'You know I was reinstated as a freelance reporter at *The London Herald*?'

'Good for you.'

'What's the matter?'

'I'm too busy to talk to the press.'

'I'm not asking as press, I'm asking as a friend.'

'Is that what we are? That's funny, I thought you wanted something.'

I coiled the phone wire around my finger, watching the blood shoot to my fingertip. 'Have I done something to piss you off?'

'How's your story going? You getting an objective view?'

'What?'

'Only I imagine it's hard to be objective when you're sleeping with the prime suspect.'

I felt the colour drain from my face. It took less than a second for my brain to piece together what an idiot I'd been. As if Durand would have released Liam without setting up surveillance on his flat. It would have been bugged too.

I swallowed hard. 'Sam –'

'Look, it's no skin off my nose who you jump into bed with.' Durand's voice hummed with a quiet fury that took me by surprise. 'But it does highlight a certain character flaw.'

'Who else knows?'

'I must thank you, actually. Liam denied he'd seen Lydia's tape during our interrogation, so that was helpful.'

'Sam, please ... did you hear what I'd just found out? The reason I wasn't ... myself?'

'Your brother, yes.' There was a pause. 'For old time's sake I'm going to let you in on a little secret. Your boyfriend is lying to you. Liam knew Lydia was being blackmailed.'

My head jerked up. 'What?'

'Perhaps you two are made for each other.'

'Sam, listen to me –' I stopped. I'd been haphazardly shuffling the case notes, piling them into the folder, when my eyes landed on a small black-and-white photograph of a group of people gathered on the steps of Liverpool Crown Court. The caption read: *Justice for Amanda's mother as Michael Farrow, 48, is sentenced to life imprisonment.* I hung up the phone and pulled the cutting towards me, the blood rushing through my ears.

It couldn't be, could it?

## 29

I belted out of Shepherd's Bush Tube Station and across the street. The wind was picking up, and the heavy wedge of clouds choked all the light out of the sky. Tadmor Road was a quiet residential street tucked away behind the roar and bustle of Westfield Shopping Centre. I ran up the steps of number fourteen – a pretty red-brick house with window boxes on the balcony – and lifted the heavy brass knocker. A few moments later the yellow front door opened.

'Isabel told me you were on your way round. This isn't a good time.' Cat gave me a startled Botox stare. She was holding a leather diary in one hand, her phone in the other, her peach silk blouse billowing in the draught.

'I need to talk to you.'

She shook her head. 'I'm up to my eyes in it. Milan is kicking off and I'm losing tomorrow morning because of the funeral. If this is about Lydia –'

'It's not about Lydia.'

She started to close the door. 'Well, whatever it is, it will have to wait.'

'It's about Amanda Barnes.'

Cat's phone slid to the floor, and she stared down at it, unable to move. Then her large frame collapsed inwards, like a cardboard box.

I glanced over my shoulder. 'You don't want to do this on your doorstep. Let me in, Cat.'

Cat bent down to pick up her phone and had to steady herself against the door frame. Then she raised a limp hand and I helped her through a narrow hallway, and into a large open-plan kitchen. The back door was open and the chill breeze brought with it a wet cement smell. A passport lay on the counter, next to a pot of coffee. Cat saw me looking.

'Milan . . .' It was all she could manage, before her legs gave way and she crumpled onto a chair.

I sat down opposite and waited, not wanting to make this any more difficult.

Cat raised her head and looked at me with flat, lifeless eyes. 'I haven't heard her name for so long.' She let out a long, shaky breath and closed her eyes. 'Who else knows?'

'Just me.'

Cat nodded, her eyes still closed. I could see them moving underneath her eyelids. Her forehead was shiny, like a bar of soap. It was odd to think of Cat as a mum. Even weirder to think that she was Amanda's mum. I searched her face for similarities, but years of plastic surgery had erased any trace of her daughter.

I undid my coat and took it off without standing up. The radio in the corner trotted out the weather forecast: rain, rain and more rain.

Eventually I spoke. 'Tell me about her.'

Cat checked her watch, then fiddled with the large gold necklace around her neck. She stood up. 'Would you like a Scotch?'

'No, thanks.'

She strode across the kitchen and, as she reached up towards a cupboard, her blouse snagged on the counter. She ripped the fabric away and a button popped off; it clicked across the wooden floor. Cat was moving oddly, exaggeratedly, as if she was in a play and was making up for missing her cue. I watched her pour a large measure, knock it back, then pour another.

'I'm sorry to be so . . . Amanda's death was . . .' She paused, searching for the right word. 'I died the day she died. The whole process, the police, the trial. It was . . .' Her solid bob swung stiffly as she shook her head.

'Do you know what the detective said to me the day my husband was sentenced? He hoped it brought me closure.' Cat gave a brittle laugh, and clutched her glass to her chest. 'Let me tell you, there's no such thing. And you don't stop being a mum, just because your child is dead.' She rocked gently on the edge of the chair, staring at nothing. 'Amanda was everywhere. The house still smelled of her vanilla perfume. Her scuffed Dr Martens were by the back door . . .' Cat drained her glass. She stood up, closed the door, sat down again. 'They say you don't know true love until you have your own child, but that didn't happen to me. Amanda's father left me when I was six months pregnant. I was sixteen. Single motherhood wasn't part of the plan. I considered all the options but couldn't go through with the one I really wanted.'

She smiled ruefully, looking down at her nails. 'It wasn't until Amanda was two that I fell in love with her. What happened to her . . . what happened to us . . . I thought I was being punished for not loving her straightaway.'

I looked down at my hands. 'Did you know about the abuse?'

Cat pulled out a tissue and started ripping it apart on her lap. She didn't speak until it was completely shredded. 'Michael was so charming at first. But a few months after he moved in, things changed. Small things at first. Commenting on my clothes. Belittling me in front of people. He became harsher and harsher until words weren't enough anymore. After a while the abuse sort of stopped. I thought he'd got bored. Turns out he was only bored of me.' Cat slugged back the amber liquid, her hands shaking. 'Amanda would have been thirty-six next week. I'd be a grandmother by now.' She gathered up the scraps of tissue and piled them on the coffee table. A sad silence settled over the room like dust.

A loud noise rattled through the air and we both jumped.

Cat sighed. 'Next door's builders. It's quieter in the sitting room.'

I followed her into a large room, with a bay window and silvery-grey walls. Cat plopped onto the cream sofa, unzipped her boots and slid them off. I settled onto the armchair in the window and warmed my hand on the radiator.

I paused, wondering where to start, but Cat didn't need any prompting.

'After Amanda died, whispers followed me everywhere. They haunted my dreams. *Why didn't she leave her husband?*

I lasted a year before I left. Giving up Amanda's surname felt like a betrayal at first. Ramsey was my mother's maiden name. Catherine was Amanda's middle name. So it felt as though she was still with me.'

'And the model agency?'

Cat fiddled with her blouse cuff. 'Amanda was killed because I didn't protect her. I had a lifetime of making up to do. When I was a girl, I used to help out with the beauty pageant my aunt ran. I massaged my CV and managed to get a job at Models International, or Models UK as it was back then. It was hell at first. Every girl reminded me of my daughter.' Cat gave a sad smile and ran her fingers through the ends of her hair. 'But the more I invested in the girls, the stronger I felt. It became my salvation. After a while, it didn't hurt so much to remember Amanda. Lydia reminded me of her in many ways. It's probably why I was so fond of her.'

It all started to make sense. The accent I couldn't place; the fierce way Cat protected her girls. I looked round the room. Barely any photographs. Cat flanked by six models at a fashion show; rowing in a scull boat; the snap of Lydia and Cat in New York. That was it. No personal effects. Symptomatic of some-one living a lie. Still, it was her lie on her terms. I understood. How many times since Tommy's death had I wished I could disappear?

I cleared my throat. 'Does the name John Bairstow ring a bell?' Cat's eyes were fixed on the floor, but a faint line appeared between her eyebrows. 'He is a convicted rapist. Amanda's friend, Melissa Wakefield-Channing, remembers

Bairstow turning up at your house the week before she died. Melissa confessed she never told the police about Bairstow. But she did tell you.' I hesitated, continuing more gently. 'Why didn't you report him?'

'I . . . don't remember. I – there was a man but . . . I'd just lost my daughter. Then my husband . . .' Cat took another slug, her eyes watering.

Suddenly, I understood. 'Another suspect meant the spotlight would shift from Michael. This was your chance to escape.'

Cat closed her eyes. 'You don't understand what he was like. Michael had a way about him. He'd talked himself out of trouble in the past. I was terrified he'd be let off. And I knew he'd killed Amanda. I watched it with my own –' Cat's voice cracked, and she leaned forward with her head in her hands.

I took a deep breath. 'I have a theory, Cat. I think Bairstow is involved in the sex ring, the killings, all of it. But I don't think he's working alone. Can you think of anyone else who knew about Amanda?' I thought back to the second DNA trace in the shed. 'Did Michael invite anyone else to join in the abuse?'

Cat hugged her knees, staring at the ground. When she didn't speak, I shifted my weight and softened my voice.

'If there's something you know, Cat, you need to speak. To me, or the police.' I didn't voice the irony that if Cat had told the police about Bairstow twenty years ago, he wouldn't have been free to kill again.

Cat turned towards me, her eyes wide and desperate. 'Sophie, you're not printing this, are you? Please don't drag Amanda into this. Please don't destroy the life I've carved out here.'

I sighed. 'Even if *The London Herald* doesn't publish the story, it's only a matter of time before another reporter makes the connection.' A siren wailed past the window. I waited until it faded to nothing. 'You could face this head-on. Get out in front of the story. Tell the world who you are. Who your daughter was. Perhaps the truth will flush Bairstow out.'

Cat stared into her glass, looking utterly drained. 'I . . . can't. I can't go back to the whispers and pitying stares.'

I considered Rowley's decision to expose the Juliets on the same day as Lydia's funeral. Wait until he heard about this story: a dead daughter, a killer husband, the friend he inspired to murder decades later. Rowley would never give Cat a free pass. I understood Rowley's choices, but I didn't always agree with them. Compassion might not sell papers, but we had to draw the line somewhere.

'Look, what my editor doesn't know, he can't publish, right? I can keep this to myself for another day or two. Until you've had a chance to get your head round things. But, Cat, the past is catching up with you, whether you like it or not. I'd rather be the one to help you through this. Think about it.'

I reached out to touch Cat's knee, but stopped when I saw the look on her face. Narrowed eyes, jutting chin, clenched jaw. It reminded me of the first time I met her, when I barged into her office. Now I understood Cat's frosty demeanour was nothing more than armour; armour that had enabled her to pack up her grief, move to a new city and start over.

I stood up, scanning the room for my bag. 'I'm so sorry, Cat . . . about all of this.'

Cat nodded once, fighting to keep her face in check. 'Your bag's in the kitchen. I'll get it.'

She swept back into the room, holding out my bag, then followed me to the front door. By the boozy waft that lingered in the hallway, I could tell she'd sneaked another Scotch in the kitchen.

Cat leaned against the front door, trying to smile. 'I appreciate you coming to me first. I . . . it's just a lot to take in.'

'Will you be OK?'

'I've survived this long, haven't I?'

I stepped out into the dark, turning just in time to catch the smile slide off Cat's face.

## 30

I powered down Sydney Street towards St Luke's Church. The cold wind threatened to rip off my hat; an oversized wedge of felt that I'd bought in a red-eyed fog for Tommy's funeral. It pinched my temples, but it hid my pale hair and today I needed all the help I could get. *The London Herald*'s Juliets exclusive had lit a fuse on Lydia's funeral. Every news site was running with the story, and the paper had come under fire for its insensitive timing. As my name was on the piece, I woke up to a flood of calls from breathless news broadcasters. I buried my chin in my scarf, feeling sick with nerves.

Hordes of people stood outside the church, packed together like pencils in a jar. Uniformed police officers stood guard behind the metal barriers that lined Sydney Street, pushing back eager bystanders who were craning their necks, eyes diamond-bright with the drama. Some held candles and signs emblazoned with *RIP LyLaw*. Most waved smartphones in the air. I hurried past the press area, which was ablaze with flashbulbs and TV crew spotlights, faltering as a wail from the crowd pierced the air behind me. A blonde Hollywood starlet, all bee-stung lips and five-inch heels, was tottering up the steps, dabbing her tiny nose with a tissue. I slid into the back row, peering out from under my hat.

The congregation fidgeted and jerked, as if it were being poked with a cattle prod. Every so often someone leaped to their feet to air-kiss an incoming guest. I recognised a smattering of movie stars and supermodels, a chart-topping boy-band, the Shadow Home Secretary, the photographer Nathan Scott. Radiators blasted out heat and grandiose displays of crimson flowers filled the stuffy church with their thick perfume. Gold easels holding giant photographs of Lydia were scattered around and a twelve-piece orchestra was playing Elton John's 'Candle in the Wind'. As I thought back to Natalia's pitiful send-off, a zingy voice made me look round.

'Too tragic, darling. I mean, no one wanted Lydia to get better more than me . . .'

The gossip columnist, Amos Adler, sailed past, blowing kisses to no one in particular. He bent down to whisper something to a statuesque black woman in a feather headdress. Next to them was Cat Ramsey. She caught my eye and gave me a cold stare. I lowered my eyes, regretting not giving her a heads-up about the Juliets story breaking.

Suddenly a roar outside split the air in half. I glanced back, then wished I hadn't. Smoky orange light filtered through the stained-glass windows, throwing shadows across Liam's face. His eyes slid across the congregation, then he shoved his hands in his pockets, scowling. The kick in my stomach was swiftly followed by the acid flare of anger. Liam had lied to me, but was that all he was guilty of? I shrank down in my seat waiting for him to pass, but when I peeked again, he'd disappeared.

The orchestra began to play Elvis Costello's 'She' and a nervous hush descended. We all stood as the double doors at the back of the church swung open and a white coffin appeared, draped in red roses. I did a double-take when I spotted the lead pallbearer. *Liam*. That was a much-needed show of support from Lydia's family. As the coffin glided past, I stared at the stone floor, not wanting to think about Lydia's mutilated face, bloated and ribboned with cuts.

The vicar, stilt-thin with a neat white beard, invited us to sing the hymn 'Abide With Me' and, as the organ's honking tones reverberated through the church, I spotted Durand leaning against the back wall, his auburn hair slicked to the side. He caught my eye and I felt my face burn.

An elderly man with Lydia's heart-shaped face and laser-blue eyes shuffled up to the front. He gripped the lectern and threw nervous glances towards the coffin.

When I gave the eulogy at Tommy's funeral, I couldn't take my eyes off his coffin. It wasn't Tommy the man I pictured lying there. It was Tommy, four years old, all skinny shins and pointy elbows. As I'd opened my mouth to speak, a memory flitted through my mind of Tommy, at that age, climbing into my bed, peering up at me through long blonde lashes. *Pease, Sops, can I have a hug?* Me pulling him close, feeling his smile against my chest. The rawness of that memory almost floored me. My speech was a disaster. Not that it mattered. My father sat like a lump of rock in the front row, my mother limp and pallid beside him, taking up so little room it was as though she wasn't there. We held the wake at Redcroft, but she never appeared. I spotted her through a crack in the drawing-room door, drifting upstairs clutching two cloudy-green gin bottles, her eyes shining like the pearls around her neck. My father flew to Hong Kong that night and I stayed at Redcroft so she wasn't alone. I was woken in the early hours by the splintering sound of glass smashing. I crept along the hallway just as my mother hurled another bottle against the wall. I knocked on her door, quietly at first, then with the heel of my hand, but the door never opened. And it had stayed that way ever since.

A husky voice brought me back to the present. I looked towards the lectern with a start. Liam was running a hand through his hair.

'I want to thank Jerry and Sarah for letting me say a few words about their daughter. Lydia was a pain in the arse. Pardon my French,' he nodded towards the vicar as nervous laughter rippled through the church. 'Lydia was a prima donna. She was a diva. That's what the tabloids want you to think, anyway. The Lydia I knew – the Lydia I *loved* – was definitely some of those things. On some days, she was all of those things. But she was also kind-hearted, funny and filled with joy.' Liam fixed his gaze on the back of the church. 'Our first date was in Los Angeles. I took her to a tiny Italian restaurant in Santa Monica, right on the beachfront. The sort of joint only insiders know about. I was trying to impress her.' Liam chuckled, and a sigh rustled through the congregation. 'I told her all the places to visit in LA and Lydia nodded along to everything I said. It was midnight when we left. She told her driver to whisk us up the Pacific Coast Highway to a hidden beach on Point Dume. We held hands, watching the moon dance across the sea. Eventually Lydia pointed to a beautiful clapboard house perched on the cliff behind us and told me she'd spent every summer there since she was eight. She'd been humouring me all night, not wanting to hurt my feelings.'

Liam smoothed his tie down and gazed down at his feet for a moment. When he looked up, a faint smile had spread across his lips.

'Lydia wasn't only beautiful, she was compassionate. Even though we'd split up, she was the first person to contact me when my sister died last year. It's a kindness I'll never forget.'

A man two rows in front of me doubled over coughing and loud tuts popped through the air as people strained to hear Liam.

'But the more famous Lydia became, the deeper she buried her real self. She was hunted, provoked, tormented by the press. It's ironic that on the day we come together to celebrate Lydia's life, a tabloid,' he spat the word out, 'runs yet another filthy story about her. That's what she was up against: soulless hacks with one agenda: to shift papers.' Liam's razor-sharp words sliced at my stomach, and I twisted the Order of Service into a cone on my lap. 'Before you get swept up in the rumours and the drama, I come to you with one request: to remember Lydia the woman, not Lydia the celebrity. She was more than just a perfect face with an imperfect personal life. And she deserves our respect and our love, today more than ever.' Liam kissed his fingers and pressed them to Lydia's coffin.

The rest of the ceremony passed in a blur of speeches and hymns and, as the coffin made its sombre way up the aisle, I caught Cat's eye again. This time she looked away, wrapping an arm round Lydia's weeping mum.

I pushed against the throng, grateful that I hadn't been busted. If I could sneak out the side exit, the path would lead me to Britten Street, and away from the crowds.

I raced through the door, straight into Liam. For a moment we just stared at each other. The fire in Liam's eyes threw me for a second. But I squared myself, refusing to look away.

'There she is, scuttling off to write her next poison-pen piece.' Liam's voice was low and deep, like muffled thunder. 'You know, you had me fooled the other night. I genuinely thought you gave a shit.'

'What makes you think I don't?'

A fat man, in a pinstriped suit, with a face resembling a Halloween pumpkin that had been carved then left to rot, charged round the corner. 'Lovely words in there, Liam.' He grasped Liam's hand between his meaty fists, and pumped it up and down. Liam gave him a curt nod, then turned back to face me, eyes flashing.

'I never said we weren't running the story.'

He nodded towards Sydney Street. A mob of paparazzi were yelling at bewildered mourners. News vans, parked at odd angles, were causing a bottle-neck in the street. The air was shrill with car horns and shouts. 'That fucking circus, there? That's your fault.'

'Liam, I'm sorry you're upset, but it wasn't my decision to run the piece today. I don't have that kind of –'

'It's a win–win for you this, isn't it? The extra impact is doing wonders for your circulation.'

'Look, I agree the timing sucks, but the Juliets is relevant to the investigation. If this sex ring has anything to do with Lydia's murder, more women could be in danger. The more people who know about it –'

'My God, you actually believe that drivel.' Liam's lips curled, baring his perfect teeth. 'Either you're a complete idiot, or you're lying, which would make you exactly the sort of person I despise.'

'Oh yes? And what's that?'

'Spineless. *The London Herald* needs to do something drastic to get themselves back in the game. But judging by the public's reaction, your little stunt may have backfired.'

I glanced over Liam's shoulder to where Lydia's parents were shielding their faces against the fireworks of camera flashes. A knot formed in my stomach. 'Liam, I –'

He closed the gap between us and, for a moment, I was knocked off balance. 'So, the other night, you were just working me for quotes?'

I stared at the curve of his mouth and a spot on my neck lit up with memory. I shook myself free of it. 'You told me it was off the record and I honoured that. You're not quoted any—'

'This isn't about me.' Liam dragged his hand over his chin, his voice catching. 'It's about Lydia. Her legacy. Do you know what today has been like for Jerry and Sarah? They're burying their child, for Christ's sake. And thanks to you, they're now dealing with this ... public bombshell. The police are looking into the Juliets. Quietly. There was no need to plaster it all over the papers. So, don't fucking come at me with a shit-show of an excuse about how your story is helping people. Be honest, the only people it's helping are the Premier News shareholders.'

The look of disgust on Liam's face sent me over the edge and I looked at him coldly. 'Honesty? Give me a fucking break.' I balled my hands into fists and jammed them into my coat pockets, my voice rising. 'You also talked a convincing game on Thursday night. You knew Lydia was being black-mailed. In fact, you knew about the Juliets a long time ago, but you didn't go to the police. Do you think Lydia's parents would give you the time of day if they knew that?' People were starting to stare, and I shifted my position, blocking out their curious expressions. 'Why did you really go back to The Rose that night?'

Liam laughed softly. 'You really want to do this here?'

'Why not? We're on sacred ground. You might think twice about lying.'

Liam reached his hand out towards me and I took a sharp breath. His fingers stopped an inch from my face. A muscle pulsed in his cheek. 'You still don't believe me.'

I shrank back from him, realising how inappropriate we looked in front of the gawping crowd. 'Can you blame me?'

Suddenly a reedy woman with a dripping red nose bowled towards us, squawking like a hen. 'Liam, darling! The cars are leaving.'

A flash of irritation crossed his face, then his eyebrows pulled low into a frown. He leaned forward and lowered his voice. 'This isn't over, duchess.'

Liam stalked off and my legs buckled. I steadied myself against the church wall and glanced across the courtyard. Durand was glowering at me.

My phone vibrated, and I was grateful for the distraction.

'Sophie? We need to talk.' It was Jasdeep. We hadn't spoken since I was fired but the urgency in his voice made me shelve the small talk. 'I've spent the past twenty-four hours on the deep web.'

'The what?'

Jas's voice was strained. 'It's a secret part of the internet; not a place you want to visit. A twisted theme park for every paedo and sex offender out there. Have you –'

The funeral procession pulled away from the curb and the crowd roared. I pressed my hand against my ear. 'Can you repeat that?'

'. . . heard the term *hurtcore*?'

'No.'

'It's rape porn. There's a whole movement of fans that pay a lot of money to watch. Unfortunately, lots of it involves children.' I leaned my head against the cold stone. 'I found a website posting links to Lydia's tapes, and Natalia's, plus loads of other models. The videos, they're graphic. Worse than the ones on the tape you found. And they're not filmed in hotel rooms either. The girls were taken to a warehouse, or a cellar or something. And,' he paused, 'I found a league table.'

'A what?'

Jasdeep's voice was flat. 'Men score points for inflicting the most amount of pain.'

*It was like they were competing with each other for a sick crown.* Eva had been closer to the truth than she'd realised.

A cold wind shuddered through the trees. I pushed myself off the wall and paced up and down. 'Can you trace the users?'

'I've gone one better. The website creator used an anonymous software program called Steal. You have to register a username to download it.' Jasdeep's phone rang and I heard him pick up and tell the caller to wait. 'Look, I've got to be quick, but his username is silver boy, spelt s-i-l-v-a b-o-i. I worked my way through everyone connected to Lydia and Natalia, and you know who uses the term *silva boi*?' He didn't wait for me to answer. 'It's appeared six times in the past year on Stitched.com.'

My head snapped up. 'Amos Adler? Are you sure?'

'A hundred per cent. I got pulled onto another story, but not before I cracked the encryption code and traced the website back to Adler's IP address. I don't know if he's running the sex ring, but he definitely uploads the tapes.'

Jasdeep rang off and I darted round the side of the church and scanned the crowd. Amos had wandered over to a sheltered corner of the courtyard to light a cigarette. He looked up when he heard me approach. 'Want a light?'

'No, ta. Just a breather. Nice send-off.'

Amos raised an over-plucked eyebrow. 'Sure. If phoney is your thing. Most of the congregation hated Lydia's guts.'

I gave him a cool look. 'Weren't you the one who came up with *Loony Lawson*?'

Amos shrugged. 'Gotta make a living, doll.' His fur coat was draped over his shoulders and his shirt was so sheer I could see the faint outline of a tattoo on his chest.

Amos's phone beeped. He glanced at the screen, swearing under his breath, then punched away at the keyboard, his cigarette dangling from the corner of his mouth. I stared at him. He couldn't be any older than me, which meant he was barely into double figures when Amanda was murdered. I heard the coroner's voice in my head: *the killer wasn't working alone.*

I reached into my bag for the cigarettes I always carried. 'I will borrow that lighter now, if that's OK?' I leaned towards the fluttering flame, shielding it with an ice-cold hand. I hadn't smoked since I was seventeen, and I didn't inhale.

Amos lit another, studied me through the veil of smoke. 'I remember you. You were at Jemima Snow's show in Berkeley Square. You're a reporter.'

'Sophie Kent, *The London Herald*.'

A flicker of something registered on Amos's face. 'You wrote the piece about the Juliets.'

The cigarette felt weird between my fingers. 'Like you say, gotta make a living.'

Amos patted his quiff. It was the colour of curdled milk. Out of the corner of my eye, I could see Durand staring at me, arms crossed. We stood in silence, Amos inhaling deeply, me pretending to smoke. Then I turned to him, feigning nonchalance. 'How long have you been running it?'

'The website?'

'The Juliets.'

Amos's hand froze midway to his mouth. 'Doll, it's not nice to make sick jokes at a funeral.'

'Who says I'm joking?'

'I've got nothing to do with that fucked-up –' Amos flicked his cigarette onto the ground and spun round to leave.

I put my arm out. 'Turns out the deep web isn't deep enough, silva boi.'

Amos turned to face me. He pulled out another cigarette, lit it, then picked something out of his teeth. His eyes gave him away. They darted across my face as if he couldn't believe I was real.

I stubbed my cigarette out and thrust my freezing hands in my pockets. 'The one thing I could never figure out was how Lydia argued with Liam, met a client upstairs, then went to DreamBox with you at 11 p.m. The timings didn't make sense. But you banked on the fact everyone was too drunk to remember whether Lydia was there or not.' Amos blew a thread of smoke over my head, watching me closely. 'So while you were hitting DreamBox, Lydia was at The Rose. You filmed it, posted it online and, then what? Made a load of money? Won the respect of perverted rape fans?' Amos licked his lips. When he didn't answer, I shrugged. 'No matter. I'll figure it out. I've got this far.'

I started to walk away, then paused. 'See that man over there, with the red hair. That's DCI Durand of Scotland Yard. He'll be over the moon when I give him the news. Oh, and in case you try to cover your tracks, we've printed off all the evidence we need.'

I had no idea if this was true, but Amos didn't look as though he was going to challenge me. A thin film of sweat coated his forehead.

'The public is after blood, Amos. Lydia was an icon, and Natalia, well, she was just a kid. Imagine what it will feel like when you're the one under fire. After all the bitchy things you've written, there's not a lot of love lost for you. I would hate to be in your shoes right now. Unless . . .' I paused, pretending to consider something. 'Unless I'm mistaken and you aren't the big chief. The name John Bairstow mean anything to you?'

Amos's head jerked back as if he'd been slapped, then he leered towards me with yellowy, nicotine breath. 'Leave him out of this.'

'Does the name Ariel Butters mean anything to you? What about Amanda Barnes?' Amos flinched. 'So you do know about Amanda. That she was murdered a week after Bairstow was seen at her house?'

Amos swayed from side to side, as though making up his mind whether to make a run for it. I took in the hard curl of his lip, the flare of his nostrils, the backwards stance. I was losing him.

I rearranged my voice, softened it. 'Bairstow needs help, Amos. Stop protecting him. You're only making this worse.'

Amos's cheeks turned white; his body stiffened into concrete. The crackle-cold air shimmered between us and I held my breath. Over his shoulder, Durand was striding towards us with a grim look on his face. I was seconds away from being sent packing.

'Amos, think. Is Bairstow worth losing everything for?'

He opened his mouth to speak, but Durand got there first.

'Amos Adler, I'm arresting you on suspicion of controlling prostitution for gain, converting criminal property and blackmail.'

I watched in shock as Durand read a snivelling Amos his rights, then led him to a waiting car. The press area erupted; the crowd swelled towards the blue flashing lights.

I called Rowley and told him what I'd just witnessed.

'But we're no closer to finding Bairstow?'

I kicked a mound of grass with my shoe. 'No, but I think the police are closing in on him.'

Rowley coughed impatiently. 'Well, there's only one way to find out. Get down to the station and pressure your police source.'

I glanced down at my hands, not wanting to tell Rowley there was a greater chance of hell freezing over than Durand sharing classified information with me. Then I stood up straight. *There is always a way.*

'Philip, how do you feel about me making a deal?'

## 31

I ducked into New Scotland Yard just as a raving drunk was being hauled through the double doors, and scooted up to the front desk.

'Wanda Woman.'

'What's up, Kent. Been a while.' Wanda was in her fifties, built like a Ukrainian weightlifter, with a fuzz of black hair and a filthy sense of humour. 'Got two words for you: Monkey Face.'

'Huh?'

Wanda grinned, revealing large stained teeth. 'Wanna hear what it means?'

I glanced past the desk to the locked door that led to the interrogation rooms. 'Sure.'

'So the guy gets a blow job, but before he does, he – get this – cuts off a handful of his pubic hair and when he, you know, ahems in her face, he lobs the pubes on top and yells Monkey Face!'

I stared at her. 'Where do you get this stuff?'

'Don't pretend you've never done it.' Wanda cackled into her coffee mug.

I waited a beat, then leaned over the desk. 'Is Amos Adler here?'

Wanda winked. 'Stretching out in the interrogation suite, waiting for the show to start.'

'What about DCI Durand?'

'Who do you think's running the show?'

'I've got information that he needs to hear before he questions Amos. Can you get a message to Durand?'

'Does the Pope shit in the woods?'

Wanda waddled to the door, swiped her pass and disappeared. My mouth went dry at the prospect of seeing Durand again. A few minutes later she appeared in the doorway and beckoned me over. 'You do know he wouldn't do this for anyone else. Room five. Go.'

I pushed open the heavy fire door and was met with a whiff of stale sweat. I glanced over at the two-way mirror, then sat down at the table in the centre. I was just pulling out my notepad when the door opened quietly and Durand slipped in.

His auburn hair grazed his collar like a copper paintbrush. Colourless eyes flicked over me once, then he folded his tall frame into the chair opposite and undid his jacket button. 'You have two minutes.'

I nodded, opening my bag. 'I have information but I need something in return. The gist of that fingerprint report from the scissors we found, and confirmation that you're looking for an accomplice.' Durand picked a hair off his suit cuff and flicked it onto the sludge-grey floor. A brittle silence filled the room.

Eventually Durand gave me a smile that didn't reach his eyes. 'I'm afraid I can't comment on a live investigation.'

Anger flared in my chest. 'So why agree to meet me?'

'Because I wanted to give you this.'

Durand pushed a piece of paper towards me. At the top in black capital letters were the words *POST-MORTEM REPORT*:

*THOMAS ANTONY KENT.* I could feel Durand's eyes on me as I scanned the document all the way down to where it said: *cause of death – inconclusive.*

'But . . . there was no investigation.' My voice sounded off, my breathing flat.

Durand's face softened a fraction. 'I made a few enquiries and it seems the whole thing was quietly dropped.'

I stared at the piece of paper, and the words started to swim. I looked at Durand through a mist of tears. 'Sam –' I couldn't bring myself to say I was sorry for sleeping with Liam. It would be a lie, and he'd know it. 'Do you know about Amanda Barnes?'

Durand looked blank. I folded the post-mortem report in half and slipped it into my bag. I didn't need any more distractions. 'I need your word I'll get something in return.'

'That PM report doesn't count?'

'Something relating to the case.'

Durand sighed and gave me a nod.

'You first.'

Durand put his forearms on the table. 'Yes, we're working on the theory that there are two killers. We found anonymous threatening emails on Natalia's and Lydia's phones. Traced them back to Amos Adler's computer. It was enough to bring him in.' Durand ran his hand back and forth across the table, obviously debating something in his head. 'Forensics found a tiny piece of latex on the carpet in Lydia's room. It's from a glove. We think the glove ripped during the sexual assault. The PM found traces of someone else's DNA inside Lydia. Results should be in later today. We're hoping they'll tally with Adler.'

'It might tally with someone else. A guy called John Bairstow.'
I opened the Amanda Barnes file and laid out the photographs
on the table. Then I told Durand everything, except for the fact
that Amanda's mum was Cat Ramsey. A promise was a promise.

Durand sat for a few moments, shrewd eyes on the ceiling,
piecing together what he'd heard. 'And John Bairstow is ...
where now?'

'No idea.'

Durand exhaled loudly. 'I'll get Waters on it just in case.' He
pushed his chair back and stood up. When he rebuttoned his
jacket, I noticed how much weight he'd lost. 'Thank you, Sophie.'

His formal tone made me want to cry. I opened my mouth to
speak, but Durand left the room before I could get the words out.


I pushed open the door of a café across the road and ordered a tea.
Then I buried myself at a corner table and pulled out my laptop.
Amos was in custody but Bairstow was still at large. I'd uncovered
a stalker, a sex ring, a twenty-year-old murder, but I still couldn't
nail the killer. Or killers. I sighed, and rooted around in my bag
for The Rose's CCTV footage. What was I missing?

Plugging it in, I watched the familiar scene unfold. An ache
twisted my stomach when I saw Lydia arriving with Leo Brand,
knowing she would be dead in two days.

Then it was time for Natalia's strange zigzag across the lobby.
I watched her lurch forward, then stop, her face etched with terror. I hit rewind. Then I hit it again. I don't know how many
times I watched. Each time Natalia's expression embedded itself
deeper into my consciousness. I was about to call it a day, when
something shifted in my head. Frowning, I opened the Natalia

Kotov folder on my desktop and pulled up the copies of Nathan Scott's party pictures.

I scrolled through them in order. Natalia striding across the lobby. Looking over her shoulder. Eyes to camera. Background sharpening. Liam's face.

Walk, glance over shoulder, eyes to camera, face crumples. My heart rate started to pick up. I zoomed in on the shot of Natalia gazing towards Liam. *The mirrored bar.*

My fingers fumbled as I dialled DI Rob Birch. He answered on the second ring.

'Twice in one –'

'Rob, that name you gave me, John Bairstow. Were there any other names on his file?'

'I'm fine, thanks for asking.' There was a pause. 'Uh, let me check.' I drummed my nails on the table, willing him to hurry. 'Yes, sorry, a middle name. Scott.'

*The trick is to disappear.*

It was another second before the penny dropped and, when it did, I slid down the chair in disbelief.

Natalia wasn't looking at Liam. She was looking in the mirror. At Nathan Scott.

Jonathan Scott Bairstow. Nathan fucking Scott.

## 32

I stared at my laptop, frozen.

My phone rang, but I ignored it. I had to be certain. I pulled a photo of Nathan off the internet and emailed it to Ariel Butters. As I hit *send*, I heard Jasdeep's voice in my head. *Users pay a lot of money to watch.*

I reached for my keyboard and searched for Operation Tike, a police taskforce that shut down an Eastern European sex ring three years ago. According to reports, founders were making half a million quid a year.

The blood pumped through my veins. Nathan was broke, living in his office. Suppose the Juliets started out as a money-making scheme. It satisfied his perverted side, but it wasn't enough. When Nathan got wind that Natalia was blabbing to the press, he murdered her. And he copied a killer who meant something to him. Ever since they had both acted out their sadistic desires on an innocent sixteen-year-old girl.

I sipped my too-hot tea, barely registering the burn on my tongue. How the hell did Amos get caught up in all this? Clarity came a moment later: Amos's chest. His tattoo. I'd seen it before, in the photographs hanging in Nathan's office.

*When I have a subject in my sights, I don't let go.*

Amos was one of the chosen few. I'd witnessed Nathan's charisma in action. I pictured the besotted face of his assistant, Margot. Heard Ariel's voice in my head: *He had a certain way about him. That's why I didn't see it coming.*

An email flashed up on my screen from Ariel and I glanced at it.

He looks different without glasses, and I think he's had a hair transplant, but, yes, it's him.

When my phone rang again, I picked up.

'Sophie, you were right.' Cat's curt tone cut through me. 'I've just had a reporter from the *Mail* on the phone, asking questions about Amanda. If this story is coming out, I want you to write it. But, listen, I'm on a flight to Milan at five. Could we –'

'Do it now?' I started to gather my things, picturing Rowley's face when I waltzed into *The London Herald* with this story.

'Sorry, I know it's not much notice. But you could ride with me to Heathrow and my driver will drop you home after.'

'I'm on my way.'

I skidded to a halt outside Cat's front door, taking a moment to get my breath back. I'd left a message for Kate to call me at once. We needed an urgent pow-wow about how to handle the Nathan Scott revelation. We couldn't accuse a member of the public without hard evidence. We'd learned that lesson after the Joanna Yeates murder. The arrest of her neighbour, Christopher

Jefferies, sparked off national hysteria, and *The London Herald* wasn't the only publication guilty of jumping the gun. Jefferies's brutal trial by press resulted in several newspapers paying out substantial damages. None of us came out of it well.

Cat opened the door, waving me in. 'My driver's outside. I need to grab my suitcase. I've just heard about Amos Adler's arrest. Can you believe it? Come in, it's freezing.'

I followed her inside, and perched on the arm of the sofa, glancing again at the photograph of Lydia and Cat in New York. For a moment, all I could hear was the tinny trill of the kitchen radio, the scratch of a bird on the windowsill, the slam of a car door. Then something stirred in my mind.

'Cat, I –'

A car horn sounded outside.

'Shit, my driver's on a double yellow. We need to run.'

Night had fallen. I slid into the black Mercedes and rested my head against the expensive leather, inhaling the damp air through the driver's open window. I closed my eyes, and when I opened them Cat was looking at me.

'Are you OK?'

I pulled out my phone, wondering where to start. 'I found John Bairstow.'

Cat slid forward in her seat. 'You're kidding.'

'Nathan Scott.'

Cat's hand flew to her mouth. 'The photographer?'

'His middle name is Scott. Jonathan Scott Bairstow. Nathan Scott. Turns out he's working with Amos.'

'Has Nathan been arrested too?'

'I don't know.' A car cut in front of us and the driver swore under his breath.

Cat's phone rang and she glanced at the screen. 'Damn it, I have to take this. Give me a sec.'

As Cat talked briskly into the phone, I tried to order my thoughts. Something I'd seen in Cat's house was bugging me. The shelf. The photograph of her and Lydia. I screwed my eyes shut, trying to think. That photograph had been in the background of the Skype call I'd witnessed at Cat's office. The call she'd made from home. The corner of the frame was chipped. But the picture I'd seen just now on Cat's shelf was as good as new. I rooted around for my phone and pulled up the photographs of Lydia's sitting room. I zoomed in on the picture of her shelves. The frame was chipped.

I scrolled through the photographs of Lydia's sitting room. Grey walls, white shelves, cream sofas. Cat and Lydia both lived in Victorian terraced houses. Lydia's sitting room could almost pass for Cat's. Except for the picture frame.

Thoughts crashed around my head. That Skype call was Cat's alibi. Why would she lie about her alibi?

I looked at Cat and the longer I stared, the more her face seemed to shift and blur before my eyes, like when you say a word over and over and it loses its meaning.

The car turned left as Cat barked an order down the phone. 'Well, they can fuck off. I'm not talking about Lydia to the press.' Her eyes flicked in my direction as she hung up. 'Sorry, Isobel is fielding calls from reporters.'

'Cat, that picture of you and –'

'The questions they're asking. It's disgusting. They're not interested in solving the mystery, they want to shift papers.' She gave me a cool look. 'You're all the same. You never know when to leave well alone. Nosy, prying, intrusive. You want to know how I *feel*? How's this: the last time I saw those girls is etched in my mind forever. Lydia slumped on her bed in that blue camisole. Poor Natalia propping up the bar, misery running down her cheeks. It's as if –'

It was a second before I realised what Cat had said.

'What did you say Lydia was wearing?'

'Sorry?'

'You said Lydia was wearing a blue camisole.'

Cat heard the edge in my voice and frowned. 'So?'

'So, Lydia wasn't wearing that camisole until after she was killed.'

Cat waved a dismissive hand. 'Then I read that somewhere.'

My phone went heavy in my hand. 'I'm the only reporter who knows that detail and I haven't used it.'

We hit a traffic jam and the car juddered to a halt. 'Well, you must have told me then. Where else would I have got it from?' All the same, her expression sharpened.

The driver turned to pass something to Cat and the headlights from an oncoming car lit up his profile.

The shock knocked all the wind out of me. *Nathan Scott.*

The realisation, when it came, was tidy and final, as if it were wrapped in paper and tied with string.

I turned towards Cat, my voice wisp-thin. 'You . . . and Nathan?' I gripped the seat. 'You're the accomplice?'

Cat plucked the phone from my hand and switched it off. In her other hand, she held a syringe.

My mouth went dry. 'What's that for?'

Cat ignored me, a smile on her lips. Then she glanced at Nathan, waiting for his order. For a moment nobody moved.

Nathan leaned forward and turned on the radio. Opera music flooded the car, soft at first, then louder as Nathan cranked up the volume. Loud enough to drown out my screams.

I hurled myself against the door just as Cat clamped a large hand round my arm. She yanked me downwards so I was sprawled across the back seat, out of sight of the other cars. Her ragged breath was hot on my face. Behind her head the car window swam in front of my eyes.

'Cat, please –'

'Lie still, Sophie.' Cat's voice was soft, almost tender. 'It won't be long now.'

A sharp sting in my arm. Cat's face split in two in front of my eyes. I opened my mouth to speak but the words wouldn't come. My body sank into the leather, heavy as a corpse.

I closed my eyes, and the silvery swell of music sang me to sleep.

# 33

The air smelled damp, dark, like a well. I licked my dust-dry lips, forcing down panic. Slowly, my surroundings sharpened in the flickering candlelight. The brick wall next to the bed was aflame with purple graffiti. An icy draught screeched through the gaps in the corrugated roof. A faint lapping of water outside. *Where am I?*

I tried to sit up. A clink of metal. Handcuffs.

Footsteps approached. I blinked, my body twitching with fear. Nathan was bent over a table. He'd removed his jacket and his sleeves were rolled up to reveal thick, beetle-brown forearms. I cleared my throat to let him know I was awake. I wanted him to make the first move.

Nathan's head snapped round, then he slithered towards me, stopping just short of the bed.

'How long have I been out?' I asked, when I couldn't take the silence any more.

'Long enough.' He looked me up and down and his mouth hooked into an ugly smile. 'You have the same hopeful look in your eyes that Natalia and Lydia had at the end. It's such a turn-on.'

I tried to keep my voice steady. 'People know where I am.'

'No.' Nathan cocked his head to one side. 'They don't.'

'Where's Cat?'

At the mention of her name, Nathan sprang up and returned to the table. I couldn't see what he was doing but a metallic scrape sliced through the air. The sound made my stomach clench.

I forced myself to look round. 'Is this where you brought the Juliets?'

'Sometimes.'

*Clink, scrape.*

'Amos has been arrested. He's telling the police everything.'

'I'm not worried about Amos.'

*Clink, scrape.*

Nathan stretched his arms above his head. 'It still fascinates me, how easy it is to keep someone quiet. It's just a matter of learning which buttons to push. Fear, shame, regret. Pick the right one, and you're rewarded with unquestioning loyalty.'

Did Nathan mean Amos? Or Natalia, or Lydia, or Cat?

'Ariel Butters wasn't loyal.'

Nathan's arms dropped to his side. 'I learned from that mistake. I learned the art of control.'

*Clink, scrape.*

'What are you doing over there?' I heard the tremor in my voice and jammed my jaw shut. My brain felt as if it was made of sandpaper. Had Cat and Nathan been working together this whole time? Since . . .

'Tell me about Amanda.'

The scraping stopped and Nathan turned round. The candle-light cast mean shadows across his face.

'She was a slut.' He laughed. 'A slutty slutty slut-slut. All curves and dimples, with skin you could eat. The kind of girl who wouldn't look twice at a man like me. Unless she was forced,' he added. 'Her eyes . . . like drops of ink. Her mum has the same eyes, don't you think?' Nathan smiled, baring large, whitened teeth. 'She vanished after Amanda died. But I always knew I'd find her. Seeing her face again, after all those years, I –'

A loud bang vibrated through the darkness beyond the circle of candlelight. I craned my neck to see. 'Cat?' I turned to Nathan. 'Where is she?' A blast of wind ripped through a crack in the window near me, sending a shiver across my body. 'Does Cat know what you did to her daughter? Or did you leave that part out when you brainwashed her?'

Nathan stalked towards me, a menacing look on his face. Suddenly his hand was on my neck, squeezing, choking, forcing hot tears down my face.

Just as suddenly, he let go. My breath thundered in my ears. I gulped down air, forcing myself to stay calm. His hand moved to my chest, my stomach, hovered over my belt. Then he pulled cable wire out of his pocket and strode to the end of the bed. As he strapped my ankles to the metal frame, his finger slid up my leg.

'Such exquisite bones. So delicate. Reminds me of Natalia. Her bones snapped like twigs.' He clicked his fingers.

I had to keep Nathan talking. All the time he was talking, I was alive. And if I was alive, there was a chance.

'Why Natalia?'

Nathan seemed surprised at the question. 'She looked like Amanda. And all roads lead back to little Miss Barnes.'

'What do you mean?'

Nathan ignored the question. 'It should have happened here. Natalia. But she opened her slut-mouth and ruined everything. We had to improvise.'

'And Lydia?'

Nathan's eyes narrowed. 'Sealed her own fate. She figured out that Cat's alibi was a lie. Decided to make it public. Her own fault, dumb bitch.'

The lyrics from Lydia's Twitter video. *She'll cut you with her smile, then laugh as you bleed.*

Lydia was singing about Cat.

Cat.

*Cat.*

The name ricocheted through my brain, refusing to settle. How could Cat, of all people, be involved in murder? It didn't make sense. I thought of the life she'd been forced to endure. Years of abuse, a psychopathic husband, a daughter murdered in front of her. Could anyone go through what she had and come out unscathed? Her past had rotted away her soul. The real mystery was how she'd been able to hide it from the world.

Nathan coughed loudly, making me jump. I turned in time to see him pick something up. A glimpse of metal. A small knife, the blade slightly hooked at the end.

An ice-cold hand swept up my back. 'What are you going to do with that?'

Nathan gave me a thin smile, before slinking away into the darkness. *Where did he go?* My heart stuck in my throat. The air shifted and Cat materialised, her large frame looming over me, her face marble-like, sculpted and stretched, shut tight against a world she felt had betrayed her.

'Please, Cat.' My voice was low and urgent. 'You don't need to do this. I know you've suffered. No one would blame you for the choices you've made. Not after everything you've been through. But men like Michael and Nathan, they're psychopaths. Manipulating people is what they do.' I glanced behind her at the blank space where Nathan had been. 'He's doing it right now. Whatever Nathan has got you into, there is a way out, there is a choice.'

Cat watched me for a moment.

'Are you thirsty?'

She held a plastic cup to my lips. The water was filthy and grit slid down my throat, but I gulped it gratefully.

'Ready?' Nathan sidled towards us, running a thumb up and down the blade in his hand.

'Please.' My voice cracked.

Nathan stopped behind Cat and stroked a hand down her back. Was it me, or did she flinch?

My breath came in shallow puffs and I grasped the bed until my fingers hurt.

Cat held my gaze for a long moment. Then she sank back against Nathan, a look of ecstasy on her face.

'Patience, my love. What have I told you about savouring the moment. You're going to spoil things.'

I stared at her. Cat's voice was clear, crisp, loud. She didn't sound like a woman who was being manipulated.

She sounded like a woman in charge.

Cat bent down and began unbuttoning my shirt with large, dry fingers. The material fell away and the air felt cold against my stomach.

'Your skin is quivering like pink jelly, Sophie. You're so beautiful. But you already know that, don't you?' Cat ran a nail down my ribs, her eyes glittering in the candlelight. 'When I was a little girl, my daddy liked to fuck me. He told me ugly girls got what they deserved.' Her face stretched into a tight smile. 'Well, my husband thought I was beautiful.'

'Your husband abused you.' The words were out before I could stop them.

Cat's face darkened. 'A lot of the time it was consensual. And when it wasn't,' she shrugged, 'it was worth it. Michael lit up my world. He filled a void I didn't know I had. I grew up wrong, you see. I had urges; a viciousness inside me. The apple doesn't fall far from the tree.'

Cat closed her eyes, fingered her necklace. 'I never dared act on it. But Michael unlocked a part of me that –' She stopped, breathless. 'I'd have done anything for him.'

The air pressed down on me. I couldn't breathe. 'Amanda.'

Cat smiled. 'The truly surprising thing was how much I enjoyed it. The power. The rush. Seeing the pleasure on Michael's face. Pleasing him became addictive. But, after a while, Amanda wasn't enough for him.' Cat gazed up at Nathan. The air between them was charged, electric.

'At first we experimented. Invited others into the circle. That's how I met Nathan, or John as he was back then.' Cat smiled. 'He was extraordinary. Could hold the room in the palm of his hand. Amanda felt it. She always behaved when Nathan was there.'

I pictured the crime-scene photographs of Farrow's shed. The filthy mattress, the restraints, the torture kit.

Bile slid up the back of my throat. 'So you turned a blind eye while men sexually abused your innocent daughter?'

'A blind eye?' Cat gave a shrill laugh, a knife against stone. 'I watched every moment. That bitch burned so brightly, there was no room left for anyone else. Well, I made room. Why shouldn't she suffer what I suffered. She was no more special than me.' Cat shifted her weight and I rolled closer towards her. The nearness made my stomach heave.

'The more we shared Amanda, the less she pleased me. She lost her allure, her innocence. We needed someone new to play with. But Amanda was a problem. A loose end. Even so, Michael took some convincing. As it turned out, he didn't have the stomach for murder.'

'So, that night . . . in the woods . . .' The words died in my mouth. I closed my eyes. 'Michael didn't kill Amanda.'

Cat smoothed her hair; her ice-blue gaze cut through me. 'I still feel her pink flesh under my fingers. Hear the throaty rasp as her breath left her body. It was the purest moment of my life.'

I stared at Cat in horror. 'But Michael –'

'Lost Amanda, and in the end that proved too much for him. Still,' Cat cocked her head to one side, a smile playing at her lips, 'he never betrayed me. The police were so enamoured with Michael as the killer that they never looked any further. No one suspected the grieving mum, especially one covered in bruises.'

Cat stood up and pulled her jumper over her head. Her but-ter-yellow blouse was damp under the arms.

'I knew how lucky I was to get away with it. Nathan and the others disappeared into the ether, and I got on with my life. But the urges, they – I tried everything. I cut myself. I self-medi-cated. I took the edge off at sado-masochistic clubs. My job at the model agency was another way of torturing myself. I wanted to tell every beautiful bitch who ran a pitying eye over me that I'd crushed a neck like hers between my large, ugly hands. I spent two decades chasing the high. But when you've tasted a pleasure that pure, nothing else comes close.'

Cat twisted her silver ring, then caught me staring and stopped. 'I wanted to hurt someone so badly. It made me want to climb out of my own skin. But I never dared. I didn't want to do it alone.' Cat's breath quickened and she glanced at Nathan. 'What we shared, it binds you for life. All these years pretending to be someone I'm not. Finding Nathan set me free. We set each other free. The last year has been the happiest of my life. The Juliets were – I can't tell you –' She laughed. 'But that was just the foreplay.'

Nathan bent down and kissed Cat's neck. The air throbbed between them, dark and meaty.

'We took our time choosing her,' said Nathan, kneading Cat's shoulders between thick, nicotine-stained fingers. 'It was my first time, and Cat wanted it to be perfect.'

Cat nodded, a faraway look in her eyes. 'Natalia had it all. She looked so much like Amanda it took my breath away. The same fragile beauty, the same little-girl-lost air about her. It wasn't supposed to happen at The Rose but, my God, the rush . . .'

I watched the two of them relive the memory in all its Technicolor glory. I pictured Natalia's mutilated body, her blood-drenched sheet, and my chest tightened.

'What about the blackthorn?'

'That we did plan,' said Nathan, laughing. 'What can I say? I try to be creative.'

Cat shrugged. 'And I like violence.'

I cleared my throat, frowning. 'But how did you get Natalia to swap rooms?'

Cat smiled. 'I couldn't book her onto the floor with no CCTV cameras because everyone knew I was in charge of her reservation. I knew all about her stalker ex-boyfriend's calling card.'

I screwed my face up. 'The blue flowers?'

'I left a bunch in her room and, *voilà*, one panicked princess.' Cat peered up at Nathan through her lashes. 'You're not the only one who can be creative.'

Nathan brushed her cheek. 'And then there was Lydia.'

Cat sighed. 'Always was a stuck-up bitch. I was delighted when she forced my hand. I pretended to Skype a make-up company from my house, but I was at Lydia's. Nathan was upstairs with her, waiting for me.' The memory coloured her cheeks.

'So that text Lydia sent to Liam –'

'Was sent by me,' said Cat. 'We needed a suspect. Alexei was no longer in the frame, and that prick Crawford has a guilty face.'

Nathan laughed, a throaty sound that curled up at the end, as excitement took hold of him.

He put a hand on Cat's shoulder. 'It's time, baby.'

Cat stood up, her eyes glittering in the candlelight. 'We're going to have some fun.'

Fear tore through me. 'I lied to you earlier, about no one knowing who you were. Durand is waiting for a DNA result. He probably has it by now. They're closing in on you. It's over.'

Nathan looked at Cat uncertainly, but her hard blue eyes never left my face. 'In that case, I'd better savour this.'

She slid to the bottom of the bed, and pulled off my socks. Her hot hands scorched my skin.

'The most frustrating thing about killing Natalia and Lydia was having to keep them quiet. But here –' She gestured round the space, arched her voice into a higher pitch. 'No drugs for you, Sophie Kent. You're going to feel everything.'

Nathan took Cat's head between his hands and kissed her on the mouth. For a moment, she gave herself to him, wholly and fully.

A stinging realisation flooded my veins, my stomach, my lungs, almost choking me from the inside. *I'm not getting out of here alive.*

Cat pulled away, her lips glistening like a wet wound. 'Fear tastes sour on the tongue, doesn't it? I can still taste it.' She held her fingers up. 'Amanda, Natalia, Lydia. Even in death they looked beautiful. But where does beauty get you in the end?' She bent down, her breath sweet and hot in my ear. 'Fuck you, Daddy. Bad things happen to beautiful girls too.'

A bubble of vomit rose in my throat.

'Hold her still.' Nathan's voice sounded far away. Two large hands clamped either side of my head. A wedge of tape across my mouth. I couldn't breathe. My bowels loosened.

I squeezed my eyes shut. Beyond the darkness, a pair of eyes. Hard and blue, like sapphire bullets.

Natalia.

Lydia.

Amanda.

Thick red tears slid down porcelain cheeks.

A burning pain in my chest. A low moan.

The eyes lightened, changed shape, softened. I stared at the round, smiling face in front of me. The face I loved more than anything in the world. All of a sudden the white-hot terror in my chest gave way to quiet acceptance. I relaxed my grip.

Tommy's eyes blinked once, then nothing.

## 34

I opened my eyes and a blinding white light blazed across my vision. I made a sound and a dark shape darted towards me.

'Sophie?' The voice was hot in my ear, then melted away. A gentle whirring noise. Cool hands on my forehead.

'Sophie, my name is Cynthia and I'm a nurse at Chelsea Westminster Hospital. Nod if you can hear me.' I moved my head a fraction and a fierce pain ripped through my neck. 'Here, sip this.' I felt a straw being pushed into my parched lips. The water felt like liquid heaven.

'Is she awake?'

'Sir, I told you to wait outside. She's in no fit –'

'He can stay.' My voice sounded scratchy and raw. The pain forced my eyes closed. When I opened them, Durand was standing over me, a deep frown on his face. His tie was pulled loose, his skin pale and taut around his eyes. He gave me a quick once over and smiled without his eyes.

'That's the second time this week I've saved your life.'

'My hero.'

Durand sat on the side of my bed, and I was hit with a memory of Cat doing the same. I swallowed the memory deep down, and fixed my eyes on Durand's face. 'How did you find me?'

Durand sighed. 'The DNA result came in. System showed it belonged to a woman who was arrested for shoplifting in 1987. A Clare Barnes. After what you told me, I figured it was Amanda Barnes's mother. Deed Poll gave us her new name and when we turned up at her house, a neighbour said she'd seen Cat leaving with a small blonde woman. When you didn't answer my calls –' Durand stopped, his jaw tight. He ran a hand through his auburn hair. 'Your phone has a tracking app that sends a signal even when your phone is switched off. Thankfully, Cat never tossed your phone.'

I frowned. A tracking app? I remembered Kate's jab at Mack. *Why don't you fix Sophie with a tracking device and save yourself the hassle?* Had Mack inadvertently saved my life? The thought was too ridiculous to process.

'It led us straight to an abandoned boathouse on the banks of the Thames. We got there just in time. We thought it would just be Cat. Bairstow took us by surprise.'

A blunt ache ballooned in my neck. I put my hand to where it hurt and felt the dressing. 'Amos didn't give him away?'

Durand shook his head. 'We leaned on him hard too. God knows what they have on him.'

I closed my eyes. 'Where are they?'

Durand put a warm hand over mine, then saw the confused look on my face and pulled it away. 'In custody. Facing life for a double murder.'

*He doesn't know.*

I pushed myself up weakly against the pillow. 'It's a triple murder for Cat.'

'There's another body?'

'Amanda. She killed her daughter.'

Durand's mouth went slack.

'Time's up, Detective. Miss Kent needs some rest.' Cynthia clicked her tongue and Durand stood up.

I grabbed his sleeve. 'Let me know what happens.'

I woke up in the dark. A sudden movement. For a heart-stopping moment, I was back in that boathouse. I sat up too quickly, and the room spun.

'Fuck.'

'That's the first thing you said to me in my studio last week.' Liam stepped out of the shadows. He was smiling, but his hooded eyes were serious.

'You're here.'

Liam shrugged. 'Got more time on my hands now I'm not a serial killer.' He inched towards me, a lazy grin on his face, and covered my hand with his. A sharp current ran through me. I pulled it away. 'Why didn't you tell me about the blackmail?'

Liam sighed. 'Because then you'd know I was a coward. When Lydia first told me, I wanted to burn whoever was responsible alive. But she told me things were being handled. When you came to my flat that night, it was as if –' Liam ran a hand up my arm and I shivered. 'I would have done anything to make you stay. If you found out I never tried to stop the blackmail, I thought you'd disappear. You already knew everything I did, so why shoot myself in the foot?'

I stared at him. 'But if you'd told me, or the police, sooner, Lydia might have lived.'

Liam's smile dropped. 'You think I don't know that? But Lydia made me promise. I'd broken so many promises to her; I had to keep that one. How was I to know she would get killed?'

I turned my head towards the window. The cotton pillow felt cool against my cheek.

'Sophie, please –'

'I'm so tired, Liam.' And I meant it. I felt wrung out. My blood was as dry as my bones. 'I can't do this.'

'I'll come back tomorrow, when you're –'

'I can't do this.' The finality in my voice surprised me, but as soon as I'd spoken the words, I realised what I wanted more than anything was to be alone.

Liam stared at me for a long time. Then he nodded once and brushed his lips against mine. 'See you around, duchess.'

I lay there, waiting for my heart rate to slow. Then I felt around for my bag and pulled out my laptop. I had several emails from concerned colleagues and friends.

I opened the one from Rowley.

Sophie, I'm glad you're OK. When you're ready, I'd like to discuss your return to The London Herald. Regards, P

I hit *reply*.

I'm ready now. Will file my first-person piece to you tonight.

I flexed my fingers, and pulled up a blank document. I was about to start typing when an email pinged in my inbox from my father, subject line: *Are you OK?* My finger hovered over his name, but

I couldn't open it. Not yet. That night in the restaurant . . . What I said to him cut me to the bone. It wasn't fair. But it was easier to turn my father into the monster than admit the truth. That I'd given up on Tommy too.

*Ugly girls get what they deserve.*

Cat's voice rang through my head. I leaned back against the pillow and closed my eyes. The image of Tommy's face from the boathouse still burned behind my eyelids. So vivid I could smell the peppermint on his breath. In the split second before death, Tommy had found me.

A sob escaped. Then another. Tears ran down my cheeks, soaking the starchy pillowcase. Outside, darkness was falling, and my reflection was pale and ghostly in the glass. A siren shrieked in some distant corner of London. Somewhere out there, Tommy's killers were going about their business. I would tread so softly they wouldn't hear me coming.

In the meantime, I had a story to write.

# ACKNOWLEDGEMENTS

Here come the thank-yous ...

This book would never have seen the light of day without my formidable agent, Teresa Chris. To negotiate a deal for a debut author who is in the middle of a transatlantic move, not to mention seven months pregnant, takes some doing. Thank you for your cool head and encouraging words when I needed them most.

I'm indebted to everybody at Twenty7, particularly Kate Parkin for her brilliant suggestions, and for pushing me into darker territory (although I'm still not sleeping at night!). Thanks also to my editor, Kate Ballard, my copy-editor Helen Gray, and to Emily Burns in Publicity. You have each made this process a complete joy.

I am very grateful to Jana Pruden, Crime Bureau Chief at the Edmonton Journal for inspiring Sophie Kent's tenacity and courage, to retired Police Inspector and owner of Crime Writing Solutions, Kevin N. Robinson for all the information (and more) concerning police procedures, and to the *Star Tribune*'s investigative reporter, Paul McEnroe. Any mistakes are entirely my own – and I apologise to them for the poetic license! Thanks also to Professor Ashley Mears, whose book *Pricing Beauty: The*

*Making of a Fashion Model* provided me with such great detail and colour.

To Anne Hamilton, my cheerleader, proofreader, sounding board and mentor, thank you for talking me down off a ledge so many times over the past two years. A big shout-out to my magazine cohorts, my Core girls and my Los Angeles clan: your words of encouragement spurred me on more than you know. And to my fellow authors at Twenty7: you are an insanely supportive bunch and I'm grateful to be on this journey with you!

A heartfelt thank you to my family, in particular my mum and dad for their endless support (sleeping giants!), and to Arthur and Evelyn, for letting me vanish into my make-believe world and, more importantly, for enticing me back out again.

Last, but not least, thank you to James.

For everything.

\*

Enjoyed *Breaking Dead*? Don't miss the next Sophie Kent Mystery, coming soon from Zaffre Publishing...

www.corriejackson.com